The Love Book

FIONA O'BRIEN

The Love Book

HODDER &
STOUGHTON

First published in Great Britain in 2012 by Hodder & Stoughton
An Hachette UK company

1

Copyright © Fiona O'Brien 2012

A CIP catalogue record for this title is available from the British Library

ISBN 978 0 340 99486 3
Hachette Books Ireland trade paperback ISBN 978 0 340 99491 7

Typeset in Plantin Light by Palimpsest Book Production Limited,
Falkirk, Stirlingshire

Printed and bound by Clays Ltd, St Ives plc

Hodder & Stoughton policy is to use papers that are natural,
renewable and recyclable products and made from wood grown in
sustainable forests. The logging and manufacturing processes are
expected to conform to the environmental regulations of
the country of origin.

Hodder & Stoughton Ltd
338 Euston Road
London NW1 3BH

www.hodder.co.uk

For Mary, my sister, with all my love

"We are each of us angels with only one wing, and we can only fly by embracing one another." - Luciano de Crescenzo

Introductory Note*

In 1835, John Spratt was summoned to Rome.

His reputation went before him. Though renowned for his preaching, it was this humble Carmelite's work among the poor and destitute of Dublin's Liberties that had won him an enduring place in people's hearts, and word had spread. John Spratt knew the real meaning of what it is to love, and he lived and shared that love generously.

When asked to preach at the Gesù, the famous Jesuit Church in Rome, the elite flocked to hear him, and he received many tokens of esteem from doyens of the Church. One such gift came from Pope Gregory XVI himself – a reliquary containing the remains of St Valentine, including a small vessel tinged with his blood.

St Valentine's relics returned with John Spratt to Dublin, where they remain to this very day, in the Church of Our Lady of Mount Carmel at Whitefriar Street.

On his feast day of 14 February, a special Blessing of Rings is performed for those about to be married.

But throughout the year, the shrine is visited daily by the hopeful, who come to write their requests of St Valentine in the book laid out for this purpose. They come from all walks of life: old and young; married and single; some celebrating anniversaries; some abandoned and heartbroken; some thankful; some despairing – but all searching, all praying for love . . .

* Adapted from www.carmelites.ie

Dublin, 18 September 1981

'Hurry up!' hisses Abby. 'How long d'you think I can keep these seats for?' She is lying across the coveted back seats of the school bus, her face puce with exertion from fighting off any takers, tendrils of dark red hair, which have escaped her ponytail, frame her indignant face.

'Jesus, Abby, relax will you?' Diana slides in beside her, indicating the seat next to her for me.

'If we were all as relaxed as you, Di, we'd be sitting up at the front, with Sr Lezzo. Or maybe that's what you were hoping for?'

'Keep your hair on,' Diana grins. 'We're here now, aren't we?'

Sr Lezzo is a reference to Sr Gallaway, an elderly nun, recently returned from America, presumably to retire. She is our class mistress, although she doesn't teach anything, just supervises study periods, during which time she has an unfortunate habit of slipping one hand underneath her brown cardigan and massaging her breasts absentmindedly, while absorbed in her reading. She cannot understand the muffled outbursts of mirth this produces. Along with her heavily accented American twang and adopted vocabulary, study has become highly entertaining. Phrases such as 'load up the wagon' (the refectory trolley) and 'put it in the trashcan' (wastepaper bin) are used by us at every opportunity to infuriate the other nuns, accompanied by the caveat, 'Sr Gallaway told us to.'

It is thanks to Sr Gallaway and another nun of nervous disposition, recently returned from the Philippines, that we are on this day trip to Dublin. A cultural tour of the city to welcome them home, a visit to the National Museum and the National Gallery, Trinity College, St Michan's Church and then back home in time for tea. A day out. Our school head, Sr O'Malley, is in charge, accompanied by our History teacher, Mr Sullivan, who looks permanently flustered.

'Right, girls,' Sr O'Malley calls us to attention after we have completed our last stop on the tour. 'You may have one hour – exactly *one* free hour – to go for coffee or have a stroll around. The bus will be at the top of St Stephen's Green at ten to five precisely. Anyone who is later than five o'clock will be grounded on Sunday. Do I make myself clear? And, girls?'

'Yes, Sister?'

'Since you are in uniform, I don't have to remind you that you are representing the school. I expect your conduct to be exemplary.'

'Yes, Sister.'

'Right you are – and no *running*.'

We're off. A sea of floating green in our abhorred school capes that billow behind us as we make our escape.

'C'mon, it's this way,' Abby instructs, as Diana and I follow her, peeling away from the others.

'Aren't you coming to Thunderbirds?' Mary, who is almost as invested in food as I am, looks incredulous.

'Later,' says Diana. 'We'll catch up with you. See ya.'

I think longingly of Thunderbirds' burgers and thick-cut chips, followed by deep-filled American apple pie, accompanied by lashings of thick, whipped cream on the side, washed down by Coke – our all-time favourite meal of choice whenever we get the chance to get in to town. But there's no time, we are on a mission.

'We might not get another chance – not until it's too late anyway.' Abby is resolute. 'C'mon, hurry.'

We set off down Grafton Street, the main shopping drag, passing by the two large department stores that face each other – Brown Thomas and Switzer's – then turn left into Wicklow Street and left, again, at the end, into George's Street, which has a more rundown feel. No big stores here, mostly decaying houses fronting offices. Farther up, we reach Aungier Street, and up ahead on the right looms a large church.

'There it is!' says Abby pointing. 'That's it, Whitefriars.' And we cross the road.

'Are you sure about this?' I say doubtfully. 'Couldn't we go to a fortune-teller instead, or something? Have our cards read?'

'Don't be silly, they're only charlatans.' Abby is defiant. 'They don't know anything – just want to take your money. Do you want to secure your future or not?'

'How do you know this'll work?' Diana looks sceptical.

'Because it just will. My mother says so. All her friends and family came here and they all got what they wanted – and *who* they wanted.' This was said triumphantly. Abby holds anything her mother says in great regard. She is always right, apparently. Infallible, like the Pope.

'My mother swears by Lough Derg,' says Diana. 'You go three times in your life, do the three-day pilgrimage, and get anything you want. You save your soul as well.'

'Lough Derg is in Pettigo,' Abby points out. 'That's in Donegal, Diana, a mere five-hour trip. *And* you have to fast for three days.' She is losing patience. 'We can do that next summer.'

The thought of fasting makes me feel weak. I have heard

horror stories of Lough Derg, people fainting with hunger, their feet ripped to shreds from stumbling over the stones barefoot and having to be carried off to the mainland to be revived.

'St Valentine is here in Dublin – right inside this church. Now are you coming in or aren't you?'

We go in.

We enter into a large vestibule, and take a moment for our eyes to adjust to the dim light. On the walls are many plaques and pictures of past members of the Carmelite order, who run the church. Names jump out at me, of robed men who have gone to their heavenly reward. *Fr Dinny Devlin and Fr John Spratt have done great work with the Poor of Dublin*, I read. I wonder mindlessly if Fr Spratt was any relation to Jack, of nursery rhyme lore.

Inside, in the cavernous nave, our eyes grow wide. The church is huge, and filled along each wall with many statues beneath which flicker a multitude of candles. On the left, there is even a miniature replica of the Lourdes Grotto. At first glance, I see St Joseph, St Anthony, St Martin, the Sacred Heart and many versions of Our Lady. I have never seen so many shrines in one church.

'Over here, this way.' Abby heads to the right, and we genuflect and make the sign of the cross as we traverse the main aisle, bowing our heads in honour of the tabernacle, and follow Abby into the south transept. And then, right in front of us, there he is – St Valentine – his statue somehow smaller than I had imagined and, beneath it, underneath his little altar through a pane of glass, there is a small cask, the one that holds his relics. Despite myself, I feel an involuntary shudder. Someone has walked over my grave.

'Here's the book,' whispers Abby. 'Here's where you write your petition.'

I am disappointed. I had expected something impressive,

intricately beautiful, like the *Book of Kells* maybe, an ancient manuscript that we'd have to put on special gloves to handle. Instead, what I see before me is just an A4, wire-bound copybook, open at the page of whoever wrote the last request – the writing is illegible, spidery. A biro lies beside it, ready for use. Suddenly, I hang back, unsure, I feel short-changed and uncomfortable, and I don't know why.

'Oh, here,' Abby hisses and snatches the biro. 'I'll go first. And there's no peeking, okay? No looking at what each of us writes, otherwise it won't come true, your petition won't be granted. So stand back until I've finished.'

I watch as Abby writes confidently, fluidly, as if she has rehearsed this many times in her head. She is word perfect. I glance behind me. Opposite St Valentine is a statue of St Jude the Apostle, the patron saint of hopeless causes, and I wonder if he wouldn't be a more appropriate choice to inter-cede for me. I catch the eye of an elderly woman, kneeling nearby with an old man, her husband presumably, and she smiles at me and winks. I feel myself blushing. I am a grade-A eejit.

But now Abby is finished, and she hands the pen like a baton to Diana, who takes her place, turns the page and begins to write her own petitions – or rather demands, I suspect. As Diana writes, quickly, methodically, she frowns in concentration. No room for slip-ups here. From what I can see, which is not enough, she appears to be writing a list, numerically ordered. This strikes me as amusing, but really I am just playing for time, distracting myself, frantically trying *not* to think of what I will write. What will I ask for? I don't even know. I am unnatural, without hopes, devoid of dreams. My mind is blank. I feel slightly sick, like I used to when I was little on Christmas Eve before I eventually fell asleep, a mixture of dread and excitement.

And now it is my turn, Diana turns the page and hands

me the pen. 'Don't bother looking,' she grins, 'I've written mine in French.'

I smile weakly and take up my position. My hands are clammy, and I can feel beads of sweat breaking out on my forehead. I turn around, like a child seeking reassurance, and see Abby nodding at me vehemently. But still there is nothing. I am supposed to ask for a lover, a soul mate, a happy marriage – but the concept seems ridiculous. For I am surely unloveable. The thought of being a disappointment to some mythical man of the future fills me with foreboding. I am not aware that I am chewing the plastic biro until I feel it crunch and taste the sourness of ink on my tongue. Oh God. I look up at St Valentine, at his kindly, or perhaps disinterested, face. Why should he care? I am one of thousands, millions maybe. I am wasting his time. And then suddenly it comes to me. I am filled with calm and I know exactly what to write. *Please, St Valentine, let me be loved, just once, in my lifetime. It doesn't have to be forever, but I would much rather be on my own than in a loveless marriage. But please, if you can, send me somebody to love me, who I can love too. That's it. Thank you very much.*

I sign it *Vonnie, 18th September 1981*. Then I heave a sigh of relief, put down the pen and turn the page. My hands, when I wipe them on my skirt, are shaking.

Afterwards, we head back to Bewley's on Grafton Street for a quick coffee before catching the bus. Well, Diana and Abby have a quick coffee, I accompany mine with a chocolate eclair and a jammy donut. Then Abby gives in and grabs a brown scone before we reach the self-service till to pay up. The place is packed, as usual, not a vacant table in sight. At times like this, I am glad we have Diana with us. She is confident to the point of brazenness about using her devastating Gallic looks and charm to her own ends, particularly where men are concerned. Her father has told her it is a woman's right. We follow, with our trays in hand, as she makes her way over to a table where a young man lingers with an empty cup in front of him, reading a newspaper. My face flames in anticipated mortification and I study my tray. I have witnessed her in action many times and the men always come off the losers. It seems vaguely unfair. But now I'm tired and hungry and my feet hurt.

'Excuse me,' she says in a charmingly put on French accent. And he looks up, startled. She smiles sympathetically at him, as if he is a bit dim, and pauses without saying anything (this is a crucial tactic she says). Then, 'I see you 'ave finished your coffee,' she glances at his empty cup and bats her heavy lashes at him.

'Er, yeah?' he says, as if to imply, *what's it to you?*

At this stage, I or any other normal Irish schoolgirl would have fled. We're in our uniforms for God's sakes! He, on the other hand, is wearing a Trinity scarf.

Diana is undeterred. 'We are very tired, and we would like to sit down – that is a Trinity scarf you are wearing, is it not?' She seems fascinated by it, leaning in closer to inspect it, as much as the tray she is holding will allow her to.

'What? Oh, yeah, why?' he is looking suspicious, and quite annoyed.

'Well, that means you are a gentleman, no? And you will let us sit down, yes?' She looks meaningfully at the two vacant chairs and the one that he is still sitting on. Her eyes narrow slightly, and her face, which he is now studying, threatens to become a mask of disapproval.

His expression is a picture – exasperation, reluctance and a grudging admiration flicker in his eyes. Then Diana smiles, full on, the dimples appear, the eyelashes flutter shyly and he caves.

'Oh, right, yeah, sure. It's all yours.' He gets up from his table, holds his vacated chair out to her, then walks away, tucking his newspaper under his arm. He looks back over his shoulder at us, shaking his head, as if he has somehow been hoodwinked, as if he is not quite in command of his faculties.

'You're shameless,' grins Abby, sitting down gratefully.

Diana shrugs, grins and continues in her stage French accent. 'Few men are born gentlemen, it is women who must make them so. That is what my papa says.'

I tuck into my eclair, relieved that our St Valentine's ordeal is over. It has rattled me, and I am grateful for the soothing effect of chocolate-covered choux pastry filled with cream, that I savour in measured mouthfuls.

I listen to my best friends as they talk about clothes and make-up in great detail. We are not allowed to wear make-up at school, so much of our time is taken up with discussing it. Anytime I have tried to do my face, I always end up looking like a badly painted clown, it just doesn't seem to work. Diana is very good with it, though, because she is half-French and therefore 'naturally sophisticated' as the girls say. One day in the holidays, she did me and Abby up, and Abby looked like something out of a pre-Raphaelite painting, with her long, dark red hair, porcelain skin, ruby lips and smoky eyes. I looked a lot better than normal, I had to admit, but there was only so much anyone could do with the raw material, even Diana.

'Why do you eat so much?' Diana has asked me many times. 'Don't you know you can never be slim if you are always eating?'

I do, but what would be the point?

I am reminded again of the unfairness that people who can eat anything and not put on weight don't seem to enjoy their food the way they could. Abby is always giving out about her straight up and down figure and skinny legs, and

Diana prefers to smoke, although she's not supposed to, even if she is half-French, but she does. Her mother would kill her if she knew.

I have what you would describe as an athletic build. That's what Barney says when she's trying to be kind. She says I'm not big, just plump, but that it's all puppy fat and will fall away naturally. But I know I'm fat. Compared to my mother and Kate, I'm *huge*. I tower over them too – all five foot ten of me. But I'm good at hockey, sporty, although Kate is a better tennis player. I stay off the courts, because beside Kate in her little white skirt and perfect, tiny figure, I feel like an elephant.

'C'mon,' says Di, draining her coffee and putting out her cigarette. 'We'd better get a move on.'

'Wait,' says Abby. 'What date is it today?'

'The eighteenth,' I say. 'Why?'

I've had an idea,' she says, grinning. 'Let's agree to meet up on this day every ten years, no matter what, to see if our wishes have come true, if St Valentine has made them happen.'

'Every ten years?' Di is incredulous. 'What did you wish for, Abby, a retirement home? If mine haven't all arrived within five years – ten max – I'm certainly not waiting around for the next twenty . . .'

'But some might take longer than others,' Abby reasons. 'We'll meet every year then! It'll be fun, make us sure to stay in touch, keep us on track, remind us of how we used to be, when we're old, like thirty and stuff . . . and married, y'know?'

We pause for a moment to imagine the unimaginable. Ten years from now, we will be twenty-five, almost thirty. Old. Settled.

'Sure,' Diana gets up. 'Why not?'

'I think it's a great idea,' I say. Abby and Di are my best friends, I can't imagine a life without them. 'We'll meet every year, on this day or as close as possible – no matter what.' I want it confirmed.

'Of course we will, but every ten years we'll have a more formal meeting, to make sure our petitions have been answered, to compare notes.'

'What if they're not?' I venture.

'Oh, Vonnie,' Abby smiles at me, 'of course they will. You mustn't be such a pessimist.'

'You're not taking that with you?' Diana looks horrified as I snatch the remains of my donut and cram it in my mouth.

'Of course I am,' I mumble. 'I can eat and run at the same time, can't I?'

The Affair

*I*n the beginning, she tells herself it is just the sex. Incredible though it is, though he *is*, it is just pure lust, a fling, nothing more – because it couldn't be anything more, not now, not ever.

They meet, accidentally of course, at an airport, he on his way to a conference, she in London for a few days to visit friends and do a bit of Christmas shopping. Their flight is delayed. They swap pleasantries and cards and go their ways, wishing each other well.

But then they meet again, just a day later, in the bar of a very hip, exclusive restaurant that happens to be in the hotel where she is staying. He invites her for a drink, introduces her to his colleagues, who are charming, and who, one by one, discreetly leave, claiming they've trains to catch, dinners to attend – until they are alone, just him and her.

'You're beautiful,' he says.

She laughs, because she can't remember the last time anyone has told her that. His eyes hold hers, just a second longer than is necessary – searching, scanning – an age-old question.

'When do you leave?' he asks.

'Tomorrow, lunch-time flight.'

'Have dinner with me.'

'Yes,' she says, 'I will.' Because she will not think about the possible ramifications, not yet, later maybe.

Over dinner, the connection she feels to this man becomes physically tangible. Her breath becomes shallower, her hands tremble. She is eating, laughing, talking. But all the time she *is thinking about what she would like him to do to her – the feel of his hands, the smell of his skin, the taste of him . . .*

He calls for the bill and they leave the table, walking together easily, already they look like a couple.

He takes her hand, there are no more questions . . .

Dublin, June 2011

Abby is ten minutes early. She puts this down to her hair appointment finishing sooner than she had allowed for, rather than her meticulous (bordering on obsessive, some might say) punctuality. The table has been booked for a quarter to one at Diana's suggestion – early enough to beat the lunch-time throng, but not so early that they'll feel like the only people in the restaurant – as Abby is now.

Privately, Abby thinks that Diana simply likes to make an entrance (she will be late by ten, possibly fifteen, minutes). She has done since Abby has known her – although she in no way resents her for it. No more than Diana would ever resent Abby for her nerve-wracking punctuality – although she is too kind to call it that – but Abby knows it for what it is.

'A bottle of sparkling water and the wine list, please,' Abby tells the waiter when he approaches with the menu. 'I'll have a look at it while I'm waiting for my friend,' she explains.

She would prefer to order a glass of wine while she waits, it would calm her nerves, but she would most certainly have finished it before Diana arrives, and she dislikes the image of a middle-aged woman knocking back wine on her own, particularly if she is left sitting with a drained wine glass in front of her, just as her companion joins her at the table.

Abby doesn't feel middle-aged. It is not an expression one

hears very often. No one is allowed to grow old at all these days, she reflects, it is considered defeatist.

Abby is only forty-five, which is, by all accounts, the new thirty, but her mother informed her the other day that she was, along with the rest of them, very definitely *moving up the ladder.*

Abby frowns, tracking her thoughts with irritation. Why shouldn't she have a glass of wine, and sip it casually? Any number of other women would do just that without a moment's thought. But that's just it – Abby thinks about *everything*, constantly, examining endless possibilities and permutations minutely. She always has done, ever since she can remember, and it is exhausting.

Take this morning. All she is doing is meeting one of her best friends, whom she has known since they were twelve years old, for lunch. There is nothing exceptional about this. Abby and Diana meet regularly, talk regularly, they always have. Abby knows she could trust Diana with her life – so why can't she relax and trust herself? Why, for instance, did she feel the need to have her hair blow-dried before meeting Diana? Why was she awake tossing and turning half the night, wondering what she ought to wear, whether or not she would weigh herself in the morning and anticipating her mother's predictable denials when she told her for the umpteenth time that she would be in town and out to lunch and therefore unable to drive her to her bridge class? 'Why didn't you tell me?' Sheila had demanded that morning.

'I did, Mum,' Abby said. 'I told you at least three times this week.'

'Humph, that's news to me.'

Sheila, Abby's mother, is not forgetful. Rather she has always had a selective memory. But now that her mother is living with her and Edward, Abby is forced to endure her personality traits on a more intimate basis. She finds it trying, but thinks it is the least she can do to look after her mother after all she has done for her, her only child.

'I'll have to ring Barbara to give me a lift.'

'Yes, that's a good idea.'

'It's very late notice.'

'I'm sure she won't mind. You're on her way, aren't you? She passes right by our house.'

'Not everyone is as vague as you about last-minute arrangements, Abby. You can be very thoughtless sometimes.'

Abby had gritted her teeth – only five more minutes, maybe less, and she would be out of the house.

'If it wasn't for my arthritis, I'd drive myself. As you know, I hate being beholden to anyone.'

'Mum, Barbara giving you a lift to the bridge class you both go to hardly makes you beholden to her.'

'You're meeting Diana, you say?' Sheila, sensing defeat, had swiftly changed tack.

'Yes.'

'I'm surprised she has time with all the gadding about she does these days.'

'She doesn't "gad", Mum, she works bloody hard. I don't know how she runs a business, travels *and* manages her family,' Abby says in defence of her childhood friend whom she knows her mother is privately intimidated by, although Sheila would die rather than admit it.

'She doesn't – that's how,' Sheila retorts. 'Any woman who doesn't put her husband and marriage first is a very foolish one. God knows how that poor husband of hers manages, never mind the children – they probably can't remember the last time they had a home-cooked meal. And don't curse, Abby, there's no need for it, using coarse language is a very unattractive trait in a woman.'

'I have to go.' Abby silently counted to ten. 'See you later, bye, Mum.'

'You're not going into town for lunch dressed like that?' Sheila looked disapprovingly at Abby's jeans, T-shirt and her tweed jacket that is fashionably frayed at the edges. 'Surely you're going to change, put on a nice suit or something?'

Abby *had* been going to wear a nice grey linen trouser suit until Roseanna, her twenty-year-old daughter, had told her she looked frumpy and seriously needed to edge up her look.

In the event, she had no time to change anyway, even if she *had* had the energy. Instead, Abby had left the house feeling both guilty and badly put together, wondering why, no matter what she did, she never seemed to get it quite right.

On the Dart, on the way into town, she had discreetly studied the other women on the train, shielded by *The Irish Times*, which she held up in front of her, glancing over it occasionally. What preoccupied her most was their individual sizes – seeking, as she was, a similar physical example to compare herself to. Abby knew she had put on quite a bit of weight lately, a stone and a half at least, since she had last stood on the scales, and that had been almost a month ago. Reading the scales was one thing, like assessing your naked self in the mirror, intimidating certainly, but at least the horror was only self-inflicted, ending the moment you stepped off, or stopped looking. What she wanted, *needed*, she felt was solid, life-sized confirmation. Was she as big on top as that woman opposite with the huge boobs? Were her hips as curvy and well padded as that one, three seats up? Or was she just deteriorating into a general blob, like the expensively dressed woman to her left, with outrageously false eyelashes that made her look like a drag artist? Abby sighed; whatever size they were, she would bet they were all quite happy with themselves – you could just tell – unlike her.

She thought about that the whole way into town, had she ever really been happy? Content even? When she was younger, she always used to think that, once she was a teenager, she would automatically become cool and untroubled by whether or not she pleased people, or whether or not she was doing the right things, making the right decisions. Instead, her teenage years had been ridden with angst, closely followed by despair at her skinny, straight up and down figure and red hair, however long and silky it was. Young womanhood proved no easier. She filled out a little, sure, but, on the inside, Abby remained as devoid of confidence as ever, permanently persuaded of her many shortcomings. For as long as she could remember, she had felt as if she was in the wrong place, at the wrong time, too early or too late. She had lost count of the number of novenas she had said, books she had read, fortune-tellers she had visited who foretold of dark handsome strangers and foreign shores, which only filled Abby with foreboding. Abby hadn't wanted a dark swarthy foreigner – or to live somewhere hot and exotic – Abby had known exactly what she wanted, she just didn't in the world know how to go about getting it. And then, although she would never have believed it possible, the manifestation of her deepest desires had materialised in the most unlikely way . . .

Abby hardly notices the restaurant filling up with people she is so lost in her reverie, until she hears the familiar voice and catches an unmistakable waft of Diana's perfume that precedes her. Abby proffers her cheek for a kiss as Diana passes her, squeezing her shoulder affectionately before reaching for her seat.

'I'm so sorry I'm late, Abs,' she slings her bag over the chair as she sits down. 'I was cursing the traffic all the way here – every light was against me – and you're always so punctual.' She pauses to catch her breath and begins to fan herself.

'Is it just me or is it hot in here?'

'I hope it's just you, otherwise my face will be the same colour as my hair in minutes.'

'Yes, it probably is just me. Hardly surprising as I've practically run halfway down the street, no mean feat in these.' Diana obligingly extends an elegant foot shod in expensively delicate leather, with a vertiginous heel.

'You shouldn't have rushed,' Abby says. 'I'm not going anywhere.' She indicates the wine list.

'Ooh, yes, goodie, I could do with a nice glass of red. Have you ordered? No? Oh right, let's get the food and wine out of the way, then we can talk.'

Halfway through the very pleasant bottle of Merlot they have chosen, and thanks to being in Diana's company, Abby has come as close as she can to escapism. The sound of Diana's voice still with its occasional French inflections, chatting away animatedly, relating hilarious details of the latest photographic shoot she has been on in the south of France, has lulled Abby into a dreamy world where exacting husbands, controlling mothers and demanding daughters are but a filmy shadow of the imagination. This exotic world Diana so easily inhabits is exactly the antidote she needs to distract her. She could sit and listen to her forever, she thinks, a smile softening the tension in her face.

'Have you done something different to yourself?' she asks Diana suddenly. 'Hair? Skin? You look amazing. I mean you always look fab, Di, but you look different somehow.' Abby studies her across the table. 'More . . . animated – yes, that's the word for it.'

Diana laughs and, most unusually for her, blushes.

Abby cannot remember, now that she comes to think of it, ever seeing Diana blush, where as she, on the other hand, with her whiter-than-white, freckled complexion has been miserably prone to it all her life.

'I'm afraid I can only attribute it to being away in my spiritual home and surrounded by beautiful people. *Young, beautiful people,*' she says, wistfully.

'Did Greg join you?'

'No. He was holding the fort. That's the deal – or at least it's supposed to be.' Diana frowns.

'How is he?'

'Greg? He's fine, better than fine, in fact, he's just back from his own little break.'

'Oh? Where?'

'California. He was meditating,' Diana explains, lifting her eyebrows meaningfully.

'I didn't know Greg was into that sort of thing – spirituality, I mean.'

'Neither did I. It came upon him rather suddenly, pretty much like all the other courses he's been exploring – life drawing, amateur dramatics, yoga . . . I could go on.'

'Oh, Di,' Abby grins. 'Is it getting on your nerves, having him around all the time?'

Greg, Diana's husband, once darling of the advertising industry, had lost his job about a year earlier. Abby, being tactful, usually never refers to it, but today Diana seems to want to talk.

'It's driving me bloody insane. That's why I was so relieved to get away when this job came up.' Diana reaches for the bottle and tops up their glasses.

'Still, it must be handy to have him around now that *you're* so busy.' Abby is good at presenting the bright side of other people's lives to them. 'To hold the fort as you say. Nice for the kids too,' she says encouragingly.

'Uh-uh.' Diana shakes her head. 'I'm with whoever said, "I married him for better or worse, but I never married him for lunch."'

Abby laughs. 'Life is never easy, is it?'

'We used to think it would be . . .'

'Only because we didn't know any better. We were just kids . . .'

'You said you had something to tell me,' Diana reminds her. 'When you were on the phone?' She takes a sip of her coffee.

'Oh, yes – so I do. You'll never guess!'

'I'm not even going to try.'

'I heard from Vonnie, just yesterday.'

'Vonnie? No way! How is she?'

'I don't know, it was just a short email, but, Di, she's coming home and she wants to see us.' Abby can hardly contain her excitement.

Di shakes her head wonderingly. 'How long has it been?'

'Almost twelve years . . .' Abby has been keeping count. There had been the occasional email from Vonnie in the beginning when she moved to LA from London, then they sort of petered out, until finally the only communication between them was Christmas cards – although, to be fair, she never forgot a birthday.

'My, my . . . where do they go?'

'I know, but I had a feeling we might hear from her sometime soon. After all, we have an anniversary coming up, don't we? Abby looks at her meaningfully. 'Don't tell me you'd forgotten?'

'How could I?' Diana says, wryly.

'Imagine,' Abby smiles wistfully, 'thirty years since we made our visit to St Valentine.' She twirls the stem of her wine glass. 'And that first day of school seems like a lifetime ago. Do you remember, Di . . .?'

September 1978, First Year

Abby

'There,' says Sheila Murphy, viewing every brand-new, name-tagged article of clothing with satisfaction. 'Everything! Every single item on that damned list – even the green knickers.'

It had not been easy, finding, selecting, not to mention buying everything on the never-ending list, which seemed to conspire to thwart her from the very outset. The woollen-weave, satin-edged blankets; the personal, engraved cutlery; the special tweed Sunday suit; even the magnificent moss-green hooded cloak had been procured, but the green knickers had stymied her. She had looked at the list in confusion. There it was in black and white, staring back at her: *Seven pairs of white cotton knickers and two pairs of green*, it said quite plainly.

Why on earth green? And where to find these elusive under-garments? Sheila had wondered wildly.

Abby had been no help at all. 'How would I know, Mum?' she had asked, wide eyed and not a little embarrassed.

In the end, although she had hated to admit defeat, Sheila had had to enlist the help of a friend of a friend, whose cousin had a daughter who was in her final year at Belmount. Word had filtered back that the mysterious green knickers were part of the sporting attire, to be worn *under* the games skirt, but *over* your regular knickers, that way there could be no occasion where a flash of feminine underwear might be glimpsed, whatever the circumstances – say, for instance, if a sudden gust of wind should whip up.

Once she had come to grips with the idea, Sheila was fully enamoured of the concept. 'Modesty at all times' was one of her favourite mottos, and you could count on the nuns to be sticklers for it. That was just one of the many reasons Sheila had chosen the exclusive convent for her only daughter's education. The fees were prohibitive, but the scholarship would take care of that. Abby had worked hard at her local national school, and, good girl that she was, had not protested at the extra coaching her mother had given her in the evenings and at weekends. (What else was being a teacher good for, reasoned Sheila, if you couldn't enhance your only child's future prospects?) It would only be for a year, she had explained to her daughter, only until the entrance exam had been passed and results exceeding and surpassing even Sheila's fond hopes had been achieved.

Now the fruits of their joint labour, the trappings of success, lay before them, stacked and piled with military precision on Abby's narrow bed, ready to go into the trunk, which Abby's father, Joe, would load into their ancient station wagon.

Joe had taken the day off work at Sheila's insistence although he would much rather have not. It was not that he was unwilling to drive his only child the hour or so to County Wicklow to deliver her to her new school – her home from home for the next twelve weeks – it was more a case of concern in case his mask might slip. In case he, the stern guard, a reliable member of the police force, might suddenly become emotional, might lose composure, might even, God forbid, shed a tear. He would much rather have said goodbye to her that morning, calmly, quietly, wished her well and gone off to work where he could have felt of some use, and at least distracted himself from the bleak prospect of just Sheila and himself home alone together for the foreseeable future.

Instead, sitting downstairs, nursing a cup of tea, dressed

uncomfortably in a new suit especially bought for the occasion, he feels in the way and useless.

In the car, all the way to Wicklow, Abby is quiet, gazing out the window from the back seat where she mindlessly fingers the pleats on her uniform plaid skirt. She is anxious, but not about leaving home or worrying how her parents will manage without her – that had been on last year's worry agenda. Her anxieties now concern her immediate destination, what might unfold, what lay in store for her, what will be expected. It is a big adventure, as her mother has been telling her for months, but Abby does not like or need adventure – she is much more comfortable with certainties.

She likes to know exactly what is expected of her so she can dedicate herself ruthlessly to the task in question. This, she has learned, is what seems to keep people happy, and keeping people happy is what makes Abby happy – or at least gives her some peace of mind. Herein lies her present quandary: she knows what her mother expects of her at school, but what about her new classmates? Thirty or so other girls about whom she knows absolutely nothing. She would very much like them to like her, to be popular – this is important at school, particularly boarding school (she has read all the books on the subject she can get her hands on, *Malory Towers*, *St Clare's*, the *Chalet Girls*) – but Abby is not entirely sure what makes a girl popular.

She does not want anyone to know she is a scholarship girl, that she has earned her place in this exclusive establishment through strenuously hard work and study rather than paying top-notch fees like the others, but she is pretty sure it will be impossible to hide the fact. Although, her mother assured her, they had scrimped and saved all the same, just in case, in the unlikely event of Abby *not* winning the scholarship. They certainly had the money to send her to Belmount

– Grandmother Harvey's small legacy had been painstakingly protected and added to for this very cause. The scholarship would just make things easier, it would pay for the school fees, but it would not cover *everything*. It would not pay for the uniform that comprised a veritable trousseau (and in its own way was just as significant). It would not pay for the inevitable school trips and excursions away, but it would be worth it. 'A good education sets a girl up for life, not just academically,' Sheila had explained many times. 'Going to a good school means you mix with the right sort of people – not riff-raff.' And the right sort of people in Sheila's opinion meant *girls*.

Abby had once mentioned innocently that she might like to attend a nearby co-ed day school some of the girls from her old school were going to, but Sheila had been appalled at the notion.

'Co-ed?' she had repeated with revulsion. 'Under no circumstances is a daughter of mine going to school with a lot of common boys.'

Abby had been curious, rather than disappointed, at the reaction this had provoked. 'Why?'

'Too many distractions,' Sheila had said, pursing her lips. 'Boys are slower learners and they hold the whole class back – then, because the girls get bored, they become lazy, they stop studying and start wearing make-up and flaunting themselves at the boys and, before you know it, the boys have passed them out and get top marks in their Leaving Certificate, while all the girls leave with is the option of a secretarial course and a "reputation".'

Abby had not been sure what a 'reputation' was but gathered it was not a good thing to acquire.

'Besides,' Sheila had continued, 'if a boy has known you since you were twelve years old there's nothing left he *wants* to know about you, nothing at all left to the imagination. Boys and young men like nothing better than a fresh face, Abby, a new girl on the scene, not some comfortable old school chum they've known since they sat in the back row together. Mystery is very important to boys when they're choosing a girl. Always keep a bit of mystery, Abby, there's nothing worse than a boy knowing your whole life story – there's nothing left for him to find out.'

Abby had not been sure what all this advice had to do with education, but she had been wise enough not to pursue the matter. Her mother knew best, and she had Abby's best interests at heart. If Sheila said Belmount Convent was the place for her, then Abby would dutifully attend and make her mother proud of her – just as she always had done.

They were here, now, turning in through an imposing entrance, up a winding drive with lawns on either side, stretching to fields in the distance, and beyond there is a glimpse of cornflower-blue sea. Abby thinks she can hear cattle lowing, she remembers hearing that the school has its own farm, and not having been allowed any pets of her own at home, she feels a glimmer of excitement. An old man wearing a cap trundles along with a wheelbarrow, a black Labrador at his heels, and lifts his hand in greeting. They swing around to the front entrance, where the old house looks on to the carefully tended front lawn, joining the many other cars discharging a multitude of young girls, some eagerly screaming greetings, some hanging back, some quietly sobbing. Abby takes a deep breath and gets out of the car. There will be no scenes, no emotional outbursts. They will proceed in an orderly fashion towards the nun who is approaching them in welcome. 'Abby Murphy, is it?' she checks her list. 'I'm Sister Byrne, welcome to Belmount! You're in St Anne's, dearie. That's to the side of the Old House, across the courtyard and upstairs. Helen will show you, won't you, Helen?'

Helen is a third year, a seasoned student and appointed

one of the Guardian Angels who will shepherd the new girls around for the first couple of days until they feel at home. 'What a lovely idea,' Sheila beams.

St Anne's is a converted stable block, consisting of the first-year classroom, common room and two dormitories above. Abby is shown her bed and locker, and begins to unpack. Her mother sets about the task briskly, her eagle eyes taking in every detail of the other girls and their families, chatting, laughing or consoling.

Once the bedclothes are laid out and the trunk is empty, Abby says she will walk her parents back to the car. 'I'll make the bed myself, there's no need for you to wait.' She smiles at her father's obvious relief. He is uncomfortable in the midst of all these women, glad to escape to the familiar sanctuary of the car. Back outside, it is almost like a party in full swing. Many of the parents seem to know each other, and are chatting and laughing easily together as they are fed tea and sandwiches on the front lawn. 'It's very convivial,' Sheila says, looking on approvingly. 'Very elegant.'

One of the older girls rings a bell – the signal for parents to depart and for the girls to say goodbye.

'Goodbye, Dad,' Abby says, awkwardly. 'Thanks for driving me down.'

'Not at all, pet.' Joe pats his daughter on the shoulder. 'Sure we'll be seeing you in no time. Mind yourself now.' He sounds stern, but Abby sees his eyes are bright and feels a pang of concern for him.

'Now, Abby.' Sheila hugs her daughter, then holds her at arm's length. 'Don't let me down. You'll do your best, won't you, love?'

'You know I will, Mum.'

'Of course you will. I'll write to you before the end of the week. And you must write and tell us all the news as soon as you can.'

Abby waves dutifully until the silver station wagon with the dent in the side that her father cannot afford to get fixed disappears down the driveway. Then she turns around and walks stoically back towards her dormitory.

She is only twelve years old, but already life's responsibilities are weighing heavily upon her shoulders.

Diana

I made my bed, then flung myself on it and began to sob noisily. I never believed that they would carry out the threat, not really. Right up to the last minute, even though they had driven me here, I still thought they would relent and take me home with them, warning me that, really, if there were to be another incident, a next time, then I really *would* be sent away to boarding school.

It's all *her* fault of course. It was her idea to send me here. Papa didn't agree with it at all, I could tell just by looking at him, he looked so sad when they sat me down to tell me. Of course, they used the excuse that because my older sister, Corinne, will be in the Sorbonne for the next few years, that it would be too lonely for me at home alone with them, that it would be better for me to be in the company of girls my own age. Papa is travelling a lot with his work and, anyway, they said Belmount is only a weekly boarding school, we are allowed home each Sunday for the day. But they didn't fool me. I know Mum has been planning this, she wants Papa all to herself. And now Corinne has gone away, she wants to get rid of me too.

Papa adores me. Everyone says so. He and I have a very special relationship. Corinne prefers Mum, I think, they are more alike. Papa says I am the double of his mother, Grand-mère Fouberge, whom I never met, because she had died by the time I was born. Unfortunately, Papa always goes along with Mum, she always has the last say. And just because there were a few little incidents, like getting caught smoking behind the prefabs at my last school, suddenly I'm told I'm going to boarding school! I'll never forgive her for this – she's going to be sorry! I'm going to be so awful they will send me home within the week, even expel me! I don't care how bad I have to be, that will teach her.

'Dear me, what have we here? Diana, isn't it?'

I look up to find one of *them*, a nun, our dorm mistress, Sr Julia, youngish, rosy-faced, sitting on my bed. She puts her arm around me and makes shushing noises. I cry even harder. Several of the girls are approaching with concerned faces, I can see them out of the corner of my eye, but really they're just curious – snooping. They haven't seen anything yet.

'Go away!' I yell. 'Leave me alone! Just leave me alone, will you?'

I sense a collective gasp. Clearly, these girls aren't used to nuns being spoken to like this. It's a first for Sr Julia, too, I suspect. I don't care, I never wanted to come here anyway. It's all a horrible mistake.

'Now stop that right now, Diana,' Sr Julia says firmly.

This is not the reaction I was expecting, and I am moment-arily shocked enough to raise my head from the pillow and turn to look at her.

'Come along now, sit up! You're a Dublin girl, aren't you, Diana?'

'What's that got to do with anything?' I hiccup. 'And no, I'm half-French, actually, on my father's side.' There, that should be rude enough to shut her up.

'Well, for starters, it means you'll be going home on Sunday for the day, doesn't it?' she says crisply. 'That's less than a week away. So there's no need at all to be crying, is there?'

Before I can reply to this ridiculous statement she goes on.

'A lot of the girls here are from the country, from all over the country, some from abroad even. Many of them won't be going home at all until the Christmas holidays, they might well be very lonely at the thought of leaving their families and friends behind for such a time, but I don't see any of *them* crying and behaving like junior infants, do you? Now, get up and dry your eyes, Diana.' Then she gets up and turns to the others. 'Tea will be served in the Refectory in fifteen minutes and, after that, seeing as it's your first night, there's a film at seven o'clock, which will be shown in the school hall. You may bring your duvets with you to keep warm if you wish. Now, run along.'

A junior infant! How dare she! Bloody old cow! I was about to scream at her but I saw a few of the girls sniggering. I wasn't going to have that. So I changed my tack and went over to the cubicles to blow my nose, brush my hair and put on some lip salve, then walked out of the dorm on my own without a backward glance.

In the refectory, first years are allowed sit together for the first meal, so we can get to know each other. *Not much point in that*, I'm thinking. I refuse a helping of the disgusting dried up chips and greasy sausage rolls that obviously pass for food here, and sit looking straight ahead sipping a cup of horrible tea – it's that or water, no coffee. Barbaric!

'You'd better eat something!' the big girl sitting opposite me whispers. She has been smiling at me since we sat down, clearly trying to engage me in conversation. 'They'll let you away with it this evening, because it's your first day,' she warns, 'but after that they'll call your parents, maybe even the doctor. You'll get into trouble.' Her eyes are wide with the thought. 'I know, you see, because I have a sister here, in third year.'

'So?'

'Well, I know it's not important or anything, but I know how things work here.'

'I couldn't care less. I've no intention of staying here – I'll be gone before the end of the week.'

'Oh,' she says, looking downcast. 'That's a pity! You're in my dorm, I was hoping we might be friends.'

Then the girl on my right pipes up. 'I am too,' she says, shyly. 'In your dorm, I mean. I saw you both earlier. My name's Abby. I didn't want to come here either, really. But don't worry, it won't be that bad, honestly.' She looks at me with concern.

'I'm not worried.' I turn to look at her. She has long red hair, pale, freckled skin and big, fearful, blue eyes. She is pretty, but she doesn't realise it. 'And I have no intention of eating this muck. My father will be horrified when I tell him we have been given sausage rolls and chips, and you couldn't even call these chips.' I hold up a rock-hard example.

'Is your father a chef?' asks the big girl, looking interested. She has been eating constantly since we sat down, and is on her third slice of bread and butter, along with several sausage rolls and a mountain of chips.

'No.' I am puzzled she should think this. 'He's an art critic. Why?'

'Oh, no reason, just wondering. I love food.' She stuffs another sausage roll into her mouth. I stare, I can't help it, even though I know it's rude. I have never seen anyone eat so much, so quickly. The girl on my right, Abby, giggles.

'My name's Vonnie – Vonnie Callaghan,' the big girl says. 'What's yours?'

'Diana.' I make sure I sound bored.

'Well, Diana and Abby,' she lowers her voice, 'I have some amazing food upstairs. If you like we can smuggle some down with us to the film tonight. In the dark, if we're careful, we should get away with it. After tomorrow, if they discover it, it will be confiscated. You're only allowed food from the Tuck Shop, and that's only open on Saturday afternoons.'

I roll my eyes. What kind of a place is this? Why all these pathetic rules and regulations? Not that I care of course.

After tea (which should be called dinner, another thing my father will be annoyed about), we undress in the dormitory and get into our 'night attire', as Sr Julia calls it. Then, duvets in hand, we troop across the courtyard, through the Old House and into the new wing where the film is being shown in the hall. A projector sits at the back and a large screen has been put up on the stage. Rows of hard-backed, wooden chairs with metal legs are lined up like soldiers.

Vonnie waves at us eagerly, indicating the three seats she has spread her duvet over. She is out of breath from running ahead. It is first-come, first-served regarding seating arrangements on movie nights, she informs us.

Silence is called for. We settle down, the lights go out, the projector whirs into action and the title rolls. *Carve Her Name With Pride* . . . I'm practically asleep already.

'Here,' whispers Vonnie, nudging me. She hands me a piece of carrot cake and something chocolaty and chewy, wrapped in cling film. 'Tin foil is too noisy,' she explains. Suddenly, I realise I am starving.

'For God's sake, don't let the nuns see,' she mumbles, already chewing away.

I bite into the carrot cake, topped with sweet, creamy icing and am pleasantly surprised. It is good, better than good, it is delicious.

'Do you like it?' she whispers.

I nod, indicating that my mouth is full.

This seems to please her. 'Good. Because there's plenty more upstairs where that came from, and we have to finish it by tonight. Tomorrow, when we're in class, they'll search the dorms.'

After the movie, we go back to our dorm, wash and climb into our narrow, squeaking beds. Sr Julia checks on us all, pulls the curtains tight and says goodnight. 'Now girls, I don't have to tell you I'm sure, no talking after lights out. Understood?'

'Yes, Sister.'

'And no food or transistor radios are allowed in the dormitories. If you are in possession of either, you must hand them in to me in the morning. You may listen to your radios in the common room during recreation. Otherwise, they will be confiscated and you will lose house marks, are we clear?'

'Yes, Sister.'

'Now, God bless and get a good night's sleep. You'll need all your energy for tomorrow.' She turns out the lights.

'Goodnight, Sister.'

For ten minutes or so, there is silence, which soon gives way to the heavy regular breathing of untroubled sleepers.

'Are you awake?' Vonnie whispers. I can just about see her in the bed across the way, sitting up.

'Mmmhmm,' I say sleepily.

Abby?'

'Yes, I'm awake.'

'Anyone else? No? Oh, well, it's just us then.' She rummages under her bed and pulls out what looks like a large sewing box, and drags it quietly across the floor, then sits at the end of my bed. 'Now, what do you fancy?' she says, opening it, and I see it is a picnic basket of sorts, packed with food, tins, paper plates and cups and plastic cutlery.

'There's enough to feed a whole family in there,' whispers Abby, wide eyed.

'Oh, Barney always makes loads of everything. She said it wouldn't be a proper first night at boarding school if we didn't have a midnight feast.'

'But it's not even ten o'clock,' Abby points out.

'Who cares? I can't wait another second.'

'Who's Barney?' I ask.

'She's our housekeeper and cook, I suppose, but she's more like family really,' says Vonnie.

'You have a cook?' Abby sounds impressed.

Vonnie considers this. 'Well, I think she just likes to cook for us, but she's brilliant at it.'

'Doesn't your mother cook?' I ask.

'No,' says Vonnie. 'I don't think she likes cooking.'

We are quiet for a while as we tuck in to various individual miniature cakes, pies, trifles and even chocolate soufflés, washed down with Coca-Cola. I eat until I think I am going to burst.

'The cakes are divine,' I sigh. 'They remind me of the patisseries in Paris.'

'You've been to Paris?' Abby says.

'My father's family are from Paris.'

'Wow, that's cool.'

I shrug.

'Your Barney is certainly a good cook, Vonnie,' I say.

I am beginning to see why Vonnie is overweight. If I had that kind of food around all the time, I probably would be too.

'I know,' Vonnie beams. 'Barney says the best way to make friends with people is to eat with them. So that makes us friends now, right?'

'Oh, good,' Abby sounds relieved. They both look at me expectantly.

'Friends? Sure, why not?' I say. There is no point disillusioning them.

We clear up any crumbs as best we can and roll back into our beds.

'Thanks, Vonnie,' Abby and I whisper.

You're welcome. See you in the morning,' Vonnie yawns.

'Night, night.'

'Don't let the bed bugs bite,' Abby giggles.

They are nice girls, Vonnie and Abby, I think as I feel sleep overtaking me – even if they are a bit immature – but we will not be friends. As soon as I go home and leave this place, we will forget all about each other. I just have to get through until Sunday. Only five more days . . .

The journey up to Dublin on the school bus feels interminable, all the more because we have to wear our stupid tweed Sunday suits, and the harsh material has been scratching my legs. Luckily for me, the bus stops quite near my house, only a ten-minute walk. Abby is being picked up at the bus stop by her parents and Vonnie lives in Wicklow, quite near to school, so her dad collected her and her sister, Kate.

'Bye,' Abby called, waving as she got into her parents' car. 'Have a great day, Di. See you later.'

Oh no you won't, I thought happily. We are required to be back at the bus stop at six o'clock for the trip back to school. But I will not be there. Papa will not force me to go back – if I have to beg, I will.

I reach our road and run the last bit of the way to our house and around the side to the back door, which I know will be left open for me. Already, I can smell my favourite food. It's Sunday lunch as usual, and I'm guessing she has done her special roast chicken with all the trimmings especially for me – out of guilt at sending me away to school.

'Mum!' I burst through the door about to start ranting how much I hate boarding school but when my mother turns around, something stops me. She is crying, there are tears on her face and her eyes are red and swollen.

'Diana!' she wipes her face quickly with a piece of paper towel. 'You're early, darling.' She laughs. 'How lovely, just give me a minute until my eyes stop streaming. It's those horrible onions I had to chop for the stuffing – it's your favourite, roast chicken with roast potatoes and parsnips and carrots and—' she hugs me and squeezes me tight.

'How is school?'

'It's horrible. I hate it! The nuns are devils and the food is disgusting. I'm not going back.' I pull away from her, angrily.

'But Diana, it's only your first week, sweetheart. Just give it a little time.'

'I don't need time. Where's Papa?' I head out of the kitchen intending to go straight into my father's study where he always sits reading before lunch. 'He'll listen to me.'

'Diana, wait!'

I turn around, something in her tone is different. 'What?'

'Not now, sweetheart. Papa is on the phone, it's business, very important, he doesn't want to be disturbed. He'll be finished any minute. Here, help me with the vegetables while I carve.'

I do as she says reluctantly, listening to her prattle, answering her questions sullenly.

After what seems an age, Papa comes in and I run straight into his outstretched arms. '*Ma jeune fille!*' he laughs with pleasure. And even though I am very angry with him for making me stay even a week away from home in that horrible place, he makes me smile, chatting away to me in French and laughing at my descriptions of school hell.

'It can't be that bad,' he says, as we sit down to eat.

'It's worse. You have no idea. They don't even let us have baths.'

'Please, Diana,' Mum pleads, 'not while we're at the table.' Her voice is strained. 'You're only home until this evening, let's have a pleasant day together, hmm?'

I shrug. Papa catches my eye and winks; he understands. I will talk to him after lunch, alone. There is no point having this discussion in front of my mother. She will only make it more difficult. So I change tactic and say how lovely it is to taste home cooking again, and ask Papa questions about his work. The atmosphere, which for a moment felt awkward and tense, relaxes.

After lunch, I help Mum clear away then run upstairs to my room to check on my stack of LPs and tape cassettes. My older sister, Corinne, who has gone to the Sorbonne, is not to be trusted – I have to make sure she has not taken any of my stuff. Satisfied that everything is in order, and looking longingly at my posters of David Bowie, Queen and the Bay City Rollers on the wall, I go downstairs ready to throw myself at Papa's mercy and plead with him not to send me back. The door to his study is closed and I am about to knock, as we always do before disturbing him, when I hear raised voices and my hand pauses before my knuckles can rap on the door panel. My mother is talking.

'I mean it! Either she goes, or I do, you decide—'

'Please, Pauline, you are over reacting.'

'Is that what you really believe?'

Silence.

'It's always her, isn't it? It always has been. You love her, don't you?'

'Please, Pauline, don't force me to choose—'

'Answer me! Do you? Do you love her?'

'I love her, yes! Yes, I have always loved her. Now, are you satisfied?'

'Oh God.' My mother stifles a sob.

'The truth is I love you both. It's possible to love more than one person, you know! It doesn't mean I love her more than you – it's just . . . different. Please don't do this to yourself, Pauline. You're my wife, we're a family.'

Silence.

'So, you won't tell her?'

'I won't do that to her, not when she needs me, if that's what you mean.'

'That's your final word? As my husband? As our daughters' father?'

'Yes, that's my final word.'

'Then *I* will leave. You leave me no option.'

'Don't be ridiculous, Pauline. Where would you go? You love me, I love you – this is just a complication. She needs me, please don't force my hand.'

I have heard enough! I back away in shock and run upstairs, back to my room where I put on my Elton John tape of *Captain Fantastic*.

I try to take it in, to understand what I have just overheard, but I feel sick. I had no idea things were like this. I know my father adores me, but I never realised my mother was so jealous of his feelings for me. I *knew* he wanted to keep me at home. He would never send me away, it was always her idea, right from the beginning. But for my mother to leave if I came home! It was unthinkable! Surely she couldn't hate me that much? I know I irritate her, get on her nerves some-times, but not like that . . . not as if she – she *hated* me. Poor Papa! He was only trying to defend me, to stand up for me.

There is only one thing to do, I decide there and then. I must go back to Belmount. I must go back to boarding school as if nothing has happened. I will behave as if it has all been a joke – as if nothing at all is wrong. Otherwise, well *anything* could happen! I might have to live with *her*, on our own together without Papa. Papa might get married to someone else if Mum left! I could have a step-mother! Papa could get sick, maybe even have a heart attack from the worry, like what happened in our neighbour's family last month. My head is filling with terrible possibilities. I am suddenly horribly sorry for the way I have been behaving. How stupid I have been! I didn't know how much of a problem I was to them. I didn't know how badly Mum wanted Papa to herself. But now I realise and it is better to know.

What was it he had said? *Don't force me to choose . . .*

Well I won't. I won't force him. I would never do that. Poor Papa . . . poor, *poor* Papa.

'You're very quiet,' Abby says to me later that evening on the bus as we head back to school.

'I'm just tired,' I say, returning to the book I am pretending to read.

Back at school, the dorm is full of girls talking about their day at home, and once we have settled, we are told there is hot chocolate in the kitchen for anyone who wants it. I don't. I am moody and uncommunicative, I don't want to see or talk to anyone.

'It's always hard coming back after spending a day at home,' Vonnie says. 'You get used to it, though.' She smiles sympathetically.

She has no idea.

And that's the way I intend to keep it. These girls think I am exotic, sophisticated, worldly – and that suits me just fine.

I have a bath. (We are allowed only two baths a week, by rote, and one of my nights is Sunday. The rest of the time we are expected to wash at the basins in our individual cubicles. *Barbaric.*)

Apparently, the bathing options improve the further up the school you get. In fifth and sixth year, they have proper showers, rows of them. I laughed at the idea when I heard it last week, but that was before I knew I would have to stay here.

In bed, I pull the covers up and pretend to be asleep, even before the lights are turned out. I wait until Sr Julia has gone, until everyone has said their goodnights, until they are all asleep. Only then do I cry – quietly, secretly – no display this time, just fierce control. But the tears that trail hotly down my face are real.

Morro Bay, California, 2011

From where I live in Morro Bay, I can hear the ocean. That should remind me of home, where I grew up in County Wicklow, a stone's throw from the sea, but, happily, it is a million miles away in every respect from the place. Here the ocean will not be ignored. Great rolling breakers, huge swells of surf or the rush of a wave cradling the shore, all have their voice – sometimes a roar, sometimes a whisper . . .

'Vonnie, how nice to see you, have a seat.' Ellen, my therapist, welcomes me warmly.

It has been some time since I have been with her, almost a year in fact. We chat about the usual things for a couple of moments and then I tell her the reason I am here.

'It's no big deal,' I say. 'In fact, I feel pretty silly even coming here to talk about it, but then I thought . . .'

'What's up?' she asks, her laser-blue eyes pinning me to the chair, although she is smiling encouragingly.

'Well, I'm going home.'

'To Ireland?'

'Yes. Not for good or anything like that,' I explain hurriedly. 'Just a visit. It's a work thing, a freelance project, but I'll be there for about six weeks or so. I thought it might be a good time to, well, to confront some things, so to speak.'

'Well,' says Ellen, watching me closely, 'in that case, it *is* a big deal for you, Vonnie. Wouldn't you say?'

I squirm a little under her eagle-eyed gaze and chew the

inside of my cheek as the question hangs in the air. Stupid, *stupid*. I had felt like a cosy little chat, some benign self-examination perhaps, a pat on the back for doing so well. Time away has made me careless – I had forgotten there is nowhere to hide in a therapist's office. Not Ellen's anyway. Already I can feel myself shifting uncomfortably in my chair.

'So, where shall we start? Are you taking Jazz with you?'

'Yes, I've rented a little house, she's very excited.'

'And what about your . . . family? Will you be seeing them?'

'I– I don't know. I'll contact them first maybe, see how it goes from there.'

'You don't owe them anything you know, Vonnie. We've been through this, right?'

'I know.'

'You're not beholden to anyone now.'

'I know that. I'd just like to, well, for Jazz. She'll have questions when she's older – she already has.'

'And your mother?'

'I haven't said anything to her yet.'

'Are you going to?'

'It's none of her business.' I sound angry, and I had resolved to be calm, which makes me even angrier.

'Well, it *does* concern her, in many ways, don't you think?'

I shrug. 'It was all so long ago.'

'Maybe for them, not for you, though, Vonnie. You're still finding your way through a lot of this stuff. They're new feelings for you, even if they've been there all along, buried, unexpressed. You've had to deal with them, live with them, let them in. Reframe it all, so it's still fresh for you, in a way, don't you think?'

'What does it matter?' I scowl at her.

Ellen smiles, unflappable. 'It matters,' she says, 'because I think it may just be a very happy coincidence, this job offer to go to Ireland. I think, in fact, it might be the ideal time to deal with all of this – to finally put all the theory into practice. You're a different person, now, Vonnie. And you've worked very hard at becoming that new person. I think it's a perfectly good opportunity to go back and tell it like it is.'

'So you *do* think it's a good idea?' Suddenly I am worried, unsure.

'That depends on you – how you handle it – but I think you're more than ready, which is more to the point. You're well able to do this, Vonnie, and you owe it to yourself, not just to Jazz.'

Our time is up before I know it, and I get up to leave. I feel drained, a bit shaky.

'You know you can call me, don't you? If you need to.'

'Thank you, Ellen, I appreciate that.'

'I don't believe in coincidences, Vonnie, as you know. It's the right time, and the right opportunity has presented itself. Let me know how you get on when you get back, won't you?'

'You'll be the first to hear,' I smile weakly.

'Atta girl.'

Back home, I check my mail, there are a few work-related ones and one from Abby, a reply to the one I sent her just a couple of days ago. I take a deep breath and hesitate before opening it, not sure of the tone it will take. It's been a long time after all, almost twelve years, I couldn't blame her if she was cool or remote. I pretty much dropped off the radar as far as Abby and Diana were concerned, but I *had* to drop everything to do with my old life in order to create a new one.

'You need to see a therapist, honey,' Jenn had said to me, as casually as if I should book a hair appointment. 'And I have a great one.'

I didn't like the idea, but I was running out of options. I had lost the weight, which had dogged me my whole life, and then, right out of the blue, the panic attacks began. I didn't see the connection, I simply thought I was going insane, losing my marbles, but Jenn, smart west coast amateur psychologist that she was, sensed something deeper was going on.

'Just humour me, hmm? Three sessions, then if you think it's all whacko, ditch it – but at least you can say you gave it a try. What have you got to lose?'

When I thought about it like that, I could see she had a point. Either way, I couldn't continue as I was.

'We've fixed the outside,' Jenn smiled. 'Now I think the inside might need a bit of work.'

And that's how my sessions with Ellen began. When, after listening to my life story, she suggested I take some time out, away from people who knew me well, perhaps too well, for my own good.

'Sometimes we all need to step back, Vonnie, to give ourselves some space to look at our life, the patterns we've established. It's a whole lot easier to do that without people in your life who may be invested in keeping you where you are instead of encouraging you to grow. You're here in LA, you've put the physical distance between your old life and your new one. I think maybe it's time to put some emotional distance there too.

'If they're real friends, they'll understand,' Ellen had said when I first started to see her and she was encouraging me to make a fresh start. 'They'll be there for you when you're ready to pick up the reins again.'

Now I wasn't so sure. I click on the email and smile. It reads simply:

To: vcallaghan23@indiemail.com
From: abs45@eirfol.com
'Well, the dead arose and appeared to many.'

Where have you been?!
Di and I longing to see you. Hurry home.
Abs xxxxxxxxx
PS Send your phone number immediately!

I check the time. I have an hour before I pick Jazz up from school, and I don't feel like working. I will go to the beach to walk, to watch the surfers, to listen to the ocean and to remember . . .

It won't be long at all now; this time next week, Jazz and I will be in Dublin. Despite myself, and all the time that has passed, I still feel apprehensive at the thought. I really don't enjoy confrontations, however therapeutic they might be. So much has happened since then, and yet it only seems like yesterday.

Third Year, September 1980

Vonnie

29th September 1980

English Essay

Topic: My Family – Discuss

I don't hate my sister. Perhaps 'hate' is too strong a word. Occasional loathing, though, that would be about right. Yes, loathing definitely features on the scale of sibling emotions that assail me on a fairly regular basis. I'm not even that emotional a person, but that's just the way it is with Kate. Everyone has strong feelings about her, she sort of elicits them. Happily, or irritatingly, depending upon your perspective, most of these feelings are unrelentingly positive.

You see Kate is perfect, always has been. This in itself wouldn't be so much of an irritation if she didn't so obviously revel in the knowledge – and believe me, she does. No one else seems to see it, but I do. There's no hiding from a sister, even a hopeless-case sister like me. If she were a friend, it would be easy, I could just disengage, drift away, but since she's a sister, I'm stuck. For the time being at any rate. But just as soon as I can, I'm getting away. From all of them, all the Kate worshippers. Each to their own and all that, but it's not for me. I know the real girl beneath the facade and, frankly, she can be pretty obnoxious. But possibly she saves those displays just for me. Either that, or everyone else is just too stupid or bedazzled to see through her. They will, one day. That's what I keep telling myself anyway. It keeps me sane. Keeps me from jumping up and smacking her in the face when she drops one of her innocent comments, inevitably a putdown, her face a mask of sisterly concern, or more often, pity – in front of a suitable audience, naturally.

It shouldn't get to me, but it does, because no one knows how to hit a weak spot like a sister – they even outdo mothers by a long shot. Apart from anything else, they know too much. This is probably why I feel exhausted a lot of the time. Nothing to do with a sudden spurt of growth or surging hormones; no, it's frantically covering my tracks and constantly thinking ahead to prevent any detail, however small or incidental, in my beyond-average life, from coming to the razor-sharp beam of her attention. This is more difficult than you might imagine. Because although Kate is generally utterly absorbed in her own successes, basking in the collective adoration of parents, extended family, teachers and multi-tudinous friends, she has an almost super-human ability to sniff out anything I'm remotely interested in or enthusiastic about, and ruin it for me.

An early memory (not a positive experience):

A doll I had been given by a favourite aunt of ours for my sixth birthday mysteriously disappeared. I left her alone in the garden sitting prettily with the other members of the tea party set, and when I came back she was gone.

Kate, two years older than me, studiously combing her own doll's hair, seemed unconcerned.

'Where is she?' I cried. 'Where's Chloe?'

'How should I know?' Kate said, without looking up.

'But she was here. I left her here, right beside you when I went inside.' Alarm began to prickle up and down my arms and my voice sounded shrill and reedy.

Kate shrugged.

I felt sick, sick with fear and something I didn't understand then, which was a horrible, unthinkable suspicion.

Chloe, my doll, did reappear, later that evening, but not as I knew her. Her clothes had gone, she was missing an eye, and her lovely, synthetic, strawberry-blonde locks had been hacked to a spiky crop. My grief (which was all consuming) was met first with confusion, then exasperation, followed by downright displeasure from my mother, who was on her second pre-dinner cocktail. My father had yet to come home.

'How could you let this happen, Veronica?' her eyes glittered as she held poor Chloe aloft in her nakedness. I felt my doll's silent, one-eyed stare even more damning. Shame overcame me.

Mrs Barnes (we call her Barney), our double-duty housekeeper and cook, looked uncomfortable, being the bearer of the bad news. 'Marty found her in the vegetable garden, in with the cabbages,' she said, fidgeting with a button on her overall. 'Sammy must have got hold of her and gone on a rampage,' she added.

Sammy, our fat, elderly, black Labrador had, along with a healthy disdain for anything that wasn't part of the food chain, lost most of his teeth, and had never in living memory destroyed anything made of something as unappetising as plastic. Even if he *had* taken Chloe, it would only have been to desperately try to retrieve her for somebody – not disfigure her. No, the culprit was definitely not Sammy, who dozed happily that day in his favourite sunspot, pressed against the glass door of the sun-room, snoring gently.

'Sammy wouldn't do that,' I said, tears beginning.

'Well, maybe one of the village lads hopped over the wall and got a hold of her. They're right little demons.' Barney looked hopeful.

'Well she's ruined,' my mother said. 'And Angela sent her all the way from America. I'm sure she was ridiculously expensive. But then Angela can afford to spend a fortune on toys and all sorts of nonsense, *she's* married to a millionaire.'

Angela, my mother's sister, is my godmother, although I had only met her once on one of her visits home.

'I told her it was far too extravagant a present for a six year old,' she continued disapprovingly. 'Maybe now she'll listen to me. Of course, not having children of her own, she doesn't understand the practicalities of suitable gifts.'

'You won't tell her.' A small noise of horror escaped me.

'Of course, she'll have to be told. And so will your father when he comes home. You have to learn to be responsible for your belongings, Veronica. I see nothing happened to Katie's doll.' She looked at Kate fondly, her voice warm with approval. 'Now, run along both of you and get washed up for your supper. And stop that crying, Veronica, what's done is done. Let it be a lesson to you.'

I took the now-mutilated Chloe with me upstairs and very gently placed her on my bed, dressing her carefully in one of the impossibly cool outfits that comprised her wardrobe. But even in her 'country weekend' red gingham shirt and bell-bottom jeans, with sunglasses to hide her empty eye socket, she looked confused and broken – just like I felt.

'Don't worry, pet,' said Barney, helping me undress for bath-time, 'we'll get her fixed up in no time. We'll send her up to the doll's hospital in Dublin, she'll come back like new. Your father can take her up with him on one of his visits.'

My father is the local GP, the irony of which was not lost on me – even then.

'No one will be able to fix her. She'll never be the same.' Of this, I was sure.

'Of course they will. You wait and see. They work miracles in that place!'

But I was beyond consolation.

Downstairs, at the kitchen table, I sat mute and miserable, despite Barney's best efforts to cheer me up. Soon I heard my father's key in the door and Kate jumped off her chair to run and greet him. I stayed put, I was far too ashamed to face him or anyone. I couldn't even take care of an expensive new doll sent to me all the way from America. *But why poor Chloe? Why my doll?* I wrestled with the unfairness of it for weeks.

That was the first memorable incident. There were others, of course, along the way but that one still rankles even now. Of course with time (a surprisingly short amount of time), I learned to anticipate, if not prevent, these sibling attacks. I learned to find my own way of coping. Withholding information from Kate is vital, and best achieved by silence. Keeping my friends well away from her is another crucial tactic. This is easy as Kate finds my friends beyond boring. I don't care, that's fine by me – they're my friends, not hers.

At home, I keep to myself, retreating to my room on the pretence of studying, but really to daydream for hours or to write in my journal. Sometimes I write stories. I don't show them to anyone, of course, they're not good enough and, anyway, they're just for me.

And then, of course, there is food. Lovely, lovely food and lots of it, doled out to me on a regular basis by Barney, who fosters and encourages its astonishing capacity to console. She is a superb cook and, understandably dismayed by my mother's lack of interest in food and my father's lack of time to appreciate her efforts, she saves her baking triumphs for me. Apple pie, sticky toffee pudding, lemon meringue pie and the stuff of dreams, treacle tart, are regularly made in my honour, and reverently consumed. There is nothing, I believe, that cannot be endured, even family dynamics like ours, after several mouthfuls of home-baked, feather-light, food of the angels. Even living with a sister like Kate.

The End.

'Jaysus,' Abby shakes her head, looks worried. 'You're never handing that in?' We are sitting in Primrose, our three-bed dorm upstairs in the turret. She passes it to Di, who speed-reads it, a grin spreading as she rouses herself to a sitting position, swinging her legs from the thin dormitory bed to the floor and crossing them. I'd give anything to have legs like Di's, we all would. Coltish is the word that best describes them. They go with her flawless skin and perfect teeth, and her hair that swings obediently into position after just one brush stroke. All the girls in our year think she could be a model, but she scoffs at the idea.

'I think it's great,' she pronounces, handing my essay back to me, a gleam in her eye. I bask momentarily in the warm glow of approval.

'That's not the point,' Abby says. 'I never said it wasn't good or anything – it is – but it's going to get you into trouble.'

'With whom, exactly?' demands Diana, fixing her with a glare.

'Well, Kate for starters. She'll go ballistic.'

'It's an essay, Abby, a matter of free expression. Vonnie can write whatever she likes. It's meant for the teacher's attention and no one else's. And, anyway, you can't go around worried what people will think about every little thing you do, you really need to relax.'

Abby looks crushed. Diana is becoming increasingly exasperated with her, but I understand where Abby's coming from. She's just trying to protect me from myself. This is her mission, I think, to protect people from getting hurt, or to make them better when they do. She wants to be a nurse, and she will make a wonderful one.

Diana will go to university. She's not sure yet what she wants to study, but she'll have her pick. She is clever and very ambitious. She will probably work in the United Nations or maybe Brussels. The words 'diligent', 'hard working' and 'a delight to teach' appear on her term reports. She will be a high achiever in her chosen field. I am sure of it, but more importantly, so is she.

'Is it true?' asks Abby. 'That thing you wrote about the doll?'

I nod.

'But that's horrible.' She looks shocked. 'I can't believe Kate would ever do something so mean. Are you sure? I mean, how do you know that it was her?'

'I found the doll's clothes later, folded in the bottom of our chest of drawers. I think she meant for me to find them. She owned up to it eventually, years later, but I always knew it had been her. She said it was just a bit of fun.'

'But why?'

I shrug. 'Who knows?'

'Jealousy,' Diana says without looking up from the magazine she is studying (we are not allowed magazines in school, but Di always manages to smuggle a few in).

'Jealousy?' There is an embarrassed silence for a moment as Abby tries to digest this. I can hear her thoughts. *Why on earth would Kate possibly, in anyone's wildest dreams, be jealous of Vonnie?* I silently echo the line of thinking, giggling nervously.

'Yes, jealousy or spite, who knows?' Diana sighs. 'But it wasn't done out of the goodness of her heart, you can be sure of that.'

'But– but Kate has everything,' Abby murmurs. 'I mean everything anyone could want.'

This is true.

'Everything isn't enough for some people, Abby.' Diana throws the magazine aside on the bed.

Diana is not just clever, I realise, she is wise beyond her years, possibly something to do with being half-French. 'Some people are born jealous, like being born with blue eyes, it's just part of their make-up. Besides, Kate tries too hard. You can't be that good at everything without trying really, *really* hard. I should know.'

'What's wrong with trying hard?' Abby is struggling to find a positive, or at least compassionate, angle to the unfolding theory.

'Nothing if you're up front about it. But when people pretend *not* to try, when really they're trying *desperately* hard, well, there's something messed up going on with them. You can be sure of it. My older sister said so, and she's studying psychology, so she should know.'

Abby is stymied by this comment, and closes her mouth, her brow furrowing. But I turn Diana's words over and over in my head. I have never considered my older sister in this light.

'Does Kate really think we're boring?' Abby asks in a small voice.

'Who the hell cares?' Diana throws a withering look at Abby. 'C'mon, it's almost time for prayers, we'd better get out of here.'

The dorms are out of bounds during day time. When you have a free period, as we had just now, you're supposed to spend it in the library, studying. But since Primrose is located in the turret right at the top of the old house, it's not as regularly patrolled by the house-mistresses.

I love boarding school. It isn't the done thing to admit this, but I do. I feel safe here. Life is simple. You follow the rules or there are consequences, the usual ones – lost marks (a courtesy mark is especially serious), detention, being grounded and, rumour has it, expulsion, but we don't know anyone so far who has been expelled. There were rumours of course, of older, past pupils, but nothing concrete. You would have to do something really, really awful to be expelled, like smuggle a boy into the place – and we don't know any boys, not really, for all our talk of boyfriends. The closest anyone in our year has got to romance during term time was a series of love letters written to a girl called Polly, which she guarded zealously, and were regarded with awe until we discovered they were in actual fact from a Nigerian pen pal, procured from the very Catholic *Sacred Heart Messenger* magazine.

Belmount is a small school, by standards. We are one hundred and sixty girls, or thereabouts, twenty-five or so in each year, and we are a happy bunch, as far as we know. Our lives are simple, revolving around class, meal times, sport and looking forward to our weekly escape on a Sunday. My family lives just under an hour's drive from school. It never occurs to me to question why Kate and I are attending boarding school when there are several perfectly good day schools within easy reach. I don't remember being consulted about the subject, just informed. I found the prospect of leaving home exciting, liberating even, and assumed any other twelve year old would too. My parents were matter of fact about it, although I remember Barney crying openly into her apron as I was leaving for my first day.

We slip down by the back stairs, quickly falling into line with the others, all trooping from their respective classrooms, and file silently into the chapel. The smell of freshly polished floors fills the air and I find this comforting. It is September, the beginning of a new school year. The evenings are drawing in, but summer is holding on, just. After tea, which is immediately after evening prayers, there might be a swimming session in the outdoor pool for those who are interested. Otherwise, we will head down to the 'lake', at the bottom of the school grounds, which is really a large pond, but it is where our year currently hang out during evening rec. There are some great old oaks around it, and a makeshift swing hangs from one, invitingly precarious, and generally guaranteed to give way after three or more goes, sending whoever is on it flying into the water. This provides us with much hilarity. We are fifteen, still young enough to be amused by 'tomfoolery' as the nuns call it, although we feel we are very mature.

In chapel, Diana nudges me and rolls her eyes as our headmistress, Sr O'Malley, launches into a decade of the Rosary. I smile and begin the countdown in my head. Only ten Hail Marys to go. It's Thursday, so if my calculations are correct, it should be lemon meringue pie for desert. Not anywhere as good as Barney's, of course, but *still*.

There are moments in your life that you always remember, however trivial. For me, this will be one of them. Unless you are in trouble for messing in class, the only other reason you are called to the headmistress's office is if something bad has happened. If, for example, someone in your family is gravely ill, or God forbid, has died. This, along with other horrible scenarios, is running through my head as I follow Sr Gallaway along the well-trodden pathways. I concentrate on the way, every step of it. Speech is beyond me and Sr Gallaway is quiet too, or perhaps I am just tuning her out. Who knows?

Out of the classroom prefabs, onto the path, right, up the steps, through the back door of the Old House and along the gleaming corridors and into the new wing, passed the library, the chapel, our third-year common room. Then left and right again, and we have arrived at our destination, Sr O'Malley's office.

Sr Gallaway knocks on the door, opens it. When I stand immobile on its threshold, she perhaps pulls, or propels, me in. Then she closes the door quietly and sits down on a chair in the corner.

And there they are. Sr O'Malley, sitting behind her desk,

and in front of her, sitting in two chairs opposite each other, are my parents.

My father is looking down, examining his hands, as if they are an object of great fascination to him. He takes out his glasses, slowly, from the inside breast pocket of his suit, and purses his mouth. It strikes me that this is what he must look like to his patients every day – a knowledgeable man, a man who thinks carefully before speaking, pronouncing illnesses, writing prescriptions, but he is not looking at me, he does not meet my eyes. I immediately feel sick.

My mother, on the other hand, cannot wait to look at me. Her still pretty, carefully made-up face is a picture of sorrow. She shakes her head, reaches for a tissue and manages a broken sob. 'Veronica.'

Kate is not here. And that is when I think it, something must have happened to Kate, something awful, that is what they are here to tell me. I feel clammy, shivery.

'Sit down, Veronica,' Sr O'Malley says, not unkindly. She looks vaguely uncomfortable. 'You must be wondering why your parents are here. Why we have called you here.'

I move to the only vacant chair, and sit, feeling lumpen, out of place in this unfolding scenario, where everyone seems to know what is happening except me.

'Why, Veronica?' my mother says, her voice a reproach. 'Why did you do it? How could you?'

I look to my father in confusion, but he is still studying his glasses, turning them around in his hands.

Sr O'Malley takes the reins. 'Ahem,' she begins. 'Veronica, an essay you wrote for English class this week has been brought to my attention.'

Oh, Jaysus. Now I get it. But they didn't, they couldn't have.

'We feel, that is, the staff feel, that although it is undoubt-edly a very good essay, well, the general consensus is that we feel you may have some issues that could be troubling you at school, and we felt it was only right to consult your parents about the situation.'

Shit. I don't believe this. *You cannot be serious.* That's what John McEnroe always says on court. But it is happening and it is serious.

'Is there anything you'd like to say, Veronica?' Sr O'Malley asks.

You could hear a pin drop. I shake my head.

Years from now, I will think of this as 'The Intervention', with me cast as the guilty abuser – but, right now, I sit mute with horror.

'She's jealous.' That's my mother, sitting up straighter now, intent. 'She's always been jealous of Kate, no matter what we tried to do—'

'I am *not*.' I have found my voice, which is a surprise, but not as much of a surprise as realising that what I say is true. I am not jealous of my sister. I don't like her most of the time, but I would not like to *be* like her. This is a revelation to me.

'It's understandable, of course,' continues my mother. 'Kate is so, well, so unlike Veronica, in every way. It's hard for her.'

Before anyone can interject, she rushes on. 'That incident about the doll, for instance, that was entirely in her own imagination, entirely made up. Dolls and toys go missing and get broken all the time. God, if I could count all the times, I certainly can't remember anything remotely like that happening. Can you Colm?' She looks to my father for confirmation.

'I don't think Veronica's childhood memories are the issue here,' says Sr O'Malley.

'Oh, but they are,' continues Mum. 'You have no idea. Why, sometimes I think Veronica is a fantasist. We've discussed this, haven't we, Colm?'

They have?

'I mean, that business about me being on my second pre-dinner cocktail, *well*,' here she gives a disbelieving laugh, 'honest to God, you'd think we were all raving alcoholics or something.' Her voice is shrill. 'We hardly ever even *have* alcohol in the house, do we, Colm? Colm's a doctor, for heaven's sakes, we have to be careful about that kind of thing. We're very particular about it. We were probably having a party that night. We do entertain regularly, of course, that was probably it. We were more than likely having one of our drinks parties that night, but to read that account, well, you'd think . . .'

Now I realise the reason for my parents' concern. This is not about me or how I'm doing at school. This is about what I might be *saying*.

My mother is still rattling on indignantly, but she doesn't notice Sr O'Malley's gaze sharpen.

'Veronica's grades are very good, I'm happy to say, Mrs Callaghan. She's doing very well in all her subjects. She's a good all rounder too,' Sr O'Malley consults her notes. 'On the junior hockey team, a keen debater, a member of the drama society, popular with all the girls in her year, plenty of friends—'

At this my mother gives a small, sad smile. 'Well, that's nice, of course. You see, it must be hard for Veronica. No one could be as popular as Kate, I mean *everybody* loves Kate, she's such a pleasure to have around. Why you've said so yourself.'

'I have said *both* Kate and Veronica are a pleasure to have in the school, Mrs Callaghan.' Sr O'Malley's voice is crisp, but the tip of her nose is going white, which means she is displeased. She doesn't take kindly to being interrupted, never mind misquoted. My mother, I realise, with something approaching interest, is skating on thin ice. This, however, does not deter her.

'You must understand, Sister, Veronica has always been

difficult – *always*. She can be very . . . awkward at home. I mean take this essay you so rightly brought to our attention, that's a perfect example. Kate would never write anything poisonous like that – never.'

'I'm not sure that "poisonous" would be an accurate description of the essay, Mrs Callaghan. Mr O'Carroll, her English teacher, has marked it as' – she reaches for a copy of the offending paper – '"fascinating and insightful, written with wry objectivity". He's given it a grade A in fact.'

'Is that so? Well, why then did you think it necessary to bring it to our attention, Sister?' Mum's mouth has settled into a thin, polite smile.

I might very well ask the same question, but I just study my feet, this could turn nasty. Sr O'Malley doesn't know them like I do.

'Because, Mrs Callaghan, the well-being of our girls is of paramount importance to us while they are in our care. Veronica is a very promising student, very promising. We would not want anything to interfere with that.' She looks pointedly at my mother, and then turns to my father.

Meanwhile, I feel myself going puce. I wish the floor would open up and swallow me.

'Wouldn't you agree, Dr Callaghan?'

'She's bright enough, all right.'

'Would it be your impression, also, Doctor, that Veronica is difficult at home?'

'She spends a lot of time in her room.'

'Is that so.'

Mum sighs. 'Looking for notice, attention seeking. And eating, of course.'

'And why do you think Veronica spends so much time in her room?' This is asked benignly, directed at my father.

'I've just told you why.' Mum again, but she is silenced by a look from Sr O'Malley.

My father sighs. 'Her mother and Kate get on very well, they're very . . . close. Maybe Veronica prefers her own company. She doesn't seem to share many of their interests.'

I am aware of Sr Gallaway listening intently in the corner behind me and writing – oh, God, she is taking notes. Is this what they do in American schools? This must be her doing, I realise. I am to be the victim of a parent-teacher counselling session, but they don't realise what a truly awful idea this is. They have no idea of the repercussions.

'I see,' says Sr O'Malley. But she doesn't, she doesn't see at all.

My mother is looking at my father meaningfully. She is not enjoying this. She likes to be in charge, the centre of attention, manipulating, not sitting in front of a nun justifying the details of family life.

It is my father's idea of hell – for a number of reasons.

My mother has had enough of this nonsense, she is about to wind things up, I sense. I wish they would just go. But I have no idea of what is coming next – even I couldn't have imagined it in my wildest dreams.

'It's quite clear to us what is going on here, Sister,' my mother says, 'I knew it the minute I read that fantastical essay.'

Sr O'Malley looks at her politely.

'Veronica is now making trouble at school exactly as she does at home. She's attention seeking, but this time she's using Kate as a scapegoat and I won't have it. You seem to forget we have *two* daughters at this school with you – at this very *expensive* school. And whatever you may say about Veronica's writing ability' – she flicks her eyes at me – 'I will not have her compromising Kate's happiness.'

'I fail to see—' Sr O'Malley begins.

'Oh, but I don't, Sister.' My mother is steely. 'I don't fail to see at all where this is going. And that is the reason we came down here to see you so promptly, to see for ourselves, why my husband has given up a valuable morning he could be spending with his patients.' She pauses for effect. 'We have discussed this between us, and we have come to the conclusion that Veronica should be taken out of Belmount. Being here with Kate is clearly having a very bad effect on her. She can attend a day school, it can be very easily arranged, where she can live at home with us – and leave Kate to progress without any further nonsense or, indeed, distractions from her sister's downright nasty behaviour.'

I gasp. Sr Gallaway's pen poises in midair. And then I am on my feet.

'No!' I cry. 'No, please, please don't make me leave school, I'm happy here, I—'

'Veronica,' Sr O'Malley's voice is calm. 'Would you go down to the refectory please and ask Sr Scully to send up the tea. I told her we'd let her know. Then you may return to the library and read, while we have a little chat here.'

I do as I'm told.

In the library, which thankfully is empty, I take out a book, sit down and stare at it, but cannot open it. I look around at the dark, panelled walls, the rows upon rows of books, then out of the windows, onto the fields, where in the distance I can make out Paddy, the aged school gardener and handyman, pushing a wheelbarrow, his dog Blackie faithfully trotting along beside him. I want to cry but I can't. Something won't let me. I was not expecting this. Anything but this. I should have thought, should have listened to Abby. She said that essay would get me into trouble. Thinking of Abby and Diana, I get a choking feeling in my throat. They can't make me leave here, they can't. My friends are here, my life is here. I can be myself here. Belmount *is* my home. And then I realise with a rush that I have ruined it all. I have pushed the self-destruct button.

I have given them the opportunity to take away the one thing that matters to me. Why did I do that?

Sometime later I hear voices outside the door, then it is pushed open. Sr Gallaway puts her head around. 'Veronica, come along.'

I join her outside in the corridor, where we walk towards Sr O'Malley and my parents, chatting in the front hall as if nothing has happened, as if it's a perfectly normal visit.

'Ah, there you are,' says Sr O'Malley. 'Your parents are off now, Veronica. You'll be seeing them as usual on Sunday.'

'Does that mean . . .?'

'You may go back to class now, Veronica, everything has been settled. Now say goodbye.'

I walk with my parents to the front door to see them off. My mother smiles tightly and gives me a peck on the cheek, a pursed rebuke. My father pats my shoulder. 'Go easy on the essays,' he says gruffly. But I see something in his eyes, a flicker of sympathy, perhaps understanding.

'See you on Sunday,' I say. Then add a mumbled 'sorry'.

I watch as they get into the car and wave as they pull away. My mother's mouth is moving rapidly. I turn away from the angry monologue I can already sense unfolding.

Around the corner, Sr Gallaway is lurking, waiting for me. 'Veronica,' she says, walking beside me, 'I want you to listen carefully to what I'm going to say.'

I keep walking, head down.

'You are a very talented, clever girl, you got that?'

I'm confused. 'Can I—? Are they—?' There is only one thing I need to know. 'Am I staying?' I look at her.

'Sure you're staying. We don't let the good ones get away that easily.' She is grinning. 'I have a lot of faith in you, Veronica, so does Sr O'Malley, so too do all the staff. As your class mistress, it's my job to let you know that.'

But I am not listening. I don't care. Sr Gallaway is American, she is mad. We are light years away from such notions as self-esteem – this is Ireland, 1980. All that matters to me is I have three more years here at Belmount. 'Can I go now, Sr Gallaway?'

'Sure, run along.'

I go back to my class and slip behind my desk. English is just winding up, then it's lunch-time.

'What was all that about?' Diana whispers to me.

'Nothing, just a visit.' I will tell her and Abby about it tonight, in Primrose.

Diana raises an eyebrow. 'You okay?'

I nod. Mr O'Carroll is passing by on his way out. He drops the essay back on my desk. 'Good work,' he says.

I look down at my grade A – the one that nearly got me taken out of school.

'Hey,' Diana gives a low whistle. 'You got an A. Mr O'Carroll never gives As. She's impressed. 'I told you it was good.'

I wonder again why I wrote the essay. What possessed me? When I must have known, somewhere, deep down, the stink it would create. The answer comes, quietly, insistently. *Look at me*, it says. *I am not invisible. I am part of this family. I have a voice.*

June 2011

Diana

I wish Abby would talk to me. I think this as I sit back in the taxi after lunch with her.

I've known her for so long I can read her like a book. She's not herself at all, hasn't been for quite a while, now that I come to think of it. But I've been so busy lately, I haven't been around much for her. It's hard when that happens between friends, because there's always that very fine line you don't want to cross of prying too much, especially under the guise of concern. Whatever's going on – and there is definitely something – she'll tell me when she's good and ready. Poor old Abs, I wonder about her and Edward sometimes, she was so frantically keen to get him, to finally nab her doctor, and she put the man on such a pedestal. I hope he was able to live up to it. I hope he appreciates her, marriage can be a great leveller in that respect.

Whitefriar Street church looms ahead of me on the right, and I think of St Valentine, still presiding over his book of petitions inside. I wonder if all our wishes came true. If we were to do it all again, would we wish for the same things?

I know what Abby wished for anyway. She couldn't believe it herself when Edward proposed to her, I thought she was going to keel over and die with delight. And she made such a beautiful bride.

25 June 1990

Abby's Wedding Day

'Hurry up! She'll be here any minute, and you don't want to show up in a corner of the bridal shots pulling on a fag, do you?' demands Vonnie. 'And, anyway, here's her mother now, and she's giving us the evil eye, better get inside the church.'

'No.' Diana flicks her cigarette deftly behind a Rhododendron bush and looks determined. 'I want to be here, to see her before she goes in, to wish her luck – besides, that guy escorting her mother is extremely cute.'

'You're pushing it.' Vonnie fixes a broad smile on her face as Abby's mother approaches, leaning rather affectedly on the arm of the usher who will guide her to her seat at the front row. 'And that's Edward's brother, Harry, so hands off – at least until everyone's respectably drunk enough not to notice.'

'Relax, Vonnie. It's a wedding. A happy occasion, one to make merry and have fun at.' Diana smiles her wicked smile, and Vonnie is immediately fearful.

'It's Abby's wedding, Di, you know how much it means to her. She wants everything to be absolutely perfect.'

'Should have chosen a different groom then, shouldn't she?' Diana fishes in her handbag, pulling out her compact mirror and applies another coat of lip gloss. Anyone else would look tacky doing this, but Diana looks simultaneously feminine and sexy.

'D'you really think so? I mean *really*?'

Diana gives Vonnie her *don't bullshit me* look. 'If you really want me to answer that question, then, yes, I do mean it – and, furthermore, you agree with me one hundred per cent. Edward is pompous and arrogant. He is everything Abby's mother aspires to on the outside, but a disaster on the inside – for Abby that is. Not that anyone is thinking about *that.*'

'But she loves him.' Vonnie looks aghast. 'You can tell she does. She's mad about him'

'Of course she is,' Diana sighs. 'Because she is making her mother's dearest wish come true.' Diana's face tightens. 'I hate that woman.'

'Mrs Murphy?' Vonnie is taken aback. 'Why?'

'Because she's ruining Abby's life, that's why – and I'm almost beginning to hate Abby for letting her.'

Now Vonnie gasps. 'You don't mean that.'

'No, of course I don't. But I want to shake Abby all the same. Still, she'll find out in her own time. Look, here she is, here's the car.'

They look on as Abby alights from the bridal car on her father's arm, attended by her three little bridesmaids and their fussing mother. Her dress is a fluttering mass of silk chiffon layers, falling away from a fitted bodice, its neckline hinting at just the right amount of creamy décolletage. Her dark red hair is piled upon her head, from which a few stray tendrils have escaped. A three-tiered veil floats behind, the first tier thrown forward, covering her face, a portrait in soft focus. Abby looks very beautiful.

'Oh,' gasps Vonnie, fighting tears. 'She looks amazing, incredible, like a fairy princess.'

'Yes,' agrees Di, tilting her head, smiling fondly as she goes to greet her.

Mrs Murphy has a quick word and then says to Abby and Diana, 'Now don't delay her girls, you can gossip all you like after it's all over. You're both looking very well.' She nods approvingly. 'Now, Abby, you're respectably late, no more time wasting.'

Mrs Murphy looks torn between wanting to shoo Abby up the aisle to claim her rightful and duly landed prospective spouse – or gliding ahead herself, on the arm of Edward's brother, to begin her own measured walk up the aisle.

'Be happy, darling Abby,' Diana says to her.

'We'll be waiting for you right outside the church when you come out,' says Vonnie. 'We're the first people you must address when you're the new Mrs Keane.'

'Wish me luck, girls,' Abby says, taking a deep breath.

'You won't need it.' Vonnie squeezes her hand. 'You've got St Valentine on your side, remember?'

'Here we go, Dad.' Abby turns to her father. 'Ready?'

'As I'll ever be,' Mr Murphy says, looking suddenly a bit blurry eyed. 'Better get inside girls.'

'She looks wonderful,' Diana says to Vonnie, as they dart inside the church just in time. 'He does not deserve her, that Edward. He is not good enough for our Abby.'

In fact, Abby's wedding turned out to be far more enjoyable than I had expected. It was held at a small hotel not far from where we went to school in Wicklow. The day was perfect, hot, sunny, and a small marquee had been put up, there was quite a good crowd, once you managed to circumnavigate Abby's mother's many relatives, most of whom barely seemed to know her, or Abby. I suspected they had been summonsed for the occasion to witness how well their kins-woman had done, managing to get her daughter to snare a doctor. I know that sounds awfully bitchy, but it was true.

Abby's mother was the worst kind of snob, a ruthlessly ambitious woman whose sights were firmly set on what *she* wanted and had very little to do with what her daughter might want, although none of us (including Abby) had ever got to the bottom of that. Perplexing though it was, Abby and her mother seemed to share one mind. Even through her teenage years when it was virtually mandatory to rebel, Abby had remained quietly acquiescent. It was a pity, too, because she was very, very clever – far cleverer than she let on. Even in the early days at school, she sat quietly in class, never putting her hand up or drawing attention to herself. It was only when she consistently got top marks in every-thing (even maths!) that we realised just how brainy she was. In fact, she's probably a lot cleverer than her doctor husband, although I bet she takes good care not to let *him* know that. Her mother would have warned her. She prob-ably told her not to tell him she was a scholarship girl either. We only found out by accident ourselves at school when one of the teachers mentioned it, and poor Abby went bright red. She was sweet, too, about helping anyone, and she always let us copy her maths homework if we found it too difficult. That's how I discovered she wanted to be a teacher more than anything – she said so often – and she would have made a great one. She'd have probably gone on to be a professor or something, but that didn't suit her mother's plans at all. Abby was going to be a nurse, and that was all there was to it.

'Why don't you do medicine, then?' I remember asking her once. 'You'll easily get the points.'

'Oh, Mummy says seven years of study would make an old maid out of me. I don't think I'd like the responsibility either, having to make all those life and death decisions.'

'But nursing, Abby,' I protested. 'It's a vocation, surely? And you hate needles, you're terrified of them!'

'Only when they're aimed at me,' she said, defensively, as if that explained everything. 'I'll be able to take blood, or give injections to patients if I have to – as long as they're not afraid of them too.'

I shook my head hopelessly. 'Whatever you say, but I still think it's an awful waste.'

So Abby became a nurse – and she got her doctor, which brings me back to the wedding . . .

Edward's younger brother, Harry, was *hot* (I have a thing for men in morning suit anyway, they look so elegant), and he couldn't stop catching my eye and grinning at me across the marquee.

It was about three o'clock, lunch was winding up and the speeches, which I can't bear, were threatening to begin. I was wearing a gorgeous red silk-lycra mix dress I'd picked up in a boutique in London when I went over to stay with Vonnie and we had gone shopping for outfits. It was off the shoulders, clung in all the right places and I topped it off with a cute little red pillbox hat that sat at a jaunty angle with red netting that covered the top half of my face, through which I could bat my eyes seductively. Red high-heeled satin pumps and a matching clutch bag completed the outfit. I looked good and I knew it.

If I was reading the signals right, Harry thought so too. We were both at tables with people old enough to be our parents and he also looked as bored as I felt. I had a suspicion that whoever had finalised the seating arrangements (Abby's mother, no prizes for guessing) had very likely conspired to keep us as far apart as possible. Anyway, there was no time to waste and no time like the present, particularly for what I had in mind. I made my excuses and left the table, presumably to visit the ladies' room, making sure to weave my way through the crowd so that I passed his table. I put my hand on his shoulder, squeezed it, smiled and murmured in his ear. 'Just pretend you know me . . . I'm going outside for a cigarette if you'd care to join me.' Then I kept on walking out of the marquee into the garden, where staff were ferrying trays of coffee and tea down to accompany the cutting of the cake.

He was beside me in less than a minute, and up close he was even cuter. Tall, well built (he played rugby for Leinster I learned later), and with a shock of dark brown hair which was fashionably long and cut so that a forelock, which he endearingly kept pushing back, fell continuously into his slanting brown eyes. Younger than me, I guessed, but a charming eagerness masked the flash of insecurity he felt as he fingered his shirt collar and cleared his throat.

'I'm Harry, Edward's brother,' he said, holding out his hand.

'I know,' I said, shaking it.

'So, who are you?'

'I'm Diana – a school friend of Abby's.'

'Well, hello, Diana. You look gorgeous, I couldn't take my eyes off you.' He grinned sheepishly.

'How old are you?'

He was taken aback by the question. 'Why? What does it matter?'

'I just like to know.' I smiled provocatively.

'Almost twenty-one.'

'Cigarette?' I offered him one.'

'I don't smoke.'

'Sweet,' I said.

He scowled. 'Look, why did you ask me out here. I thought—'

'What did you think?'

He looked uncomfortable.

I locked eyes with him 'Do you want to know what *I* think?'

He swallowed. 'What?'

I think we should go upstairs to my room, right now. I don't know about you, Harry, but I'm not into speeches.'

He licked his lips nervously and coughed. 'I, that is, I'm making a speech. I'm on after the best man.'

'So, the father of the bride will speak, then the best man

. . .' I tilted my head. 'That gives us ten, possibly even fifteen minutes. I guarantee to have you back in twenty at the latest, although you might not want to rush. They can always get someone to fill in for you and you can take the next slot if you miss it. What do you say?'

I almost felt sorry for him. I could tell he had never had such a proposition in his life. It was unfair of me, but it is flirting with danger, the possibility of being found out, that is thrilling, no?

He hesitated for only a second. 'Lead the way.'

'Oh, I will, Harry.' I gave him my sexiest smile. 'Follow me to Room 215 in thirty seconds. I'll be waiting for you.'

When he came in, I was already naked, except for my shoes and hat, and a cigarette in my hand, of course. I was looking out the window, and slowly turned around to face him.

He caught his breath when he saw me, then laughed out loud and shook his head. 'You are something else.'

Slowly, he took the cigarette from my hand and put it out. Then took off his morning coat and hung it on the chair, and undid his tie, never taking his eyes off me. I unbuttoned his shirt, helped him out of his trousers, then it was my turn to inhale sharply. He had a great body, better than great.

'Well, well, well, look what you've been hiding,' I said, my glance trailing downwards.

And then things happened very quickly. I had planned to seduce him, slowly, tantalisingly, speech or no speech. But before I knew it he had lifted me up easily, one hand under my bottom, the other around my back, supporting me, and I wrapped my legs around him, feeling him rock hard against me.

'Wait,' I gasped.

'What for?' he said steering us towards the wall behind, so I could lean against it. 'Are you okay?' he murmured.

'Yes, but—'

Then he was inside me, thrusting, holding me tight against him. And, *oh God*!

It wasn't meant to be like this. It wasn't meant to be this hot, this frantic, so *unbelievably* sexy. And it was supposed to be *me*, not him, setting the pace. He was just a kid, for God's sake! Not even twenty-one. But he had thighs of steel and—

'Shhh,' he murmured into my neck, and kissed me every time I tried to speak. He kept thrusting, harder and harder, until I felt an unmistakable throbbing begin, one that usually took quite a while and not a little effort to arouse.

'Oh God,' I mumbled. I clung to him, melting, helpless, slick with sweat, as he kept on and on. And then it overtook me, consumed me – an orgasm of such intensity I would have collapsed had he not already been holding me up. 'Oh, my God! Oh, sweet Jesus!' He rocked me back and forth and, seconds later, clenched his teeth and climaxed. Then after a few moments, or maybe eternity, he gently put me down, led me to the bed, where I collapsed gratefully against the pillows and he bent down and kissed me, lingeringly.

'What are you doing?' I asked, as he checked his watch, and began pulling on his clothes. I struggled up on my elbows, dazed.

'I'd love to stay,' he grinned, 'but I have a speech to make. Thank you, Diana, that was most enjoyable. I must have a smoke with you more often.' He fixed his tie, pulled the rosebud from his buttonhole and stuck it behind my ear. 'Save a dance for me later, won't you?'

And then he was gone, the door closing softly behind him.

When I could summon the strength, I staggered over to the mirror and leaned on the dresser. Minus my pretty hat and shoes, with my hair tousled and scarlet lipstick smeared from my swollen mouth to my ears and neck, I looked, well, ravished and felt unusually vulnerable. I looked around for my hat, and saw it sitting atop the bedpost, vaguely remembering Harry throwing it there. I wasn't quite sure what had just happened. *I* was the one who was supposed to walk off and leave *him* looking longingly after me. Now, well, *oh pull yourself together, ma fille,* I said sternly to myself, as I showered and redressed. He's just a kid, a very accomplished, sensual young man, to be sure, but just a kid. We could, or would, have absolutely nothing in common. It was just a bit of fun.

I sauntered back to the marquee about an hour later. The speeches were over (thank God), the guys were hitting the bar and the band was gearing up to get started. I was pretty sure no one had missed me, until I saw Vonnie, in a shapeless silk dress, eyeing me sternly from her table and waving me over.

'Where were you? You missed all the speeches.'

'I had a headache. I had to get some fresh air. You would too if you'd been at our table.'

'I don't believe you,' she said suspiciously. 'Funny, Edward's brother almost missed them all too – just about made his own, in fact.'

'Really?' I looked innocent. 'Was he any good?'

'Maybe I should be asking you the same question.' She raised her eyebrows.

'Vonnie! I don't believe you just said that! Are you insinuating—?'

'Tell me you didn't, Di,' she pleaded.

'All right, I didn't.'

'You did, didn't you? Oh, God, I don't believe it.' She put her hands to her face. 'Not Harry, he's only twenty, Di. He's Edward's youngest *brother.*'

'So?'

'Abby would *die* if she knew.'

'Well she won't, will she? Unless you tell her.' I helped

myself to a glass of champagne from a passing waiter. 'Anyway,' I took a sip, 'there's nothing to tell. It was just a bit of fun.' I smiled wickedly. 'And it's not as if I deflowered him, Von. If you must know, he was pretty spectacular—'

'Stop!' she held up her hand. 'No, I really do not want to know.' She shook her head at me in despair. 'You're something else, you are.'

'Funny, that's what Harry said too.'

He asked me to dance of course, later, but I said no.

'Why not?' he looked puzzled.

I shrugged. 'I don't feel like it.'

'Oh, I get it,' he smiled. 'You don't want anyone to know – to see us – well, all right, give me your phone number then.'

'I don't think so.'

'What? Why not?'

'Because there's no point. We won't be seeing each other again. It was just a bit of fun, Harry.' I smiled disarmingly, not sure why I was being so horrid to him.

'But what about later, then, at least, I mean we're here for the night.'

I shook my head. He looked hurt.

'Oh, right.' He took a deep breath and pulled himself up to his full six feet two inches. 'I see. Well, it was lovely meeting you, Diana. Really lovely.' Then he turned and walked away.

I watched him, surreptitiously, of course, for the rest of the night as the band played on and gave way to the disco, as I danced with countless other men, none of whom I found the slightest bit attractive.

He was surrounded by girls constantly, relentlessly pulled onto the dance floor, and was equally relentlessly charming about it. Harry was lovely, I thought, absolutely lovely. I'd forgotten what impeccable manners those English public schoolboys have. I had thought Edward rather pompous when

I met him, but now I could see what Abby found attractive in him. Men like that knew how to treat a girl. And if he shared any other similarities with his brother, well, Abby was in for a memorable honeymoon! What a pity Harry was so young.

I resolved to put him out of my mind. We were just ships that passed in the night, even if I had to admit the sex had been incredible.

Just *how* incredible, I wouldn't admit until much, much later.

But even now, twenty years on, I always smile when I think about Abby's wedding.

The taxi pulls up at my studio and I go in through the private entrance reserved for celebrities who need to come and go discreetly. The hair salon is busy, I see, peering through the smoked-glass screen, and there are four girls having their make-up done, one with a mother issuing instructions from beside the reclining chair. Poor Freda doing the make-up is trying hard to look serene, although I can tell she would like to punch the pushy mother.

There's nothing I can't tell you about a person if I study their face. Faces are my business, and I love them. People always talk about things being revealed in the eyes – the windows to a person's soul and all that – but that's just a teeny part of the conversation. If you want to get the whole story learn to read the other features too. A forehead, for instance, can be smoothly untroubled (even with lines), or tightly harbouring a whole Pandora's box of worries. And it doesn't matter how much Botox you've had, just because the skin is smooth and taut doesn't mean I won't see through it to what lies beneath. Noses, too, tell me a lot, particularly how the person feels about them, and that will tell you a lot about the person. Mouths, of course, are my favourite thing. I could go on for hours about mouths – shapes, sizes, their whimsical little risings and fallings, the soundless exclamations they make, and of course the most wonderful thing of all about the face, the smile. All smiles are beautiful. So if I can give you any advice at all, this is the most important – whatever else you put on your face, wear a smile at every opportunity.

I'm a make-up artist, in case you haven't worked it out already. A very good one, if I say so myself. And I'm lucky (and hard working) enough to run my own business now, a hair and make-up studio in town called Chic2Chic. Paris was where I trained initially, going on to work in London, Milan and LA. But Paris was the toughest; if you can survive the couture shows in Paris, you can survive anything.

I've earned my stripes, as they say. I had a chain, three studios in Dublin, but I scaled back and sold off the other two five years ago. It was the right move to make, not just financially (although I had no idea then of the hideous debacle that was about to unfold globally, especially here in Ireland) but because I wanted to cut back, to focus, to take things a little easier. Expansion sounds like an impressive thing to do, and it *is* exciting, but, believe me, it's not easy to spread yourself across three different studios and still maintain the same level of impeccable service – and I am rigorous about providing just that. If you're the boss, you have to be there, that's the whole point. Any business is a reflection of the person who runs it.

I also believe, regarding work, as with life in general, that it is important to know when to get out, when to let go – listen to your instincts and not your ego. Follow your passion, that's my motto; it may get you into trouble but at least you'll enjoy it.

My parents were horrified, you know, when I decided to become a make-up artist. They had notions of me being some sort of Eurocrat. I went to university, of course, partly to keep them happy and partly because I wanted to. I got my law degree with languages and then went on to do a year at the Sorbonne.

But although I flirted with the idea of international law, or interpreting – even the Corps Diplomatique – I always knew the lure of the greasepaint would win out.

No one who knew me well was surprised. My parents were disappointed initially, but when they began to see how well I was doing and how happy I was they relaxed about it. Actually, my mother was a big support to me. I used to think we didn't get on well together when I was a teenager (I was probably a horror!), but we have become very close over the years and she was adamant that I should follow my heart, not just in my career but in everything. And once my father realised I was not going to run off with someone crazy from the fashion or film world, he even began to show a tentative interest in my career. He's French – how could he not be interested in a daughter who has access to the faces (and therefore even the minutest of flaws) of some of the most beautiful women in the world?

Some of my friends from university raised a few eyebrows, but only in surprise, and there was one boyfriend (a rather sexy intellectual) who was almost as aghast at the idea as my parents had been initially. I bid *him* adieu pretty quickly, I can tell you. But my *real* friends, they were not surprised at all. Especially Abby and Vonnie, who had very obligingly sat for me as guinea pigs when I was trying out my fledgling talents.

I had to travel a lot back then, but it was fun and I loved it. Vonnie was in London, Abby was doing nursing in Dublin, and we managed to meet up as often as we could and stay in touch. It was easier for Abby and me, of course, being based here, but we got over to see Vonnie as much as we could, finances permitting. Vonnie rarely if ever came home and we didn't press her about it – in fact, I think the only time she did was for our respective weddings.

★　★　★

I met Greg at a photographic shoot in South Beach, Miami in 1996. It was a television commercial for pizza, I think, and there were some seriously good-looking actors both male and female involved. The director was English, cute too, and very serious. The atmosphere on set was quite tense, because the client had flown out too, and that always makes the advertising agency nervous, which, in turn, makes the production company antsy, which meant everyone was a bit stressed. That's when it's a relief to be in 'make-up'. Compared to the fashion shows, television commercials are a walk in the park for a make-up artist. Defining features and powdering away perspiration from foreheads and noses is something most of us can do in our sleep.

The crew were just about ready to run through the first take when the main actor began to fluff his line. He only *had* one line, one really easy line, but once he started getting it wrong, he couldn't seem to stop himself – it was pitiful. It got to the stage where we were all silently mouthing it for him, to no avail.

And then I noticed this guy walk up to the actor, take him aside and talk to him for a few minutes. When I saw him, my breath caught, quite literally. It wasn't just that he was good looking, although he was, it was just that I knew, right then and there, that he was 'The One'.

How did I know? It wasn't any sense of wild attraction or chemistry, not at that exact moment, it was simply because I had described this man down to the last detail, the very last *written* detail, in Whitefriars church. I had written down a description, a physical description of the man I wanted to meet (well all right, I might as well be honest here, to marry) and he had somehow materialised and walked off the page into my life. I couldn't believe it – in fact, it quite frightened me. Until that moment, I had actually forgotten about the stupid list I had written to St Valentine. But here it was, walking around breathing, all six foot three inches of it. Right down to the crooked, but character-giving nose, the lopsided grin, even the dimple, right there on the right-hand side of his mouth when he smiled. And those footballer's legs . . .

Whatever he said to the actor seemed to work and, a few minutes later, the same man ran through his line without a hitch, and everyone breathed a huge sigh of relief.

'Who is that guy?' I whispered to Maria, the local production assistant, nodding in his direction.

'Oh, that's Greg, he's with the agency. He's the copywriter on the script. And before you get any ideas,' she warned, 'he's engaged. Although I can't say I blame you. If I wasn't safely married myself, I'd be gazing in his direction too; he's like a taller and younger-looking version of Gabriel Byrne, isn't he?'

He was. And he was taken. *But not married,* my inner voice reminded me. I decided I was being ridiculous and to dismiss the whole thing as a weird coincidence. I was letting my imagination run away with me. When he turned and caught my eye, I ignored him, even though I could feel my heart beginning to do a little rhythm skip thing that was quite alarming. I had read about things like that, of course, and always considered them to be a complete cliché. Now here it was doing a version that was not quite hip-hop, but close enough. And it happened every time Greg showed up. It was inevitable that we would meet and be introduced. Shooting a television commercial is just like shooting a movie, except it's a much shorter timescale. When you're at home, it's usually a couple of days, but when it's a shoot being filmed abroad, well, it can be up to a couple of weeks, sometimes more, depending on the scale of the thing. And since you're all staying in the same place, working together all day (sometimes nights) and socialising after work, well, it's pretty hard to avoid anyone.

After that first time I caught him looking at me, he seemed to be doing it quite a lot, and equally regularly I would look away. Finally, on the last day of the shoot, when we were packing up our stuff, he came up to me while I was talking to Maria.

'Can I get you girls a drink?'

'Shouldn't we wait for the others?' I said.

'We've got a whole night ahead with the others, including dinner,' he pointed out. Which was true, we were going to Michael Caine's restaurant later that evening, for the wrap party.

'Sure,' grinned Maria. 'Make mine a Cosmo.'

'Thanks, I'll have a Mojito,' I said, a tad unenthusiastically.

'What's the problem?' asked Maria, not unreasonably, looking at my scowl as Greg went over to the outdoor bar of the hotel to get the drinks.

'Nothing,' I said. 'I just would have preferred to wait and join the others.'

'Well, one drink isn't going to hurt you. And, as Greg said, we've got all night with the others.' She was looking at me speculatively.

But it wasn't the drink I was worried about.

We had our drinks and then, as soon as I could, I excused myself to go and shower and get ready for the evening ahead. And to call my boyfriend; I made sure to say that.

And I did call William. I called him to tell him I missed him and that I couldn't wait to get back home to see him, and I made myself believe that was the truth.

At dinner, I found myself seated next to Greg, every other chair had been filled. So I made it my business to talk to the director, who was on my other side, all evening. I was doing very well, really, all things considered. I was a grown up now, in a proper, adult relationship – my days of flirting were behind me.

When dinner was over, and the others decided to head to a nightclub in the area, I made my escape, claiming a headache, saying I would make my way back to the hotel. Just as I got the cab I'd hailed, Greg jumped in beside me.

'What do you think you're doing?' I immediately slid over to the far corner of the seat.

'Seeing you back to the hotel, it's not safe to be wandering around on your own at this time of night.' His teeth gleamed white in the dim light of the cab. 'And you needn't worry, I don't bite.'

'I'm perfectly capable of looking after myself.'

'I don't doubt it for a minute, but what's your problem?'

'I beg your pardon?'

'Why do you keep glowering at me and ignoring me?'

'I have not been glowering.'

'You're doing it again.'

'Where to?' the cab driver asked, looking bored.

'The Delano,' Greg told him.

'Have a drink with me, just one drink, before you go. I want to talk to you. We can sit outside by the pool. C'mon, humour me, a poor Irish guy going back to get rained on tomorrow.'

So I did, even though I knew it was a mistake. As we sat up talking for most of the night, I had to keep myself from staring at all of those features, those sculpted body parts, right down to the beautiful hands, that I had listed in my ideal man.

'You're Irish?' He was surprised. 'How come you didn't come out with the rest of us?'

'Half-Irish, half-French. I'm doing a freelance gig out here for American *Vogue*. The make-up artist they usually work with broke her arm, I was able to fill in for her.'

'Lucky for me.' He gave a lopsided grin and I felt my heart turn over slowly, although I was determined not to succumb to his considerable charms.

'I can't imagine why.'

'I would have thought that was obvious.'

'You're engaged.' I played my trump card.

'And you have a boyfriend.'

'Exactly.' I stood up and turned to go, but not quickly enough.

'Wait.' Greg was beside me, his hand on my arm. 'Don't go, not just yet.'

I wanted to go, I really did, but I seemed to be rooted to the spot, mesmerised by that beautiful mouth of his as it came closer to mine and he kissed me. And that was it, I was done for.

Greg left the next day, early, with the rest of the agency and production company. I had another two weeks left. When he called me to say he had broken off his engagement, I didn't know whether to feel appalled or delirious, but I was suddenly scared, because I knew I was going to have to break up with William – and he wasn't going to take it well. Neither would my parents. But there was no point fighting the inevitable, and that's what it was.

We were married six months later.

I think that must have been hard for Vonnie when Abby and I were dating and going on to play happy families. Even though she wasn't living here, she must have felt like the odd one out. But her career in London was going well, even though her love life obviously left a lot to be desired.

Then Vonnie moved to LA and we sort of lost touch after that.

I heard on the grapevine from various media people I worked with that her career as a freelance writer had taken off and she is a regular contributor to all the big American glossies – *Vanity Fair*, *Harper's Bazaar* and even *The New Yorker*. I was so pleased for her.

Poor old Vonnie. She was such a lovely girl, but she never

had any real self-esteem, never made anything of herself. She had the most wonderful bone structure, you know, even though she was determined to hide it under a layer of fat, hardly surprising with all that rubbish she ate. I always wondered why she took refuge in food. With her height, and those cheekbones, big brown eyes and naturally arching brows – well, let's put it this way, I wouldn't have been hiding them.

I hope she met somebody, I hope she found love, she deserved to – we all do.

Anyway, that was all so long ago now – fifteen years – funny how life works out. Greg and I have two great kids, a boy and a girl, and we've had some great years and some pretty tough ones. I'd like to say that ours was a fairytale romance, and parts of it were, but the truth is, any relationship is a work in progress and a lot of that work comes down to the woman, no matter what the relationship gurus tell you. Take it from me – it's the Frenchwoman in me, I'm ruthlessly practical.

Would I do things differently with the benefit of hindsight? Well, let's just say I'd have amended that list I wrote all those years ago to include some inner attributes, they're the important ones – the ones you end up living with, tolerating, sometimes enduring, day in, day out. And before you know it, the years have flown by.

That's when you begin to scrutinise your life, your choices, and that's healthy because otherwise we would always keep repeating the same mistakes, never learning from them. Don't get me wrong, I'm happy with my life, as much as anyone can be. I have a loving family, a good marriage and I love what I do – although, lately, I had been thinking of giving it all up, my career that is. I've worked all my life, and I'd like to have had the opportunity to spend some quality time at home, to really relax, get to know myself again – instead of always promising to take a sabbatical and never getting around to it. Not that I work anywhere near as hard as I used to, I don't, but all that may be about to change if things continue as they are with Greg.

These days, I mostly confine myself to supervising things at the studio, although I still work freelance for a very select few (like that job I was on in the south of France recently), but only at my own discretion, if I feel like it. At this stage, I can pick and choose. Life's too short, no?

The only exception to this rule is regarding my daughter's friends, who, at fifteen, are constantly begging me for make-up lessons, which I gladly give them. This is not just out of the goodness of my heart, I am determined to eradicate this awful habit too many young Irish girls have of plastering their faces with make-up, especially foundation, when their skin needs it least – when they are at their most beautiful, with a fresh-ness no cosmetic can supply – but I draw the line at their mothers. They know where the studio is. It's amazing how many people always want something for nothing. I have to make a living out of this, you know, it's not a hobby, I don't run a charity service.

Well actually I do – just every so often – and that's the part of my work that gives me the greatest pleasure of all. I visit a variety of centres, along with a few hand-picked members of my team. Sometimes we go to homeless shelters, sometimes refuge shelters (for abused women and children) and, of course, hospitals. No amount of money could give me the pleasure I get when I see the looks of amazement on those women's faces after I've worked on them. As they say in the Mastercard advertisement, *priceless*.

But I could still do all that, even if I sold the business.

That was my plan, this time last year. I'm forty-five, not getting any younger – if not now, when?

I'll sit Greg down over the weekend and tell him, once and for all. I know he's not the most responsible guy in the world (creative types always plead that), and he always said he loved the fact that I was financially independent and had a career and life of my own. But we don't need two incomes now. Greg's salary as creative director in KPFT was quite enough to support us. We'd have to cut back, of course, but who isn't these days? And with me being at home, we could save money lots of other ways – I might even start up a business from home, but not for a year or two. I reckon I owe it to myself to take a gap year. Stop and smell the roses for a while.

That was what was on my mind, anyway, that fateful Friday evening last year as I finished up at the studio and drove home. I say fateful, because although I was blissfully unaware of it – domestic life as I knew it was about to change rather dramatically.

'I've been fired,' Greg said. He was sitting in the kitchen, his feet on the table, a large glass of red wine in front of him.

'Oh, Greg, no, I'm so sorry. What happened?' I took off my coat and dumped my bags.

'Charlie called me in before lunch, man-to-man chat, laid it on the line, we're falling like flies.' He took a swig of wine. 'I knew things were tough, but I never thought it would be me – never thought it would come to this.'

'Oh, darling.' I went over and sat beside him, kissed him. 'How horrible, what a shock, you poor old thing.'

'You got the *old thing* bit right anyway. Seems I'm super-fluous to requirements, it's all about the young turks now, digital marketing, social networking, no need for old farts like me anymore.'

'You're not an old fart.' I gave him a squeeze.

'Of course I am. I'm nearly fifty.' He turned and smiled at me, dropping a kiss on my forehead. 'You and me both.'

'You're forty-seven, Greg. I'm forty-five—'

'Same thing. Anyway, it's happened, it's over. There's nothing I can do about it.'

'D'you think you might be able to get another—'

'Job in advertising? Are you kidding? At my age? The best I can hope for is the odd bit of freelance, maybe a bit of consultancy work, but even that won't be easy. Thank God I have a working wife, eh? Knew you'd come in handy some day.'

I said nothing. Just smiled.

'What about the financial package?'

'Oh, it'll get us through a year, at a push, if we're careful. And I can sell my shares in the agency, not that they're worth anything much, but every little helps, right?'

'Right,' I sighed.

'Tell you what?'

'What?'

'Let's go out to dinner – let's celebrate!'

'Celebrate?'

'Yes, the beginning of a new phase of our life. I can look at retraining, maybe starting a business of my own. Things are changing, Di, people are sick of the rat race. There's a fortune to be made in teaching people to slow down, find their inner peace . . .'

'Yes,' I murmured. A variety of thoughts were running through my head, none of them appealing or peaceful.

So we did go out to dinner, to our local Italian, and had a very good bottle of Chianti, even a couple of liqueurs to follow.

'To us.' Greg raised his glass, smiling at me, and I wondered, not for the first time, at his ability to repackage a scene – transform it. What was faulty or problematic was now to be reframed as hopeful, brimful of possibilities. That was what had made him good at his job, of course. The job he didn't have any more.

'You said there was something you wanted to talk to me about this morning?' Greg looked interested. He was being unusually attentive, charming.

'Oh, it was nothing,' I brushed it off. 'I can't even remember now,' I lied, clinking glasses with him.

'I'm looking forward to this, actually, now that I think about it,' he said. 'It's fate . . . a sign. The universe is telling me it's time to redirect my life.'

I smiled gamely. I didn't doubt it for a minute. But of far more concern to me, selfishly perhaps, was my own life, and how this would impact on it. What was the universe saying to *me* in that case?

LAX Airport, June 2011

The staff in Hudson News at LAX have an ongoing competition with the guys across the aisle in Starbucks to see who can photograph the most celebrities per week on their smartphones. The losers get to buy the first round of Friday night cocktails.

Today Max, the assistant manager, is on duty. Business is brisk, and the new guy, Sam, is working out well and handling the line of customers with ease – giving Max crucial time to keep his eyes peeled. He is alert, vigilant, still stung by the fact that only yesterday he missed George Clooney walking straight past him. A woman catches his attention. She is heading to her gate, oblivious to the admiring glances that follow her. She is not famous, although her face is clearly one people feel compelled to study, unaware they are doing just that, looking away quickly, embarrassed, if they catch her eye.

She could be an actress, a model or just any one of the many beautiful people that pass through LAX every day – and yet there is something different about her, something arresting, that makes Max pause and wonder for a moment.

She is tall and lean with long brown hair streaked with caramel and honey, cut in layers around her face, which is striking. She is lightly tanned, dressed casually in jeans, leather boots, and a white cotton vest, although she pauses to pull a long cashmere wrap around her shoulders. She looks right at him, catches him staring at her and smiles. Then she stops at the news stand, browsing for a couple of minutes with her little girl.

'Mommy?'

'Mmhmm?'

'How long before we get to Ireland?'

'Oh, just about as soon as you wake up.'

'I'm *not* going to sleep, Mommy. I'm going to watch movies all night with you.'

'Well, *I* might fall asleep,' she says, smiling.

'That's okay. I'll wake you up when we get there.'

'Thank you, sweetheart.'

'I can't wait to get to Ireland. Are you excited, Mommy? How long has it been since you were there?'

'Twelve years,' she says, rather thoughtfully, picking up a couple of magazines.

'Wow, that's like before I was even born.'

'Yes, Jasmine, five whole years before you were born.'

'That's like almost my whole life.'

'Mine too.'

'It can't be your whole life, Mommy!'

'Sometimes it feels that way, Jazz, that my life began with you.'

Jasmine giggles, pleased with this. 'That's what Daddy says too.'

The woman pays for the magazines and heads for her gate, before disappearing down the walkway.

'Wow, who was that?' Sam gives a low whistle.

'No idea,' Max says.

'She's beautiful.'

'She sure is,' Max agrees. 'Welcome to LAX, Sam, that's just one of the perks of this job.'

On the plane, we settle into our seats and fasten our seat-belts for takeoff. Jazz has flown before, but only on internal flights in smaller aircraft, and she is suitably impressed with the Airbus and informs me she now thinks she would like to be a flight attendant when she grows up.

'Did you know what you wanted to be when you were my age, Mom?'

'Didn't have a clue.'

'So when did you know you wanted to be a writer?'

'I'm not sure when, honey. It was more a case of *how* I knew.'

'Well, how did you know?'

'I used to spend a lot of time writing stories when I was young.'

'Inside?'

'Well it certainly wasn't outside.' I grin, just thinking about it. It was cold enough inside the Old Rectory growing up, never mind outside.

'I'd only like to write stories if I could do it outside.'

Jazz has no concept of rainy, miserable summers and I hope desperately the weather will be good or at least reasonably dry while we are in Dublin.

I watch her, as she sets up her individual viewing screen and plugs in her headphones, happily flicking channels. She has no idea, I think, and I am grateful for that. I want Jazz to grow up happy and secure, confident of her place in this world and excited by the possibilities of her life. Not like me, never like me . . .

The Old Rectory, August 1978

Vonnie

'This is boring.' Kate turned to her friend and scrambled to her feet after I'd beaten them both at Monopoly. 'C'mon, Holly.' She linked her arm. 'Let's walk down to the tennis club. Pete Hogan is playing at three o'clock and I want to watch him.'

'Pete Hogan is sixteen years old and doesn't even know you exist,' I said, annoyed at being abandoned for the afternoon. It was the school holidays and both my best friends were away at the same time, leaving me dependent on Kate and her friends, who clearly found it beneath them to hang out with me. Even though I could beat them at most sports, games and cards – they were almost two years older – and that was the great divide when you were only twelve and a half as I was then. If I beat them, as I had just now, they sulked. If I let them win, they laughed at me and called me thick. I could never get it right.

Holly giggled and Kate glared at her.

'He does too. He was looking at me all last week when I was playing on the junior team. And Larry Fegan told Sarah O'Reilly that Pete thought I was cute, didn't he, Holly?'

Holly looked blank.

'Anyway. What would you know about boys? You're only a kid.'

'I know he's not interested in you, 'cos he's mad about Ciara's sister, Ann. He rings her all the time asking her to go out.'

This was true, I had it on authority from my friend Ciara. I hadn't realised how accurately I hit an obvious sore point with Kate, who flushed angrily upon hearing this nugget of information.

'You're pathetic, you and your stupid friends. And Ann McCarthy is a slag, everyone knows that.'

'Doesn't seem to bother Pete though, does it?' I knew I was being too smart for my own good with this comment, but I didn't care. I wanted to hurt Kate the way she was always hurting me and, besides, it was the truth.

'C'mon, Holly, let's go.' Kate put on a bored expression. 'You, Vonnie, are just too tiresome. And you're not even my real sister.' She turned to Holly. 'She's not, you know.'

'Who'd want to be?' I retorted. 'Clearly there was a mix up at the hospital – my bad luck.'

'I'm going to tell mum you said that.'

'Tell her what you like. I'll tell her you and Holly left me on my own all afternoon when you're meant to be playing with me.'

Holly looked worried.

'Nobody'd want to play with you, except morons. Anyway, I'm always being nice to you – only because mum told me I have to be – and I'm sick of it. C'mon, Holly, let's go and leave my non-sister to her weirdo hobbies. D'you know she makes up stories? She sits in her room writing them,' Kate sniggered. 'You know why?'

Holly shook her head.

'Because she has to make up stories and people to write about because she doesn't have a real life – in the real world.'

'That's a lie,' I said, my face flaming.

'Now, now, girls, what's all this shouting?' Barney came out the back door, wiping her hands on her apron. There was flour in her hair and she looked cross. 'God help us,' she said, 'can you girls not get through one afternoon, one tiny afternoon, without squabbling like a bag of cats?'

'Holly and me are going to the tennis club,' Kate announced to Barney, who didn't look exactly pleased at the news.

'Didn't your mother say to you—'

'Yes,' Kate said, 'but we can't stand it a minute longer. Anyway, we've already played two games of Monopoly with her and let her win. We're going to meet our friends, people of our own age.'

'You did not let me win,' I shouted at their retreating backs. 'I beat you fair and square.'

'Don't mind them,' Barney said. 'They're only being typical teenagers, full of self-importance and no regard for anyone. Come inside, pet, and have a cup of tea with me. I've just taken an apple tart out of the oven, we can have a nice warm slice with cream.'

'Well I'll be a teenager soon,' I grumbled, sitting down at the kitchen table. 'Will that make a difference?'

'To what, pet?'

'Will Kate start liking me more then, when I'm a teenager?'

'Heaven help us, child, she likes you already, of course she does. Isn't she your sister? Don't all sisters squabble? And older sisters are the divil himself to younger ones, that's just the way of the world.' Barney poured boiling water into the teapot and began to cut a generous slice of the apple pie.

'She says I'm not her real sister. That she's only ever nice to me because Mum says she has to be.' I took a mouthful of pie and began to chew mindlessly, letting the velvety fruit and feather-light pastry melt in my mouth.

Barney made a clicking sound with her tongue. 'It's all a lot of nonsense, that's what it is. Pay no heed to her.'

'We don't look alike, though, do we?' The thought had suddenly popped into my head.

'I came from a family of seven sisters and one brother, and not one of us looked alike. My mother said we were all changeling babies – the fairies had taken her real children away in the night,' Barney grinned. 'Anyway wouldn't the world be a very boring auld place if we all looked the same? Now stop blathering and eat up that pie before it gets cold. Then I'll show you how to make an angel cake.'

I immediately perked up. Spending an afternoon baking with Barney and listening to her stories about growing up on their small farm was one of my very favourite things to do.

'Veronica?'

It was later that evening in my bedroom where I was reading before dinner when I heard my mother's voice calling me from the bottom of the stairs.

'Come down here, would you?'

I put my book down, carefully marking the page, straightened my bedspread and went downstairs. I assumed Kate was already ahead of me, but when I walked into the sitting room, there were only my parents. My father was in front of the fireplace, leaning against the mantelpiece, smoking a cigarette, something he rarely did. My mother sat on the sofa, a drink in hand. She had had her hair done, I noticed, and was wearing a floaty summer dress and big gold-hooped earrings. She looked like a lovely blonde gypsy. I wondered if I was in trouble for something, but she was smiling at me and beckoned me over.

'Veronica, pet, come over here and sit down.'

She patted the couch beside her and immediately I felt a sense of foreboding. For a moment I thought I couldn't breathe, that the floor was slipping away beneath me. If she was being nice, then something bad must have happened or was about to.

I sat down, and waited.

'There's something Daddy and I want to have a little chat with you about, isn't there, Colm?' She looked up at my father, who sighed, put out his cigarette, then nodded and smiled tightly.

'Well?' she said to him expectantly.

He shook his head.

'What is it?' I asked. 'What's wrong?'

'Nothing's wrong, pet, nothing at all.' She smiled again, but I saw her flick her eyes at my father.

'Your mother has something to tell you,' he said.

'We both do—'

'What?' I cried.

'For God's sake, Carmel.'

'Are you sick? Is someone ill? What is it?'

'Nobody's sick, Veronica. The thing is, well, we feel that you're old enough now to know some grown-up things – things we didn't feel we could talk to you about before.'

A rush of colour flooded my face; surely to God she wasn't going to have another go at the birds and the bees talk – not in front of my father? My mother never referred to sex. Kate and I had respectively been given a small booklet titled *Everything Your Child Needs to Know about Growing Up* and informed we could ask her any questions about anything we didn't understand. Kate, having been divulged this information two years ahead of me, had taken instant delight regaling me with her new-found knowledge on the subject, which I had felt squeamish about ever since. Now, though, I thought, anything was preferable to going through the whole icky subject again.

I was wrong.

'I already know about babies and everything.'

My father looked alarmed and coughed.

'This isn't about babies, Veronica.' My mother began, and then gave a little laugh. 'Well, actually maybe it is, in a funny sort of way, isn't it, Colm? It's about you as a baby.'

'Me? What about me as a baby?' A variety of scenarios flashed through my mind. Maybe something happened at the hospital, maybe I was dropped on my head, fell out a window – any number of things could have happened to explain why . . . 'Is this about why I— I'm different?'

'Not different, Veronica – special.'

'Special?'

'Yes, you were a special baby because you were meant for us. Isn't that right, Colm?'

'Meant for you?'

'Yes, Veronica, we chose you.'

'I don't understand.'

Impatience flashed across my mother's face, replaced by a determined smile. 'We chose you, Veronica. Out of all the other babies we could have taken, we chose you. Didn't we, Colm?'

My father cleared his throat and seemed to be about to say something, then thought the better of it. 'We did. We chose you.'

Slowly, exquisitely slowly, the truth began to dawn on me, but when I tried to say the words they stuck in my throat. 'That means, that means I'm . . .'

'You're adopted, pet, that's right. We wanted Kate to have a little sister and, well, we chose you.' Something fell flat in her voice, her delivery faltered. Even this presumably well-rehearsed dialogue couldn't hide her disappointment of how her 'choice' had turned out. I tried to imagine what it must feel like, having one blonde, beautiful, God-given daughter and choosing, inadvertently gaining, a big, plain lump of a girl to go alongside her. A girl you could only be embarrassed about. No wonder I felt different. No wonder Kate had been told to be nice to me. No wonder . . . oh God, Kate – this meant she had known all along and, worse, she had been right when she said I wasn't her real sister. She said that in

front of Holly, which meant the whole class would know –
my whole school – maybe they'd always known. I felt my
head begin to swim and horror crawled lazily up and down
my spine.

'Veronica? Veronica, child, are you all right?' My father's
voice interrupted my nightmare reverie. I pulled myself
together.

'I— I'm fine.'

'We realise this must come as a bit of a surprise,' my
mother, my adopted mother, said.

'A bit,' I said faintly.

'But you're a big girl now, you're able to understand things
properly, and now that you'll be joining Kate at boarding
school next month, well, it's better that everything's straightened out, that we're all clear about how things are in the
family.'

'Yes.'

'That's another thing, Veronica, it's best if you keep this
to yourself . . . at school I mean. Don't go telling anyone, no
matter how friendly you get with them. These kinds of things
are best kept in the family. Kate won't say anything about it
either. Is that clear?' her voice rose sharply.

'Yes. I mean, no, I won't say anything to anyone.'

'Good girl. So everything's all right then?'

'Yes, fine.'

There was an awkward silence. 'Are there any questions
you'd like to ask us?'

'No.'

'Well, if you change your mind about that,' said my father,
'you can always ask us, can't you?'

'I suppose.'

'What would she want to be asking? Sure hasn't she
everything here a child could want? You're a clever girl,
Veronica. Leave the past in the past, where it belongs. Isn't

that right, Colm? You have a lovely family and you were
chosen especially, a lot of children weren't so lucky, you
know?'

I'd heard enough. 'Can I go now?'

'Yes, yes, of course you can.' There was a brief pause during
which my parents exchanged glances. 'Dinner's in ten
minutes,' my mother said. 'Don't be late.'

The flight is long and uneventful. I watch a movie, eat dinner,
try to get Jazz to eat something and beg her to sleep, even
for a little while, to no avail. I leaf through the current issue
of *Vanity Fair*, the magazine that changed my career, and
remember the early days in London, and the giddy excitement when I got the job as a copy-editor on one of the big
English glossies. We worked flat out, twenty-four-seven, all
of us on the magazine, but I finally felt as if maybe I was
amounting to something. Maybe, after all, I had done the
right thing getting out of Dublin. I was still a girl on the run
from my family, but the magazine had become a surrogate
family to me, and, of course, even though they were both
back in Dublin, there was always Abby and Di. That was
when we were young, free and single, and the girls came over
to visit me whenever they could. I loved seeing them and
lived for their visits, but I was also becoming aware that I
was changing, becoming more confident in both myself and
my abilities, and that much as I loved Abby and Di, and they
me, I could see that maybe they weren't quite as comfortable
with those changes as I had imagined.

London, 1988

'I can't believe we're actually having this conversation,' Diana exhales a plume of smoke, and rolls her eyes dramatically.

We have driven to Oxford and are having Sunday lunch in a darling little pub. Abby and Di have come to stay with me for a long weekend. One of the guys I share a house with in Wandsworth is away, and he very kindly offered me his room if I wanted anyone to stay, so that's where they are bunking up. There are four of us in the house, two guys, two girls, and we all offer our rooms to the others if we are away for any length of time.

Abby is nursing in Dublin and has met a doctor she likes, and Diana is making a name for herself as a make-up artist and travelling to a lot of the big fashion shows. We hang on her every word as she tells us of the behind-the-scenes goings-on and the famous supermodels she has worked with. She looks amazing, with big teased hair, pale skin and red lips, and thinner than ever in a white T-shirt and high-waisted, belted Levis 501s.

She looks pointedly at Abby. 'I mean you're what, twenty-two now?' Diana goes on. 'Abby, what the hell are you waiting for?'

'The right man obviously.' Abby is indignant.

Di shakes her head. 'The right man is the one you marry. The wrong ones are the ones you have fun with, practise on.'

'I don't want to practise. I only want to ever make love to

one man, and that's the one I marry. So,' she turns to me, 'do you think I should go on the pill? Do it with Edward?'

Before I can answer, Di interjects. 'Jesus! You're a bloody nurse, Abby, and he's a doctor! You've been dating for three months and you haven't even had sex yet?'

'Shut up,' hisses Abby. 'Keep your voice down. We're not all as liberal as you, Di. Besides, Mummy says the minute you let a man have sex with you, it's all over, he thinks you're easy and cheap and he'll never marry you.'

'Your point being?' Diana asks.

'I think what Abby's trying to say is that she doesn't want to get it wrong, to give this Edward – that's his name? – the wrong impression.'

Abby sighs with relief. 'That's exactly what I mean.'

'Well, I'd say *not* having sex with him is giving him the worst impression possible . . . you really think a guy's going to marry someone he hasn't had sex with in this day and age? I take it you *do* want to marry him?' Diana says rather sarcastically. 'That's what this is all about, right?'

'Well, yes, as a matter of fact I do but, well,' she lowers her voice, 'what if we do it and it goes wrong? What if I'm not any good, you know, in bed?'

'Do you fancy him?' Diana demands.

'Oh yes,' she breathes.

'Well, then, it'll be fine. Unless *he's* rubbish between the sheets, then you're in trouble.'

This thought obviously hadn't occurred to Abby, who looks panicked.

'Oh, God,' she says. 'I'm damned if I do and damned if I don't. I couldn't bear to lose him.'

'Abby,' I say gently, 'I don't think you should do anything you're not ready for. Surely if he loves you, this guy will understand. When you're ready and the time is right, you'll know.'

Abby suddenly looks at me in astonishment. 'How would *you* know? Have you? No, you haven't! I mean, have *you* done it, Vonnie?'

Diana sits back in her chair and regards me with amusement. 'Well, *ma petite*?'

'Not that it's any of your business, but, yes, I have.'

'With who?' And how come you didn't tell us?' Abby splutters.

'Because it's none of your business,' I say with a smile. It is meant light-heartedly, but I can see a flare of resentment in Abby's eyes. Clearly, it is all right for Diana to have a sex life, but not for me.

As it happens, I have had very enjoyable sex with several men in the five years I've lived over here. Men are comfortable around me, they like me, I am just not really girlfriend material. But that's okay, I am happy to listen to their woes, give advice when asked for, and sometimes I have ended up having the odd relationship. It's just that they never seem to last for long. But that's okay too, I have always remained friends with them and, more often than not, am invited to the inevitable weddings that follow.

'I am glad to hear that, Vonnie,' Diana grins. 'You have a lot of sex appeal, it would be a great waste not to use it.' This is news to me.

'How do you know,' Abby asks Di, clearly put out at the turn the conversation has taken, 'if a girl has sex appeal or not?'

Diana shrugs. 'I don't. It was my father who said it, years ago, he said that girl Vonnie has sex appeal but she doesn't know it.'

I go bright red with mortification, but inside there is a flicker of hope – Diana's dad is French, he knows all about women, Diana has always told us. If he says I have sex appeal, well, maybe I do.

Abby shudders. 'Well, seeing as I'm the only girl here who hasn't got around to it, I'd better do something about it.'

'I would if I were you, Abs,' says Di. 'And just for the record, he shouldn't be able to keep his hands off you.'

'Thank you for your kind advice, but I'm sure I'll be able to figure it out for myself.' Abby is miffed and a little embarrassed, which is understandable.

'There's just one more thing,' Diana says conspiratorially.

'What?'

'My father always told me a woman should only marry a man who loves her more than she loves him.'

'Why would he say that?' I wonder.

Diana shrugs. 'He just said it was good advice, makes for a better marriage – for the woman naturally.'

Abby is quiet as we ponder this latest remark.

'I don't think I'd mind either way,' I muse. 'As long as we really did love each other. I mean, how can you measure love? It can't stay the same, can it? Surely it must change? Maybe it shifts like a see-saw, one person loves more, then the other.'

'Obviously this is not a view that should be expressed to the men in your life,' Diana grins. 'I'm just passing on the advice. What you do with it is up to you.'

I thought about that as I drove the girls back to London. I thought about my adoptive parents and my birth parents – who loved who more? And I wondered how I hadn't acknowledged before that love didn't appear to feature much in either situation.

People talk about love an awful lot. Songs, poetry, stories, art have all been created in its name, but back then, as far as I was concerned, love seemed like a pretty dangerous word to me and I'm not sure that I've ever revised that opinion.

June, 2011

Abby

Abby is sitting in her kitchen, methodically working her way through a packet of oatcakes. She only meant to have two, but consoles herself with the fact that they are low GI and therefore can't be *that* bad. Besides, Edward approves of them.

Dinner is in the oven, her mother will be down shortly from her afternoon nap, and her children and husband will be home. Abby loves it when everyone is home, when they can sit around the table and be a real family, even though Edward is away quite a lot these days.

She thinks of the lunch she had with Di, and reminds herself how lucky she is, having a husband who supports her, enabling her to make a home and look after him and their family. Although Di's life is terribly glamorous, and she's often jetting off to wonderful locations, meeting celebrities and everything, Abby can't help suspecting it must be quite a strain for Di with Greg being unemployed. She pretty much said as much at lunch. She admires Di hugely, always has, but secretly Abby thinks she got the better deal. St Valentine certainly hadn't let her down on that front. She got exactly what she had asked for in a husband in Edward – a successful doctor, who would take care of her and make her happy – so she, in turn, could make her mother happy. And it had all worked out perfectly – well almost perfectly, but she wouldn't think about that now. Instead, she summons up her favourite memory – her wedding day.

25 June 1990

Abby is happier than she ever thought possible. She is the first of all her friends to get married, although this is not the reason for her happiness. She is in love, very much in love. But, better still, she has made her mother happy, and that is something she thought she would never be able to manage in her wildest dreams.

It has all been worthwhile, she has been assured. The years of saving, of sacrifice, her mother's constant haranguing of her father, the sheer, back-breaking *effort* of it all – everything has finally amounted to something. Abby is marrying a doctor. She is the embodiment of her mother's ultimate ambition.

Edward is not just any doctor, either. He is a catch, in every sense of the word. He is tall, blond, good-looking and he played rugby for Trinity. If he hadn't been so dedicated to his medical studies, he would, he assured her, have played for Ireland. The thought occurred to Abby, fleetingly, that it is not unheard of to do both, plenty have done it before him, but she wisely kept this comment to herself. Edward has sometimes been described as arrogant, but then, as her mother reasons, doesn't he have plenty to be arrogant about? He is from a Very Good Family, those sorts of people are naturally confident, it's been bred into them for generations, along with his fine straight features and elegant bearing. He even went to public school in England, all his family did. A Catholic one of course – Ampleforth – which means he is very posh indeed. Her mother has read up on it. She knows someone who knows someone whose uncle went there, she thinks he became an archbishop, maybe even a cardinal.

That had been one of the extremely worrying aspects about the prospective wedding for her mother, who to get to perform the ceremony. It couldn't just be any old priest. Not even their parish priest, old Fr O'Sullivan, would do. She needn't have worried, though; Edward's parents have an old family friend, a Jesuit, very high up, who was happy to do the honours. In fact, there was no avoiding it, Edward told Abby, he would be mortally offended *not* to be asked. Abby hadn't liked him when she met him, this tall, austere, man, but it kept Edward's parents happy and therefore her mother was happy too.

Meeting Edward's parents had been nerve-wracking. His father is a prominent solicitor, who, along with his two brothers, owns one of the biggest and most respected legal firms in the country. Abby had been introduced to them over dinner at the Royal Irish Yacht Club, although they didn't seem to do much sailing. Edward's mother suffers with her nerves. This, at least, was something Abby could relate to and sympathise with – although she quickly learned it is a subject never to be mentioned.

She had wanted them to like her, she very much wanted to make a good impression, but at dinner Edward's father was gruff and disinterested, preferring to fire questions at Edward about rugby and whether or not he had made up his mind about what he wanted to specialise in – vascular surgery was proving to be the thing, he had heard from a medical chap in his club.

Abby tried to join in the conversation. Being a nurse, she could at least contribute knowledgeably on this front, but George, Edward's father, didn't seem to be interested in her opinions.

His mother, Daphne, looked pained, although she had

asked several times how Abby could stand to be a nurse. 'Hospitals, such depressing places.'

'People do get better, occasionally, Mum,' Edward pointed out. 'That's why I decided to become a doctor, remember?'

Daphne looked pained to be reminded of that too.

But today Abby is not thinking about any of that. Or about the excruciatingly embarrassing meeting between Edward's parents and her own, although her mother is under the illusion it all went very well – *such elegant people, so discerning.* Her late grandmother, Abby's great-grandmother, whose house used to be the Old Famine Hospital in a west Cork village, would approve. 'I come from good stock, you know,' Abby's mother had said. 'My people had breeding, money, before it was all drunk away by The Waster.'

Edward is not a 'waster'. Abby is sure of this.

Mostly, it doesn't bother Abby that she is an only child but, today, it occurs to her, fancifully, that it would be nice to have a bit of noise in the house, some sounds of life, a few brothers, moaning about hangovers and struggling to get into stiff, unfamiliar shirts and jackets, larking about with her father. A sister or two to rush about with, wailing about lost stockings, gained inches and where, oh where, was the blue garter? Something old, something new, something borrowed . . .

But nothing has been left to chance. This wedding has been planned with military precision *for years*. Abby's mother has seen to that. The last of Grandmother Harvey's inheritance had been put away especially for this purpose. The house they live in had been hers too. It is shabby now, but in a respectable area. No shame in that. Sheila Murphy knew she could afford one child – to give that child the best life she could. That's why Abby had been sent to the most exclusive school in the country so she could mix with the right kinds of girls, who would, in turn, include her in their circles. All in all, Sheila Murphy was very pleased how things had turned out. Her husband Joe hadn't contributed much, but he was a good-looking man, and Abby, it was acknowledged, had done well in the gene pool, inheriting her mother's tall, slim figure and her father's slanting green eyes and dark red hair, which she wears long and in rippling curls.

Abby looks in the mirror one last time.

'You look beautiful, pet,' her mother says. 'Now hurry, the car is here and the bridesmaids have gone ahead. Your father's ready and waiting downstairs.'

Abby wishes that Di and Vonnie could have been her bridesmaids – that's what they had always planned for each other's weddings – but her mother had thought it a bad idea. 'Children are much more appropriate, and doesn't Edward's sister Sarah have three little girls who are only *dotes*.'

Abby knows privately that her mother would not have been happy with Diana, who might steal the limelight, and Vonnie who, she says, would just look awkward, 'not easy to dress that girl'.

But at least they will be there as guests. Abby will know they are in the church, wishing her well, and they will talk later. They had met Edward, of course, and pronounced him wonderful, although Abby had noticed Diana watching him speculatively as he held forth over dinner, and caught Vonnie yawning and looking at her watch. But then Vonnie often did that.

'You'll be the most beautiful bride any of them has ever seen,' her mother says triumphantly. 'They'll all be green with envy.' She fixes Abby's gossamer veil and looks fondly at her. 'You're a good girl, Abby. A very good daughter, you've made me very proud.' And then she leaves, hurrying to make her own much anticipated entrance as Mother Of The Bride.

On the way to the church, in the hired vintage Bentley, Abby pats her father's arm. 'It'll all be over before you know it, Dad,' she smiles.

'He's a lucky man, that Edward,' he says, rather grimly. 'I hope he knows it.'

Abby thinks he does. Although, sometimes, he isn't very good at showing it – but, then, he is not from an emotionally demonstrative family, any more than she is. They have been going out for two years, engaged for one. Edward made no secret of pursuing Abby and, even though she had fancied him wildly, she had made sure to be elusive, reserved, not too easy, and it had driven him mad and set her apart from the hoards of other girls who had chased him shamefully.

For the past six months, though, Edward has been a little remote for her liking, nothing major, just not quite as keen to spend time with her, not looking at her longingly with such tenderness, the way he used to. It is not her imagin- ation, because Abby is very sensitive to how people feel around her. It is part of her nature. She understands how marriage might frighten a man like Edward, even marriage to someone like her, who will work so hard to make him happy. That is why, three months ago, she had stopped taking the pill. *What was the harm?* she'd reasoned. *We were getting married anyway, it was just a little experiment, and one month was all it took.*

She hugs her secret to her happily. No one else knows, except Edward, not even her mother. And no one else need ever know. This baby will be a honeymoon baby, they happen all the time. Edward is an honourable man, he comes from a family that takes duty and responsibility seriously. He will make a wonderful husband and father, even if he does not know this yet – even if, as Abby suspects, he might have been having second thoughts.

A creak in the stair as her mother descends after her after- noon nap brings Abby back smartly to the present. Two more creaks and she will be down. That, and the stick her mother has taken to walking with, which she is quite well able to walk without, have been irritating Abby to screaming pitch lately. She takes a deep breath.

'Oh, there you are,' Sheila says. As if she is somehow surprised that she should find her daughter in the kitchen at ten past six in the evening when she is here every day at this time.

'Hello, Mum. Did you have nice nap?'

'What's for dinner?' Sheila joins her at the table, sitting down heavily and picking up the TV remote, deftly changing channels to the news, which Abby could well do without.

'Fish pie, you like that, don't you?' The low-fat version of Edward's favourite fish pie is baking in the oven. Sheila will have some of this too (it agrees with her delicate digestive system). Roseanna, Abby's daughter, will hardly eat anything as she is constantly watching her figure – and Abby's fifteen-year-old twin sons will have sirloin steaks – they are bulking up for their school's rugby camp.

'Oh, I'll take whatever I'm given,' Sheila sighs. 'That dog next door is a disgrace, I couldn't get a wink. You'll have to have words with them.'

There is no dog next door and Sheila's room has been treble glazed, you couldn't hear a heavy metal concert outside her window, but Abby is not about to dispute this now.

'Well, you look nice and rested,' she says instead.

Sheila looks at her. 'Are you not going to put on a bit of lipstick or something? Edward will be home any minute.'

Abby ignores this and gets up to check the fish pie.

'You've put on weight,' Sheila observes.

'I know I have, Mum. I don't really need to hear it, thank you.'

'I'm only telling you. It's very unflattering. It's a shame, you know, you always had such a nice figure. You should go on a diet.'

'Maybe next week,' Abby says.

'You can't afford to let yourself go, Abby, not with a husband like Edward. He could have any woman he wants, you know.'

'Thank you for that, Mother. But he chose me, remember?'

'That was then, Abby. I know what you're thinking, that I'm being mean, but I'm only trying to protect you. It's a mother's duty. And Edward must have noticed, even if he's not saying.'

Edward has said. But Abby will not think about that now.

'I know Roseanna has, because she said to me. She said—'

'Mum, why don't you pour yourself a little sherry?'

'What? Oh, yes, good idea. I'll just have time, before dinner, won't I?' Sheila gets up and heads swiftly for the drinks cabinet in the sitting room, forgetting her walking stick.

Her mother can move with surprising agility, it occurs to Abby not for the first time, when there is suitable motivation involved.

'Hey, Mum!' Timothy says, coming in through the back door, closely followed by his twin Tom. Fresh from rugby camp they are covered in mud, and look like a pair of black and white minstrels. They dump their stuff in the back hall, off which there is a shower, especially installed for their use. This means they can clean up before dragging all of their combined dirt through the rest of the house. It was Edward's idea, one of his better ones, and one Abby is grateful for. It means she can chuck all their gear in the utility room and not have to drag it downstairs from their bedrooms to be washed.

'What's for dinner?' asks Tom.

'Steaks for you guys,' Abby smiles at her boys as they blunder into the kitchen, seeming too big and unco-ordinated for the modern streamlined room.

'Great, rare for me,' Tom says.

'Medium,' says Timothy, frowning.

'I *know*,' says Abby. *As if they need to remind me*, she thinks fondly. Hasn't she anticipated every one of her children's needs since they arrived in this world? Abby adores her children – even Roseanna, who can be a right pain these days – but it's hard for them, Abby thinks, they are living in such uncertain times. We all are. She hopes she is not spoiling them, but she doesn't think so, they are good kids, no trouble so far, thank God.

'Hurry up,' she tells them, 'dinner's almost ready, get showered and changed.'

She hears the front door slam. Edward is home – no time for lipstick now.

She listens as he goes into his study. There was a time when Edward would always come into the kitchen and kiss her the minute he got home, but this happens rarely now. But they have been married for twenty years, Abby reminds herself, what does she expect? A constant honeymoon? Besides, everyone needs their space, especially after a hard day's work, and Edward works very hard. His new clinic is doing very well and has been relatively unaffected by the recession.

'I got out just in time,' he says, proudly, of his former career as a vascular surgeon. 'Best move I ever made.'

Edward owns a cosmetic surgery clinic now, the best in the country, he says. He doesn't operate himself (that would have meant retraining), he doesn't need to when he can get surgeons from all over the world to fly in and out as needed. He has, however, mastered Botox and hair transplants, and has the most up-to-date, state-of-the-art laser machines available. Anyone who is anyone goes to him to buy new hair or shiny new skin. He has become quite a celebrity in Ireland – cosmetic doctor to the stars – though she preferred it when he was a surgeon, she's not sure why.

'What's for dinner?' Roseanna wanders into the kitchen and opens the fridge, peering inside, while Abby sets the table.

'Fish pie.'

'Ugh.' Roseanna wrinkles her pretty nose (it used not to be so pretty, but Edward allowed her to have it 'done' and although Abby put up quite a fight about that, she was outnumbered). She takes a pot of yoghurt from the fridge and peels off the lid.

'Don't eat that now, Rosie,' Abby pleads. 'Not just before dinner.'

'This *is* my dinner. I hate fish pie. Anyway, I ate earlier, there was tons of food at the shoot.' Roseanna is trying to become a model, although she does not seem to be getting an awful lot of work. Neither Abby nor Edward were keen on the idea of their daughter doing modelling, but she got a good degree at university and begged for them to allow her a year to at least try her luck. After that, if she wasn't getting anywhere, she promised she would do something else. Her gap year travelling with her friends has been sacrificed to this end, so Abby felt she must be serious about it. Anyhow, she has always vowed to encourage her children's passions, not to thwart them.

'Hello, dear,' Sheila returns with her sherry and sits down at the table. 'That's a lovely rig-out.' She looks at her grand-daughter fondly. 'Is it new?'

'Sort of,' Roseanna grins.

'Well it's lovely on you,' Sheila says approvingly. 'Sure, what wouldn't be? You're so gorgeous and slim, you remind me of myself when I was young. Where's your father? I thought I heard him come in?'

'So did I.' Roseanna frowns, then yells, 'D-a-a-d?'

Edward trots down the three steps to the kitchen. 'Hi, hi, hi, everyone, I'm home.'

'Well, here he is,' beams Sheila, 'the working man. What sort of a day did you have?'

'Terrific,' Edwards grins.

'How did the shoot go today, sweetheart?' he asks Roseanna. 'Boring.'

'Well, Sheila, did you work out four down and three across? Think I might have beaten you today!' Edward and Sheila enjoy sparring over the crossword. They have a great relationship, Sheila boasts to her friends, not like mother and son-in-law at all, more like friends. They have great banter, the pair of them.

Edward, Abby notices, has taken to talking with an inflection at the end of his sentences, an American affectation. She doesn't particularly like it, but nobody else seems to notice. Maybe she is imagining it, but she doesn't think so, and why should it matter? Edward goes to the States on business quite a lot, he probably can't help it, doesn't even notice it. But all the same, it grates on Abby. It also reminds her of someone, but she can't think who. And then it comes to her – a flash of memory, a classroom, and an old American nun whose accent they used to laugh at. Happy days.

'What's for dinner?' Edward asks, picking up one of Roseanna's magazines and flicking through it.

'I had a great day too, thanks for asking.' The words escape before Abby can stop them, although there is a smile fixed on her face.

'Well,' Edward raises an eyebrow, 'someone obviously got out of the wrong side of bed this morning.'

Abby bites her bottom lip and shrugs, turning away.

Edward never gets out of the wrong side of bed. He is always up and out of the house at a quarter to six to hit the gym before going to the clinic. He is in great shape, of course; that's important in his line of business, he says. In fact, he is in better shape than when they got married, which is saying something – leaner and remarkably unlined. Abby preferred him when he was more rugged, which was a word she enjoyed using to describe his good looks. Now, while he's still undeniably good looking – no arguing with that – there is something contrived about it all. He looks younger than his forty-six years, certainly. She knows he uses Botox, although very sparingly, and naturally he availed of his transplant facilities at the clinic to restore his own receding hairline. He has had his teeth fixed too, straightened and whitened with veneers. Edward is considered handsome, but he always was, and Abby privately thinks he looked better without the retouching. He is not *her* Edward anymore, in so many ways – perhaps that is the problem – instead he seems to belong to everyone else.

'Fish pie.' Roseanna answers her father's question, giving him a rather-you-than-me look. She pulls out a chair from the table and sits down with her yoghurt, licking the entirety of her first spoonful thoroughly.

'Rosie, *please*,' Abby chides, 'you could at least wait for everyone else to begin dinner.'

'Oh, she's all right,' says Sheila, indulgently, but throws Abby a meaningful look.

'Tell *Timmony* to get a move on then,' says Roseanna. 'The rest of us are all here.'

Abby smiles, despite herself – *Timmony* is what Tom and Timothy have been jointly labelled at school – in the manner of Jedward, the infamous Irish *X-Factor* twins. The boys are good-natured about it, but Edward doesn't like the term being used at home. Roseanna uses it at every available opportunity. Abby rather likes it.

'I don't understand this *Timmony* thing,' says Sheila, deftly seizing her chance to side with Edward and avert any potential tension. She is still looking at Abby, silently warning her not to be narky, not to annoy anyone, especially Edward.

'It's a lot of nonsense,' says Edward, frowning. He is opening a bottle of sparkling water and filling his own glass, leaving the jug of filtered water on the table for everyone else.

Abby would like to fill her own glass with a generous helping of white wine, but Edward says it plays havoc with the blood sugar and makes women bloated. You can tell women who 'drink', he says, by just looking at them, and he is watching her.

She takes the fish pie from the oven and begins to dish up at the counter.

The boys come in and take their plates eagerly, Abby deftly spearing a steak on each one.

Edward walks over and peers over her shoulder at the fish pie. 'What, exactly, is in that?' he asks, suspiciously.

Abby turns her head to look at him, pausing for a split second as she arranges the food on his plate. 'Fish,' she says.

'Yes, I can see that, obviously,' he says, exasperated. 'But what *kind* of fish, exactly?'

'Whale,' says Abby. 'Oh, and there's a bit of Piranha in there too, for extra flavour. That all right for you? And it's the low-fat sauce, just the way you like it.' She hands him his plate and serves herself.

'There's no need for that,' Edward says thinly. 'You need to get your hormone levels checked, you know,' he mutters, heading back to the table to sit down.

Abby is grateful for the noise around the table. No one will have noticed Edward's comment. Except her mother, of course, who has the ability to lip read when it suits her – or perhaps it just always seems that way.

Dublin, June 2011

Vonnie

'M om, I *love* this. It's a real cottage, just like in story-books.' Jazz runs around investigating every nook and cranny, exclaiming with delight.

'It's not really a cottage, Jazz,' I point out, 'it's a little house, but it *is* cute.'

'But it has roses growing up the walls in front and around the door,' she protests. 'And it's pink – my favourite colour.' In her world, this is textbook cottage, and I am too tired to debate the finer points.

The rental agency did well, and the house is just what we need for our two-month stay.

Silversands is one of the last proper villages in Dublin and is right on the coast. It is much as I remember it, although it has developed considerably, but has managed to retain its character and prettiness in the process, thanks in no small part, I imagine, to the local residents (among whose number are Diana's parents) who have always been fiercely protective of it. It is also conveniently close to the city centre, although you would never imagine it. In Silversands, you could be in a seaside village almost anywhere in the country; only the occasional rumble of a heavy lorry heading for the port or the busy early-morning traffic along the coast road heading into town gives any clue that you are minutes away from a major European city, if Dublin could be called that. But all the same, its proximity to town will be helpful for the occa-sional research I will need to do, especially in Trinity College.

You can walk into town in under half an hour, or hop on the Dart, the light rail system that chunters up and down the coast between Howth on the northside and Greystones to the south. I make a mental note to investigate bicycles later. I have no intention of driving if I can avoid it. I have always hated it. But in California, not having a car wasn't really an option.

It is June, and the sun is promising to shine, although it is just seven a.m., but jet lag always makes me feel cold, and I fling open a suitcase to begin some rudimentary unpacking, just the essentials. Someone from the agency has left milk, teabags, bread and eggs, and I am ridiculously grateful; the thought of going out to shops now would finish me off completely, I just want to crawl into bed for a couple of hours.

'C'mon, Jazz, help me make up the bed.' I take the freshly laundered sheets from the airing cupboard.

'Can we go to the beach, Mommy? I want to explore.'

'Later, sweetheart, we need to sleep first.'

She looks downcast, but her energy is a short burst of excitement. Jazz was true to her promise and stayed awake for most of the flight watching movies – in minutes we will both be wilting and cranky.

I make tea, strong for me, milky for Jazz, while she wriggles out of her jeans and into her current favourite nightdress. Nightdresses are her latest obsession, and she has abandoned her enormous and varied collection of sleepwear in favour of them. Since I read to her from *Little Women*, by Louisa M. Alcott, Jazz has embraced everything feminine, longs for a sister, and wants to put a clothes peg on her nose at night to make it thinner – just like Amy. I drew the line at that.

This particular nightdress is whisper-thin, white-gathered cotton, sleeveless, with broderic anglaise detail on the bodice and hem, which reaches her ankles. She looks so cute in it my heart contracts. We bought it with her dad on a trip to New Orleans, which along with Disneyland has become her other favourite place in the world.

Thinking of Jake, I am mindful that he asked me to call him as soon as we got in.

'I'm getting into your bed, Mommy.' Jazz clambers under the cover clutching George, a soft and much-confided in toy monkey, who has seen better days. When she was younger, Jazz chatted away to him all the time quite unself-consciously, even in public. There was a time when I found it worrying, now I kind of wish she still did. I often wonder about the secrets George holds so close to his bedraggled little chest.

'How's George doing?' I put her tea on the bedside locker and undress, pulling on a long T-shirt and slip in beside her. The sheets are starched and silky. Bliss.

'He's fine.'

'Do you guys still talk?'

'Sure, but we don't need words anymore. George knows what I'm thinking and feeling.'

'That's nice. What *are* you thinking?' I push a dark, silky curl out of her eye.

'I'm thinking I can't wait to meet my Irish grandpa and grandma. George is excited to meet them too. When will we meet them, Mommy?'

The question catches me off guard. 'I don't know, honey. We've only just got here, we'll think about it tomorrow. Try to get some sleep.'

Her grandparents. Boy was that one loaded question, and one I was going to have to face while I was back in Dublin. I feel my stomach go into knots of frustration just thinking about it. As far as grandparents go on my side of the family, Jazz has been pretty short changed. I've barely met my own mother on a handful of occasions, and I have no clue about my father. I feel a surge of anger run through me and take a deep breath, stroking Jazz's hair as her eyes begin to close.

The ringing of my cell phone makes me jump, and I reach for it as Jazz's eyes fly open. Jake's name flashes on screen.

'Hi,' I say, 'I was just about to ring you.'

'How're my girls?' The dark velvet of his voice reaches across the ocean and into a place deep inside of me that used to make me shiver. Still does.

'Daddy!' Jazz shrieks.

'Sleepy, but one of them wants to talk to you, I think.'

'Put her on.' I can hear his smile as I hand the phone to Jazz.

I am not Jake's girl anymore, technically speaking, or rather his woman – but that is what he always calls us, 'My girls.' I don't mind. Old habits die hard. And part of me will always belong to him. He knows that.

Jazz, though, will always be his girl. They have a mutual adoration society and I am grateful for that, and Jake is a wonderful father.

They chat for a couple of minutes, and when Jazz demands to know when he is coming to join us, I signal to her to hand the phone back to me.

'Bye, Daddy. Love you too.' Jazz hands the phone back to me reluctantly.

'So, when can I come over?' Jake asks, as I knew he would.

'We've only just got here.' I am playing for time. 'We need to get settled in and, you know, I have some things to figure out.'

'I know. Vonnie?'

'What?'

'Don't let them get to you. Things are different now. You're a different person. You can handle it. Right?'

'Right,' I say. But nothing feels that way. Not for the first time, I wonder if I am making a huge mistake.

'You know you can. And I'm here for you. You know that, don't you? You just have to holler.'

'I know. Thanks.'

'Okay. I miss you guys. Let me know when I can come over.'

'I will. Bye, Jake.'

'When is Daddy coming over?'

'Soon, Jazz, but not just yet. We have to get settled in first.'

'But he'll stay here, with us, won't he? Not in a hotel. There's three bedrooms if you count the really small one. Or he can have my room and I can sleep with you, can't I?'

Her little face is full of longing, but I also see the worry there, the rapid blinking of her almond-shaped, brown eyes, and I am awash with guilt.

'We'll figure something out, sweetheart, don't worry.'

This seems to reassure her and she snuggles down beside me, suddenly weary. 'Are you glad to be home in Ireland, Mommy?' she asks sleepily.

'Home for me is wherever *you* are, Jazz.'

'Me too, Mommy.' She looks up at me and smiles, looking for a split second so like her father I catch my breath. An expression, something fleeting, something I can never quite put my finger on. 'So we'd better always stay together then, hadn't we?'

'We certainly better had,' I agree. She has no idea how fiercely I mean that.

A text alert bleeps. It is from Abby, reminding me of our lunch date with Di. I reply that I'll be there, that I am looking forward to it. This is true, although part of me is apprehensive. It's been a long time, and a lot has happened, but I do not have to justify myself. I am not that person any more. I have boundaries, and if people can't respect them then they have no place in my life.

Jazz is asleep in minutes, but I stay awake for a little while longer – watching her, my beautiful girl.

The Affair

*T*here are days together, sometimes nights – not often, but
enough. Enough for her to be insanely happy, enough for her
to know that this is not enough, that she wants – needs – more.

Her husband travels occasionally. He doesn't suspect anything,
why would he? She is a good wife. He takes her for granted, she
tells herself, and perhaps that is true, although not entirely fair.
But she won't think about that now. Instead, she will enjoy these
two days in Paris, blissful days, heightened by the edge of danger,
of being seen, possibly found out.

Would it be so very bad, she allows herself to wonder briefly,
if that were to happen?

She is sitting, waiting for him, nursing a cup of chocolate in the
Boulevard Saint-Germain, in a window table at Brasserie Lipp.
He has a meeting this morning, part of a conference, but the afternoon
will be free. They will wander around, soaking up the atmosphere
of Saint-Germain-des-Prés, the church, the sights, the smells.

A crowd of students stroll by, laughing, carefree, and she jumps
at the feeling of a hand on her shoulder.

'Hello!' says the vaguely familiar woman. 'Fancy meeting you
here!'

She tries to remember her name and fails, she doesn't know
her, not well, their children attend the same school. She forces a
bright smile and says, 'Yes, what a coincidence. A few days shopping, what about you?'

'Oh a conference,' the woman says. 'Michael promised he'd bring
me the next time it was somewhere nice.'

She listens to the woman prattle on, silently willing her to go before her lover arrives. Out of the corner of her eye, she spies the woman's husband, his eyes scanning the room for his wife. Oh no! *she thinks.* Please don't let him join us.

The woman catches sight of him and waves for him to come over, but thankfully he seems impatient and motions for her to go.

'So lovely to see you,' *she says.* 'Better dash.'

When the woman has gone, she breathes more easily. She mustn't be so uptight; so what if someone sees her with someone who is not her husband? It could be anyone, a friend, a relative, a totally innocent meeting.

But it's not. There is nothing innocent about it. She looks up and sees him at the door, he spots her and grins, making his way through huddled tables to slide into the seat opposite her.

'I'm sorry I kept you waiting,' *he says.* 'I thought we would never wrap it up.'

'It doesn't matter,' *she says smiling.* 'You're here now.'

It begins to rain. Tumbling out of heavy, summer, storm-laden clouds, hammering on roofs, sliding down the windows. Doors are quickly shut, collars and umbrellas put up, hats pulled down, as pedestrians hurry along steaming pavements.

She feels safe, cocooned, protected from the outside world. There is still tonight, she thinks, still most of tomorrow. It is not over yet.

The Old Rectory, 2011

Carmel and Colm

'She's back, you know. I told you she would be, sooner or later.' Carmel's tone is heavy with foreboding as she rearranges medical magazines and papers in her husband's study, dusting them impatiently. It is her housekeeper's day off and this gives Carmel a good opportunity to snoop.

'What of it? It's highly unlikely she's going to pay us a visit after all this time. She's made her point and I can't say I blame her for feeling hard done by.'

Colm Callaghan knows this is a dangerous tack to take, particularly as he is a prisoner in his own home for the duration of his enforced recuperation. The hip replacement operation was not undertaken lightly. Being a doctor, albeit a retired one – he is seventy-seven now – he has a healthy suspicion of both surgeons and hospitals. But Carmel was having none of it. 'I'm not having an invalid around the house to run after. I have quite enough to do as it is,' she had said. 'You can get your hip done like everyone else, can't you?'

There is a price to pay for everything, reflects Colm. The price of getting about with renewed agility and without pain is that he must endure his wife's silent reproach that he is there at all. He feels it keenly. Almost as much as the irritation he feels when she now walks into a room. He can sense her these days, long before she even enters the room in question, as if her combined and long-accrued resentments have become an entity in their own right, preceding her in a cloud of disapproving gloom wherever she goes.

'Hard done by!' Carmel looks at him scornfully. 'Are you in the early stages of dementia, or what?' The dusting has come to an abrupt halt. 'We took that girl in when her own mother dumped her. *Dumped* her. And you're saying she should feel hard done by!' She shakes her head in exasperation. 'If it wasn't for us, she'd have been taken into care. And the more I think of it, it would have been the better decision all round.'

'She wasn't any trouble, not when you think about it.' Colm is feeing maudlin now, and is assailed by the stirrings of guilt more frequently with the accumulation of years.

The same cannot be said of his wife, who is still intent on blaming everyone else for anything in her life that she finds less than satisfactory. This gives her a considerable amount of material to work with, and now that the two of them are alone, Colm must endure her increasingly resentful diatribes. It is making him grind his teeth, even in his sleep. So much so that a recently implanted dental bridge in his mouth has to be reconstructed. Even his dentist was impressed.

At least before the hip operation he was able to slip out of the house on the pretence of running an errand or attending to some business, but now he is trapped – for twelve insufferable weeks (he can't bear to think of it in *months*). He can't even drive the car for six weeks. Not that he would feel up to it, he can just about negotiate his way around tentatively with the walker, or Zimmer frame as Carmel insists on calling it. It is driving her mad, the Zimmer frame, she is tripping over it everywhere, she says.

Colm takes a small, perverse pleasure from this.

'I don't suppose there's any chance of a cup of tea?' He thinks it worth a try, and it is time to change the subject.

'What am I? A waitress? You're well able to make it

yourself. Didn't the physiotherapist say you were to practise walking on the Zimmer?'

Carmel dusts with renewed violence, and Colm weighs up the effort of getting himself to the kitchen, as opposed to staying in the comfort of his study, but there is no telling how long the dusting could go on. The kitchen wins – even if making tea will be a prolonged and complicated, one-handed procedure, supporting himself on the walker. At the mention of the physiotherapist, however, he brightens. Her visits, two days a week, have brought a glimmer of light into the whole intolerable hostage situation. She is young, bright and pretty. Most of all, she is kind to him, even when she must be firm. In her company, though, he is an old man, but he allows himself the odd fantasy of what might transpire if he was forty years younger.

To his dismay, Carmel follows him into the kitchen. 'Kate told me, when she called in on Wednesday,' Carmel continues. 'Veronica had had the nerve to ring her, after all these years, to say she's back. Here, give me that, I'll do it.' She snatches the milk from him and bangs the kettle on. 'Sit down for God's sake, I don't need you scalding yourself on top of everything else.'

'I could go back to the study,' he offers. 'You could bring it in to me there?'

'I will not. Sit down at the table and I'll have a cup myself. I've been running around all day.'

Colm does as he's told. *Foiled again.*

'Is Vonnie back for good?'

'Not likely. She's here on some work assignment apparently.'

'She must be doing well, all the same, living in California.'

'What would you know about anyone doing well?' Carmel pours tea and sits down opposite him. 'Isn't she only writing for magazines? Not even on the staff of any of them.' She sniffs. 'Sure any eejit could do that. If she had a real job, a career, like our Kate, then she'd know what it's like to be run off her feet. Poor Kate is very stressed at the moment.'

Poor Kate, Colm thinks, is only doing what he did for most of his life. She is a doctor too, a dermatologist, a rather nice career for a woman, he reckons. Regular hours, no late-night emergency callouts, and a steady supply of business. But, unlike her father, Kate is a consultant, as Carmel continually reminds him.

As a GP in a small country town, Colm's time was everyone's and anyone's – at all hours of the day and night – and all Carmel ever expressed then was exasperation, never sympathy. Poor Kate she feels, though, is worked off her feet.

'Why is she stressed?' Colm senses the chance to perhaps score a point.

'Why do you think? That waster she married has lost most of her capital. The property fella who got them into that syndicate has gone bust, the whole thing has collapsed.'

'It was Simon's money to invest too,' Colm points out. 'I seem to remember Kate being very keen to get in on the syndicate. I don't think he had to twist her arm. Sure, didn't she want us to invest in it as well?'

Carmel glares at him. 'She was badly advised. They were all at it, all the medical crowd, and the legal – it's not as if she was rash about it.'

Colm does not point out the pun – a dermatologist being rash – which he thinks quite amusing, but Carmel does not enjoy irony.

'Doctors should stick to what they know,' he says. 'They're not meant to be property speculators.'

The minute the words are out of his mouth, he realises his mistake. The operation has left him dopey, not as alert

as he should be. He is not on his guard. In his day, Colm
had been a great man for the horses and the cards and
pretty much anything else he could put a bet on. Now he
has handed Carmel the proverbial stick with which to beat
him.

Astonishingly, she doesn't, although he sees the familiar
contempt flare in her eyes.

That is because she will save it for later. For now, Carmel
has more pertinent information to impart. 'Kate told
Veronica about your hip replacement, of course, and she
didn't even ask after you, nor offer to lift a finger to help
out here.'

Carmel always refers to Vonnie by her full name, *Veronica.*
Even though Vonnie hated it, even as a child, Colm
remembers.

'I can't say I'm surprised.' He is not, truthfully, but Colm
feels a little hurt that Vonnie did not even enquire after
him. Carmel knows how to wound, he thinks, hardly
surprising seeing as she has made it the practice of a lifetime. But all the same, there was no need for her to mention
that.

'Well, here's something that might surprise you,' she says.
'She has a daughter. She has the child with her, seven years
old.'

'That's nice,' Colm says, carefully. He would like to have
been a grandfather, but Kate and Simon have been unable
to have children. He would like to meet Vonnie's daughter,
perhaps even build a relationship with her, but he thinks it
unlikely he will be offered the opportunity.

'No husband, mind, just the child.' Carmel looks triumphant.
'Like mother like daughter.'

Ah, thinks Colm.

'Well?' Carmel's eyes are sharp.

Colm declines to comment. Two can play at this game,

and he is no slouch at it. His wife is not the only one to have mastered the art of mutual irritation. Forty-eight years of marriage can teach you a lot.

'How is Angela?' he enquires. 'Have you heard from her recently?' Angela, Carmel's younger sister, who lives in New York, has always been a thorn in her side.

'Of course I haven't heard from her. Not that I'd want to – not after that last phone call, not to mention the vile letter she sent us. That woman is the most selfish creature on the planet. How she can live with herself I don't know.'

Colm suspects Angela lives quite easily with herself. Her conscience never seemed to trouble her much or, if it did, then she had certainly paid handsomely to beat it into submission. But all the same, it couldn't have been easy for her either – even if she *was* married to a Wall Street millionaire and had a lifestyle to match. He was about to say as much to Carmel but then thought better of it. Some things were better left unsaid. Especially when they had all been part of the ghastly business themselves. But Angela had been generous – extremely generous – he would give her that, at least.

Upper East Manhattan, 2011

Angela

T hings were very *different* back then, you have to remember. Ireland in 1965 was not a fun place for a young girl. And we didn't even live in Dublin, we were outside it, in County Wicklow, living in the Old Rectory, in a sleepy little town about an hour or so by car from the city. My parents were very strict, very straight people, both dead now of course. Whatever was swinging in 1960s London certainly hadn't made it to our neck of the woods – and even if it had, it would have been stamped out pretty damn quickly.

I couldn't stand it living there, I found it suffocating. My older sister, Carmel, didn't seem to mind it, she was into horses and dogs and tennis parties – but me, I was different. I wanted more out of life than marrying some boring pen-pusher or farmer, and ending up a suburban Stepford wife. Hell, no. I was getting out of there, as fast as I could. How to arrange that was the tricky part. But where there's a will there's a relative, as they say.

In my case, I knew my mother had distant relatives who lived in the States – Boston, I thought, correctly. I also knew that they corresponded perfunctorily once a year, usually at Christmas, the usual stuff. It didn't take me long to find a quiet moment when my mother was out to rifle through her writing desk. I found a card with our relatives' address on it, and the rest was easy.

I wrote to them, and said it had always been my dream to visit America, and that as I was finishing my last year at school, this coming summer would be perfect timing. I explained of course, that my parents were very conservative, protective people, with a great fear of travelling and foreign places (this was true), but that I was a more adventurous spirit, with a healthy curiosity and a great desire to travel the world and educate myself (Americans love that). I also mentioned, of course, that times were very hard in Ireland, and I had been saving up my pocket money or allowance for the past five years for a plane ticket (not true). I explained that I felt that if my parents could only be given some assurance, some little encouragement, such as an invitation to me from their *own people*, to come and stay that they would surely be unable to refuse. For good measure, I included a very flattering family shot, well it was flattering of *me*, but then I always photographed well, even back then. I was a looker, and I knew it, and I wasn't about to let my good fortune in that respect go to waste.

That afternoon, I took Bessie, our spaniel, for a very unaccustomed walk, which included passing the post office. There, I sent off the letter in crinkly thin airmail paper and envelope (even that felt exotic) and went home to begin the long, agonising wait. I didn't tell anyone, not even Carmel – perhaps especially not Carmel – even then she was wildly jealous of me, but that was *her* problem. Still is, I guess. But we all make our own choices in this life, some of them difficult, and you have to stand over them. I know I have and, believe me, it hasn't been easy.

June 2011

Abby

Abby is sitting in the hairdresser's. She is having her colour done, then a treatment and a blow dry. She has a party to go to tonight although she would rather not. She is not in the mood. But Diana was talking to her on the phone this morning and insisted she go. 'You must, Abs, really, it will do you good.'

The people giving it are friends of Edward, and although the invitation says 'barbecue' and 'dress casual', she knows from previous experience this probably involves an al fresco sit-down dinner and full-on glamour. Either way, it requires work. The work of getting herself ready, and then later on chatting and being charming when she would rather be at home watching *Modern Family*.

'You still have a great head of hair, Abby,' Dermot her stylist says. 'Still in great condition. Soon as we hide those sneaky greys, you'll have the hair of a twenty year old.'

Abby wonders how old this must make the rest of her seem, if it is just her hair that is holding up. She is forty-five now, and although she doesn't feel much older, not really, she is aware of the fine lines fanning out around her eyes and the deepening of the grooves around her mouth, even the dimple on her left cheek is now a permanent dent. Edward, of course, could soften and erase these markings of time with Botox and some facial fillers, but since Abby has a pathological fear of having injections, attempting this proved an exercise in futility. She tried it once, just to please him, but

once she caught sight of the syringe coming towards her, she
burst into tears. Although Edward had been patient (he had
given it five attempts) and said it didn't matter, Abby sensed
his exasperation and displeasure with her, which, of course,
had made her want to cry even more. It was not the pain
she feared, she explained, only the needle and, even in
Edward's hands, a needle is still a needle. But she felt she
had let him down, that she was weak. She is not a coward,
just irrational – the fact that she had her three children without
an epidural because of her fear of needles should confirm
that much at least.

Edward only has her best interests at heart, she reasons,
and, of course, in his line of business, looking good for your
age is important. People expect it. The unspoken implication
is that Abby must look good too. It is ironic, she reflects, that
so many women would give anything to have access to her
husband's skills, and indeed many pay exorbitant prices to
do just that, when she could have it done for free. Which
reminds her, Edward has acquired several new machines
recently (not involving needles), a laser (for skin resurfacing)
and a radio frequency one that claims to tighten sagging jaw
lines. The former requires a certain amount of downtime, or
hiding, for fear of frightening people with your raspberry-red
face while it crusts and sheds, and the latter is rumoured to
be extraordinarily painful, but Abby thinks she will be
expected sooner rather than later to undergo one or probably
both.

An article in the magazine she is flicking through catches
her attention. It is written by an eminent psychologist debating
whether or not women are naturally inclined to be 'people
pleasers', given that they are taught from such an early age
to acquiesce and, on top of that, are genetically programmed to
nurture.

Abby settles back happily to read it. She has always

maintained that she is a people pleaser, and although she would like to be more assertive on occasion, secretly she feels that if it were not for her people-pleasing abilities, her family, and life in general, would be a lot more difficult. What was wrong with wanting to keep people happy anyway?

Five minutes later, she is frowning, her foot tapping absent-mindedly on the steel bar beneath her chair. The article has taken an unexpected twist. People who claim to be people pleasers, the psychologist writes, are in fact serious egotists. They want everything to be about *them*. The only difference between them and other obviously egotistical characters is that people who claim to be people pleasers are using this as an underhand weapon to make people like them, to depend on them, to garner sympathy. That their need to be needed and most of all liked is, in fact, nothing more than a symptom of their bottomless pit of self-obsession.

The woman writing the article (Abby had rather hoped it had been written by a man) is well-respected in her field, and quotes impressive research and case histories, one or two of which seem eerily familiar. The same woman also writes a problem page for a national English broadsheet that Abby looks forward to reading every Sunday. Abby loves the problem page, she identifies with a lot of the people who write in and with their problems, and feels she could answer and shed light on the various problems herself. Now she is not so sure.

The article ends by saying that people pleasers are undeniably harbouring deeply buried (often vast) reservoirs of inner anger, which ideally should be accessed through the help of a qualified therapist.

Abby snaps the magazine shut. What a lot of rubbish, she thinks. Really.

She focuses instead on the reunion she and Diana will have with Vonnie, who is back in Dublin for a work assignment, and is dying to catch up with them both. It has been years since they have seen Vonnie, and Abby is excited at the prospect of reconnecting with her. Excited . . . and something else too, though she is not sure what. She shifts a bit in her chair as Dermot begins her blow-dry.

They were inseparable when they were younger – her, Di and Vonnie – but, of course, that was before they got married and had families to look after and other commitments. At least, she and Diana had got married – poor Vonnie, as far as she knew, hadn't. And she would have known about something like that. Vonnie would have told them – even though she did disappear off to the States without a word to anyone. But then, she had been living in London before that, and Abby had been busy with small children back then. But word would have filtered back about a wedding – it always does.

'Are we doing the ghd curls?' Dermot enquires.

'What?'

'For tonight? You want the waves, don't you?'

'Oh, yes. I suppose so.'

Dermot raises an eyebrow at her in the mirror. 'Doesn't Cinderella want to go to the ball?'

'Not if she could avoid it.'

'Tut, tut, Abby. It's going to be brilliant. Another client of mine is going and I hear the select gathering will feature in the society pages, which means photographers, darling. I'd go for the ghd waves – more impact.'

Abby's stomach sinks. This is worse than she thought. Suddenly she blurts out, 'Dermot, tell me honestly, do you think I've put on weight?'

Dermot is a committed, if camp, heterosexual and very good-looking. He has also been Abby's hairdresser for fifteen years. He will be honest, although she is not sure if she is ready for honest.

'Since when?'

'What do you mean since *when*?'

'Well, do you mean have you put on weight since we first met, when you were gloriously resplendent with the twins, or since, say, last month?'

Christ, Abby thinks. 'So I have! I have put on weight.'

'Abby we've *all* put on weight.' Dermot pats his washboard stomach. 'Men don't like skinny women; you look fabulous, gorgeous, voluptuous, edible – like a lush peach.'

Abby is glad she is sitting down. She swallows.

'You mean fat.' She glowers at him.

'I did *not* say that.'

'You might as well have. Oh well, you're only confirming what my mother has been telling me for the past year.'

'Abby,' Dermot looks at her sternly, 'you are beautiful. You will look amazing tonight. Put on your highest heels and have a good time for heaven's sakes. And, after that, get out of the house, away from your mother, and take some exercise. It's a terrific mood booster.'

The rest of the session passes in silence. Her hair looks wonderful when Dermot has finished with it but she hardly notices. It is only when she has paid and left and is getting into her car that she realises she forgot to tip him. Abby never forgets to tip. She thinks briefly about going back to rectify this and then instead says sod it. She will make it up to him next time. Or maybe not.

The Affair

*H*e *is the first thing she thinks of each day and the last thing she thinks of before she sleeps fitfully. Sometimes, on waking, in the fleeting seconds before the day becomes real and claims her, she imagines he is beside her. She breathes in his warmth, his smell and turns drowsily to reach for him. And then she remembers, retreats to her side of the bed, slipping out, quietly, quite awake now, already agitated. What will today bring? Will it be a good day? Will she hear from him? Might they speak? Perhaps even meet?*

The morning is full of eagerness, unspoken possibilities. As the day wears on, her spirits wane, hope is leaving her, she becomes irritable, forgetful. Work suffers, chores intrude – she snaps and snarls, and hates herself for it. Her phone, which she checks repeatedly, is silent.

Somehow she gets through the day, holds it together. Appears normal to her husband and children. After dinner she goes for a walk, willing him to text or ring her. The evening wears on, giving way to night. She runs a bath, safe in the sanctuary of the bathroom, and wipes away tears of frustration along with her cleansing cream. Here she is safe, no one will intrude. In the bath, she lies back in the water, closes her eyes and prays for tomorrow – maybe tomorrow. She hears her husband come upstairs and into their room, a wardrobe door bangs, she squeezes her eyes shut to block out the images. A saying she can relate to comes to mind: There is no lonelier place in the world than a double bed when you are in it with the wrong person.

She hopes, desperately, that her husband is tired, that he will not want sex, she could not bear it. Cannot abide the touch of anyone but her lover. She is a traitor – to them both, to herself. But she cannot think about that. If people think affairs are glamorous, exciting, she reflects, they do not know the abject misery of the married lover.

2011

Vonnie

I am not familiar with the restaurant Diana has chosen for lunch, but she has told me it is casual and cosy. It was good to hear her voice after all this time, still just the same, and I can't wait to see her and Abby – although, if I'm honest, I'm a little nervous, having lost contact with everyone when I left London for LA, even though I needed to.

I needed to wipe the slate clean, stop running from myself, try to figure out who I really am. It's a lot harder than it sounds and it's an ongoing journey, as they say. I just started out later than most, or at least it feels that way.

It all began when I lost the weight. It had been my body armour in a way, the wall I hid behind, the excuse I used to avoid becoming who I knew I could be. Food filled all the emptiness inside me, took away the loneliness and numbed the sadness – for a while, at least. So it was no coincidence that when I found myself without it, the panic attacks began. Later, once I had started therapy with Ellen, I learned to understand the connection. The fear that was raising its ugly head, the feelings and voices that made themselves known with a vengeance – that I had never been any good and never would be – particularly now I had nothing to hide behind. I was exposed. I had lost my shield. Although I was loathe to do it, I followed Ellen's advice to cut all my ties with home, for a while at any rate, until we could get to the bottom of my problems.

'Surely not even with my best, my oldest friends?' I had asked her, astonished.

'Perhaps especially your oldest and best friends,' she had said calmly. 'We're going to be doing a lot of tough work together, Vonnie. I need to know you're really committed to this, or we won't get the results. I know it's hard to understand, but sometimes the people we think are holding us together are really just holding us back. They don't mean to.' She smiled. 'Well not always, but established patterns are hard enough to break on your own, but they're even harder to break when you have well-meaning people reinforcing them for you.'

So, difficult though it was for me (and it took a superhuman effort in the beginning), I pulled back from Abby and Di. I contacted them less and less and, gradually, without any big deal, we just drifted apart, as friends sometimes do. And Ellen was right. The changes did come. Some painful, some joyful, but all brought their own special triumphs for me, building blocks of inner strength and pride that I never in a million years thought I could have achieved. So it was little wonder I was nervous now; after all it was almost twelve years since the three of us had sat down together.

Jazz has been dropped off at an art class – she loves painting – and is spending the afternoon with one of the little friends she met there who lives just around the corner from us. I will pick her up after our lunch. I grab my bag and head out to begin the walk into town. The sun is shining and Dublin is preening. Despite the recession, there is a carefree atmosphere as people stroll along wearing sunglasses, girls in pretty dresses, men in rolled-up shirt sleeves, chatting to each other or on mobile phones. Sun-roofs are open, soft tops are down and everywhere people seem to be drinking coffee. Although I am glad to be back (I can't quite think of it as *home*), it is unnerving too. I am still treading water, still playing for time.

'You need to confront this, Vonnie,' Ellen, my therapist had said. And I knew by the level of reluctance that arose in me at the thought that she was right.

My decision to return to her a couple of months ago, when I was offered this assignment and when Jake and I, well, when everything became complicated again, hadn't been easy. I thought I was fixed, you see, I thought I had sorted everything out, done the therapy, done all the work – but when all this came up, I found I was just as confused as ever. Relationships were never my strong point. I find it hard to trust people. This is hardly surprising, Ellen has said, and that's why I began therapy in the first place, because whatever about me, I wanted to be the best mother possible to Jazz – and I hadn't exactly had a good role model in that department.

I had been in London for almost fourteen years by then – and had established myself as a journalist – before I moved to California. The job offer from the paper in California took me by surprise. I was head-hunted on the advice of a former colleague who had moved to LA and, within two months, I had packed up my old life in London, said my goodbyes, sold my small flat in Wandsworth and found myself in Los Angeles. My big break came when I did a piece on Irish actors in Hollywood and got some really interesting stuff. I have always put it down to the fact that the actors got such a shock that I wasn't the usual pocket-sized Venus, polished and honed to perfection, showing off my buff body in a suitably skimpy outfit, that they were relaxed enough to really open up with me – of course, it helped that I was Irish myself. *Vanity Fair* ran the piece. After that I was able to go freelance, which was a dream come true – my own life, on my own terms, professionally speaking at any rate – as long as I delivered the goods and met the deadlines. I wound up in San Luis Obispo kind of by accident. I went there on a wine-tasting tour organised by a newspaper I had worked for in LA, and I decided to stay on for a couple of days' holiday and explore. The moment I got to Morro Bay, I knew it felt like home – or at least what I imagined a home would feel like – and that was when I started to get myself together, well, a bit anyway.

San Luis Obispo, or SLO County as we call it, entranced me. This was slow-paced, laid-back, old romantic California that I didn't think existed anymore, from the rolling hills and miles of unspoiled beaches, to the vineyards and mountain trails, and the series of quirky coastal villages with their vibrant communities nestled between San Francisco and Los Angeles.

After spending a lazy day in Morro Bay in the shadow of the Rock, watching the surfers on the beach and paddling a kayak in the bay, I knew that was where I wanted to be, so I left my details with a local real estate agent and a week later got the call to come and see some properties.

I knew 160 Island Street was meant for me the minute I saw it. Single storey, renovated, with two good-sized bedrooms and bathrooms, a huge great room (as they call the living room out there) leading into a small open-plan kitchen, hardwood floors throughout and a cute deck out back. But what clinched it for me was the rooftop terrace, where you could sit and listen to the ocean or watch the sun go down.

It was also on a pretty street close to local stores and amenities. I leased it for a year, with an option to buy, and never looked back. I always think that house was lucky for me, because that's when things began to turn around. I began to have a life, albeit a tentative one. I liked that Morro Bay was a holiday town, and quiet out of season except for the locals, who welcomed me in their own laid-back way. I was able to take things slowly and, bit by bit, I could feel myself unwinding, relaxing into the rhythm of the place. I began to run on the beach with my friend and neighbour Jenn, a stylist, and wander in for breakfast or coffee to Rollers, more of a shack than the cafe/restaurant it claimed to be, run by a die-hard old surfer dude called Luke, who was so tanned, bleached and tattooed it was impossible to tell how old he was. He had a great craggy face and an unending supply of one-liners. Rumour was he'd been an actor at some stage and came out to Morro Bay after his movie-star wife left him for the big time. He'd been around since anyone could remember and he still surfed every day.

Despite the newer, smarter cafes that had sprung up over the years, Rollers was the real hub for us locals who came to eat, drink or just hang out. I worked for the rest of the day, at the desk I had set up in a corner of the living room (it was too distracting to take my laptop outside) and then, in the late afternoon, I would wander back to the sea front and go for a swim or cycle and have an early supper with friends.

It was just what I needed; nobody asked any questions, no one found it strange that I was living alone at the age of thirty-six, or if they did they never asked why. Pretty much everyone was living an alternative lifestyle, following a dream, or avoiding the rat race – surfers, hikers, artists, from the painters, to the crafts people and jewellery makers, the wildlife photographers and writers, like me, or Luke, whose cocktails were an art form all of their own.

So it wasn't surprising that after six months I began to feel happier, got fitter and began to lose weight, almost without noticing. Living by the ocean, in a year-round Mediterranean climate, it's hard *not* to start living more healthily, it kind of creeps up on you despite your best efforts. I got to know a few other artists and writers, and made some friends – everyone else seemed to run on the beach every day, so I thought why not? And just like they told me, I found it was a really great way to start the day. It really cleared my head, and I found settling down to work each day easier; I could concentrate, instead of getting up from the computer every twenty minutes to prowl restlessly. Then the first few pounds dropped off, and my clothes started getting looser and, before I knew it, I was hitting the gym too. I was probably addicted to exercise at that point, but better that than a whole lot of other things I could think of – and believe me I can eat. I ate for Ireland in my day. Surprising what you can pack inside when you're determined to numb your feelings into submission. And as I was about to learn with Ellen, I had a lot of unresolved feelings.

I still wore my old baggy T-shirts and sweatpants, until one day Jenn looked at me critically and said, 'Vonnie, honey, you've really shaped up. If you'd stop hiding under all those tents you wear you'd see how much weight you've lost. C'mon girl, I'm taking you shopping.' And she did.

It was a revelation. I know that sounds like a cliché, but it's true. I genuinely didn't notice how much weight I'd lost, how the flab had vanished, replaced by totally unfamiliar muscle tone. I didn't buy much – you don't need much in the way of stylish clothes out there – but I bought a couple of pairs of jeans, some T-shirt dresses, and shorts and tops, and some really nice working out gear – and no one was more surprised than I was at the tall, lean person looking back at me from the store mirror.

After that, there was no stopping Jenn, I became her personal mission. Not content with the shopping spree, the next weekend she insisted on a complete makeover. Since it was the weekend, and I had nothing planned anyhow, I went along with it. My hair, which had grown much longer than I used to wear it, was restyled, still long but artful layers were cut around my face, suddenly drawing attention to cheekbones I never knew I had. Honey and caramel highlights

were added and then a make-up lesson. I wanted to draw
the line at teeth whitening the following week, but this was
California, and I have to say the end result was worth it.
We finished up that day with a massage, manicure and pedicure at a local spa, where over margaritas Jenn assessed her
handiwork and pronounced me a knockout.

'What are you grinning at?' I asked warily as she studied
me.

'I have a feeling,' she said, raising her glass to me, 'that
today, Vonnie Callaghan, is the first day of the rest of a whole
new life for you!'

I laughed at her then, my new friend, for her enthusiasm,
her boundless American optimism, but I never for a moment
thought any more about it. But Jenn, as I have learned many
times over since, usually turns out to be right about things
and this pronouncement proved to be no exception.

The outside had been taken care of, but on the inside it was
a very different story. At least in California it was easy to
pretend – no one had ever known me there, but now that
I'm back in Dublin, I can already feel myself starting to feel
like big, lumpen Vonnie again. The girl who could never get
it right, who was always in the way. And that's when I thank
God for Jazz because every time I look at her, I am reminded
that the most extraordinary gifts can come your way when
you least expect it.

I reach the restaurant, and check to make sure I am in the
right place. It is tucked away off Grafton Street and up a
little road behind the Powerscourt Centre. There are a few
tables outside, but these are full, and no sign of Abby or Di.
Inside, I check with the girl on the desk, who tells me my
lunch companions are already here, and I search for them
as I follow her, my eyes adjusting from the bright sunlight
outside. And then I see them! At a corner table deep in

conversation, and at the sight of their dear, familiar, faces, I almost want to cry. Di is looking as groomed and beautiful as ever and Abby, with her porcelain skin and dark red hair cascading round her shoulders, is listening intently to whatever Di is saying. They look up as I am shown to the table, and there is a split second of surprise – hesitation – then they are on their feet, we are hugging and laughing, and suddenly it feels all right again. I am with my friends, my dearest, oldest friends, and we have an awful lot of catching up to do.

Diana

I was sitting there, looking at her, and I could feel myself gaping. I had to pull myself together. And as for Abby, I thought she was going to faint. Vonnie, *our Vonnie*, had morphed into this most *incredible*-looking woman. Neither of us could take our eyes off her. I was happy for her, thrilled, of course I was, but it was such a shock. Really. When she walked in to the restaurant, she literally turned heads. I almost didn't recognise her, except for her height and the smile. And then, once we got talking, well, all I can say is, it was like listening to a soap opera unfold. And I thought it was just *my* life that was turning out to be, shall we say, unconventional.

First of all, naturally, Abby and I wanted to hear all about Vonnie.

'Well,' she said, 'the first thing I have to tell you is that I have a daughter.'

Then she took out a photograph and I found myself looking at the most adorable little girl I've ever seen. 'Her name's Jasmine,' Vonnie said. 'We call her Jazz.'

'Oh, Vonnie,' I breathed, 'she's just beautiful, absolutely beautiful.'

And then Abby, who had already knocked back two glasses of wine, goes and says it. 'That's so wonderful, Vonnie. When did you get her?'

'Get her?' says Vonnie, and I felt ice cubes melting down my back.

'Well, yes, when did you adopt her?'

'Who said anything about adopting?' Vonnie said lightly. 'She's mine. All mine.'

I don't know about Abby but, God, I wanted to slide under the table I was so mortified for her. And angry.

Let me explain something here. Jazz, Vonnie's daughter, is 'mixed race', I think is the politically correct term these days. Not dark, more coffee-coloured and really, exquisitely beautiful. But still you couldn't blame us, it was a shock. She might have warned us. But at least I had the sense to keep my mouth shut. In fact, if I'm honest, what I was really thinking is *Christ, if she's that gorgeous – I want to see a picture of Daddy.* But poor old Abby had rushed straight in and put her two big trotters in it. Luckily, Vonnie didn't seem to mind, perhaps she was expecting it. I wondered if she got that reaction a lot of the time.

'Oh God, Vonnie, I'm so sorry,' says Abby, 'I didn't mean to, I mean—'

'It's okay, Abby, really.' Vonnie put a reassuring hand on her arm. 'It's an understandable assumption to make; after all, I was thirty-eight when I had her, apart from anything else.'

After that I *had* to cut in because Abby would have spent the whole lunch apologising, she was practically gibbering. And anyway, this was Vonnie for heaven's sake – even if she did look like a supermodel (a supermodel with little or no make-up I would like to point out, just a lovely, healthy, enviable glow) – and we had always told each other everything.

'So,' I said, mischievously, cutting to the chase. 'Is this adorable child's father in the picture?'

'It's a long story but, yes . . . in a manner of speaking.'
And then she grinned, that big Vonnie grin, and I knew we
were all okay.

'Well, I'm in no rush, are you, Abby?'

'Certainly not.'

Turns out she met this guy called Jake in New Orleans, at
a newspaper convention. And, at the time, this Jake was a
war correspondent for the *Los Angeles Times*. Could this *get*
any more glamorous, I asked myself? It was instant attraction,
I could tell that much even though she tried to play it down,
and they began a relationship. Then Jazz came along and,
for some reason, they split up when Jazz was three years old.

'It wasn't working out,' Vonnie said simply.

Although when I saw the photo of Jake, which Vonnie
reluctantly produced (it was one of the three of them
together), all I could think of was, *how could you let a guy
like this get away?* He was quite simply beautiful – there was
no other word for it. Mixed race, obviously, and tall, about
six three, I'd guess, well built and he had the most amazing
face (and you know how I am about faces). It wasn't just
that he was good looking, it was so much more than that.
His was a face that told a story, one I very much would have
liked to hear. Broad forehead, longish, swept back, jet black,
curly hair (the kind you could run your fingers through
forever, I'd bet), straight, high-bridged nose, razor-slash
cheekbones and slanting, ebony eyes. But it was his mouth
that was so arresting; I think it was the most sensual mouth
I've ever seen, and, of course, he had one of those big, perfect,
all-American smiles, complete with white, straighter-than-
straight teeth. It was a proud face, too, a face that spoke of
proud peoples – at a guess part-African, part-Native American,
maybe a dash of Asian and, of course, part-European. I was
mesmerised. You could forgive a man who looked like this *a
lot* I reckoned.

'But we're still close, still the best of friends,' Vonnie was saying, interrupting my drooling, 'and Jake's a wonderful father to Jazz.'

'You can be friends with a guy who looks like this?' I said incredulously. I couldn't help myself.

At that, Vonnie blushed. 'I think we've managed it pretty well.'

I wanted to push for more, this was riveting stuff, but decency forbade me.

Abby showed no such reticence. 'Did he leave you? You poor darling.' She patted Vonnie's hand, and I noticed the first flash of irritation in Vonnie's face.'

'Actually, Abby, no, he didn't. I left him. Like I said, it wasn't working out – and it was unsettling for Jazz. She's the most important person in my life, always will be.

'But do you really think living with a single parent is a more positive situation for her?' Abby asked, quite insensitively, I thought.

Abby, I realised, was becoming a little drunk by this stage. Not quite slurring, but close enough. There was something going on with her, but I couldn't think about that just yet. And she had gained quite a lot of weight, lately. She definitely wasn't herself.

'You never considered marriage?' I ventured.

'No.' Vonnie paused just a fraction. 'It never really seemed necessary.' She took a deep breath. 'The marriage I grew up in wasn't exactly encouraging in that respect. Kind of put me off the whole idea, to be honest.'

'I sort of got that impression,' I had to say, 'that when I met your parents, even way back then, when we were just kids, there was an undercurrent. I didn't understand it then, but I suspected things weren't great for you at home.'

There was another pause. Then Vonnie said. 'Actually, that was one of things I wanted to tell you – they're not my parents.'

Luckily, the waiter came along just then with the main course and topped up our glasses. I refrained. I was taking it easy, I just can't stomach a hangover these days. The recovery isn't worth the procuring I find and, anyhow, I had to be somewhere later. Vonnie was still sipping her first glass and drinking a lot of water but Abby was knocking it back.

'Abby, are you all right?' I had to ask.

'I'm fine. I just feel like letting off a bit of steam, that's all. It's not as if I'm driving.' She glared at me before turning back to Vonnie. 'So, you mean you were adopted, Von?' she regarded her with interest.

'Not exactly,' Vonnie said carefully.

'It's none of our business, Abby,' I said firmly.

'It's okay,' Vonnie said. 'I need to set the record straight, and I don't mind talking about it. Briefly. I just don't want to dwell on it. But it's part of why I went away.'

'Go on.' We were agog.

'Well, the woman I thought of as my mother is actually my aunt. She and her husband, Colm, brought me up. Turns out my real mother, my birth mother, is her younger sister, who I obviously thought of as my Aunt Angela, who lived – still lives – in New York. She paused for breath.

'No way! How did that happen?' Abby asked.

'She got a better deal in the States, it seems.' Vonnie shrugged. 'She left me as a baby with Carmel and Colm, promised to come back and never did. That's about it.'

'And you never knew?' I probed.

'Not about my mother – no.' The first hardness entered her voice. 'Not until I needed my first passport, you remember when—'

'When we were going on that au pair holiday.' I remembered instantly. That explains a lot, I thought to myself. I remembered Vonnie hadn't been herself at all at the time, we must have been eighteen, but she hadn't said a word, and

Abby and I had put it down to nerves about going away on her own for the first time.

'Yes, well, they had to tell me then. So that's when I found out.'

'What about your mother, your real mother?' Abby was riveted. This Angela one. What did she have to say about it?'

'Not a lot. I've only met her a couple of times; well, obviously, I'd met her before as a kid. But it was only in the last year, I wanted to hear what she had to say.'

'And . . .?'

'Well, she told me the unvarnished truth,' Vonnie said, matter-of-factly. I was the result of her losing her head and her virginity on her first trip to Boston to stay with relatives. The guy in question was going off to war, Saigon, as it happens – she didn't even know his second name – I think he was of Swedish extraction. He doesn't even know I exist, that's if he's still alive. My mother got married to a very rich man a few years later and decided it was better if her husband didn't know about me. And I really don't want to talk about that just now.'

'Of course you don't,' I said quickly. 'And you know what? I think you're right about the whole marriage thing. It can be a royal pain in the arse.'

And that was it. There was no going back then.

'How is Greg?' Vonnie asked.

'Oh Greg's fine, he's never been better. Wish I could say the same for myself.'

'What is it?' Vonnie looked concerned. 'You're not sick, are you?'

'Lord, no. We've just been having a period of . . . readjustment.' I paused. 'Greg lost his job almost a year ago.'

'Oh I'm so sorry to hear that, Di.' Vonnie said. 'He was creative director wasn't he, with that big advertising agency?'

'Yes, the whole industry has been very badly hit.'

'Can he get freelance work, you know, consultancy stuff?'

I took a steadying breath. 'Yes, he probably could if he was bothered to.'

Abby looked uncomfortable and Vonnie curious. 'How d'you mean?'

'Well, Greg has decided to take a sabbatical of sorts.'

'A sabbatical?'

'Yes. He feels he's been selling out to the rat race all his life, and that this redundancy is a sign, an opportunity for him to discover his real calling in life.'

There was a vaguely embarrassed silence.

'Does he have any idea as to what that might be?'

'Not yet, but he's having lots of fun and spending lots of money trying to find out. He's just back, in fact, from a meditation course on developing your spirituality – in your neck of the woods, Vonnie, somewhere in California.' I mentioned the name of the centre.

'Oh right, yeah, well, I've heard of it. It's very well known, I believe they do great work there,' she said encouragingly.

'Expensive, great work.'

'And what about you, Di? How do you feel about all this?'

'Funnily enough, Vonnie, that's the first time anyone has asked me that very relevant question.' I tried to keep the bitterness from my voice and failed.

'Di was hoping to scale back herself,' Abby explained. 'Maybe take a gap year.'

'Abby's right. Ironically, it was *my* dream to sell up completely and take some time out, you know, have some home time, embrace my inner domestic goddess, but Greg got there first and now there's not a chance.'

'That's men for you,' said Abby.

'Couldn't you, you know, negotiate something?' Vonnie suggested.

'Not while we need to keep food on the table, no,' I answered curtly. 'Sorry, Vonnie, I didn't mean to snap, it's just that this whole thing is really getting me down.'

'I don't blame you, honey.'

'Well, at least he must help out with the housework?' Abby said brightly.

'Greg? Not likely.'

'So what are his plans? I mean he just can't opt out,' Vonnie said.

'Try telling him that. Of course he has the perfect excuse with my business. I can support us, just, but it means putting in more hours, working a lot harder and I *was* hoping to take things a bit easier. And the way things are going, well, who knows just how long I'll be able to keep the business going. My accountant called me this morning to set up an urgent meeting – he didn't sound happy.'

'That's tough,' said Vonnie.

'It's putting a strain on the marriage, if I'm honest.' I frowned. 'He was talking about holding meditation classes in the house while I'm out at work – can you imagine? A bunch of chanting strangers in my house while the kids are on holiday? I can tell you I put my foot down about that right away.'

'What about you, Abby, how are things with you?' Vonnie enquired.

'Oh, I can't complain,' she sighed. 'They're fine, really. Edward's still Edward, the kids are great – and Mum is living with us now.'

'Oh, that's nice,' said Vonnie. 'If you've got the space.'

'Well, her arthritis has got quite bad and she's had one or two nasty falls. So she, I mean we, decided that it would be best if she sold her house and came to live with us.' Abby paused. 'Edward was fine about it. Mum and him get on very well, they always have, and the kids adore her and we do have the space. It was the obvious thing to do really.' She said it lightly, but the muscle flexing at her temple didn't escape my eagle eye. Neither did the quick swig of wine she took.

'It must be great if you can have that kind of relationship with your mother,' Vonnie said.

'I would never live with my children,' I said emphatically. 'Never, no matter how much they begged me. It's not healthy – or fair to them. Put me in a home any day.'

'Yes, well, luckily not everyone thinks like you do, Di.' Abby motioned to the waiter. 'Another bottle, girls?'

'Not for me, thanks,' Vonnie checked her watch. 'I'm going to have to go quite soon. I have to pick up Jazz.'

'Nor me,' I said firmly. Then when the waiter arrived, I got in before Abby could. 'Could we have some coffee please and the bill? Oh and another glass of white here,' I indicated Abby's place, 'when you're ready.'

'What's the matter with you both?' Abby was peeved. 'We haven't sat down together for years, we used to gossip for hours.'

'It *has* been hours, Abby, two to be precise. I don't have to rush off right away, but much as I would like to get completely blotto and forget about the soap opera that my life is turning into, I think one pixelated parent at a time is quite enough for my children and, indeed, one household to contend with. Anyway, you don't want to roll home as high as a kite, do you? In my experience, it's never a good move, especially when you've got kids at home or a husband – not to mention a mother. Gives them far too much ammunition.'

'Oh, Mummy's not like that,' Abby said. 'She enjoys a little drink now and again – and Edward's away on business. We'll probably all get a takeaway tonight.'

Ah, that explained it, I reasoned as the lightbulb went on. Abby had a free pass so to speak. No wonder she wanted to let her hair down. I couldn't say I blamed her.

'Do you remember,' I said, 'our trip to St Valentine all those years ago?'

Vonnie smiled. 'Yes, I remember it well. I often think about it.'

'Well, did you get what you asked for?'

'Yes, actually,' said Abby. 'I got exactly what I asked for.'

'Me too,' I said. 'It was uncanny, right down to the last detail.'

'I wasn't that specific,' Vonnie mused, 'but, yes, I got everything I could have ever hoped for with Jazz.'

I thought about that, all the way home after lunch and throughout the following days. Not because we all got what we asked St Valentine for, but because Vonnie was the only one who was smiling as she said it.

When I got home, and let myself in, I was assailed by a wave of incense. Greg was sitting at the kitchen table, the entire surface of which was covered with various books and journals he was poring over.

'Hey!' He looked up as I came in. 'Good lunch?'

'Yes,' I said. 'Lovely.'

'How are the girls?'

'They're great.' I paused. 'Vonnie looks amazing. She's lost all the weight and is in incredible shape, we hardly recognised her – and she has a little girl now.'

'Ah, that's great. I always liked Vonnie. She had a really good aura. I guess she's got her stuff together now, that's what living in California does for you. Abby, on the other hand, phew, that's one real uptight woman, bet nothing's changed there.'

I went to pour myself a glass of wine, torn between agreeing with him or defending the sisterhood. I mean what the hell do men know about women anyway?

I took the home-made casserole I had defrosted earlier and put it in the oven.

'What makes you say that?' I asked lightly, sitting down and clearing a space for my glass. Greg, I noticed, had already poured himself one.

He shrugged. 'She's always been uptight, ever since I've known her anyway.'

'You've only ever met her with Edward,' I pointed out.

'True, can't be easy living with that moron. How *is* the cosmetic doctor to the good and the great?'

'Very busy, apparently.'

'Hardly surprising. No wonder society's going down the tubes when women are encouraged to do their damnedest to change everything about themselves on the outside, when it's what's inside that's important – and no bloody doctor can give you that. In my opinion, someone who plays on people's outward insecurities and gets paid for it is sick.'

'That's ridiculous,' I snapped. 'This is the twenty-first century, Greg. If a woman wants to change something about her appearance then she has every right to – if she can afford it. Besides, Edward's making a fortune. Abby said his business hasn't been affected by the recession at all.'

'Ah,' Greg leaned back in his chair and stretched his legs under the table. He twirled the stem of his wine glass thoughtfully, and suddenly a wave of irritation surged through me.

'Of course, it's still all about the money, isn't it?' He went on, 'No one has learned anything. Well they will. This recession is going to bring a lot of timely lessons along with it.'

'Yes,' I agreed. 'One of which is that it is very nice to have enough money.'

'That's not what I meant.'

'Of course you didn't, because you've never had to do without it.'

His eyes narrowed ever so slightly. 'I could – if I had to.'

'Really?' I said. 'Somehow I can't quite see you slumming

it, Greg. After all, you enjoy the good life as much as anyone. Good wine, good food, nice clothes – not to mention holidays. Oh, and what about annoying little things like school fees and stuff for the kids?'

'Children are far too materialistic for their own good these days – that's going to change too, and not a second too soon. You've said so yourself,' he said, neatly avoiding my previous observations.

I was too tired to argue. And this was heading towards dangerous territory. I got up and took my wine glass with me. 'I'm going to have a bath.'

'Good idea. You seem a little uptight yourself.' Greg looked at me speculatively. I might come up and join you.'

'No thanks,' I said. 'The kids are upstairs and, anyway, I need a bit of space. Oh, and Greg, can you keep the joss sticks to your office, please, I can't stand the smell of them in the house.'

'Sure,' he went back to his book. 'I didn't think you'd mind, you're out all day anyway.'

'Not out, Greg, *working* – there's a difference. Oh, and clear that stuff off the table and set it for me, would you? We'll be eating in about half an hour.'

Upstairs, I checked on the kids. Sophie was in her bedroom, at the table that doubled as a desk and work table for her dress-making practice, cutting out pieces of fabric to make one of her many designs. Her room was as meticulous as always. Ever since she learned to draw and handle a scissors, she has displayed a completely natural talent for making clothes, handbags and other accessories. Seeing as I could hardly thread a needle, I assumed she had inherited this skill from my father's mother, long dead, who had been a renowned Parisian seamstress. Now, at fourteen, Sophie was happily determined to become a famous designer herself.

'Hey, Mum, did you have a good day?'

'Yes,' I smiled. 'I did. I had our reunion lunch with Abby and Vonnie. What're you making?'

'It's going to be a top or a dress – a kind of shift.' She pulled back to examine the silky, translucent material. 'I'm not sure yet. I might make you try it on later for me, I need to see how it's going to fall, and the dummy is never exactly right.'

'Maybe tomorrow, sweetheart, I'm really tired right now. I'm going to have a bath, dinner's in half an hour.

'Good, I'm starving. Oh, and Mum?

'Yes?

'Can you get Dad to stop burning those disgusting joss sticks? The smell is getting into all my clothes.'

'Why don't you mention it to him yourself, Sophie?'

'Can't you?' she frowned.

'It's your house too, you know. But if it's any help I already have had a word about them.'

'Good.'

Philip was reading, when I popped my head around the door. At twelve, he seemed to me too diligent a child. Always earnest and eager to please, he was as sensitive as his sister was self-possessed – and I worried about him. Since Greg had lost his job, I had noticed Philip spending more time at his schoolbooks and not enough hanging out with his friends being generally ridiculous in the way only twelve-year-old boys could be.

'Hey.'

'Hi, Mum.' He yawned and stretched. 'What's for dinner?'

'Beef casserole, and tons of mashed potatoes.'

'Wicked.'

'We'll be eating in about half an hour. Why don't you go down and talk to Dad? He's on his own downstairs.'

'It smells weird downstairs.' He sniffed and made a face.

'I think you'll find it should be smelling of casserole round about now.'

'Cool.' He grinned at me. 'I'll go down in a minute.'

In the bedroom, I undressed, then closed the door of the bathroom and ran a hot bath to which I added a generous helping of my current favourite Jo Malone oil. Then I lit some scented candles and cleansed my face thoroughly. I had a nagging tension between my shoulder blades I couldn't get rid of. Sinking into the silky water I closed my eyes, let the heat seep into my body and tried to relax. But try as I might, my mind kept drifting back to that day all those years ago, in the church, with St Valentine – I had the distinct impression that he was laughing at me.

The Affair

*S*he has been beside herself with excitement all week. This Friday, a whole evening together.

Her husband is away, she has organised someone to supervise the children. She will not have to be back until midnight, possibly later.

Every spare minute is filled with preparations – hair colour, waxing, self-tan.

She is happy, giddy, careless with love. Nothing has been left to chance. Her outfit (jeans and a silk jersey off-the-shoulder top) is hanging in the wardrobe. All that is left to do is to shop for what she will cook for them. She loves to cook for him, loves to be part of his day, his life, even a fraction of it, to pretend, however fleetingly, they are together.

She is not at home when she gets the phone call. An accident, they say, not to worry, they say, but her son is in hospital, in A&E, a broken wrist they think, perhaps a fractured femur, but can she come and get him?

'I'm on my way,' she says, hearing the panic in her voice escalate. She drops everything, any mother would. But all the while, all the way driving to the hospital, her world is crumbling around her. What has she become? How did this happen? Only a monster would resent her own child for unwittingly spoiling her illicit rendezvous. Even then, wildly, she wonders could she still make it once she had got him home and settled. But already the dull ache of reality begins to tug somewhere in her solar plexus. She parks her car and, sitting in it, phones him. It goes to voicemail, *he is at work, of course. 'So sorry, so terribly sorry,' she says, 'but I can't make it, not tonight, something's come up – one of the kids, an accident, nothing serious, but I have to be with him, at home for the night.'*

She walks from the car park to the hospital, her face is white, her stomach churning, she feels as if she might be sick.

'Sorry, Mum.' He looks guilty, subdued, her son, bandaged up on a trolley.

She hugs him. 'Thank God you're all right,' she says. 'That's all that matters.'

And it is, of course it is. She says it again and again to herself, listening to the words reverberate in her head and in the hollow place that is her heart.

June 2011

Vonnie

Meeting the girls had been great, better than great, after the first couple of minutes – it was just like it had always been between us. And yet, there was no denying that so much had changed, and not just with me. Life had happened to us all in the intervening years and it was shaping us in different ways.

As I left the restaurant, arranging to meet or at least talk soon with the girls, I decided to walk back through town, the way I had come in, just to let it all settle. It had been a big deal for me, showing up again, venturing details of my current life and what had happened in the years I had been away. Telling them about Jake was hard because I knew the minute they saw a photograph of him that they would assume exactly what they did – that he had left me. Abby at least articulated it, but I could tell Di was probably thinking the same thing, she just didn't come out and say it – that Jazz and I had been left behind by this man who was far too handsome to be serious about me. *Stop it!* I heard my inner voice say. *Do not put yourself down! You know the truth – what they think doesn't matter.* But that didn't make any of it any easier.

New Orleans, 2002

L ife was good. Work was going well, I was beginning to finally like myself, feel that maybe I did have a right to be happy (or at least left in peace!) but still I was ignoring the big white elephant that stalked me – the one that had followed me into every relationship I ever had, the voice that told me I could never be happy, fulfilled or worthwhile, and still I couldn't confront her – the woman who was my mother.

Then, when I least expected it, I met Jake.

Jake Kurkimaki was a legend in his own lunch-time. Of course I'd heard of him, in my line of work everyone would have. He was a Pulitzer-winning photojournalist, and at that time was the war correspondent for the *Los Angeles Times*. As guest speaker at the American News conference taking place in New Orleans that summer, I was just one of hundreds who turned up to hear him, see him, say they'd been in the same room as him. As it turned out, I barely *could* see him, squashed as I was on a tiny chair at the back of the conference room, straining to see this paragon of modern frontline reporting.

When he came on stage to rapturous applause, I got a glimpse of a tall, dark, broad-shouldered man and, though he was leaning on a crutch at the time, the sense of charisma he generated made the room fall silent as a still night. When he began to speak, you could have heard a pin drop. I'd read a lot of his stuff, of course, but I'd never heard him speak, and his voice, which was mesmerising, made every cell in my body quiver. Judging by the rapt expressions of the other women, I wasn't the only one he was having that effect on. Even the men were looking as if they were having a mystical experience.

He spoke about Iraq, the conflict, the people he had come to know and respect, and the American involvement and what he thought would come of it. He spoke about the book he was working on and, by the end of it, the electricity in the room was tangible. I left the room hurriedly, just as thunderous applause was breaking out, and grabbed a seat in a quiet corner of the lobby to quickly write up my notes, which I would later polish and send back to my paper. I was doing great until some idiot guy brushed by my small table, sending my coffee cup flying, and he didn't even stop to acknowledge it. I watched in horror as the hot liquid spilled right onto my laptop, which I knew instantly would be history. That's when I heard that voice again, this time right beside me.

'Hang on,' he said, suddenly materialising before my eyes. 'I think I have a memory stick on me; if you're quick, you might just be able to save that.'

He handed me the small gadget which I immediately plunged into my about-to-be-disabled laptop. And I did manage to save my stuff, thanks to his quick thinking, and could hardly gibber my gratitude I was so relieved. When I had collected myself enough to thank him properly and introduce myself, I thought I was hallucinating when he asked me out to lunch, right there and then. I mean this was *me*, Vonnie Callaghan from Ireland, talking to, well, a legend – and he wanted to have lunch with me!

He took me to Galatoire's, in the French Quarter, and even though the line snaked around the block (it was Friday, their biggest day), Jake was ushered straight in. Luckily, he suggested we have some bloody Marys, which I needed to steady my very unnerved nerves, not because of the laptop incident (that had been resigned to ancient history), but because I was so blown away by him, I was afraid he would notice my hands were trembling. I wanted to sit on them, but instead I held the huge menu as best I could, firmly pressing my wrists against the table for support. I was holding on to it so tightly he must have thought I hadn't eaten in weeks. While he was greeted by the staff as the old friend he was, and listened to the waiter talk about the specials, I was able to sneak a large gulp of my drink, and slowly the jitters subsided, replaced by a warm glow that had very little to do with the vodka, although it did, I admit, definitely help.

Jake didn't need to look at the menu – he was a local I soon discovered and had grown up in New Orleans – so I asked him what he recommended, seeing as the unending list of dishes was swimming before my eyes. I don't know if he realised how nervous I was, but he was funny and warm and, eventually, I felt myself relaxing in his company – although I had to stop myself from staring at him he was so god-damned handsome. After lunch (which went on for quite a while, they don't rush these things in New Orleans), he took me to Audubon Park, and we strolled around the lake, along with roller-bladers and dog walkers, dwarfed by the giant oaks cloaked in Spanish moss. It was so beautiful. I had always heard New Orleans had a special kind of magic, but nothing really prepared me for the sultry headiness of it – the warmth, the humidity, the indolently relaxed atmosphere that radiated from the people and place alike. And what a gene pool! They were all so good looking, men and women with every blend of skin from darkest black to porcelain white and in between, and all gorgeous and wonderfully dressed. This wasn't like America – this wasn't like anywhere. If I'd lived here, I don't think I could ever leave, and I said as much to Jake.

'It's a small town, by standards,' he said, 'not unlike your Dublin, in many ways.' He had been to Dublin several years earlier when he was travelling through Europe.

'That can get claustrophobic, as I'm sure you know,' he grinned.

Personally, I didn't see any similarities between the two, but you know how Americans can be – they all have this incredibly romanticised view of Dublin, particularly writers, and perhaps they are right. Jake even claimed some Irish ancestry, way back, from the days of the Old South, although there were obviously a lot of other more predominant nationalities in his combined gene pool. But he was adamant his sense of humour was Irish and his love of literature. I was beyond caring at that stage, I was just drinking him in, listening to that incredible voice and wishing the afternoon would go on forever.

When he pulled me close and bent to kiss me, it felt like the most natural thing in the world, although I really did think my knees were going to give way. Jake kissed the way I was to learn he did a lot of things – with total and utter dedication – as if he had nothing more important to do for the rest of his life.

He came to visit me the following weekend and we spent a perfect three days together. When he left to catch the Sunday evening flight back to LA, I smiled encouragingly, waving as he left, willing myself to be strong, to accept this for what it was, just a wonderful romantic interlude in my life that I could always cherish. At least Jake didn't bullshit me. There were no whispered promises, no I'll call yous, just one last lingering kiss that left me reeling, then he was gone. I closed the door behind me and looked around a room that seemed suddenly too big and bare and wandered to the kitchen, to pour myself a glass of wine and flick through television channels. I could do this. I was used to being alone. It's just that everything had changed somehow, and I didn't quite know why or how.

Looking back, it was so obvious, but I wasn't ready to admit it then – that in the space of three short days I had met the person who would change my life irrevocably, and having met him, I couldn't ever imagine or contemplate a life without him.

So instead I busied myself, did some housework, sent some emails, had a long hot bath and finally got into bed, where I read, or attempted to read, and tried unsuccessfully to shut out the images that floated before my eyes – of our bodies, relaxed and lazy with love, effortlessly entwined, a tangle of limbs so startlingly natural and familiar to me. And the memory of his touch, that made me shiver involuntarily, reminding me that this new aloneness was something very different from what I had been used to. Before, I could fool myself that I had never lost anyone really important to me (or so I stubbornly believed), whereas, now, without Jake, every cell in my body seemed to be shrieking with deprivation.

It was crazy, I thought, *I'm* crazy. It was ridiculous, but without him I felt as if part of me had been secretly stolen, and without that part I was lost, confused, agitated. I couldn't give it a name, this elusive part of me, which was hardly surprising, considering the fact that I had kept it so deeply buried and out of bounds even to myself, *especially* to myself. It was only natural then that it came to me as quite a shock to realise that I had lost it – given it away, thrown caution to the wind. My heart, it dawned on me, closed and shuttered though it was, was now entirely in the keeping of a virtual stranger, one who I might never see again, and that thought filled me with despair.

Which was why, when my cell phone rang shortly after I had turned off the light, I hurled myself at it, groping blindly, knocking over a glass of water on the bedside locker in the process, and tried not to gasp as the cold liquid ran down my arm.

'Hello?' I said in the darkness.

There was the briefest of pauses and then Jake's resonant voice saying, 'I hope I didn't wake you. I just got in and I wanted to call you.'

'Oh, that's nice. It's good to hear you,' I gabbled inanely.

'I wanted to tell you how much I enjoyed our weekend.'

'Me too.'

'And . . .'

Oh God, I thought, *don't let him hang up, not now.*

'. . . and I wanted to ask if I could see you next weekend, and maybe the one after that too.'

I could hear the smile in his voice.

'I'd like that.' I wanted to weep with relief.

'Great. I'll call you during the week. Don't work too hard.' And he hung up.

I held the phone for quite some time after that, looking at it anew, as an instrument of wonder, a bearer of heavenly tidings. Then I sighed with happiness and fell into a deep, untroubled sleep.

And that was how it all began.

Los Angeles

Jake

How do you begin to find someone?

Someone you never knew existed, never dared to imagine, someone who could change your life – maybe even complete it.

And what if that person was you?

That's what they say, all those self-help gurus, and maybe they have a point. In the heel of the hunt, we all have only ourselves to rely on, to answer to.

But there's another line of reckoning too. I'm not sure where it started, exactly, somewhere in the ancient world; Greece, perhaps – a myth – that as a punishment from the gods, all human souls were torn apart, condemned to wander the earth miserably until (if they were lucky) they found their missing half, their twin soul, soul mate, call it what you will. Then, and only then, would they know real peace and fulfilment.

Call me a romantic sucker but, personally, I think there's something in that. I've seen it, too, time and time again, when someone meets the right guy or girl, and two people suddenly come together to make perfect sense. And sometimes it even works. Goes the distance.

The rest of us? You'll find us hiding out in all the usual places. Staying too late at the office, working out excessively in the gym, drinking too much in dimly lit bars, or laughing too loudly at brittle, noisy, social occasions – and picking up too many wrong women in whose arms you only ever find an emptiness even lonelier than your own. Any place, really, will do, as long as it can numb the all-consuming sense of loss, keep it at bay, for just a little while longer.

I'm not even sure when I began to know I was lost. It's not the kind of thing a guy admits. And I was good at fooling myself, really good. In my line of work that was easy. A war zone is a pretty good place to get lost, plenty of skewed perspectives to delve into, bullets to dodge, lives hanging by a thread. Everything takes on a surreal quality that becomes addictive in itself. And everyone is high on adrenaline or terror, whatever it takes to just survive. It's easy to kid yourself then that you have a life, a necessary, fearless one.

It's only in the brief, dangerous moments of solitude, which we go to almost any lengths to avoid, that you realise the war zone is yourself.

I met her in New Orleans, my home town, although, on that occasion, I was there for a news conference as guest speaker. I had already won the Pulitzer for a shot that captured the death of a mistaken Inkatha supporter set upon by ANC members; he was kicked, slapped and knifed, before some kid emptied a Molotov cocktail over him and he was set alight. I captured each blow to his body as the mob grew more fervent, finally catching him engulfed by flames in the throes of death, his skull being cleaved by a machete. That was Soweto, a lifetime ago. Then I was involved in Iraq. I had seen too much, but still it didn't seem to be enough, there was always another war to chase, deadline to meet, shot to claim and, of course, it was an excuse to keep running from the person I feared most of all, myself.

I was with the *Los Angeles Times*, recovering from surface wounds to a leg I had narrowly missed losing. My colleague hadn't been so lucky. He had stepped on the landmine.

I had given my speech, taken the question and answer session and was about to get out of there when I saw her. She was sitting in the lobby, working on her laptop, when some jerk brushed by her table and the paper cup of coffee beside her spilled right all over the keyboard. The guy didn't even stop.

Her face registered what you'd expect – shock, dismay and, of course, anger, then near despair. That's the trouble with laptops – spill something on them and they're history. Luckily, I had a memory stick on me and we managed to save what she'd been working on, which gave me an unfair advantage I wasn't going to waste.

'Oh, I can't tell you how grateful I am,' she said in this gorgeous accent that I knew straight away wasn't British, but took me a little longer to work out as Irish. Her voice was low and gentle, washed over me like a breeze, and when she looked up at me and smiled, I felt a deeply buried tight-ness loosening in my chest that felt simultaneously foreign yet familiar. It was several months later before I identified it as hope.

'How can I thank you?' she stood up, tall and lean, and held out her hand. 'I'm Vonnie,' she said, as I clasped it. 'And I know who you are, of course.'

And right then, right there, I knew I wasn't going to let her go.

'Let me buy you lunch then,' I said. 'You could probably use a drink after that. I know I could.'

I took her to Galatoire's – a New Orleans institution, bastion of French Creole cuisine and still my favourite restaurant. Right in the heart of the Vieux Carré, the French Quarter – though we just call it the Quarter.

It was late June, and the humidity was already kicking in, but still the familiar line of hopeful Friday lunch patrons snaked around the corner. If you were a regular, and I was (having celebrated every family occasion there since I could sit at table with my parents), you got to skip the queue. And that's where Vonnie and I had our first lunch.

Better still, I learned it was her first time in New Orleans, and that's a magical time for anyone.

We had bloody Marys while we waited to order. I didn't need to look at the menu or the wine list, I knew what I was having. Besides, I was far too busy looking at Vonnie. While she studied the menu, I studied her, discreetly of course.

She was beautiful, no doubt about that, but there was something else about her, something I couldn't put my finger on, something that made me want to sit there with her all afternoon and try to decipher every beat of a heart I could tell held a story.

She was in great shape, she obviously worked out, but it was her face that was arresting – wide high cheekbones, big soulful brown eyes, full lips and a smile that lit up the room. When she laughed, really laughed, she threw back her head, and as her hair fell down her back I wanted to kiss the hollow of her throat so badly I almost winced.

'What do you recommend?' She looked up to find me gazing at her.

I concentrated on the culinary options and refrained from suggesting that we skip eating and go back to my hotel room forthwith. Okay, I would never have said that, but it is what I was thinking, albeit wishfully.

Over lunch, I learned she was a writer, like me, who had learned the ropes the hard way – the only way as far as I'm concerned. You can have all the fancy degrees and diplomas under the sun after your name, but if you want to work for the real papers or publications, the ones that matter, that kind of writing has to come from a different place, one no writing degree can give you. It has to come from inside, from a place in your deepest core, a place that is often strange, unchartered territory, but the result, if you have it in you, is generally riveting. And that's what Vonnie was to me, right from the get-go.

After lunch, I took her to Audubon Park and we strolled

around the lake, oblivious to the skaters, dog walkers and joggers. When we kissed in the shadow of one of the great live oaks, I felt I was drowning, and never wanted to come up for air.

That evening, since I was in town, I was expected for dinner at home with my parents, both lawyers. I brought Vonnie with me, and as I knew they would, she was welcomed warmly and unquestioningly by the large unruly gathering that was my family and others. My parents' home was on Harmony Street in the Garden District, and my mother, an excellent and instinctive cook, was always happy to include an extra guest.

In the kitchen, when I brought in some dishes, my sister and mother stopped their muted conversation. 'She's beautiful,' said Gloria. 'Where did you find her?'

'Oh, stop it,' Mom said, but she looked at me eagerly.

'What can I tell you?' I said truthfully. 'I just met her today.'

'Today is all it takes, sometimes,' Mom said, and swatted me with a towel.

'There have been a lot of todays, Mom, with Jake,' Gloria reminded her. 'Don't get your hopes up.'

'Who's hoping?' She bent over the dishwasher. But I didn't need to see her face to know she *was* hoping. I didn't tell her I was too.

I went back to the dining room, where my two other sisters, their husbands and respective five kids were still eating and laughing. Dad was talking to Vonnie, his deep voice resonating with the pleasure of recounting one of his many favourite law case triumphs in his heyday to an untried audience. He sounded almost young again, although the years were taking their toll in the creases and lines of a face that had weathered its share of sadness. We lost my younger brother, Luke, in a car wreck nine years ago. And at times like those, when I walked through the door after being away for any length of time, I could feel my parents' split-second hopefulness that he would be following me so palpably that, on occasion, I would look around myself, unwittingly, just to check whether or not he had somehow materialised behind me.

Vonnie and I were both heading back to the west coast the following morning. The next weekend, I took the short flight from LA to San Luis Obispo to spend the weekend with her. I stayed in a local guest house in Morro Bay for the first night. But the next night, after a Saturday spent hanging out at the beach and picking up some food at the local market, we went back to her place, where I barbecued steaks, then we sat on the roof terrace drinking red wine, talking and listening to the echo of the ocean and our respective dreams.

When I took her in my arms and held her, breathed her in, it felt as natural as the faint smell of sunlight on her skin. Later, when we made love, I felt the fire in my blood, in the melded heat of our skin, and it didn't scare me. I didn't feel the familiar urge to cut and run. I should have known then that this girl was trouble with a capital 'T' – trouble I wasn't ready for, but I didn't. Because all I felt was peace, and the answering beat of her heart.

I felt I had come home, had found the one person in the world who held the answer to myself.

What I didn't realise back then was that Vonnie was just as lost as I was. It was just that the landscape was different.

Manhattan Upper East, 2011

Angela

I'm sixty-two now. I don't look it – but, God, I feel it, every lousy year of it. That's what they *don't* tell you. It doesn't matter how damn young you look on the outside, there's no denying those accumulating years on the inside. But looking good is important to me, always has been. And it's certainly important to Ron, my husband. I was twenty-two when I met him, and he fell in love with me instantly – him and the rest. I'm not being arrogant, really, but I was gorgeous back then. I knew it, I'm not ashamed to say, and I was determined to make it work for me. That's why I had to get out of Ireland, out of our terribly repressed, restricted, one-horse town. Oh, sure, Wicklow is beautiful – 'the Garden of Ireland' they call it – and we had a pretty little home, but there were no opportunities there, not the kind I was after anyway. I didn't want to be a big fish in a small pond. I wanted the ocean and that's what I got, sharks and all.

My first stop was Boston in 1965, where my relatives were based. I can remember it as if it was yesterday, that first sweet summer of freedom. That was where it all began, the parties, the boating and those long, lazy summer days in Cape Cod. God, I thought I was in heaven – and maybe, for a while, I was.

Of course later, when I realised I had no intention of staying in Ireland, I moved to New York. That was where the modelling scene was and that was when things really took off. I had 'the look', and timing is everything in modelling. It doesn't matter how beautiful you are if you don't have the look that's in vogue. Luckily for me, I did, and it all happened very quickly. Oh, I wasn't discovered on the street or anything like that (it rarely happens that way, the publicity people just always *say* that because it makes the business sound glamorous and accidental, as if a girl just happens to be in the right place at the right time and is plucked from obscurity). No, I headed straight for the Ford Modelling Agency, and Eileen Ford herself interviewed me and took me on right away. If you stuck to the rules and I did (for once), it was your passport to fame and occasionally fortune, although the money was nothing like it is these days. I had to live in the Fords' house with the other models from out of town, the chosen few that Eileen and Gerry supervised, and they were strict, believe me, but once your career got going, then you could afford to move out and your life was your own.

But I was on my way – Suzy Parker, Jean Shrimpton, Ali MacGraw, Cheryl Tiegs – all the great models started out with Ford, and now I was joining their ranks. They said I was the new Lauren Hutton, which will give you some idea of how cut-throat and bloody that industry is when Lauren is only two, maybe three years older than I am (she still looks incredible too by the way). But that's America for you, everyone is the new someone else. You have to grab your chance and run with it, before someone else does. They were heady days, and I threw myself into the whole thing. I wanted to extract every possible ounce from the good times while they lasted. Also, if I worked hard enough, and long enough, I didn't have to think. And I certainly didn't want to have to do that.

I met Ron (Ronald E. Douglas III) at a dinner party. I didn't know the couple giving the dinner, they were friends of Jamie, the guy I had been dating briefly, and he brought me along. The party was in an incredible apartment on the

Upper East, not far from where we live now, actually, and I had never seen anything like it.

There were pre-dinner drinks, and I remember Ron making a late, and very noticeable, entrance. Not just because of his good looks, although he was very handsome in that square-jawed, blond, waspish, American way, but because an indecipherable flutter passed through the women in the room, and the men stood taller and started making more noise, talking and laughing more loudly – you know, that classic Neanderthal stuff they do when an alpha comes into the pack.

I must have been the only one in the room who didn't get *exactly* how alpha Ronald E. Douglas was. He was guest of honour, of course – that much was plain from the start, as our host and hostess hovered around him anxiously – and the girl who had been lined up for him, a beautiful, sleek, brunette and close friend of the hostess, practically swooned. But she didn't stand a chance. From the moment he entered the room, Ron couldn't take his eyes off me. My date, an advertising executive, already had possessive tendencies, which I found irritating, but now he was all over me like a rash. I had to tell him to back off, which didn't go down well, as you can imagine.

Throughout dinner, Ron, who was seated opposite me and to the left, continually tried to make eye contact, but I was having none of it. Not out of any altruistic intentions, you understand – I could flirt with the best of them, still can – but because I found it insulting that he assumed I would be so susceptible to his rather indiscreet advances. Ron might have been master of the game in financial circles but, in me, he had met someone who could match him move for move and outmanoeuvre him romantically. It was important he understood that. He may have been the east coast's most eligible bachelor but by the end of the night, Ron E. Douglas

III knew I wasn't like any other woman he'd come across. He had met someone who was as predatory as he was. I was just making sure he did the hunting. But the truth was that I really wasn't that interested. You can't fake that, not really, and that's what drives men crazy, if they're a *real* man, that is – and let's face it, who needs the wimps?

We were married a year later, that's forty years ago now – a whole lifetime. The wedding was small by American standards. I didn't need to ask to know that Ron's parents weren't exactly thrilled with his choice of bride. Sure, I was a top model, and I was making a good living, but they had in mind one of those Grace Kelly-type lookalikes with inherited fortunes and pedigrees as long as their thoroughbred legs. I was a wild card – an Irish one at that. But once they realised Ron was hell bent on marrying me, they gave in, on the condition that I attended a finishing school in Switzerland for six months. It sounds ludicrous now, I know, but in hindsight it was pretty smart of them, and because *I* was smart I went along with the idea.

I had been well brought up, of course, in Ireland, but I wasn't exactly *educated*. I had no clue about the kind of full-time job I was taking on in becoming Mrs Ronald E. Douglas III. And I had to learn the rules and regulations of what that entailed, entertaining vast numbers of people I hardly knew on a regular basis, throwing effortlessly casual dinner parties at a moment's notice, how to handle fleets of staff and supervise our three homes – our apartment on the Upper East Side, the house in The Hamptons and our hideaway in Barbados – immaculately. Not to mention boning up on art and culture. Believe me, that stint in Geneva did me a favour. Being married to a billionaire isn't easy, especially when you haven't produced the much-longed-for son and heir. That was hard. Ron and I don't have children. We tried everything, but fertility treatments were only in their infancy when we were trying to get pregnant. And neither Ron nor I were keen on adopting. I had my own reasons for that and, luckily for me, Ron didn't want kids if he couldn't have his own.

It put a strain on the marriage, for sure, but I wasn't going to let it break us. Not after all I'd been through, after all the hard work I'd put in. I could have married anyone, but I chose Ron not just because I did fall in love with him (he can be pretty persuasive), but because he was the only one who could give me everything I ever wanted, and he did – no question. I wasn't about to let anything change that.

Of course he's had affairs over the years, that's par for the course with men like Ron. You can hardly blame him when every drop-dead beautiful model or actress or wannabe was throwing themselves at him. I do what all smart wives do who are married to rich, influential men. I turn a blind eye. Give him some space, and make sure the show goes on as effortlessly and entertainingly as possible. Sooner or later, he always gets tired of the girl in question – even if he briefly falls in love with her.

Of course, the real danger would have been a girl getting pregnant, then I'd have been in trouble. But that wasn't going to happen, because Ron was the one who was infertile, not me. The doctors figured out that much. That was tricky to deal with too, I can tell you. Doesn't do a lot for a man's ego, finding that out. I had to work pretty hard to get things going again in the bedroom, if you get my drift. But at least he couldn't blame me. In fact, I think he's always felt a bit guilty about it all – feels he's deprived me of a family – but we've done pretty well on our own.

At least we did until recently. But I'm not going to think about that now, I can't. I just have to sit back and see what happens next. Sometimes, even the best laid plans go wrong, and if I'm honest, I knew it was only a matter of time before life caught up with me, so to speak. But, like I said, you have to stand over your choices – own your failings – even if it hurts. The chips fall where they fall, it's how you play the game that counts. That's what I keep telling myself anyway because, right now, there's nothing I can do but wait. And that's the toughest thing of all to do.

Abby

The party that Abby had been dreading had, in fact, turned out to be quite a lot of fun. This was due in no small part to the fact that she was sitting beside a lovely American man from Texas, an energy investment consultant colleague of their hosts, who was visiting on business and then going on to drive to the southwest of the country on a golfing and fishing tour. He had proved very entertaining company, so much so that she had hardly exchanged a word with Edward all night, even though he was seated to her right. Jim, the American, had even asked Abby playfully if she might consider joining him on his trip. He had no idea how close she came to saying yes and to hell with it! Instead, she engaged eagerly in the mutual flirtation that, as the night wore on, attracted quite envious glances from around the table.

When their hostess, a thin, coiffed woman called Rachel, had made her way around the table and put a hand on his shoulder, enquiring if he had everything he needed, Jim confirmed loudly, 'Hell, yes, I'm doing great, thanks, Rachel. Good wine, excellent food and the sexiest woman at the table sitting next to me. It doesn't *get* any better!' This was followed by polite laughter from the other women, and envious glances from their accompanying men. Jim, realising his rather over-enthusiastic and unintentionally excluding compliment to Abby, added hurriedly, 'Couldn't get any better except, of course, it's the lucky guy on her *other* side who gets to take her home!'

This was greeted by more polite laughter and a smile from Edward that never quite reached his eyes but, for once, Abby didn't care. She was enjoying herself too much. Jim was great fun, told terrific jokes, topped up her glass regularly but discreetly and, most of all, he listened attentively to what she had to say, as if it really mattered. Abby had forgotten what that felt like. But she had enjoyed the evening thoroughly, particularly when Jim said pointedly how she reminded him of the smoking hot redhead actress who played the part of the glamorous secretary in *Madmen* – another of her favourite programmes. Abby found herself becoming more vivacious by the minute, telling stories and jokes herself, and even mimicking a few well-known celebrities. Before long, she had the table in hoots of laughter. When the dancing started, Jim whirled her onto her feet, and pretty soon all the other men were cutting in for a turn themselves. All but Edward, who sat talking intently to a group of older couples, his back turned resolutely on the revelry.

On the way home in the taxi, he was withdrawn.

'Wasn't it a great night?' Abby asked. 'Didn't you enjoy it?'

'You certainly seemed to be having a good time.'

Abby allowed herself to wonder, hopefully, if Edward perhaps was jealous of the attention she had been attracting. Usually, it was she who had to sit back dutifully while he was surrounded by eager, admiring women.

When they went upstairs to bed, Abby undressed carefully, hanging up her dress, so that when Edward emerged from the bathroom she was down to her sexy new lacy underwear and was casually unrolling her sheer black stockings. Slipping in to bed beside him, she curved into his back and stroked his chest tentatively.

'Not tonight, Abby,' he said, tersely. 'I have an early start.'

Abby rolled over to her own side of the bed where she lay awake long after Edward's regular breathing told her he was asleep. All the good of the evening seeped out of her. All the trouble she had taken to look her best had been for nothing. Her own husband didn't find her attractive any more. He could hardly be more obvious about it. Sleep eluded her, replaced instead by the unsettling realisation that she had tried so hard to avoid thinking about during the day – that it has been months, many months now, since she and Edward had had sex.

'Must have been some party.' Sheila is sitting in the kitchen reading the newspaper when Abby comes down the next morning. The remains of the cooked breakfast she has made are congealing in the pan and the smell makes Abby instantly nauseous.

'We weren't late.'

'Oh I heard you come in. You look awful. I suppose you had too much to drink?'

'No, I did not.' Abby is feeling a tad hungover, but that is not the cause of her white face and red-rimmed, sunken eyes.

'Well, pardon me for asking.' The newspaper in Sheila's hands is rustled defensively. 'There's some bacon left. Edward was up early, so I made him breakfast. He was delighted.'

'I'm sure he was.' Abby goes to make some fresh coffee, she cannot stomach the thought of food just yet. Later, she will have sugar cravings, but she will deal with that when it arises, not in front of her mother.

'What's the matter with you?' Sheila demands, looking at her. 'You're like a briar lately.'

'I'm tired, that's all.' Abby sits down wearily.

'Tired? Sure we're all tired, Abby. I'm seventy-six and I have arthritis, but I can still manage to get up and make a man his breakfast and put a cheerful smile on my face.'

Something stirs in Abby, but she says nothing. She is trying to identify the unsettling emotion.

'No wonder Edward is up every morning at an ungodly hour and out of the house if he has to face you, mooning around like a misery. Have you not thought about that? Asked yourself why?'

'Edward likes to start the day early, Mum, you know that,' Abby says. 'He goes to the gym before work – that's what he's done for, well, for ages.'

Sheila snorts. 'And what about all the trips away?'

'He has to keep up to date with every advance in his field. It's a very fast-moving business, cosmetology.'

'That's what he says.' Sheila's eyes are piercing. 'Do you want to know what I think? I think he's having an affair.' Sheila sits back in her chair. 'I think my son-in-law is having an affair and my own daughter is too stupid to see it – or, God forbid, to do anything about it.

Abby looks at her, as if she is seeing her mother for the first time, feeling an odd sense of detachment. She notices the carefully made-up face, the lines that have settled around the turned-down corners of her mouth, the deter-mined set of her chin, beneath which folds of skin have settled. Most particularly, she notices her eyes, alight now with eagerness for potential drama, a desire to inflame her daughter into acting out whatever course of action she thinks appropriate. But also, for the first time, she sees lurking in their depths the unmistakable gleam of jealousy.

She wonders now what it was like for her father, living with her mother for all those years, in the shadow of her forceful personality, unshielded from her thinly veiled disap-pointment of him. Her father has been dead for five years. He slipped away, quietly, after a brief illness, just three days in hospital, leaving her mother vaguely surprised, but far from bereft. On the contrary, she had assumed the mantle of widowhood lightly, shedding the skin of her marriage as easily as an over-worn overcoat.

Regarding her daughter dubiously from across the kitchen table, Sheila tries a softer approach. 'Let's go into town, Abby, and have lunch, my treat. Make a day of it,' she says conspiratorially. 'We'll go and get our hair and nails done, maybe book a facial or a massage in that nice new salon that's opened in town, the one they're always talking about on *Xposé*, where all the celebrities go.'

Abby's jaw tightens at the thought.

'No thanks, Mum, not today. I'm not really up to it.'

'But that's the whole problem,' Sheila persists. 'You're never up to it. You won't take care of yourself at all, Abby.' She pauses emphatically. 'There's no other way to say this Abby, but you've let yourself go. It's a crying shame, but it's never too late to do something about it – and it's not as if you can't afford it. We'll start today and we'll go once a week, every week. And maybe you could go to one of those weight-loss places—'

'I said no.' Abby gets up from the table, taking her mug of coffee to the sink.

'I don't know what the heck is the matter with you.' Sheila looks perplexed. 'Can't you see I'm only trying to help you? Before it's too late—'

'Too late for what?'

'For God's sake, Abby, wake up, will you. If you don't take yourself in hand, Edward will leave you. We'll lose him. Though the way you've been behaving lately, I can't say I'd blame him.' Sheila's face has flushed angrily.

'Perhaps you wouldn't,' Abby says evenly, although her heart is racing, 'but, then, he's not your husband to blame. Is he, Mum?'

Abby leaves Sheila sitting open-mouthed in the kitchen and goes upstairs to get her bag. She has to get out of the house – anywhere. She is not dressed up, just wearing a pair of comfortable sweat pants and a long-sleeved T-shirt. They are both grey, and match the colour of her face, the thought occurs to her as she catches a glimpse of herself in the full-length mirror. She grabs her phone and handbag and heads downstairs, brushing by a sleepy Roseanna on the landing.

'Mum?' she yawns. 'You're giving me a lift into town for twelve thirty, aren't you?'

'Sorry Rosie, I can't – I have to go out.'

'But how am I supposed to—'

'Get the Dart or a bus, whatever. I'm not a taxi service.'

'I can't,' wails Roseanna. 'I have to be at the audition *in* my outfit, I can't get on the Dart in it.'

'That's your problem.'

As she runs out the door, Abby hears Roseanna mutter some obscenity directed at her, but she doesn't care. She doesn't care about anything except getting out of the house.

Once she is in the car, she heads for the main road and drives aimlessly, finally taking long, deep breaths. She turns on the radio but hardly hears whatever song is playing.

She thinks of the lunch last week with the girls, and what a shock it had been when she saw Vonnie. Why, she was almost unrecognisable. Even Di's mouth had dropped open. And the photo of her gorgeous little daughter, and that incredible looking man who was the father, and by all accounts (if Vonnie were to be believed) still her 'close friend'. A former war correspondent, no less, a photojournalist-turned-writer. God, it was so unbelievably romantic, and . . . and exciting – even if he *had* left her, if they had split up. Vonnie now had this amazing life in a small town in California. It was, well, pretty unbelievable really. Not that she didn't deserve it or anything, but it suddenly made Abby feel horribly inadequate – and boring, terribly boring.

And then there had been Di, looking as groomed and glamorous as ever, of course. But her face, when Abby had talked about her mother living with her, had registered utter

horror. I mean who did she think she was? And all that talk
about how she would never, ever live with her own children.
Well, Abby reasoned, that's possibly because they would never
invite her to. And, of course, Di was still thin, sure she hardly
put a morsel in her mouth over lunch, but instead had
managed to watch and log every sip of wine Abby had taken
with an eagle eye. I mean what the hell was that about?
Di was half-French for Christ's sake. She had been drinking
wine at home with her parents before Abby had ever heard
of the stuff.

Abby tries to make sense of it all and fails. It wasn't
supposed to turn out like this. *Vonnie* had been the fat one
– the one they all felt sorry for – and now . . . Abby looks
down at her comfortably spreading thighs underneath the
steering wheel and wants to cry or scream. Maybe both.

She fishes for her phone on the seat beside her and calls
Diana. Maybe talking to her will make her feel better, make
sense of it all. They haven't had a chance to have their usual
post-mortem about the lunch, never mind Vonnie and her
extraordinary story. But Diana's phone is busy or switched
off; whichever, the mailbox voice tells Abby to try later.
'Story of my life,' she mutters to herself.

And the worst thing, the very worst thing of all, worse
even than the thought of Edward having an affair (she won't
think about that now, she can't) was that Di had been absolutely right. Having Sheila come to live with them had been
a terrible, horrible mistake. Worse still, a mistake that there
was no foreseeable way out of. Because what Abby hadn't
mentioned was that when Sheila had sold her house, she had
put the proceeds into bank shares, along with everything else
she had. So to all intents and purposes, her mother, apart
from her small pension, was penniless. Edward didn't appear
to mind her living with them – why would he, when the
woman virtually fawned over him constantly? – and the kids

thought she was great fun altogether. It was Abby who could hardly bear another minute in her presence. And the weird thing was that, up until all this, right up until she had moved in with them, Abby had thought she and her mother were very close, that they had a great relationship.

Taking a left turn, Abby finds herself heading towards the coast road, and realises she is only ten minutes or so away from Sliversands, the village where Vonnie is renting her house. She has her address, too, somewhere in her handbag. She will take a chance and call around to Vonnie, see if she's in. Vonnie has always been calm and understanding, not bossy and dictatorial like Di and, anyway, Abby couldn't talk properly at the lunch, she felt too intimidated. Suddenly she wants to open up, to talk to someone, very much, about what is going on in her life. Vonnie will know what to do. She must, she has completely transformed her own life. Surely she will know what Abby should do? And she will not be judgemental. Abby has had all she can take of being judged and found wanting. But there is no hiding from old school friends, not when you have lived together for six years since the age of twelve.

Abby finds the address, parks her car and stands on the porch of the small, pale-pink, flat-fronted house that wouldn't look out of place in a Grimm's fairytale. Wisteria and summer roses twine under the windows and around the small front door. She rings the bell and waits nervously.

'Abby,' Vonnie says as she opens the door. 'What a lovely surprise, come on in.'

'Sorry for descending on you like this.' Abby steps inside. 'I hope I'm not disturbing you.'

'Are you crazy? It's great to see you, don't you dare apologise. As a matter of fact,' she wipes her hands on a tea towel, 'I was just putting a picnic together, Jazz and I were going to go to the beach, you'll join us, won't you? It's only down the road, and it's such a lovely day.'

'Well, if you're sure?'

'Sure I'm sure. And Jazz is dying to meet you. She's always asking about my school friends, I don't think she really believes I have any. Come into the kitchen and help yourself to a drink and I'll just finish getting this stuff together.

'Jazz, honey,' she calls out through the open back door. 'C'mon inside. I want you to meet a friend of mine.'

The photograph does not do her justice. The thought comes into Abby's mind as the small figure, with bare feet, wearing what looks like a Victorian lace nightdress, hurtles through the door and stops dead, appraising Abby from the doorway. The child is exquisite, like a miniature Halle Berry, with a long, dark, tangle of curls cascading down her back. But when her face breaks into a delighted grin, she is very much her mother's daughter.

'Oh, Vonnie, she has your smile.'

'You think?' Vonnie grins. 'Jazz,' she says to her daughter, 'this is Abby, one of my best friends. We went to school together.'

'Wow.' Jazz runs to Abby and flings her arms around her waist. And, for a moment, bending down to hug her back, Abby fights back tears.

'You're honoured,' says Vonnie. 'Not everyone gets that reception, I can tell you.'

Jazz stands back and looks at Abby. 'You're beautiful. My mom said you were. And I love your hair. It's fierce.'

'Fierce is good,' Vonnie explains.

'Well thank you.' Abby is taken aback. 'I think you're beautiful too.'

'Jazz, go get changed, we're going in a minute.'

'But I want to wear *this*.'

'No way, put on your shorts and T-shirt. *Now*.'

'I can't get her out of that thing, she'd live in it if I let her,' Vonnie says as Jazz does as she's told and runs upstairs.

Vonnie puts the rest of the food in a straw basket, and catches sight of Abby's feet, encased in her most comfortable trainers. 'Aren't you too hot in those things?'

'I wasn't thinking, really.'

'Here, take a pair of my flip-flops – we're the same size, aren't we?' She throws a pair over to Abby, who sits down to peel off her shoes. Luckily, she thinks, her feet are present-able, she had a pedicure for the party, and the varnish is still pretty much intact.

'C'mon, Jazz, let's go,' Vonnie calls upstairs.

They leave the little house and stroll through the village, Jazz chattering ten to the dozen, firing questions at Abby about what her mother was like when she was young, which make Abby smile.

Perhaps it is feeling the sun warm upon her back, or the carefree 'slip, slap' of the flip flops as she and Vonnie stroll along, or watching Jazz skip ahead of them, without a care in the world – whatever it is, suddenly the years seem to fall away for Abby, taking with them, to her relief, the blistering sense of resentment that has been shadowing her.

A little while later they are settled beside the rocks, sheltered from the breeze. Jazz is playing by the water's edge, collecting shells in a plastic bag. She is wearing a bright pink bikini, which makes Abby shiver just to think about. It is a warm sunny day, but only June, still Ireland. And Vonnie and Abby are sitting cross-legged, fully clothed, munching on bread and cheese.

'Vonnie, can I ask you something?'

'Mmhmm.' Vonnie looks up from brushing crumbs off her chest and meets Abby's enquiring gaze. 'Sure, shoot.'

'How did you do it?'

'Do what?'

'All this.' Abby waves her hand gesturing towards Jazz and

back to Vonnie. 'How did you change everything? Transform yourself – your life? You seem so happy, and . . . serene.'

'Are you kidding?' Vonnie laughs. 'I'm far from serene. How long have you got?'

'All afternoon, as long as it takes.'

'Well, first of all,' Vonnie begins, thoughtfully. 'It wasn't a conscious decision. I just knew I had to get away. After I found out about my mother, a lot of things started to make sense. Like how I never fitted in at home, how I always felt like an outsider. But I knew without a shadow of a doubt that I had to get out of there, away from them and here, if I was to have any chance of finding out who I am.'

'And have you?'

'Well, I've found out who I want to be. I'm not sure if I'm there yet. But when Jazz came into my life, she simplified everything. Nothing else mattered, none of the small stuff, the pettiness, the dishonesty. As long as I don't repeat it.'

'How do you ever know if you're being a good mother?' Abby wonders. She thinks of her twin boys and Roseanna, they seem happy enough. And then the image of her own mother, Sheila, floats in front of her, crowding them out.

'You don't, I guess. You just have to do the best you can with what you've got. But you don't have to repeat the past. You don't have to let it define you.'

'Things happen for a reason, I think,' Vonnie says. 'I think the right people come into your life when you need to learn something – do the relevant work.'

'So everyone that comes into your life is work?'

Vonnie grins. 'Well, everyone has something to teach you about yourself, and you them. Nobody's saying it's easy.' Vonnie pauses, and then goes on. 'At the risk of sounding very Californian, I have a great therapist – she's helped me a lot.'

'You've done therapy?' Abby's eyes widen.

'Quite a lot of therapy. I still do, when I need it.'

'But what did it do for you? What did you learn? I mean, I suppose I'm not surprised, *everyone* in America goes to a therapist, don't they?' Abby laughs a little nervously. 'I mean it's a rite of passage.'

'Not everyone, but maybe everyone should. A couple of years should be mandatory I reckon – and not just in America.'

'Well, you're certainly a good advertisement for it.'

'It's not that simple, Abby, unfortunately. I still have a lot of stuff. Take my word for it.'

'But you *look* fabulous.' And that, Abby can't help thinking, is all that seems to matter.

'Well, thank you,' Vonnie smiles. 'But that's mostly down to a lot of hard work.'

Abby is intrigued. The old Vonnie would have brushed off the compliment, any compliment, however well deserved, and made a joke.

'What is it, Abby? What's going on with you?'

'Me? Oh, I don't know . . . nothing and everything.'

'Like what?'

'Well, look at me. I've got fat and I'm boring and—' She lets out a long breath. 'Edward's having an affair.'

'Oh, Abby.' Vonnie reaches over and takes her hand. 'I'm truly sorry to hear that. That's devastating. How did you find out?'

'My mother told me.' Abby gives a mirthless laugh.

'Your mother?'

'Yes. Apparently, I'm too blind and stupid to see it. But, of course, I've driven him to it.'

'Abby that's not funny.' Vonnie sounds cross.

'She's right. I just didn't – don't – want to face the fact.'

'Has he admitted to it?'

'I haven't said anything to him yet.'

'Abby, you have to talk to him.'

'He doesn't have to say anything. He's made it perfectly clear he has no interest in me. We haven't had sex for months – a year almost.'

'Oh, Abby.'

'It's like he can't bear to touch me anymore.'

Vonnie seems at a loss for words. 'But surely you can talk to him. I mean you have to, otherwise you'll drive yourself crazy.'

'I will, if my mother doesn't get there first. I wouldn't put it past her. She and Edward have a mutual admiration society going on.'

'But it's your marriage, Abby,' Vonnie says gently.

'You think I don't know that? Sorry. I didn't mean to snap. I'm a complete rat bag these days, pay no attention to me. It's my own fault.'

'How can it possibly be your fault? You and Edward were crazy about each other. I remember.'

'That was a long time ago, Vonnie. I was pregnant when I married him.' Abby pauses to let the words sink in. She has never said them before, not out loud. 'Oh, don't get me wrong, that's not *why* I married him. I was thrilled, it was deliberate actually, and we were engaged when it happened, it was just a month before the wedding. But I suspect it's probably why he married *me*. I could feel him pulling away. I was terrified he was having second thoughts – that he was going to break off the engagement. I couldn't have handled that.'

'So what if you were pregnant, Abby? You've been married for what? Twenty, twenty-one years? Nobody stays together that long because of an unplanned pregnancy. I mean look at me . . .' Vonnie looks over towards Jazz, still playing at the water's edge. 'Jake and I didn't get married.'

'I don't know what to do.' She looks at Vonnie helplessly. 'I couldn't bear it if he left me. If it were just me and mum on our own together. I couldn't stand it.' There, she has said it. 'And yet, I can't help myself. I can feel myself driving him further and further away. It's like I can't help myself.'

'Your mother . . . Does she . . . Do you have to have her living with you?'

'I do now. She lost the proceeds from her house and pretty much everything else in bank shares.'

'Oh, no, Abby, how awful.'

'So, yes, we're stuck with each other now. I thought it would be a good idea, initially – I mean we've always got on well together – but, now . . . oh, Vonnie, I can't stand the sight of her.' Abby tries to laugh, but finds instead tears running down her face. She brushes them away angrily. 'So, you see, it *is* all my own fault. I made my bed and now I have to lie in it – with a man who clearly would rather be in someone else's, whoever she is.'

'Please, Abby,' Vonnie urges, 'talk to Edward. You have to, you can't just let this situation drift, you have to deal with it. It doesn't have to mean the end of the marriage – you have to give him a chance to tell you what's really going on. And, remember, you don't have any actual proof he's having an affair, do you?'

Abby shrugs. 'I have all the proof I need. I'm sorry for dumping this on you and being so pathetic. I can't think about anything else, I'm going out of my mind.'

'Of course you are, any of us would. But it may not be what you think – or what your mother thinks. Please, promise me you'll talk to him.'

Abby nods and wipes her nose on her sleeve. 'Speaking of which, I'd better get back. They'll be wondering where I've got to.'

'Don't rush off, Abby, not like this. Come in and have a cup of tea with me at home, or something stronger if you like. C'mon, we'll pack up now. It's getting chilly anyway.'

On their way back, Vonnie drops Jazz off at her friend's house, two doors down, to play and stay for tea. 'Lindsay's a godsend for Jazz, she's just her age and her mother Anne is a sweetheart. It makes things a lot easier for me, having her so close, gives us both a bit of flexibility, and it's meant Jazz has got to know the local kids too.'

In Vonnie's little house, Abby looks around while Vonnie makes tea. On a table under a window that looks out onto the back garden sits a laptop, surrounded by an unruly pile of books. The garden itself, which is narrow and winding, is a tangle of colour – hollyhocks, roses and clematis, all growing in a haphazard muddle of flowers and foliage. There is a little path weaving through it all, and at the end in a clearing, a small wooden table and chairs.

'What a gorgeous garden,' Abby says.

'I know, classic 'English country'. The woman who owned the house was an artist, and a keen gardener. She died last year, so her family are renting the house out. I feel I should be taking care of her garden, but I haven't a clue about plants.'

Inside, over tea and deliciously chewy caramel and choco-late pralines (Abby has four) they talk – about men, mothers and daughters, and the twists and turns of life.

'I never asked you what you were working on,' Abby says, mid-mouthful. 'Your assignment?'

'It's part of a piece I'm researching on the influence of Islamic art in Europe,' Vonnie says. 'I'm writing up the Chester Beatty collection here – it's fascinating.'

'That's in Dublin Castle now, isn't it?' Abby remembers vaguely.

'Uh-huh, manuscripts, miniature paintings, prints and rare books. You should come up and have lunch with me there one day, it's really interesting.' Vonnie pauses. 'Have you thought about going back to work at all, Abby?'

'As a nurse? No. It's been over twenty years now. And, to be honest, I was glad to get out of it. I'd probably have to totally retrain now.'

'But your experience and qualifications will always stand to you. The health industry is huge these days – what about nutrition or something holistic? It might be just what you need, you know. Get you out of the house, give you a life of your own again.'

Abby nods but looks miserable.

'Abby, sweetheart,' Vonnie sighs. 'You can do anything you want to, you know. You're clever and funny – you've just lost your self-belief. Trying out something new, anything, a course maybe, something that will build up your confidence again. You could even go to college – you were a scholarship girl for heaven's sake! You have brains to burn.'

Abby knows Vonnie is right, but all she can think about is how hopeless she is. She wouldn't know where to start.

'Just think about it, will you?' Vonnie says gently. 'Take it one day at a time. But I think it would really help you, get you some perspective on things. It can't be good for you being cooped up at home all the time.'

'I will, and thank you for today, I really needed it.' Abby finishes her tea and gets up to leave.

'Call me,' Vonnie says. 'Anytime, if you need to talk. I mean that.'

Vonnie watches her from the door as she heads down the path.

'Abby?'

'What?'

'Promise me you'll talk to him.'

But Abby only smiles and waves before disappearing into her car.

Vonnie

I was worried about Abby – and shocked by what she had told me. Not so much the affair she was convinced her husband was having, but rather her strangely acquiescent acceptance of it. It was almost as if she felt she had no right to be in the marriage, just because she had been pregnant going into it.

But I remember Abby's wedding well, and how Edward's face shone with pride every time he looked at her or introduced his new bride to someone. He was very much in love with her, it was as plain as the nose on his face.

As for what had happened in the intervening years, well, that was anyone's guess. All relationships and marriages go through rough patches, and we all bring our own baggage into every new development. Nobody knows that better than I do.

Having Jazz changed everything.

She wasn't planned, and through my daze of shock and confusion I remember telling Jake, worrying how he'd take it, what it would do to him – to us.

'I'm pregnant,' I said, putting down the bowl of pasta on the table and turning to pick up the salad on the counter.

'Say again?' he looked up from his laptop.

'I'm pregnant.'

There was a split-second pause, and then he threw back his head and laughed. 'Get outta here! Really?'

'Jake, I wouldn't joke about something this serious.'

He leapt off the couch, grabbed me and swung me off my feet, around and around until I was dizzy.

'Baby, that's wild! That's fantastic! That's the best thing I've ever heard in my life.' He had put me down and kissed me.

'You mean you're okay with it? You're not, well, upset?'

'Upset? Are you crazy? It's a surprise, I'll admit, but I like surprises – and I *love* you. This calls for a celebration, I think.' He headed for the fridge. 'If my memory serves me correctly, there's a bottle of champagne lurking here waiting for an excuse to be opened.'

'I can't drink now,' I said.

'Oh come on, you're allowed one glass, then I'll make sure another drop never passes your beautiful lips until you're holding our daughter in your arms.'

So I did have a glass, just the one.

'Here's to you, Vonnie, you're the best thing that's ever happened to me.'

'What makes you so sure it's a girl?' I said.

'Oh, it's a girl all right. I just have a feeling. A very lucky little girl.'

'Why?'

'Because she's going to have the most gorgeous, incredible mother in the world, and a father who'll be hopelessly in love with both of you.' He took my hands across the table.

'I'm scared, Jake.'

'What of?'

'Well, I'll be thirty-eight when the baby's born, and—'

'Honey that's young, you're fit and healthy – you'll breeze through it.'

'And, and I don't know if I, well, I don't know if I can ever be a good mother, you know. With my background and everything.'

'You'll be a natural. I know it.'

'My mother wasn't.'

'Things were different back then. Besides, what happened to her was really bad luck, not you, baby,' he smiled, 'but you know, with the guy and everything, she hardly knew him, he was a virtual stranger from what you tell me. You can't compare that to us.'

'I don't. But what kind of woman could leave her own child? A baby.'

'A very disturbed and unhappy one, I should imagine.' Jake looked at me. 'Have you ever asked her? I mean really, face to face?'

'No.' I felt every muscle in my body tense.

'Then this might be a good time to confront that, don't you think?'

'I can't go there.' I stood up quickly, and took my plate over to the sink.

'For you, Vonnie, I can understand that, but maybe, for this baby, you need to.'

'Oh please,' I said.

'No really, Von, I mean it. Why don't you go see your mother, have it out with her? At least get some answers.'

'I don't want to see her.'

She had written to me, of course, many times over the years, ever since it was made known that I had 'discovered the truth'. I had never replied to any of the letters.

'One day, she won't be around. You might regret it. Then there won't be any answers.'

'Good. Can't come soon enough. She's dead to me anyway. I certainly didn't ever exist for her, except as a monumental inconvenience.'

'You don't know that.'

'Excuse me?'

'Look, all I'm saying is at least hear her side of the story. It might be interesting.'

'This is not a plot line, Jake. I am not looking for the missing pieces in a script of my life marked "mother". I think, everything considered, I've done pretty well without one.'

Jake's reply to that was silence.

I put my face in my hands.

'Hey,' he said, coming over and wrapping his arms around

me from behind. 'You're the only thing that matters to me in the world, Von – you, and our baby of course. You don't have to do anything, you know that. I just think it might help, addressing the past can sometimes put the present in clearer focus, that's all.'

He turned me to face him.

'I'll think about it,' I said, feeling suddenly weary.

'Remember,' he said, tilting my chin, 'you're the one who's in charge now. You're in the driving seat. You were powerless then, but not now. That has to make a difference.

When I thought about it like that, he was right. I knew he was. But even the mention of the word 'mother' made me feel small, defenceless and, most of all, unwanted.

Thinking back, I am seventeen again, off to work in France for the summer with my two best friends. We have all secured jobs as au pairs with local families in the same town and I am beyond excited. Our flights have been booked, the only thing left to do is pack and begin the long, agonising wait for our Leaving Certificate results in August. But that is almost three whole months away. My French is quite good and, of course, Diana is fluent so that is not an issue for her. We are not leaving for another two days, but I like to be organised, so I have my clothes laid out, suitcase ready and tickets packed in my on-flight bag, all I need is my passport which I know is in date because we have gone on holidays abroad before, with my parents, and mine has a dorky photograph of me aged twelve on it – but there's nothing I can do about that for another four years. Dad promised he'd leave it out for me for the past week but he keeps forgetting, so I pester him.

'Dad?'

'What is it now, Vonnie?' he says wearily as I put my head around the door to the TV den, where he is sitting with a whiskey. He seems tired and I hate to bother him, but I have to.

'My passport. You said you'd get it for me, I need it for Tuesday.'

He looks perplexed, then brightens. 'That's right, I did, and I left it out to remind myself. It's on top of my desk, you can get it yourself.'

'Great,' I say, relieved that I don't have to disturb him after all. 'Thanks, Dad.'

Downstairs all is quiet. Mum is having a bath, Barney has gone home and Kate is out. I swing by the kitchen and help myself to a generous slice of fruit cake that Barney has baked that day. I take it into Dad's study and bite into a mouthful, which I pause to savour as I look around the room. It smells vaguely of disinfectant, medicinal, the walls covered with books, not medical ones, those are all kept in the surgery, but these books reveal his real passions – horses and cards. I go over to his desk, an antique writing bureau, where, as he said, my passport is sitting. I pick it up gratefully, flicking through it, reassuring myself that it is indeed in date. And then I notice that the bureau has been left open, the lid down on its brass hinges, revealing a leather inlay, and mysterious miniature drawers and slots where papers and old cheque and bank books are neatly stacked and stored. I can see the other passports and I take up Kate's, opening it at her photo – in contrast to mine, she looks like a sophisticated teenager smiling prettily.

I take another bite of cake, spilling crumbs on the desk interior, and brush them off hurriedly, knocking a folded paper off in the process. I pick it up distractedly and open the first fold as a matter of casual interest. And then I realise it is my birth certificate. For a moment, I am transfixed. I have never been denied this document, nor have I ever asked to see it. I didn't want to. Since that hideous exchange with my parents before I went off to boarding school when I'd learned I was adopted, I had never mentioned the subject. Neither had they, at least not in front of me. Neither had Kate, I assumed she had been warned not to. I had visions of them discussing it and me at length between themselves behind closed doors. All I wanted was to forget about it as best I could – now here I was holding the damning evidence in my own hand, which began to tremble. I wanted to throw it away, tear it up or just put it back, folded as I had found it and run away, but my brain seemed to have other ideas.

I put down the remainder of the slice of cake and slowly unfolded the certificate that harboured such tantalising information. Mesmerised, I scanned it; my date of birth was there, just as it should be. Astonishingly, it claimed my place of birth had been here, right here, in this very house. Under the column headed 'Name of Father', there was nothing, it had been left blank, but my mother's name was printed clearly: Angela Mary Cunningham. The words swam before me. Even then, I don't think I quite grasped it. Cunningham rang a bell of course, it was my adopted mother's maiden name . . . which meant . . . slowly, I joined the dots and realisation dawned on me, horrible, unwanted, bewildering realisation. I stared at the document with hatred. Now I would have to ask, I would have to seek an explanation, I would have to discover the reason why I had been so unwanted.

Forgetting my slice of uneaten cake, I took my birth certificate and headed back to my father with leaden feet. I was pretty sure he wouldn't want to have this conversation either. I was also sure I would get into trouble for 'snooping' through private documents. Or maybe they had planned it that way? Maybe they had arranged for me to discover this incriminating evidence for myself. Either way, it didn't really matter. All I knew was I was about to hear something I didn't want to, and my brain felt as if it would buckle in two trying to assimilate yet more confusing information about myself and my fragmented family.

'We didn't want to upset you.' Carmel is in her dressing gown, looking annoyed at being summoned downstairs by her husband who, when presented with my demands for explanations, went up and physically retrieved her from her nightly bathing ritual. Colm (I cannot now think of him as 'Dad' in any respect) is sitting back down, blowing out his red veined cheeks, alternately taking swigs from his whiskey and running his hands through his hair. He is looking at Carmel with an I-told-you-this-would-happen expression.

'You told me I was adopted,' I say. 'That you chose me especially.' Even at the time I heard that version, I had known somewhere, in the back of my mind, that it was not the truth. Who would choose me?

'It was a difficult situation,' Carmel says, carefully.

'Tell me,' I demand.

She looks uncomfortable.

'Tell the girl, for God's sake,' Colm says wearily.

'Your mother . . .' Carmel begins and stops.

'Angela?'

'Yes, my sister, Angela, she was in America, she, well she got herself into trouble – that's the only way of putting it.'

I pale. 'Go on,' I say through gritted teeth.

'She came home, of course – what else could she do?' At this, Carmel gives a short, bitter laugh.

'What about . . . What about the— my father?'

There was an awkward silence. 'I think he was engaged to someone else, he was in the army, off to Vietnam. I don't think there was any contact between them after.'

'You mean he wasn't interested.'

Colm interjects. 'Angela was young, around the same age

as you are now.' He shakes his head. 'Things were different in those days.'

'Well,' Carmel continues, 'she came home and had the baby.'

'Me.'

'Yes, you.'

'So what happened? Why did I end up here with you?'

'She couldn't cope,' Colm says.

Carmel snorts derisively. 'You can say that again.'

Something inside me is turning to cold, seeping dread. But I prod them on, I have to know. 'So what happened?'

'She left. That's what happened.'

'Left?'

'Yes, left. She told nobody, she just went. She wrote a letter asking us to take care of you, and that she would be back when she had made some money and a life for herself.'

'But she didn't come back for me, did she?'

Carmel looks at her hands.

Colm tries again. 'She wasn't well when she left, was she, Carmel? She was depressed.'

'Oh for God's sake,' Carmel snaps at him. 'She cheered up pretty quickly when she got back to America.'

'Then she got married,' Colm said. As if that explained everything.

'So why didn't she come back and get me then?' I ask, hating the pathetic bleating of my voice.

'She never told him. That's why.' Carmel lights a cigarette. 'She put herself and her new husband before her daughter, her own flesh and blood.'

'Carmel,' Colm protests.

'Well that's what she did.' Carmel is defiant. 'Angela was always good at looking after number one.'

There is a long silence, during which shame crawls all over me.

'I— I suppose I should say thank you, then,' I say. 'For taking me in. For, well, looking after me.'

'There's no need for that, Vonnie.' Colm looks uncomfortable.

'You've been a good girl, Veronica,' Carmel says. 'I know this can't be easy for you, but, well, at least we're family. You're with your own people.'

'Yes.' I agree. 'Yes, you've been very good to me.'

'We've done our best. So you can see now why we didn't want to tell you? We wanted to spare you.'

'Yes, I see now.'

'Put the whole thing out of your head,' Carmel says. 'Go off and enjoy your lovely holiday in France and forget all about it. When you come back you'll be off to university and a whole new life.'

I smile weakly. 'Yes, yes, I'll do that. I think I'll go upstairs and do some packing now.'

'Goodnight, Vonnie,' Colm says.

'Goodnight,' I say, not meeting his eyes. But there is nothing good about it.

Upstairs I sit on my bed and try to think rationally. What difference does it make? It doesn't change anything. I am still part of the same family, chosen or not. In fact, I should feel better about it all, I reason. At least, as Carmel (my Aunt Carmel now) pointed out, I am with my own family, my relatives. There are blood ties. Kate and I share grandparents, even though they are now gone. But I can't fool myself. Everything has changed. I am even more unwanted than I thought I was. Even my dead grandparents must have been horrified to hear of my imminent arrival.

I was not chosen, or longed for – I arrived, unasked for and unwanted. A hideous intrusion on everyone's orderly, proper life, the embodiment of disgrace. No wonder my mother had wanted to get away from me. Who could blame her? I thought about my family, my Aunt Carmel and Uncle Colm and my cousin Kate. My cousin! I had known we weren't sisters, of course, but as cousins the lack of any similarity in our appearance became even more of an affront. Why couldn't I have been more petite, prettier, blonder? Just a tiny bit? And then I would be overcome with shame again. What an ungrateful girl I was. I should be thankful for any kindness shown to me. Poor Kate, having to put up with me all these years, share her home and her parents with me as if they were my own, my right. How unfair I had been about her. Who could blame her for occasionally being unkind to me? I didn't deserve their kindness, their tolerance, their generosity. I didn't deserve anything.

Two days later, I set off for France with Diana and Abby. It was a blessed escape. I didn't say anything about my latest discovery, I was too shell-shocked. And there was something else too. I was at that awkward age, I suppose, trying to strike out in the world, trying things on for size, and I felt as if every time I got a handle on life, or myself, the goal posts changed. I didn't know who I was, quite literally. And when I found out, I turned out to be someone else entirely, and neither version felt real in any way. It was horribly unsettling for me. So I kept it to myself, and tried not to think about it as much as I could. Instead, I threw myself into my summer job, looking after two small, badly behaved boys, and tried to learn as much French as I could, while trying to teach them English. I was used as a cook and housemaid as well, which was not included in our duties specified by the agency who had placed us, but I didn't care. The more I had to do, the less time I had to think, and that suited me fine. It also gave me access to the kitchen, which meant access to food, and since I did the shopping, I was able to include a few treats for myself. I also discovered that I was a better cook than I realised, as a result of spending all that time with Barney in the kitchen growing up. If the French couple I worked for had any problem with me digging into their bakery supplies, they clearly felt they were getting the better end of the deal in respect of my work load. By the time we were due to go home, I had put on at least another stone, and had decided to change my flight.

'What do you mean, you're not coming home?' Abby looked at me in horror as I informed her and Diana over cafe au laits and pastries in the town where we were based.

'You're staying here?' Diana said.

'No, I'm going to London.' I might as well have said the moon, the way Abby was looking at me.

'But why? I mean why don't you come home like us and then go to London if you want to?'

It was a fair question. One I had asked myself. But I couldn't tell them that I just couldn't face my family again. Something had flipped inside me. I had to get away.

'Has something happened, something gone wrong, out here?' Diana asked. Did anyone—'

'No,' I quickly reassured her. 'Absolutely nothing has happened out here. I've had a great time. I just need to get away.'

'But why leave from here, I don't understand.' Abby looked bewildered, as well she might. 'I mean what will we say? What will we tell them? They'll think something awful has happened.'

'They won't,' I said. 'Because I will tell them before I go and I will ring them from London to say I am absolutely fine.'

'I don't like it,' said Abby.

'Neither do I,' Diana frowned.

'My parents would kill me if I did that.'

'My father would be on the first plane after me,' Diana agreed.

'Yes, well, my parents will understand, they're quite liberal in many respects.' Well, that was putting it mildly, I thought, ironically, not knowing them but still the track record spoke for itself.

'You would tell us if something was wrong, wouldn't you?' Diana looked at me keenly.

'Of course I would. There's no big deal, I just want to get a life – spread my wings.'

'But I thought you wanted to go to university?' Abby protested.

'I've changed my mind.'

Diana shook her head. 'Well, it's your life. I don't know what's got into you but if that's what you want, who are we to stop you?'

I smiled my relief.

'When do you leave?'

'The day before you guys.'

'You'll phone us, won't you? Stay in touch?'

'Of course I will. It's only London, not the other side of the world. You can come over and stay with me when I'm settled.' I was winging it, but these seemed like the normal kind of things to say.

'What are you going to do? Where will you stay?' Diana asked.

'I have a cousin there,' I lied. 'I'll stay with her until I get a job. Then I'll get my own place.' The point was I was getting away, I assured myself – not running away, that would have been cowardly. I would write the letter to my aunt and uncle tonight. Then I would post it so they would get it the day I was due home, when it was too late to try and stop me, although privately I thought they would be relieved. I didn't care. I had had enough of living my life on other people's terms. London might not be too far from home, but it was the first step of the journey. And one step at a time was all I could take.

Abby

Half an hour later, Abby let herself in to her house. Roseanna will not be back until later, and the twins are at rugby training camp. She has not organised anything for dinner, but there is always plenty of food in the house and everyone is well able to fend for themselves. She will suggest to Edward that they go out somewhere local, just the two of them, for a bite to eat – maybe test the water.

Then she smells it from the hall, the unmistakable aroma of roast chicken, and she follows it all the way to the kitchen, where Edward and Sheila are sitting over the remains, enjoying a glass of wine.

'Where on earth did you get to?' says Sheila.

'I was out.'

Sheila's mouth clamps shut.

'I was going to suggest,' Abby looks at Edward, 'that we go out for a bite to eat.'

'Oh there's no need for that now,' says Sheila. 'I went out myself and got a chicken, we've had a lovely roast dinner with all the trimmings, haven't we, Edward?'

'Yes, it was lovely.'

'There's plenty left, Abby.' Sheila gestures to the stove. 'I kept a warm plate in the oven, on the off-chance you might eventually show up.'

Abby ignores this and says to her husband. 'Pity, maybe we can go out tomorrow then. I'll book the Indian.'

'I can't, I'm afraid,' Edward replies, checking his iPhone. 'I'm away tomorrow, I'll be gone until Thursday – the Atlanta conference.'

'I thought Sarah was going to that.' Sarah is Edward's chief nurse at the clinic.

'She was, but her daughter's sick. She doesn't want to leave her.'

'Well, that's that, then,' says Abby. She takes the plate from the oven and removes the tin foil covering. Roast chicken is one of her favourite dinners, but somehow she has lost her appetite.

Sheila makes a great show of getting up from the table to clear the plates.

'Sit down, Sheila,' Edward says, jumping up to take them. 'I won't have you clearing up after cooking that lovely dinner. Allow me.'

Sheila sits down again. 'Well, isn't that nice of you. You're a real gentleman, Edward.'

This is said innocently. But as she looks at her mother, Abby sees triumph in the curve of Sheila's smile.

Diana

It is Tuesday evening, and I am finally home after a long day at the studio. We are all clustered around the TV for what has become crucial viewing in our house.

In a few moments I will have to leave, to go for dinner in my parents' house but, for now, I listen to the excited comments from my children and the obvious pride in their voices as they watch their father.

The presenter talks intently to camera. He is bending down, on one knee, a consoling arm on the shoulder of the man he has just spoken with, who is sitting on the pavement, leaning against a lamppost, huddled in rugs, a woolly hat pulled down over his head.

Presenter, wrapping up the segment, 'This is Rob, and this is where you'll find him, propping up a lamppost. Hoping, if he's lucky, that someone might take the time to buy him a cup of coffee. Or, if it's a good day, that he'll cadge a couple of cigarettes, maybe collect enough change to make it to the shelter, get a bed for the night. Ordinary things that you and I take for granted.'

Camera pans across to Rob, who looks up at him and nods in agreement.

The presenter continues, 'There are a lot of Robs out there at the moment, hungry, cold and without any place to call home. Sometimes, the only difference between them and you is an unlucky break. That's how easy it is to fall through the cracks – and become one of "them".'

There is a close-up of presenter looking grim. 'This is Greg O'Mahony, coming to you live from the Streets of Dublin.'

I watch, from my living room, as the camera lingers on the angles of my husband's attractive, concerned face, before the screen fades to black and the credits roll.

I am not sure exactly how it happened, but, somehow, in the past few weeks Greg has ended up presenting a reality TV show that has become a household hit. *The Streets of Dublin* is the brainchild of an art director he used to work with in the advertising agency, who is trying out his directing talents. Greg gets to be the front man. One of the many courses he undertook during the year (television presenting, two hours every Tuesday evening in the Irish Academy of Television) has paid off. Basically, they go around Dublin talking to the unemployed, the dispossessed, the homeless – they edit the footage and write a script around it. It is basic stuff, but whether it is an idea whose time has come or the morbid curiosity that reality TV generates, it has become insanely popular in a very short space of time. The ratings are going through the roof and Greg, as they say, gives good interview. He has found his niche, he is a natural, he has a gift for interviewing without sounding patronising or irritating. It also helps that he is easy on the eye. He has become a small-screen media star. My husband is the new Bob Geldof!

Of course everyone has been very nice about it, very supportive. Vonnie and Abby were the first to congratulate us. Abby and Edward sent a huge bouquet of flowers, and Vonnie invited me to lunch up in Dublin Castle to celebrate. And I'm pleased for Greg, I really am – so pleased – but I can't go along with all the bravado either, all the false 'I'm back in the saddle, watch out here I come, I'm on a roll,' Greg-style PR. Because the fact is that he isn't making any money out of it. The television station concerned has taken it on as a trial pilot, and the small amount he's getting is ploughed straight into editing and production costs, which means I am still left shouldering our financial burdens.

The other day, when I went to one of the women's shelters to do hair and make-up, all any of them could talk about was Greg O'Mahony. How gorgeous he is, what a caring person he must be, what a sense of humour he has. They didn't realise I was married to him, of course, and I didn't feel the need to point it out. I thought, instead, how ironic it is that while I have been giving my time and expertise freely for the past ten years, it is Greg who is hailed as the new local hero. I wanted to say *you should try living with him,* but that would have sounded churlish and bitter – feelings, I am aware, that are making themselves known to me with alarming regularity.

'Are you sure you won't come along? Change your mind?' I ask, although I already know the answer.

'No.' Greg stretches his arms behind his head, then stands up, looking purposeful. 'I've got to meet the guys later for an editing session. We've got some really interesting material for the next tranche. I'll wait until you get back before I leave, tell them I said hi.'

'Sure,' I say.

'Mum?' Sophie says. 'Don't forget to remind Gran about the vintage dress she has for me.'

'I won't,' I smile. 'See you later, I won't be late.'

I try to see my parents every Tuesday. It has become a ritual, this weekly supper they insist on. In the beginning, Greg used to come too and, when they were younger, we brought the kids but these days, with everybody's diverging interests and schedules, it's usually just me who pops around. They are getting older now, and the realisation that they won't be around forever is constantly perched on my shoulder. Greg laughs at me for worrying about them, saying they will outlive us both, but lately I have noticed a difference in them, a sort of melancholy has enveloped them, and I find it unsettling.

I get the Dart to Silversands station. My parents' house is about two streets away from where Vonnie is staying and, if I have time, I might call in to see her afterwards. I could do with a proper chat. It's not that I can't talk to Abby, of course I can, I do it all the time, but Vonnie has done so much work on herself, and seems so transformed, so confident, I'd really like to sit down and thrash a few things out with her, get her opinions, about me, my life, where it's all going. Meeting up with her and Abby is great, but I'd forgotten the calm, quiet, wisdom Vonnie always used to have, and obviously still does (she was the one we used to always turn to for advice). I was just so thrown by her outer transformation, I forgot how soothing talking to her could be. I make a mental note to take her up on her invitation to lunch in the Chester Beatty Library as soon as I can.

As I arrive at the pretty terraced villa where my parents now live, my mother answers the door before I even ring the bell.

'I thought I saw someone coming up the path,' she says, breezily. And I lean in to kiss her. 'We don't get many visitors these days so I guessed it had to be you.' Her smile has a girlish quality about it, although now in her late seventies, my mother's face, still beautiful, is lined. When in repose, in the odd moments I catch her off guard, I notice she wears a resigned expression that I used to think of as pensiveness, but now I sometimes wonder about that.

You never really do know your parents, do you? Not as real people, not as adult to adult. Even in moments of great honesty, mutual openness or attempted intimacy, the protective gauze that binds the parent–child relationship together serves to soften edges of truths elders may want to share but fear youth may not be ready to shoulder. And, to them, we are always young. I know that, now I have my own children. That's just the way it is. We all want to protect our children – from hurt, from the world, from themselves.

When I was young, just a kid, I got it into my head that my mother didn't like me. I particularly resented her for sending me away to boarding school, which I unfairly blamed her for. This was due in a large part to the heroic adoration I held my father in (probably still do). He had a very unfair advantage over her in that respect. My father was, without doubt, the head of the family in all things, but he left it to my mother to dispense the day-to-day disciplines, preferring to be the bearer of good tidings and, of course, his own wisdom, his particular take on life. Later, of course, I realised my mother loved me and my sister devotedly. She just never got much of a chance to shine as a parent when Dad was around. Now that I'm a mother myself, I can understand what she sacrificed for us in playing 'bad cop'. It's not a role any of us want thrust upon us.

All the same, my mother is not quite telling the truth. They have plenty of visitors. She and my father lead a very active, albeit retired, life. In fact, I'm not sure what, exactly, they have retired from. Dad was and is a well-respected art critic and collector. Officially he is retired, but unofficially still writes for the odd periodical, still ventures his opinions to trusted colleagues and old friends, still visits his old club. Art has been his life's work, his passion, and, happily, a subject he can continue to keep abreast of indefinitely, albeit in a more sedate fashion.

My mother, too, studied art history. She met my father at the Sorbonne, where she was studying for the summer. She had intended to return to the small town in County Kerry she called home to teach. But what followed was a torrid romance, and my father, unwilling to lose this shy but head-strong Irish girl who had won his heart, made the ultimate sacrifice a Frenchman can make. After six months of daily written love letters, he resigned himself to the fact that she would never move to Paris and, instead, he came to set up house and home in Ireland. Dublin had to be their home, that was his only stipulation. He was not ready for life in rural Ireland, and it certainly would not have been a suitable base for his work, although we spent many happy holidays in Ballyvaughneen, my mother's family home. My father would leave us there for the summer, and come down from Dublin every weekend to join us, returning to work on the Monday, except for the two weeks he would spend full-time with us.

'He's inside,' my mother says, inclining her head towards my father's study. 'He's a bit low lately. It'll do him the world of good to see you.'

'Can I give you a hand?' I ask, handing her the freesias I know are her favourites.

'No, it's all under control.' She smiles. 'And, thank you, you shouldn't have. Let me get you a glass of wine.' I follow her into the kitchen. 'We'll be eating in about ten minutes.'

I take my glass of wine into the study, where Dad is sitting in his favourite winged armchair, a book on his lap, staring into space. When I come in, he starts, repositions his reading glasses and turns a page in the book as if he has been reading. It is one of those moments I am encountering with increasing regularity, when one or either of my parents suddenly appears frail or vulnerable to me, and I feel both angry and afraid. Anger towards my sister, who blithely ignores the very obvious signs of increased fragility on their part and anger, in general, that encroaching old age is slowly but surely diminishing these two stalwarts of my life. The fear I cannot even think about – what shall I do without them? They have always been part of the story, my life story. I have always been able to rely on them, particularly my father, to help me construct a better script, rewrite passages I might have skipped entirely or taken too quickly. Without them, I am not sure of the plot that lies ahead or how it will unfold. I am thinking, in particular, of my marriage.

I drop a kiss on my father's head before he can go through the motions of getting up to greet me. At eighty-three, he is still a handsome man and still, of course, dresses immaculately in his fashion. Today he is wearing an olive-green linen shirt, matching corduroy trousers, with turn-ups, and his signature silk cravat with a paisley pattern. On his feet, red socks and brown suede loafers.

When I was younger, my friends used to tease me about the long-running Renault advertising campaign featuring the lovely Nicole and her dashing Papa that first aired in 1991, comparing me and Dad to the fictional father and daughter who drove around having romantic adventures in their matching Renault Clios. What a difference twenty years can make, I think now.

'Diana,' he says, '*ma jeune fille*. How lovely to see you.'

I sink into the chair opposite him and relax in the familiar surroundings of faded elegance. Not ones for unnecessary purchasing, my parents' house is filled with furniture, paintings and *objets* from previous houses and incarnations – even the thickly interlined silk curtains have been remade by my mother to fit the lower, wider windows. Yet every single item looks as though it were handpicked for its place and function in every room throughout the house. That, my mother tells me, is the evidence of 'good taste'. She has always had a good eye, but claims it wasn't until she met my father that she really developed any real style either in her dress sense or home decorating skills – neither of us believes her. My father, in fact, has said many times that apart from her fresh-faced good looks, it was her flair for colour and many ingenious ways with a headscarf that entranced him, quite apart from her gentle but wickedly observant wit.

Dinner is fillet steak done just the way I like it, medium rare, with baked potatoes and salad. Simple fair, but delicious, and I am hungrier than I think. Washed down with a nice Bordeaux and followed by baked apples with spiced cream, I feel warm and satisfied.

'How is Greg?' my mother asks.

'He's fine.' I am noncommittal.

'It's been a while since we've seen him now.'

I wondered how my mother had had held off asking until now, even with her innate tact. My father is watching me over the rim of his coffee cup.

'He's very busy with his new programme,' I tell them. 'The hours are very unpredictable. I hardly know when I'll see him myself.'

'Is he making any money at it?' Dad cuts straight to the chase.

'Not yet, these things take a while apparently.'

'You look tired,' Mum says, the very words I don't need to hear.

'That's because she is working too hard,' Dad shrugs. 'I don't understand how neither of my daughters could manage to find a man who would support them – how hard can it be?'

'I love my work. You know I do,' I protest. This is the closest I can get to defending Greg to my father, who has always been silently disapproving of him. Even when Greg was creative director at the agency, Dad dismissed advertising as being for failed would-be artists and writers – not a popular opinion, not even in France. But my father would have criticised any man his daughters became involved with (my mother reassured me on this score). It's just the way he is, protective and a tad possessive of his darling girls. If it hadn't been for Mum, and my sister's headstrong streak, I don't think we'd ever have got to date at all. Poor Dad had harboured hopes of marrying us off to dashing Frenchmen, preferably equipped with a chateau or vineyard.

'Of course you do,' Mum says. 'But Dad's right, you work too hard. Weren't you thinking of scaling back. I thought you wanted to—'

'Of course she wanted to,' Dad interjects. 'But how can she when her husband has taken it upon himself to retire? *I* do more work than he does.'

My father is warming to his theme, getting worked up. For someone who taught me to be practical, competent and, above all, financially independent, I wonder why it bothers him so much that I am all of these things. It is not the theory, but the practice, that seems to rankle. For all his protests at being open-minded and liberal, when it comes to family life, and women in general, my father is pretty old fashioned. He is adamant that a man should support his wife and the family home, and that a woman should raise her children and take care of her husband. It worked for him and Mum, but things (I have pointed out many times) have changed a little in that respect. It annoys me, though, more than usual, although I am well used to his opinions. I know why, too. It is because he is right about me, on this occasion at any rate.

My father knows me inside out and I could never fool him. But I cannot let him know that, at least I cannot verify it. He may well be entitled to think it, but I will not confirm it. I have some pride left. I cannot let them know that I ache with tiredness these days. And, tired though I am, that I wake up on the dot of three a.m. every morning, to hear Greg, asleep, breathing peacefully beside me. My job is the easy part – at least *that* is something I can do with my eyes shut. But there are other things I cannot shut them to, like the fact that business, although steady, has decreased considerably. I am wrestling with the agony of having to let one or even two dearly loved members of my team go. And, for the first time in my life, we are in arrears with the lease – nothing half the country isn't going through, too, but my husband's untroubled attitude to the situation is what's doing my head in. All he cares about is *The Streets of Dublin* – his new baby. What he studiously fails to realise is that we too may be joining the people that live on them, if he doesn't wake up and smell the coffee.

Most of all, I am tired of always, *always*, having to be the responsible one. I didn't sign up for this, you know. When I met Greg I was independent, free, a bit of a wild child. He was too – that's what attracted me to him. I never saw us as what we have become, a couple stifled by our own lack of ability to adapt and grow together. Any family can ill-afford one irresponsible parent, but two is the death knell. So a couple of years into our marriage I was forced to grasp the nettle. We had two small children and Greg's lack of any career longevity or staying power meant I had to step up to bat.

'The Organiser', Greg began calling me then, teasingly.

'I'll check with The Organiser,' he used to say to his mates if he was asked to anything. I often wonder now if he secretly meant 'The Controller'. That is what he said when we had our most recent row. 'Your problem, Diana, is that you're a control freak. Always have and always will be.'

That is the trouble when you marry someone who is charming but irresponsible. You can't win. They expect you to keep everything happening smoothly – bills are paid, holidays booked, meals cooked, children organised and their social diary kept up to date too. Life must not, under any circumstances, interfere with their creative pursuits. In return, you get fun, spontaneity, wit and charm, oh, and the envy of other women who think your husband is hot. Entertaining though these are, none of these qualities will pay the bills. Or keep you warm when you are sick, or calm you when you are tired and worried, as I am now. And if you protest, query or, God forbid, question the sanity of some of the more alternative projects they become enamoured of, you are labelled a control freak.

'More coffee?' Mum asks.

'No thanks,' I say, 'I'd better get going. Thanks for dinner, it was lovely.'

'Oh, and tell Sophie I've found that 1950s cocktail dress she was interested in, it was packed away in a trunk in the attic. I'm just having it cleaned.'

'She'll be thrilled,' I say, feeing immediately guilty. 'Come for dinner next week and you can give it to her then.' Mum and Dad adore their grandchildren, but getting everyone around a table these days can take quite some doing, especially Sophie, whose social life is unpredictable to say the least and who conveniently forgets to tell me any of her arrangements until about five minutes before she leaves for them. She gets that from her father, and I'm not even going to think about Greg and dinner right now.

'Give me a ring later,' Mum says as they see me to the door. I kiss them goodbye, and wave as their faces disappear behind the front door. I know what they will be saying, as I hurry to the Dart. My father will be saying that Greg should have at least come to pick me up, and come in for a coffee, that he is not taking enough care of me, that he does not deserve me. My mother will tell him not to worry, that Greg and I have made it through this far and that we're just going through a rough patch. All marriages do, she has always told me, but I never saw any rough patches with her and Dad.

On the way home, I think about Vonnie, and how she seems to have really found herself, turned her life around, how happy she seems with her circumstances, in her skin – *bien dans sa peau*, as the French say. I am happy for her, truly I am, but I cannot help thinking that the opposite is happening to me. That I am anything *but* comfortable in my skin at the moment, that life as I knew it has changed irrevocably, and this change, when it happened, was so insidious that I hardly noticed, until it had wound its way into my marriage and my home. Or was I simply not paying attention? Being too caught up in myself? I don't think so, but then I don't know what to think about anything anymore.

The Affair

*T*he deceit is the hardest thing to live with. She is bound by it, suffocated, even before the guilt strikes. It is like being two separate people. She feels fractured, divided, warped. Loyalty becomes a twisted word, bent at will to protect her family, her lover, herself. She cannot even tell her friends, especially not her friends. She must protect him — and protect them from the reproachful knowledge she carries within herself day and night. She wonders sometimes what they would think if they knew. Would they judge her? Hate her? Pity her?

The strain is getting to her. It always does eventually. It has been five years now, five blissful, agonising, ecstatic, tormented years. They have finished it several times throughout those years, vowed to stay apart, to stop this insanity, but the madness always wins. They are like a tornado together, gathering speed, greedily consuming everything in their path.

Even though when they are apart stillness is restored, sanity regained, for a few weeks, maybe even a month, the lack, the absence, the utter abyss of a life without him threatens to destroy her.

She loves him beyond reason. And still she feels unable to leave. How can she? She has almost worked up the courage, once or twice, to say it, but the words, however couched, resonate with cruelty. 'I'm in love with someone else, I need to be with him. I'm leaving you . . .'

But they cannot go on like this. He has made it clear — even if she will, he will not. He will not force her to choose, he *understands how hideously difficult it is for her. But he has to think of his own life . . . he has waited five years, but now he has given her an ultimatum. When the time comes, he will move on, with or without her, even though it tears him apart, even though he tells her, no matter what, she will always be in every breath he takes.*

July 2011

Jake

It was just as well I was living in Los Angeles when Vonnie and I got together because, right from the start, I found it hard to stay away from her. In the beginning, I told myself it was just infatuation. She was so different from any woman I'd ever been involved with (and there'd been more than a few over the years). I'd never before felt the need to settle down, much less slow down.

I was the kind of guy you really didn't need to meet if you were thinking of weddings and babies – and whatever they said, sooner or later that's what all the women I ever knew wanted, no matter how much they'd pretended otherwise. And they had every right to want it, it just didn't interest me and I didn't want to waste their time. Anyway, who in their right mind would choose a war correspondent to have a relationship with? I hardly knew what country I'd be showing up at never mind what day of the week, and I didn't want it any other way. But then fate intervened.

I was still recovering from surgery to my injured leg when I met Vonnie, so I had to stay put in one country for a while, which wasn't something I was ever very good at. Now I thank God every day that that injury came my way. If it hadn't, I don't like to think where my life might have ended up – though the way I was headed, it wouldn't have been pretty, I can tell you that much. Looking back, I can see so clearly now that Vonnie was the turning point for me. She was the internal compass I could never seem to access, the gentle brake to my constant acceleration. Wanting to get to know her made me pause and, almost without realising it, I found myself getting to a place where I could slow down just enough to glimpse the sweetness of a life that was less driven, less frenetic, a life where it was possible to maybe contemplate not running. But that would all come later. In those early days we were both caught up in the heady delight of discovering one another. As usual, I charged right ahead, too drunk with exhilaration and wonder to reflect even briefly on whether or not this was a good idea, whether or not I could really show up for this woman, really be there for her, because Vonnie, I was soon to learn, hid a lot of hurting behind a fiercely independent facade.

She lived alone and worked alone and wasn't entertaining any thoughts about changing the status quo. She didn't say much about her family either. She mentioned a sister once, briefly, that they were never close and had gone their own ways a long time ago. And there appeared to have been some kind of falling out with her parents. Whatever it was, she was adamant she was better off without them all. She certainly didn't seem to miss them.

Yet I knew instinctively that Vonnie was a woman who needed to belong to someone more than she needed to breathe. She just didn't know it yet. That was part of what made her such a wonderfully alluring contradiction to me. I knew for sure that she had a story, even if it was one she wasn't ready to share with me. But that was okay, we all have stories, and I wasn't in any rush. She would tell me when she was good and ready. In the meantime, there were more important things to concentrate on, like learning every little thing about her that I could, and strenuously telling myself that I was not falling in love, even though I was living for the weekends when I would see her.

I would get a flight to San Luis Obispo on a Friday

evening, or as early as I could, and get the red eye back to LA Monday morning. The minute that plane touched down in SLO County, my heart began to beat faster. We would get off the plane, stroll outside, weary commuters all, smell the grass, feel the warm air on our skin, and then I would see her, waiting for me, and I would be taken by surprise every time for just a second – not just because she was more beautiful than I remembered from the week before, but because the minute I took her hand in mine and looked at her, I could feel a connection that went way beyond any words.

The time always went too quickly. There was plenty to do in Morro Bay and the surrounding county, if you were so inclined, it was a nature lover's paradise. It was equally perfectly suited to doing nothing. Mostly we'd go for a quiet dinner, sometimes we'd do the Embarcadero Art Walk, where waterfront art galleries held open evenings every first Friday. Saturdays, depending on the weather, we'd go hiking, visit a vineyard or spend the day at one of the beaches along that glorious eighty miles of coastline. Sundays we'd be lazy, go for brunch at one of the local inns, or drive to the Mission, which San Luis Obispo is named for. Vonnie loves that place, and I can understand why.

The old church and surrounding gardens are pretty special. I'm not religious, but it's an interesting spot. San Louis Obispo was the fifth Californian Mission founded by Franciscan Father Junipero Serra on the first of September in 1772. Not impressive by European standards, I know, but, if you're American, that's *old*. Father Serra was following orders from Spain to bring the Catholic faith to the natives of Alta California, and that's what he did. I have a healthy respect for Catholic missionaries (some of my ancestors were Creoles), seeing as, along with other notorious achievements, they are responsible for some of the most esteemed alcoholic

beverages known to man – Benedictine, Dom Perignon and
Green Chartreuse to name a few (the recipe for the latter
being so guarded that apparently only three monks at any
one time in the order ever know it, until one of them dies
and it is passed to his successor). Not a lot of people realise
the tradition of wine making in California originally started
with the missions, the first being Mission San Miguel. In my
opinion, that alone was a commendable contribution to
modern American society. But I digress, it's the journalist in
me, I'm awash with obscure facts. As I was saying, Vonnie
loves the place, she even goes to mass there occasionally, says
she gets a peaceful feeling when she's in the old church, with
its big oak doors, the old Spanish chandelier hanging and
the religious oil paintings that hail all the way from Lima in
Peru. Afterwards, she says she sometimes talks to the local
priest, who had an Irish grandfather. He likes to stroll with
her under the outdoor archway covered with wine grapes (I
suspect he's in love with her too). I asked her if she went to
church because it reminded her of home and she said it
couldn't have been more different, and that was why she
liked it so much. I left it at that, but all the same I was
intrigued. Home certainly didn't conjure up any good vibes
for Vonnie.

Of course, pretty soon, weekends weren't enough, no
amount of time was, I wanted to be with her twenty-four-
seven. I wanted her to be the first thing I saw when I woke
up, and the last thing I looked at before I went to sleep. It
was simple and selfish, that's what love reduces us to, craving
the beloved, the object of our desire. True devotion, and the
myriad of extraordinary lengths we will go to to achieve and
maintain it, are what make up the real tests of love, the ones
that separate women from girls and make men out of boys.
But that doesn't figure in the beginning, in the first giddy
flush, which is just as well, because learning to love someone,

really love them, can be tough. But like I said, I wasn't thinking along those lines back then.

When I think of that time, I think of blues, a million blues – the rolling blue of the sky, the deep blue of the ocean and Vonnie in blue. She wears a lot of that colour and it suits her. There was a lot of blue stuff in her house too, throws, cushions, rugs. Her style is mostly boho, except when she dresses up for a business meeting with a prospective editor or highbrow publication, and then she has this pared down elegant thing going on – those deceptively simple little dresses, all fitted and ladylike, worn with heels, and she has no idea how goddamn sexy she looks. I have real trouble letting her out the door dressed like that, because I immediately want to undress her, and I am happy to say I have managed that too, on the odd occasion.

At any rate, I fell in love with her, big time. I was a marked man from the beginning, and no one was happier about that than me.

Over a plate of guacamole and margaritas in September, I asked her if she would consider living with me, moving in together, my place or hers – commuting wasn't a problem for me, I pretty much worked my own schedule anyway, and my days at the frontline were losing their attraction. I was planning to work on another book, seeing as the first one had been well received by the critics.

To my great joy she said yes, without missing a beat. We decided to stay in Morro Bay, in her little house, and I would rent my place out. To celebrate we had more margaritas. Then we dropped by Rollers, and a bunch of her friends joined us and helped us celebrate some more. The old surfer dude, Luke, who ran the place, took me aside and said very amiably that if I ever hurt Vonnie he would track me down and break my neck. Something about the look in his eyes told me he meant it. Vonnie just has that effect on men. She brings out our protective streak. I assured him nothing was further from my mind.

'You're a lucky man,' he growled, slapping me on the back.

'Tell me about it,' I said, and ordered another round of drinks.

Later that night we made love on the roof terrace, under a crescent moon and a clutch of stars.

In bed, I fell asleep watching her, the rise and fall of her breathing the only lullaby I needed.

This is it, I remember thinking. *This is as good as it gets. Don't screw it up.*

And I was right. That was the beginning of the good years.

Angela

The years have been kind to me in many ways. I'm the first to acknowledge that. I have a good marriage to a good man, no financial concerns, no elderly parents to worry about – and no children. It could have been very different, but I try not to think about that. That kind of thinking can destroy a woman. I've survived this long, and I've no intention of going under now. Occasionally, though, I allow myself to remember the halcyon days, all three of them in that very special weekend way back in 1965.

'Hey, Angie, wanna beer?' I caught the bottle my distant cousin Bill threw me deftly. We had driven to the beach in Dennis Port, Cape Cod, in a jeep borrowed from a friend whose parents were on vacation. There were twelve of us, in three cars, a convoy headed to the Cape, escaping parents and a sweltering weekend in Boston.

I had been in America two whole weeks, and I felt as if I was on another planet; compared to home, it might as well have been.

After my carefully written letter earlier that year, plaintively illustrating my great desire to visit my relatives and further my education, the unthinkable had transpired and they had written to my parents expressing their fondest wish that I should come and spend the summer with them. A plane ticket had also been included, much to the consternation of my father – 'We're not paupers!' – the value of which I readily assured him I would spend the summer working off.

My mother, bless her soul, thought it a grand idea. She had already married off my sister Carmel to Colm, a local doctor, and they had just had their first baby, a little girl called Kate. Carmel liked the idea of being a doctor's wife, I think she felt it gave her a certain status in the community and, God knows, she was organised enough to run a surgery blindfolded for half the country if she put her mind to it.

Carmel was very pretty, there was no disputing that but, beside me, men just didn't seem to notice her, including her own husband. I didn't care or get it back then. But now I know what the vital difference was – I had sex appeal, oodles of it. And, as anyone who has it will tell you, sex appeal has nothing whatsoever to do with sex itself. That's just an accidental consequence that usually follows suit, as I was to learn to my very considerable cost.

But that day, that first day of that glorious weekend, nothing could have been further from my mind. I was seventeen, and on the biggest adventure of my life. Three whole days away with my cousins and their friends, unsupervised. Well the older guys were in charge, of course, and took it quite seriously, in fact my two cousins, Bill and Wayne, were almost too protective of me. That could have been to do with the fact that once I had arrived, and word got out that the guys had a 'smokin' hot' cousin from Ireland staying with them for the summer, a steady stream of male callers began to appear at the house on mindlessly innocent pretexts, until the guys had to tell them to get lost. Their younger sister,

Marie, who was a few years older than me, wasn't any too happy about it. I could tell her nose was out of joint even though she was icily if studiously polite to me. I didn't care. I had made it to America, the land of the free, and I was going to enjoy every blessed second of it.

The minute we got to the beach, I went for a swim and was just out of the water, dripping from head to toe and ravenous for food. I caught the beer bottle, grabbed a towel and wrapped it around me, then I opened the bottle on the edge of a rock, a trick I had mastered with great difficulty and not a little practice with some of the local lads back home. Marie looked disapprovingly at me from under her lashes although she pretended to busy herself with unloading our picnic basket. She opened a bottle of Coca-Cola, found a straw to put in it and sipped demurely. Clearly, she thought it most unladylike that I should be drinking beer at all, never mind straight from the bottle.

'Don't you want to cover up, Angela?' she asked, pointedly looking at my new two-piece bikini I had bought in Filene's Basement.

'No, I'm fine thanks.' I said breezily, getting to my feet. 'In fact, I think I'll go for a run along the water's edge so I can dry off.'

'Great idea, I'll come too,' said Brent Smithson, who, it was plain for all the world to see, Marie had a giant crush on, though it didn't seem to be reciprocated. Judging by the look on her face, the thought of him accompanying me on my run was an idea to be discouraged at all costs.

'But we're just about to eat, Brent,' she wheedled, 'I was counting on you helping to bring the drinks down in the cooler. There's a lot more beer to get through,' she added slyly.

Brent looked torn.

'I won't be a minute, Brent,' I said. 'There's absolutely no need for you to come with me, I'll be back before you know it.' And I set off at a reasonably slow jog, much to Marie's relief.

The day was beautiful. At half past twelve, the sun was high in the sky and hot, but a refreshing sea breeze was whipping the few wisps of cloud across a blue sky that seemed to stretch forever. I revelled in my new-found freedom and almost had to pinch myself to believe I was really here, that I had really escaped. To my right, waves pounded the shore, and to my left, the dunes rose in orderly ranks behind the sun-bleached boardwalk.

By the time I got back, a few more people had joined us, and the guys had set up an impromptu barbecue that was turning into a regular beach party. I helped myself to some food, got another beer and sat down beside the rocks to eat. Soon, although I could have done without it, I was surrounded on all sides by guys, who sat down to join me and ply me with offers of food or drink. It was a bit like the barbecue scene at Twelve Oaks in *Gone with the Wind*, when Scarlett was besieged by hopeful beaus, although I was rather more scantily clad. Declining their generous offers and answering their questions as best I could, I looked around distractedly to try and catch Bill's or Wayne's eye and make my escape. That's when I saw him, and suddenly everything else receded into the background – voices, faces, the feeling of the sand beneath my feet – and I studied him, every gesture, every minute detail, as if I somehow knew I would have to remember this moment, frame by frame, for as long as I lived. He was tall, about six foot three, with an incredible body (we were all in our swimwear, remember), light-brown, sun-bleached hair and a handsome chiselled face. He was talking and laughing with Bill, although he caught my eye once or twice, and there was a definite flicker of interest. I had to meet him.

'Excuse me,' I said hurriedly, getting to my feet on the pretext of having second helpings.

'But you've still got a half-full plate,' said a muscular but observant law student.

I ignored him, naturally, and dodging around by the board-walk, I found a litter bin and discreetly emptied the remaining food he'd been referring to. Then, taking a deep breath, I strolled towards the trestle table, making sure that Bill and his companion were right in my pathway.

'Hey, Angie,' said Bill, obligingly, putting an arm around my shoulders, 'Gus, have you met my Irish cousin, Angie? She's staying with us for the summer.'

So that was what the vision was called – Gus. I rolled the name around my mind, silently trying it out in a myriad of different inflections, all of which sounded perfect. He was talking to me now, this Gus, and looking vaguely amused.

'You're really Irish? That's cool.' His eyes met mine and then briefly flickered over my body and I shivered despite the warmth of the day.

We chatted for a while although I could hardly tell you what I said. I must have answered the usual questions, made some sort of acceptable conversation, but all I remember is gazing at him. He was super fit, with broad shoulders, rippling muscles and long, tanned legs. When he smiled, he reminded me of a better looking version of Bobby Kennedy, with the same cheeky grin and mouthful of white teeth. While we were talking, Bill took my plate to refill it, and I hardly noticed until he was back a few moments later.

'Nice to see a girl with a healthy appetite.' Gus looked approvingly at the plate piled high with food that Bill handed to me.

'It's all this fresh air,' I lied. 'It's making me hungry. I'll have to watch it or I won't fit in to any of my clothes soon.'

'Shouldn't be a problem,' Gus said. 'You look pretty perfect without them.'

'Hey,' Bill laughed, as I blushed furiously, 'take it easy, Gus, that's my kid cousin you're talking to.'

But something in the way he was looking at me told me Gus didn't think of me as a kid at all. I tucked gamely into my second plate of food and tried to find out as much about him as I could. Bill tactfully left us alone, although he added as a parting shot, 'Don't believe a word he tells you, Angie, Gus is quite a lady killer.'

But I wasn't listening, I only had eyes for Gus. I learned he was the eldest of a family of five, and his parents were of Swedish origin; that would explain the stunning looks, I thought to myself. He had an easy, relaxed manner I found engaging and, despite his jocular exterior, there was a serious side lurking beneath, especially when he spoke about his family – I could tell they meant everything to him. 'How about you?' he asked, as we left the others and walked along the shore.

'There's not much to tell,' I shrugged. My life seemed so parochial compared with the kids out here, who all drove around in their own cars and seemed to have a freedom Irish young people could only dream of. 'There's just me and my older sister, Carmel, who's married with a baby girl, and my parents. We live in the countryside, on the coast in a place called Wicklow, about an hour outside Dublin.'

'I'd like to go to Ireland sometime,' Gus said thoughtfully. 'Maybe you can take me!'

I tried to imagine him at home, this glorious hunk of maleness, and failed. The girls would drop dead. He looked like a movie star, even beside the other American guys who all seemed to be good looking. It must be the mix of races, I decided, and the healthy outdoor way of life that was such a part of things. I loved America, I told him, and felt like I belonged there already, even though I'd only been there for a couple of weeks.

'Maybe you'll stay.' He smiled at me.

'I'll have to go back home after the summer, there's no way my parents would let me stay, but I intend to come back as soon as I can.' I couldn't even bear to think of going home.

'Then I'm sure you will. You seem like a girl who knows her own mind. I admire that.'

I wasn't used to being treated with this new-found respect, especially by a guy. At home most of the boys my age were just that – silly, spotty, tongue-tied kids – and the older, more confident men were married, although that never stopped them looking at me whenever they could get away with it, when their wives' backs were turned; some of them didn't even bother that much to conceal their interest. I hated it. And I hated the subsequent coolness with which the women treated me, even some of my parents' friends, I mean it was ridiculous! As if I was going to be interested in one of their doddery old men.

But everything was different here. Even though America was still reeling from the death of their beloved John F. Kennedy, it was still a country where anything seemed possible, a place where dreams could come true if you really wanted them enough and were prepared to work for them. Everyone was living for the moment, not with the past hovering over them like in Ireland, where the older generation in general, and my parents in particular, were still stuck in a hopeless rut that was positively Victorian.

Gus was older than me, twenty-two to my seventeen, but I told him I was nineteen, going on twenty. It made me feel more confident. He was a trained engineer and flying out to San Francisco where he would join up with his platoon who were off to somewhere called Saigon. 'Where's that?' I'd never heard of the place.

Gus laughed and swung me up in his arms, wading into the sea. 'That's what I like about you Angie, you're probably the only person on this side of the Atlantic who isn't obsessed with Saigon. For your information, it's in Vietnam,' he said, dropping me into the freezing water despite my screams of protest before diving under himself.

We swam out for a bit – I was a strong swimmer and could keep up with him easily – then we headed back, knowing the others would miss us. We had just reached the shore, and were wading in waist-high water, when I felt Gus's arm slip around me and he pulled me to him, before bending to kiss me. When I eventually came up for air, I felt dazed. No one had ever kissed me like that before. The couple of incidents I could remember were hastily orchestrated events, at local dances, fumbling efforts at best – and huge letdowns. What was all the fuss about? I had wondered then. Now I knew. Now I understood.

'Jesus, Angie,' he murmured. 'You're hotter than Ursula Andress in *Dr No* – way hotter.' And he kissed me again. I'm not sure how long we would have gone on for, I was dizzy with excitement and a surging feeling I had never experienced. I shivered, and it was nothing to do with the coldness of the water.

Gus pulled away reluctantly. 'C'mon, let's get you back. I don't want you to catch your death of cold out here.'

We walked back to the others, who had hardly noticed our absence, or, if they had, made no comment. The guys were busy setting up a game of volleyball and Gus went to join them. When the game started, the girls gathered round to watch admiringly and cheer. I was going to lie down and sunbathe, but I thought that might seem a little rude and standoffish, so I grabbed a Coke, pulled on a T-shirt and joined them. I mustn't have been able to take my eyes off Gus, because I heard Marie's voice murmuring in my ear.

'Don't get any ideas about Gus, Angie, he has a steady girlfriend, you know. Rumour has it they're about to get engaged any day now.'

I turned to her and smiled, even though my heart sank as I spoke. 'Well, isn't that just peachy!' I said, borrowing one of her more annoying expressions. 'I couldn't be more happy for him.' And I turned and walked away. I was shaken, but I wasn't going to let her see she had got to me. I'd been used to girls like Marie all my life. Gus might have had a girlfriend, I reasoned, in fact it would have been astonishing if he didn't, but he wasn't married, not yet anyway – and that made him fair game as far as I was concerned.

The next day I didn't see him, not on the beach at any rate. But that night there was a dance at the local yacht club and I was informed we were all going. I had got quite a lot of sun over the past couple of days and I tanned easily, but I took extra care all the same getting ready, washing my hair and blow-drying it straight and long in the current fashion. Luckily, I had brought one dress with me – a simple white cotton halter neck, and a pair of high strappy sandals to go with it. Wayne and Bill drove the short distance to the club, while Marie sat next to me in the back seat radiating resentment. I didn't know if her brothers were aware of the under-current of tension between us, but I made an effort to be particularly chatty and witty to cover up any bad vibes, which only made her scowl more.

When we got to the yacht club, the party was in full swing, with a band warming up to play and huge tables groaning with food. I still couldn't get used to the scale they did things on. I scanned the room quickly for Gus, but there didn't appear to be any sign of him. But pretty soon I had a group of eager admirers surrounding me, and a chorus of voices urging Wayne and Bill to introduce me. American men, it was refreshing to see, were not shy about coming forward when a pretty girl was involved. It made a nice change from Ireland where guys were too intimidated to approach me or, if they did, it was at the end of the night when they had drunk themselves senseless and were incoherent and swaying.

I was inundated with dance partners and was just taking a breather to sip a drink I had never heard of (I think it was a screwball) when I looked up and saw him, shouldering his way through the throng of people, steadily making his way over to me. Our eyes met and I immediately felt a bolt of excitement ripple through me.

'Hey! You look gorgeous,' he said, taking me by the elbow and steering me through to a quieter part of the room. 'I was afraid you wouldn't be here.'

'Why?' I asked, flirtatiously. 'What would you have done?'

'Well,' his eyes roved over me and he grinned, 'I'd have had to come and find you.'

'You weren't on the beach today.' I hadn't meant to say anything, I was going to play it cool and pretend I hadn't even noticed, but the words just tumbled out.

'I had some stuff to take care of back at my folks' place. My dad's old truck was acting up and I promised him I'd take a look at it; it turned out to be more work than I figured on. Believe me I'd rather have been at the beach.'

'Well, you're here now,' I said.

'Dance with me,' he said, as the band launched into a slow number. And when he took me in his arms and held me close, I wondered if he could hear the beating of my heart.

We danced together for the rest of the evening. Gus never left my side and although we were causing quite a lot of speculation, I didn't care. I was living for the moment, and I was right where I wanted to be.

'Let's get out of here, Angie. What do you say? And go some place quiet.'

I nodded, because I couldn't quite trust myself to speak.

Gus wanted to be alone with me. Gus took me by the hand and found Bill, my cousin. 'I'm taking Angie to the ice cream parlour, I'll take her home afterwards.'

Bill looked at us both, then asked me, 'You okay with that, Angie?'

'Sure,' I said. I was trying to sound nonchalant.

'Make sure you have her back before midnight, Gus, that's the curfew deal.'

'You have my word.'

Outside, Gus walked me to his car, which was a gorgeous red convertible, and opened the passenger door for me until I was comfortably inside.

'Wow,' I said. 'What a groovy car. What is it?' I knew men loved talking about cars and, besides, I couldn't think of anything else to say. Now that we were alone together, I was suddenly shy.

'It's a T-Bird,' he grinned, gunning the engine. Then, seeing my lack of comprehension, added. 'A Ford Thunderbird.'

'Oh, we have Fords at home too, but I've never seen one like this.' I sat back as we pulled out of the yacht club and on to the coast road, feeling a thrill of exhilaration as we roared away, the wind blowing my hair every which way, and I looked at Gus and laughed, as we sped along under a star-spangled sky.

I wanted to drive all night with him, but we really did go to the ice cream parlour. And I felt as if I was in an American television show, everything was just the same. We slid into a quiet booth and ordered the house special and coffees. A jukebox was playing in the corner, I remember that, crooning out some country song, romantic and plaintive. We talked and talked. I could have listened to him all night. Eventually, I asked him casually, 'Do you have a girlfriend, Gus?'

'Not anymore.' He looked me directly in the eyes and I felt my heart skip a beat.

'Since when?'

'Since yesterday. That's why I wasn't around. Fixing my father's truck was only part of the story. I had a long talk with her on the phone, she's at home in Connecticut, it was better to be straight with her.'

I wanted desperately to ask him what he had told her – had it been on account of meeting me? Did he feel the same way I did? That this was fate, that both our lives had been leading to this very moment, that nothing could have kept us apart.

'She must have been upset,' I ventured.

'Oh, Gracie'll be fine. She's a popular girl, we were college sweethearts for a while, but really the spark had gone, we wanted different things from life, we were just really good friends, but I could never have seen Gracie as an army wife.' He smiled and shook his head. 'She's an east coast society gal at heart. She'll find herself a nice WASP millionaire and everyone will be very happy.'

I didn't envy this Gracie her prospective 'WASP millionaire', whatever *that* meant. (I later discovered it stood for 'White Anglo-Saxon Protestant'; of course, I was so unbelievably green back then.) But, all the same, I felt sorry for her – for anyone who'd loved Gus only to lose him, well it didn't bear thinking about. I knew instinctively he'd broken up with her because of me, although he would never say that for fear of making me feel guilty, although I wouldn't have because I really and truly believed we were meant to be together. This was my knight in shining armour. Remember, I was only seventeen and, looking back, my natural sense of adventure was leading me way out of my depth.

Gus was as good as his word and had me back at the house well before midnight. In fact, I was disappointed; it was only eleven thirty, we could have had a whole half an hour more together. Looking up from the car, I saw that the light in the bedroom I had to share with Marie was on. Damn!

She was probably waiting up for me, probably spying from behind the lace curtain right now.

'What's the matter, sweetie?' Gus asked when he saw me scowling.

'Oh nothing, it's just that I was hoping Marie wouldn't be home. I have to share a room with her and let's just say I'm not her favourite person. In fact, I think she hates me, she's constantly on my case, no matter how nice I am to her.'

'That's because she's jealous of you, baby, all the girls are. There's not one of them can hold a candle to you, you've put their pretty noses out of joint. I don't notice any of the guys having a problem with you.' Gus's arm slid around my shoulders.

I smiled in the darkness. Gus sure knew how to make a girl feel good. 'She's probably spying on us right now, timing how long I stay out here in the car,' I grumbled.

'Then let's give her something to talk about,' he said, leaning in to kiss me – and I kissed him right back. We continued like that for quite a while, must have been fifteen or twenty minutes, until finally Gus pulled away and grinned ruefully. 'You are something else, Angie. I don't see how any man could trust himself around you.' He sighed and opened his door. 'C'mon, sweetheart, much as I would like to run away with you right now, I'd better see you safely to the door. I don't want your cousins coming after me with a shotgun.'

At the door, Gus said the words I'd been longing for. 'Can I see you tomorrow, Angie? It's my last day here and I'd really like to spend it with you.'

It was my last day on the Cape too, and I couldn't think of a better way to spend it. I wouldn't think beyond that, I couldn't. 'I'd love to spend the day with you, Gus.'

'Great, I was hoping you'd say that. I'll pick you up at ten, and I'll have a surprise for you. Make sure you bring a swimsuit and sneakers.' With that enigmatic comment he left me, sliding behind the wheel of the T-Bird and revving off into the night.

The house was quiet downstairs, and I went into the kitchen to pour myself a glass of water to take up to bed with me. Climbing the stairs, I braced myself to go into the room I shared with Marie, then paused, as I heard the unmistakable whine of her voice coming from Bill's room. I know I shouldn't have, but I had to listen, I couldn't help overhearing anyway.

'It's not right, Bill, it's just not right. I'm going to telephone Gracie tomorrow. The way Angie's behaving, well she's nothing but a tramp. There's no other word for it. I wish she'd never come here. I can't bear the thought of her staying for the rest of the summer. I'm going to talk to Mom and Dad about her.'

'Oh, come on Marie, the kid's just having a bit of fun. What's it to you anyway?'

It's something to me when she's stealing my best friend's boyfriend right from underneath our noses.'

'Gus has a say in this too you know.'

'Oh you men, you're all the same, of course you'd take his side. Well he's only using her, he knows he's leaving for Saigon, and she'll be back in Ireland. She can be as cheap and as fast as she likes with him, but it's not going to get her anywhere!'

'Then you have nothing to worry about, Marie, do you? For heaven's sake mind your own business and go to bed.'

I'd heard enough. I slipped quietly into our bedroom and hurriedly undressed. Luckily, I heard Marie go back downstairs, maybe she couldn't bear to face me either. I left the reading light on beside her bed and turned off my own, then snuggled down beneath the covers. So I was a tramp, was I? Cheap and fast? But I hadn't done anything, had I? I'd just responded to a guy who was drop-dead gorgeous and spent a little time with him. And he told me himself he'd finished with his girlfriend. If it was a guy doing the same, nobody would bat an eyelid. I pushed Marie's cruel words from my mind and thought instead about spending a whole day with Gus. And whatever she might think about me, there was absolutely nothing Marie could do about that.

The next morning I was awake bright and early, and giddy with excitement. I crept around the room like a mouse, trying not to wake Marie, who was a shapeless mound under the covers, and snoring lightly. I gathered the clothes I needed, and then headed for the bathroom to shower. I had my swimsuit and bikini, a pair of shorts and a T-shirt and a couple of towels. I wore my summer dress and my sneakers, just like Gus had told me. I figured I was ready for anything. Cape Cod was extremely casual dress-wise, even by Irish standards. In the kitchen, I fixed myself a good breakfast, just in case we might not be eating until a lot later. Then I sat outside on the rocker on the back porch and willed the minutes to go by. Judging by the lack of activity in the house, the others were enjoying a lie in. So I left a note for Bill, saying I'd be out for the day with Gus. Let Marie chew that one over and see what she makes of it, I thought grimly. Eventually, although it felt like an eternity, I heard Gus's car wheels crunch on the gravel and, grabbing my bag, I ran out to meet him.

'Well, aren't you a sight for sore eyes.' He jumped out of the car to take my bag.

'Where are you taking me?' I asked as we set off, the roof down and the radio blaring out a Beach Boys number.

'It's a surprise. You'll have to wait and see.'

We drove for a while, and when we reached West Dennis I thought it looked vaguely familiar, and I realised we were headed back to the yacht club where the dance had been last night.

'This is where we were last night,' I said.

'Yes, but today we're going sailing.' Gus patted my knee and grinned.

'Oh,' I said, trying to sound enthusiastic. It wasn't that I didn't enjoy sailing, I hadn't done very much of it, but I'd liked it, it was just that this sounded like it was going to be group activity and I had been so hoping to have Gus to myself all day. I had pictured a romantic picnic perhaps or a drive and a long walk. I certainly hadn't thought of any serious activity, and sailing could prove quite strenuous, if I remembered correctly. And, the thought occurred to me, there were bigger fish over here! Whales, and even sharks patrolled these waters on a regular basis. I swallowed briefly and fixed a smile on my face. Gus was an outdoor, sporty type, he wouldn't think much of a girl who was going to be wimpy about this, so I resolved to make the best of it.

We parked the car and got out, but instead of going into the club, Gus walked me around to the harbour side, where hundreds of boats were moored along the marina. So far so good. Then we took a turn to the left, and came to a stop before a beautiful motor boat.

'This is yours?' I asked.

'I wish.' Gus helped me aboard. 'It belongs to my uncle, but he allows me use it whenever I want.'

'When are the others coming?' I looked around.

'What others?' Gus seemed surprised. 'It's just you and me.' He suddenly looked concerned. 'Is that okay? I mean I thought, that is—'

'That's just perfect,' I reassured him. 'I didn't want to have to share you with anyone else on our last day here.' I said 'here' deliberately, because I couldn't even contemplate the idea of not seeing him again. I had to think of this as a beginning, not an end, or I would have fallen apart there and then.

Out in the bay, the weather was perfect. The sea was calm

beneath a cloudless sky and gulls laughed and swooped over-head. We dropped anchor, dived in for a swim, fooled around a bit, and felt like we were the only two people on the planet.

Gus hauled himself out before I did, and reached out to help me up the drop ladder. When I stumbled aboard, he caught me, and I fell into his arms laughing. We kissed then, and I could taste the salt and sunlight on his skin, and something else, something more urgent. I suppose I might have known then, had some sort of inkling, a vague memory of the kind of things the teachers warned us about – like giving in to corporeal urges, avoiding at all costs being alone with a man, none of whom were to be trusted to control themselves, but we, we girls were made of sterner stuff. Men, poor creatures, couldn't help themselves, but we women held the reins of power when it came to things carnal. We had to set the boundaries. It was all love, somewhere, like a distant drum beat in my mind, some limbic part of my brain warning me I was in danger, mortal danger, my very soul was at stake. But this ancient voice, wherever it came from, was no match for the present, more insistent one, alerting me to more pressing needs and pleasures that were being heaped, sensation upon delicious sensation, upon my dimming consciousness.

I would like to think that I said, 'stop', 'wait', 'don't', but I didn't. I remember lying, both of us, on the yellow-striped sun mattress that sat on the deck, I remember with the barest flick of a clip Gus undoing my bikini top, I remember wriggling out of my damp bikini bottoms, until we were together skin on skin. I remember how gentle Gus was with me, and I remember burning up with desire at his touch and longing for him. So much so that I put all thought of anything but that exact moment as far out of my mind as I could. I knew it was insanity, of course I did, but I was way beyond caring.

So we made love, with the intensity and eagerness of the

young people we were. 'I love you,' Gus said, over and over. 'You're incredible.'

And I believed him, because I had no other choice. I felt incredible, I felt loved, I felt as if my whole world had somehow shifted. Later we ate, Gus had brought a picnic lunch and a bottle of champagne and strawberries, which we fed each other in between kisses. We talked about the future, which seemed endless, the things we wanted to do, anything but Gus's leaving for San Francisco from where he would go to Saigon, or me going back to Ireland, which at that very moment seemed more unthinkable than going to the moon. Gus promised to write to me the minute he arrived; I would still be at my cousins' house for six more weeks which now, without him, seemed interminable. We went for a last swim, then turned back and headed for shore. I told Gus it had been the most perfect day of my life.

'We'll have lots more of those, Angie.' He squeezed my hand. 'I promise.'

I wanted to be happy, but a creeping sense of desolation was beginning to build inside me. We tied up the boat, gathered our stuff and headed back to the car; it was only four thirty in the afternoon, a perfectly respectable time to show up. The others would more than likely be at the beach, grabbing a final few rays before we all headed back to Boston the next day. Before we reached the beach house, Gus turned off into a small clearing and stopped the car so he could kiss me properly one last time. That was where we said our goodbyes. I was strong, I was determined not to cry. Gus cradled my head on his shoulder and told me that this was just the beginning. 'I'll think of you every single hour of every day, Angie.'

'Promise you'll write?'

'You know I will.'

And I did.

So I waved him off, cheerfully, because that was the way I wanted him to remember me, to think of me while he was on duty – upbeat and happy, not moping and miserable.

Inside the house, I hoped desperately to have it to myself; my illusions were shattered. I was hoping to go to my room or at least lock myself in the bathroom to shed the tears I had been so valiantly holding back. I was halfway up the stairs when Marie met me on the return. Something in her expression made me steel myself.

'Did loverboy give you a good send off?' she enquired icily.

'Gus and I went sailing, not that it's any of your business.'

'Oh, but it *is* my business, cousin Angela, especially when Gus happens to be the long-term boyfriend of one of my dearest friends.'

'Used to be, you mean.' My heart was beating double time but I was determined to stand my ground. 'Gus called his girlfriend yesterday and broke up with her.'

'Is that what he told you?' A supercilious smile played on Marie's mouth.

'That's what he told me.' I was tired now, weary from the emotions of the day and I just wanted to get in the bath tub.

'Strange then that Grace never received *that* telephone call.' Her eyes glittered as she studied me.

'What do you mean?'

'I mean Gus did call Gracie, just as he always does, every day he's away from her, but only to tell her how he missed her, how he wished she were here, oh, and how much he loved her of course.'

'That's a lie.'

'Is that so?' she looked at me pityingly. 'Face it, Angela, you're way out of your depth with Gus, you don't understand how relationships are conducted in this part of the world. Perhaps in *Ireland* (she made it sound like a dirty word), blow-ins like you think they can muscle in on any man in trousers and consider him fair game, but in America the girls men marry are the girls men respect. Whatever you and Gus have been getting up to on your sordid little excursions – he was only amusing himself with you, using you, to put it bluntly.' Here she paused to draw breath. 'Gus and Gracie will get married, you can count on it. His very career depends on it, and Gus is ultra ambitious; whatever he told you was just to keep you happy for the weekend. You know what men are like, surely? Anyway, if I were you, I wouldn't count on hearing from him any time soon. According to the guys, Gus was boasting about how easy you were – so, congratulations, Angela, in the space of – what, less than two weeks in Boston – you've got yourself a name. No one else will want you, unless it's for a series of cheap thrills. As far as I'm concerned, the sooner you get yourself back to Ireland the better. Frankly, we don't need your type around here.'

God, how I hated her at that moment, the prissy bitch! I could have hurled all manner of abuse at her, but something told me I would only be playing into her hands. I managed a tightly lipped, 'I'm sorry you feel that way, Marie. But I have no intention of cutting short my visit on either your or anyone else's whims. Now if you'll excuse me, I'd like to take a long bath.'

Once inside the bathroom, with the door locked and my small transistor radio playing, I felt safer and calmer. Marie's outburst had shaken me, but I knew where she was coming from – she was jealous of me, plain and simple. As for Gus and this so-called girlfriend Gracie, well, I knew who I believed, and time would fill in the other details. To be honest, I was far too overwhelmed to take everything in. I focused on the only lovely thing I could, which was our last heavenly day that we had just spent together, and the words of love Gus had whispered to me. He wasn't faking it, I knew that,

I was sure of it. I had to be, because otherwise the thought that I had just lost my virginity to a guy I might never see or hear from again who had a bona fide girlfriend was just too terrible to even contemplate.

Back in Boston, I tried to put the whole thing out of my mind. But of course that was useless, because I couldn't stop thinking about Gus. But I kept myself busy, played a lot of tennis and helped out my Aunt Nancy, who was very involved in the local women's association. It had been two weeks since the Cape Cod weekend, and so far no word from Gus, although I realised it was still early days. I was beginning to find the heat oppressive, and was irritable and out of sorts. I had done all the sightseeing I wanted to and, since I couldn't go anywhere without one of my cousins to chaperone me, I was longing for some time on my own. This opportunity came about when I discovered Uncle Joe in his small library, shaking his head in exasperation. 'The entire History section is out of order,' he announced. 'Not to mention English Literature. Can't abide disorganisation, how am I supposed to find anything. If I had the time to, I'd do it myself, but—'

'I could do it,' I offered.

'Could you, Angela?'

'Sure, I've worked in our local library at home. I could do a new index system for you. I'd be happy to.'

'Well,' he smiled broadly, 'if you'd care to take on the job, I'd be mighty happy to give it to you. Let me know if you need any help.'

So that was where I retreated to most days, the cool of the library, out of Marie's way and her spiteful looks thrown regularly in my direction. Wayne and Bill seemed just the same as ever, which was a relief; I guessed they were used to her carry on and didn't pay her much attention. They both had girlfriends, nice girls, I had met several times and they had always been pleasant to me.

Marie didn't appear to have a boyfriend, which, of course, was part of her problem. She was twenty going on twenty-one and a lot of her girlfriends had serious boyfriends and one or two were even getting married. I think Aunt Nancy was beginning to worry about her. With good reason, I thought to myself grimly. Marie was pretty, in a contrived, Grace Kelly sort of way, but with her sour-puss face and constantly disapproving manner I didn't see anyone wanting to run away with her any time soon. Her brothers' friends made an effort to be polite, but none of them asked her out on dates. And even though I was asked out all the time, after that magic weekend I had spent with Gus I had no interest in going out with anyone anymore.

I still hadn't heard from him, and Marie went out of her way to say every morning at the breakfast table, 'Daddy, I'll just get the mail for you now and sort it in your study, just the way you like it.' With a pointed glance in my direction. I knew instinctively she wouldn't ever let a letter from Gus find its way into my hands – and there wasn't a damn thing I could do about it short of waylaying the mailman on his morning rounds. I wished desperately I had thought of that when Gus said he would write to me here – I should have thought of another address, anything.

Something else had been worrying me too. I had missed my period. I felt perfectly fine, or persuaded myself I did, and put it down to the vagaries of transatlantic travel and my body clock being out of whack, but I was experiencing a growing unease. Then, about a week later, I was sick, violently sick; luckily I was in the library on my own when it happened, and I made it to the bathroom. But as I looked at my white, petrified face in the mirror, I knew I had to confront this . . . horror, and deal with it.

I needed to see a doctor, but of course I didn't know any, and I couldn't just walk in off the street, and I couldn't possibly say anything to Aunt Nancy. In desperation, after a match at the local tennis club, I cornered Bill's girlfriend, Sue, and asked if I could talk to her in private.

'Sure.' She looked concerned. 'Are you okay?'

'I— I don't think so,' I said, as she took my arm and we walked away from the others. 'I need to see a doctor.' I looked her in the eyes. 'In the strictest privacy. I was hoping, that is, I know it's awkward, but I was hoping you might be able to . . .' I trailed off, shame and desperation overcoming me.

'Don't worry, sweetie,' she said firmly. 'I have a doll of a doctor, this is women's stuff, right?'

I nodded miserably.

'I'll make an appointment for you right now. She'll see you tomorrow, I'm sure. I'll ring you at the house and the code is we're going shopping together. I'll tell you the time then and you can meet me and we'll go together.'

'I can't tell you how much I appreciate this, Sue.'

'It's probably nothing, you know,' she said cheerfully. 'I'll call you this evening.'

Sue was as good as her word, and picked me up at twelve o'clock on the pretext of lunch and shopping. 'Have a nice time, dear,' Aunt Nancy said, waving us off. For the short drive to the doctor's rooms, in an old brownstone in an exclusive part of the city, Sue was chatty and upbeat. I tried to smile and respond, but I really would much rather have been on my own for this ordeal. Having someone with me, however well meaning, was straining my already stretched nerves.

'I'll wait outside in the car, sweetie. 'Your appointment is for twelve forty-five, you're right on time.' She parked across the road.

Inside, I sat numbly in the wood-panelled waiting room,

full of leather chairs and overstuffed couches. The magazines were new and upmarket. This was a ritzy practice, no mistaking it. For a moment, I wondered had I brought enough money with me, and then before I knew it a girl in a tight summer dress put her head around the door and called my name.

'Angela Callaghan? Dr Segal will see you now.'

I followed her upstairs into a bright, tastefully decorated room where a good-looking woman in her forties looked at me over the top of her glasses and stood up from behind an antique desk to greet me. 'Have a seat, Miss Callaghan,' she smiled, indicating the chair opposite her. 'Before we begin, I'll just need to take a few details.'

Half an hour later, I left with assurances from Dr Segal not to hesitate to contact her if she could be of any further help. She was a nice woman, she had been kind to me, and unemotional under the circumstances. It didn't make it any easier hearing her tell me what I already knew.

Outside, I braced myself to face Sue, who leaned over to open the passenger door for me. 'How'd it go?' she asked.

'I'm pregnant,' I said dully. Realising the moment the words were out of my mouth that I had got myself into even more trouble than I was already in. At least up until now it had been my secret. But I was in shock, I couldn't even begin to think straight then. To be fair to Sue, she handled the announcement with a commendable lack of drama.

'Oh, honey,' she said, shaking her head. 'You need a drink – you and me both. I'm taking you to lunch, we gotta talk this through.' And that's what we did. And for an hour or so I felt better, felt there might, after all, be a sliver of light at the end of this terrifying tunnel. But only for an hour, after that I was queasier than ever.

That afternoon I went to bed claiming an upset stomach, something I ate at lunch must have disagreed with me. I had to think, or at least not be around people making normal conversation about their normal lives when mine had been thrown into complete and utter turmoil. I skipped dinner too, although Aunt Nancy had some chicken broth and toast sent up to me which I was grateful for. Despite everything, I was ravenously hungry – eating for two now, the thought looped around my brain.

For a while I cried, muffling the sobs under my pillow. Then I blew my nose, sat up and told myself to get a grip. I had to be rational about this. But how could I be? Logic brought the bleak realisation that I had very few options. I had no idea where Gus was and I hadn't heard from him. What could I do, ring up the US army and ask for him? I didn't even know what platoon he was with. And anyway, what good would that do? He was gone for a year at least. Desolation threatened to overcome me. I was seventeen and pregnant, with no support from a boyfriend and far away from home – which, depending on how you looked at it, might have been a good thing. Thinking of home brought a whole other set of terrors to light. But I couldn't think about them right then. I decided to sleep on it, and maybe in the morning things would seem clearer. Isn't that what people always said?

But in the morning it just all seemed like a bad dream I couldn't wake up from. I forced myself to go down to breakfast and act normally. Was it my imagination, or was Bill finding it difficult to meet my eyes? Either way, he finished up his breakfast in quite a hurry and left the table.

'Why the rush, dear?' asked his mother.

'Got an early tennis match at the club, I have to warm up, see you.'

Marie, on the other hand, was taking her time, eating daintily, seeming more prim and proper than ever.

I excused myself as soon as I could and headed for the

library to continue my work, which, if nothing else, was a blessed escape.

Half an hour later, I jumped when the door opened and Marie appeared, closing it softly behind her.

'You're wanted in the drawing room, Angela. My mother would like to see you there – now.'

'Wh— What?' I heard her, but my brain wasn't quite computing what I heard, and the tone of her voice was scathing. It could only mean one thing. I cursed myself for saying anything to Sue. Of course she would have told Bill, and Bill mustn't have been able to help himself telling Marie. After that, well, I didn't even like to think how much glee she had telling her mother.

'You heard me, Angela. You're wanted in the drawing room. I knew you were trouble, but even I didn't think you were this stupid.' She grinned. 'You've ruined yourself all on your own.'

I tried to walk past her with my head held high, even though I was so frightened I wanted to throw up. When I went into the drawing room, Aunt Nancy was standing looking out the large bay window. When I came in she turned to face me. Her voice was calm but cold.

'Sit down, Angela.'

I did as I was told, holding my hands very tightly together to stop them trembling.

'A rumour has come to my attention, Angela, a very disturbing rumour, that you find yourself in a very compromising situation, and I would be grateful if you would be straight with me. Is this true?' She looked me in the eye and I wanted the ground to open up and swallow me.

'Yes,' I whispered.

'I see. Well that *is* very unfortunate, very unfortunate indeed. I was hoping there might have been some mistake.'

'I— I'm afraid not.' I studied my hands.

'Do you know who the father is?'

My face burned. 'Yes.'

'Is there any chance he might marry you?'

'N— No. That is, I don't think so. He doesn't know, he's gone away on a tour of duty.'

'I see.' Her tone grew chillier by the minute. 'You realise I will have to telephone your parents immediately.'

'Oh, please, no!'

'I'm afraid I must insist on it. You see, we cannot have you here in the house a moment longer under these . . . circumstances. In fact, my husband as we speak is instructing his secretary to book you on the next flight home available. With any luck, she'll be able to get you on this evening's one.'

I gasped. 'But—'

'Therefore it is imperative that I inform your parents of your imminent return, you understand.'

'Please, don't say, I mean . . .' The horror of it all was dawning on me and every way I looked at it, the prospective scenes became more hideous. 'I understand you have to speak to them, Aunt Nancy,' I babbled, 'but please, let me be the one to tell them why, allow me that much, please, I'm begging you.'

There was an interminable pause and then she said, 'Very well. But I will be saying that it is unfortunate circumstances that have led to your early departure. They may make of that what they will. I must say, Angela, I am extremely disappointed in you. You have brought shame on your family and abused our kindness and hospitality to pursue your own selfish, immoral and very, very stupid agenda. I don't think I have to explain that you will not be welcome here ever again. I will inform anyone who might ask that your mother was unwell and you had to return home to be with her. Now, I suggest you go upstairs and begin to pack immediately. I will let you know as soon as your flight is confirmed.'

'Aunt Nancy,' I stood up, shakily.

'Yes?'

'I'm really sorry, truly I am.'

'I don't doubt it. Most girls would be, if they found themselves in your position.' She shook her head sadly. 'And to think that I thought we were getting a sweet, innocent, Irish girl to visit. Someone who would be a good example to our own children. And instead, well, words fail me.'

I couldn't take any more. I fled from the room and ran as fast as I could upstairs, pushing past a sneering Marie on the landing. In my bedroom, I dragged down my suitcase and began flinging in clothes. I didn't want to stay a second longer in this place, I couldn't bear any more cold contempt. Yet the prospect of going home seemed equally bleak. I understood for the first time in my life, but not the last, what it is to feel trapped, imprisoned by your own actions. What it feels to have utterly and totally run out of options.

Jake

Vonnie changed my life for sure, no question about it. I retired from the paper to write full time, working on the first of a three-book deal I had secured. Money was good. I didn't miss the war zones, the adrenaline rush, the whisper of death brushing by – at least not at first. And even then, that wasn't really what I missed, although it took a lot longer to figure that out. What I missed was an excuse to get loaded, to drink my way to oblivion.

It's easy to hide a drink problem, especially if you don't admit you have one. Even easier if you're a war correspondent because it pretty much goes with the territory. Dangerous people, exotic locations, stories and pictures snatched from the jaws of death – as many reasons to open a bottle as there are to celebrate life, or what you kid yourself is one. Whether it's sitting in the bar of a glamorous hotel or crouched in a corner of a building under attack, your throat thick with dust and fear, waiting the night out, liquor will reach the ragged, uneven places inside you and smooth them over. And for a while the world takes on a warmer glow. You feel safe, powerful, you have stilled the voice of fear, the whispering one, replacing it with something more stealthy and insidious than any enemy.

Don't get me wrong, I can hold my liquor – most of us can, I could very probably drink anyone under the proverbial table – but that doesn't mean it doesn't have a hold on you, and that's the one thing we will go to any lengths to avoid confronting. I wasn't a messy drunk. I didn't fall over or do embarrassing stuff, didn't get loud or combative; on the contrary, I was a very controlled drinker, a functioning alcoholic as they call it. If you call functioning messing up every relationship you've ever been in – or, even better, avoiding them altogether. Especially the 'big one' – the one with yourself. I didn't want to go there because I was scared. Scared, guilty and very, very angry. So I did what anyone does when they don't want to face or fix themselves, I focused on fixing someone else. And it didn't take me long to discover that Vonnie's family (or lack of) was one very toxic situation.

'There's something you need to know about me,' she said, shortly before we moved in together.

'I need to know *everything* about you,' I said, grabbing her and nuzzling her neck. 'That's why I'm going to live with you.'

'No, really, Jake, I mean it, seriously.' She sat down and I threw myself on the sofa beside her.

'There's nothing you can tell me about yourself to make me change the way I feel about you, Von, as far as I'm concerned the past belongs in the past. But if you really want to, well, shoot.' I leaned back and put my hands behind my head.

'Well, my upbringing was kind of unusual.' She took a deep breath. 'My parents, my family, are not who I thought they were. I'm not who I thought I was.' She chewed her lip.

'You were adopted?'

'No, no, not adopted, more, well, given away.'

'I'm not following.'

'I told you I had a sister, right?'

'Uhuh.'

'Well, she's not my sister, she's my cousin. Her mother, who I thought . . . who I was brought up to believe was my mother, is, in fact, my aunt. My real mother, my birth mother, is a woman I thought was my aunt. She gave me away to her sister and her husband and they brought me up.'

'But why? She must have been in trouble, right?'

'Well, she got herself in trouble, as you put it. It's a long story, but basically she couldn't hack being home in Ireland as a single mother, she was only seventeen. So she ran away, promised it was just until she made some money and could provide some kind of life for me. In the interim, her sister, my aunt, and her husband took care of me.'

'And?'

'And when it became apparent that she . . . that she wasn't coming back, they kept me, so to speak.'

'Oh, honey, I'm so sorry, that must have been so hard for you.'

'Well it wasn't, not really. You see, I didn't know anything about it until, well, until much later. I wasn't adopted, not officially at any rate.'

'Just duped, huh?'

'That's it in a nutshell. I feel pretty stupid about it, as you can imagine.'

I pulled her to me. 'When did you find out the truth?'

And that's when she said something that really surprised me.

'Well, I'm not sure I have. Not all of it, anyway. There's been a version, of course, but you know what? I'm not sure I want to know. Like you said, sometimes the past is best left in the past.'

Sometimes, I thought to myself, but not with this kind of stuff. This kind of past hangs around in the present. As I got to know Vonnie better, I could see she was beset by ghosts, something I could relate to – except, in her case, most of them were still alive.

Angela

My daughter was born on 12 July 1966, at 3.45 a.m. It was an easy birth, so I was told. I was a young and healthy eighteen year old, and everything went according to plan. I went into labour at half past six, right before supper. By midnight the midwife had arrived, under cover of darkness, and was able to leave before daylight. Everything about my daughter's arrival showed consideration. She didn't even scream loudly when she was smacked briskly on the bottom to welcome her to our world and ways, she just gave a little wail. Then she was quiet and calm, sleeping almost immediately, as if she was as stunned and exhausted as I had been these past months while the reality of her inappropriate and life-changing conception slowly dawned on me. When I held her in my arms, the overriding emotion I felt was guilt.

I was one of the lucky ones. My parents were Church of Ireland, respectable, God-fearing people, but genuinely Christian. They were shattered when I returned home with my news, but they stood by me in their way, I was not abandoned as so many Irish girls of my generation were in similar circumstances. I was not sent away. There was no incarceration in some viciously Catholic institution for 'fallen women', where my daughter would have been wrenched away from me and sent on to some unknown and faraway family. But there were proprieties to be observed nonetheless. It was decided that I should not leave the house once my condition became apparent. Seeing as I had already been away in America, people had become used to my absence, and my parents kept to themselves mostly, except for a small circle of friends – mostly Protestants like themselves – who, if they suspected anything amiss, were decent enough not to probe or speculate. We were a small community in a largely Catholic country and that, if for no other, was reason enough to close ranks.

That summer was glorious, which made the last three months of my pregnancy stifling. I helped in the house, sat outside reading until I was so hot and bored that I thought I would go insane. I slept a lot too, and in every waking hour in between it seemed I had to listen to Carmel, who had a baby girl of eighteen months, relate increasingly gruesome tales of labour and childbirth.

'I'm still not the better of it,' she said, with a shudder, while Kate, blonde and blue eyed like her mother, sat on her knee regarding her with solemn eyes.

I think Carmel wanted me to have a terrible time of it. She felt it was my due. What she didn't realise was that I was beyond caring. I just wanted it to be over. I wanted my body back, and my life, both which I knew would be altered forever. But anything had to be better than being cooped up in this house of quiet accusation, being an incubator to this unimaginable and uninvited imminent arrival. I know that sounds horrible, but it's the unvarnished truth. I'm not going to pretend that I was overcome with love and excitement at the thought of meeting my baby. I was numb – and beneath that numbness was terror.

So the day came when my daughter finally arrived; all I could think was *it's over*. I couldn't think any further than that. I was alive, I had survived. I would cope, somehow.

'What will you call her?' my mother asked quietly as she took her from her cot to bring her to me.

I looked at her blankly. Then I opened my mouth but no words came, only tears.

'There, there, Angela,' said Mother. 'It's all a bit overwhelming, I know. Don't worry, dear, it's perfectly natural to feel emotional at this stage.'

'Well,' said my father, who had just come back from church and couldn't bear tears or scenes of any kind, 'today is the feast of St Veronica. That seems like a perfectly good name to me.'

So Veronica she became.

I never even liked the name.

That year was hell for me, sheer and utter hell. I tried, I really did, to feel something, anything, for my daughter, but all I felt was a permanent exhaustion and a piercing sense of resentment. At first I was told it was 'the baby blues' and would soon pass. I was sent to our family doctor, who prescribed sedatives, which only made me feel as if I was walking through pea soup. Time would be the cure for everything, they said, time would make everything better – only I knew it was making things infinitely worse. I was trapped and there was no getting out. And every day, a little bit of me died.

I thought of Gus a lot. Not with rancour, I didn't blame him, not even then. How could I? I had willingly followed where he led. It was strange, too, having had such an intense encounter with someone, such a connection with a virtual stranger and now not even knowing if he were alive or dead. Or married, perhaps.

Maybe it would have been easier if Veronica's father had been a local boy. I could have married quietly, settled down and gone about having more children, people would make allowances, forget.

The trouble was that, quite apart from Gus, America had given me a taste of freedom, and now there was no way I could envisage a life without it.

Jake

My daughter was born on 31 August 2004.

Jasmine Mary Gloria (after my mom) Kurkimaki-Callaghan was born as dawn was breaking. She brought with her a new world and new sense of bewilderment on my part. I had never experienced anything so beautiful and fragile, yet powerful. When I held her for the first time and looked at her perfect little face and waving, fighting fists, something fierce unleashed in me that threatened to slay me – every parent knows it, the overwhelming terror of unconditional love.

If Vonnie and I changed each other, then Jazz changed both of us. I'd like to say for the better and, in Vonnie's case, that was so, she was and is an incredible and instinctive mother. Watching her and Jazz together is something I could do forever. Maybe women are natural parents, maybe it's part of the whole nurturing thing. I wanted to be a good parent, the best, better than best, because that was what Jazz and Vonnie deserved. But the road to hell, as they say, is paved with good intentions. Besides, I was still in denial, and well on the road to quiet self-destruction.

It's funny how you can be meticulous about hiding the evidence of your drinking from another person, and yet convince yourself that it is totally normal behaviour, nothing at all out of the ordinary. That may sound insane (and it is, of course), but to a drinker it's entirely reasonable, and I was nothing if not meticulous in that respect. Initially, it was easy. I wasn't a daily drinker, I could go for weeks, sometimes months, without a drink. I could even go out and drink with a crowd, being careful to match my pace to theirs, giving nothing away. And when I needed to drink – really drink – I would go away. That was easy too. Research was an ally, I had books to write, locations and facts to check on, I even used that age-old excuse of needing a few days of complete peace and quiet to go away to write, and that's when I could get well and truly slaughtered. There were friends too, old drinking buddies, journalists, cops, soldiers, photographers who had seen too much, lived too much, who had looked at themselves too little and hadn't liked what they'd seen. One or all of us were always at the end of a phone or email. Ready to catch a flight or a story, anything that would lead to lunch, dinner, inevitably a bar.

Initially, and for quite a while, Vonnie had no clue. Why would she? And then, when Jazz came along, she became the focus of our lives, except I wasn't being entirely truthful. I was there, of course I was, but not all of me, not truly *present*. There was another love affair I was conducting – clandestine and demanding – thinking about, longing for, constantly, and I was willing to betray both Jazz and Vonnie to maintain it. When she did begin to suspect, as partners will, I think she didn't want to know, not really. And who can blame her? Here we were, to all intents and purposes a perfect little family. A family that I loved beyond reason and who loved me back. No one wants to be the one to shatter that, to pull the card that makes the whole house come tumbling down. Eventually, of course, the alcoholic will do that for himself or herself, that is the nature of a beast more destructive than any mythical creature, the multi-headed one with deep-reaching tentacles to whom nothing is sacrosanct, the monster we call addiction. It takes you over, you see. You think you're in control but you're not. You become a different person, maybe several, you end up living so many lies you can hardly tell fact from fiction, daylight from living nightmares.

I began to get careless. Maybe it was a desire to get found out, to get help – or maybe it was just selfishness. I like to think the former, but suspect the latter. I remember one particular time, when Jazz was about eighteen months old. I was in New York, on a genuine meeting with my publisher, but I had scheduled in another two days to do some serious drinking, factoring in the recovery day of course. I rang Vonnie as I always did, several times a day, but the last time I didn't press 'end' on my phone properly, so the call ran on with Vonnie hearing every sound. I had lied about where I was, which was obviously in a crowded bar.

On my return she was distant, disturbed.

'What's the matter?' I asked.

'Nothing.'

'Come on, Vonnie, don't do this,' I said wearily. 'I know you, what's up?'

She looked at me and said, 'Maybe I don't know you, I'm wondering if I ever did.'

'What the hell is that supposed to mean?' I asked, hackles up, ready for an attack.

'Well what were you doing hanging out in a bar or wherever you were when you called me Wednesday night and said you were in your hotel room?'

When I looked blank she said, 'You left your phone on. I couldn't help hearing the background sound effects. You were having quite a time for yourself.'

'Look—'

'I'm just saying.' She went to pick up Jazz from the floor and disappeared around the corner to the bathroom. 'If you're finding this stifling, if you're cheating on me, well, don't bother coming back.'

I was floored. Really floored. But underscoring that was heavy relief. Vonnie didn't know. She just suspected that maybe I'd been cheating on her. The idea was so absurd I almost laughed out loud. But I didn't try to dissuade her either. Instead, I used her comment as an excuse to be remote and distant for a couple of days, and watched her warily watching me, fear replacing anger in every gesture and expression.

We made up, of course, I made sure of that. But the seed had been sown. I had handed Vonnie a reason to distrust me and, to my enduring shame, I shrugged it off. Told myself she was being paranoid, possessive.

That's what I mean when I say addiction changes you. You won't even notice it. It will stealthily erode everything good in your life until you are left alone, utterly alone. But I was a long way from that unthinkable scenario – or so I thought.

Abby

Abby had seen her, plain as day, with her own eyes. She was tall and slim, conservatively dressed in a well-cut, charcoal-grey suit, displaying long, shapely legs and wearing heels high enough for her to have to hold on to the railings as she took the steps from the house down to the pavement tentatively, as if she might trip or fall, making her immediately seem fragile. She had light-brown hair that swung to her shoulders and was wearing little or no make-up. When she looked up, smiled and waved, she had an open, inviting expression, one people would find it hard not to warm to. Abby swallowed hard from her vantage point in her mother's ancient Mini. It had been Sheila's idea to follow Edward, and Abby wonders now what madness possessed her to go along with it, to think, however fleetingly, that any good might come of it.

She remembers doing this before with her mother, many years ago, when she had first met Edward, and her mother had persuaded her to drive under cover of darkness (it had been an early evening in winter then) to sneak a look at the house where he and his parents lived. Sheila had been impressed, Abby terrified. But they had got away with it. 'It's only research,' Sheila had said grinning. 'Better to know as much as you can, then you can tailor your plan of attack.' She had made it sound like a military offensive, procuring a suitable husband for her daughter, and Abby had gone along with it all, playing hard to get, keeping her cool – and it had worked. Edward had married her, and if Rosie had arrived a couple of weeks prematurely, no one had so much as raised an eyebrow – sure weren't they the perfect couple, she and Edward, and honeymoon babies were the icing on the cake.

Now here she was, twenty years later, sitting in her mother's car, stalking her own husband. What did that make her, she wondered?

Sheila, worryingly, was silent, as she sat hunched behind the wheel. Abby thinks her mother is more shocked than she is. In a strange way, Abby is relieved. Things are finally beginning to make sense. She had begun to think she was going mad, imagining things to be out of kilter that were perfectly normal, thinking her mother was just being sensational in venturing to think that Edward was having an affair – but, well, now the pieces are falling into place, like a menacing jigsaw. It is a weekly rendezvous, this Thursday appointment, and this is the third week that they have followed Edward but the first occasion that Abby has seen *her*, the embodiment of reasons for Edward's coolness, his distance towards Abby.

Edward had left the tall, terraced house a respectable couple of minutes before. He got into his car, started the engine and looked up, and that was when the woman had waved at him, when her face had lit up into that beaming smile.

Abby had found the card, quite accidentally, in the breast pocket of Edward's jacket, which she was taking along with the usual bundle of clothes that accumulated for monthly dry cleaning. The girl behind the counter had very obligingly handed it to her, examining the clothes, as she always did, for any lingering contents. At home, Abby had looked at it, turning it over and over in her hands. It said simply: 'Olivia Fitzgerald, Psychologist', followed by an impressive number of letters after her name. There was also an address.

At first, Abby was inclined to dismiss it, but her intuition was bothering her, urging her to look harder, so she did. She went through the rest of Edward's jackets and suits and found three more identical cards. Of course, there could be a perfectly plausible explanation, Abby reasoned. Edward could be seeing this woman on a professional basis; after all that was what she did – she ran a therapy practice. A renowned one by all accounts (Abby had immediately Googled her), she had even attended Harvard and left with a masters, among many other accomplishments. She was sporty, went running early every morning and raised money for several charitable causes. She was married with young children too, but since when did that prove anything? Abby shut down the glowing website feeling fat, foolish and very unfit – in every sense of the word. There was just one glaringly obvious reason why the plausible explanation was unlikely, and that was because Edward, along with many other pet hates, had a derisive and profound dislike of therapy, counselling or any of 'that kind of codswallop' as he referred to it. He would no more see a therapist, Abby would bet, than start meditating or smoking dope. Which reminded her of Diana and Greg. Diana had not been happy about her husband at the lunch either. Abby wondered briefly were all marriages doomed to evolve into unwieldy, unrecognisable entities where one partner (usually the woman) was tested to their limits and either had to leave, or shut up and put up with an arrangement that had long since ceased to resemble the mutual exchange of vows to love and cherish each other until death or inconvenience drove them apart.

In a weak moment she had confided this latest information about the card to Sheila, who had immediately mooted the drive-by. In the absence of any better ideas, and enjoying the sympathy and conspiratorial support Sheila had instantly bestowed, Abby had agreed. And now here they were.

'Well,' says Abby, 'that must be her.'

'Looks like it. And that was definitely Edward she was waving at.'

'It was. Obviously they're being discreet,' Abby observes. 'Wouldn't do to traipse down the steps together.'

'She's a psychologist, you say.'

'She is.'

'Hmm. So she'd know how to worm her way into a man's mind.'

'I expect so.' Abby sighs. 'Let's go, Mum, I need to get back to do dinner.'

Sheila guns the engine and reverses out of their parking space, where they have been discreetly hidden at the other side of the square.

'They're always the worst ones.'

'Who?'

'The ones that look as if butter wouldn't melt in their mouths. Brazen, that's what they are.'

'I thought she looked rather nice.'

Sheila looks at her askance. 'Nice?'

'Yes. She's nice looking, has a nice smile, a nice figure and she's younger than me, obviously.'

Something has been unleashed in Abby, although she doesn't quite know what. Seeing that girl, thinking about Edward and her. Thinking about how quietly distraught she has been for the past few months, while Edward's been seeing this happy, chirpy-looking young woman without a care in the world. Thinking about how Edward has been quietly putting her down, when she's his wife; it is all suddenly enough to—

'What are you thinking?' Sheila is staring grimly ahead over the wheel as they turn into the road where they live.

'I'm thinking that I don't really care anymore.'

'What do you mean you don't care?' Sheila slams the car door shut and follows Abby up the three steps to the front door. Abby turns the key, then bends down to pick up the two supermarket bags of groceries she bought before the stakeout.

In the kitchen, as she unpacks them, she puts on the kettle, while Sheila sits at the table, looking defeated, which is most unlike her.

Abby goes to the fridge and takes out a bottle of chilled white wine.

'What are you doing?' Sheila asks suspiciously.

'I'm opening a bottle of wine.'

'You never drink in the middle of the day.'

'It's four thirty, Mum, I'm going to have a drink, you're welcome to join me if you like – otherwise I'm more than happy to drink alone.'

'Edward won't like it.' Sheila looks torn.

'Pity about him, then.' Abby pours a glass for herself and waves another one invitingly at her mother.

'Oh, go on then. I'll have a glass. My nerves are in shreds.'

'Cheers,' says Abby, clicking glasses.

'What are you going to do?'

'About what?'

'About her.'

'Nothing.'

'What? What do you mean, nothing?'

'What do you want me to do, Mum? There's not a lot I can do, really, when you think about it, is there?' Abby sits down across the table from Sheila.

'You could try being nicer to him.'

'Nicer?'

'Yes, you think *she* isn't playing up to him morning, noon and night? That's what you're up against. You have to do something, you can't just sit here and . . . take to the bottle.'

'I have no intention of taking to the bottle. I've always enjoyed a glass or two of wine, I just don't have it very often because Edward doesn't approve, but from now on I'm going to do a lot more of what I want to – and if he doesn't like it, well you know what he can do.'

'What can he do?'

'He can get lost, quite frankly.'

'That attitude isn't going to get you anywhere.' Sheila looks mutinous. 'Why won't you listen to me? I only have—'

'My best interests at heart.' Abby finishes the sentence for her. 'I know you do, Mum, but I have always listened to you, and that's part of the problem.'

'What problem? Are you insinuating *I'm* the reason your husband is having an affair?'

'Of course not, I'm just saying that I don't really know who I am anymore.'

'Oh for God's sake, don't start with that nonsense.'

'It's not nonsense.'

'It is, it's American claptrap. You've been watching too much of those *Oprah* and *Dr. Phil* – they're full of nothing but whingers. That's what's wrong with this country, no one does anything but whinge and whine these days, and talk complete rubbish. Of course you know who you are. You are my daughter, you are Edward's wife and you are your children's mother – who else do you think you might be?'

'I don't know.' Abby takes a sip of wine. 'I just know that it wasn't meant to end up like this.'

'Listen to me, Abby. You have to think about this, have a plan, otherwise you will lose Edward, then what?'

Abby looks at her mother. 'Do you know we haven't had sex for almost a year now?'

Sheila splutters on her mouthful of wine. 'I don't think that's any of my—'

'Well you seem to be great at giving me advice on everything else, Mum, why not my sex life? And what about me? Forget Edward, what if I've had enough? I'm sick of pandering to his every need. That's all I've done since the day I married him. And I'm supposed to be grateful for that? I've cleaned for him, cooked for him, cajoled him and done the same for my children – and this is how he repays me?' Abby is surprised to see she is quivering with rage.

'Men are all the same, Abby. Even Edward. They're always susceptible to a clever woman. But it doesn't do to take them for granted, they don't like it. You've been very dismissive to him lately and that's not good.'

'I don't care.' Abby's voice is almost a shriek.

'Calm down will you, you're like a raving lunatic. Here, have another glass of wine and relax.' Sheila tops up her glass. 'I'll get the dinner on.'

Sheila potters about the kitchen muttering to herself. She looks older to Abby, suddenly, and rather frail, as if all the fight has gone out of her. 'Don't worry about it, Mum, I'll do it. You go and have your lie down.'

'Are you sure?'

'Of course I am. I like having something to do, takes my mind off things. Here,' she adds, handing the glass to Sheila, 'take a glass of wine up with you, it'll help you sleep.'

'Oh, right, then,' Sheila's face brightens. 'I will. See you later, then.'

When her mother has gone upstairs, Abby mechanically takes the shoulder of lamb from the fridge and begins to stud it with sprigs of rosemary and slivers of garlic. Then she sets it aside and peels the potatoes for roasting. She wonders why she is not feeling devastated, why she is not crumbling, falling to pieces. Isn't that what is supposed to happen when you discover your husband is cheating on you? Perhaps she is in denial, she thinks, perhaps she hasn't quite grasped the reality of the situation. Where are the floods of tears, the prepared accusations she will hurl at him? Why are they not lining up, standing to attention like well-drilled soldiers in her mind?

She puts the lamb in the oven, sets the timer and flicks on the television, sitting down with her wine on the blue-check sofa and curling her legs under her. Abby loves the kitchen, she has always felt happy here, and this is the kitchen of her dreams. Welcoming, cosy, spacious but not intimidating, with room for a lounging area in the small room they knocked through where they could watch TV on the sofa, and eat at the big scrubbed pine table where the children used to do their homework when they were younger. But nowadays everyone seems to retreat to their own private space, to computers and phones and, in Edward's case, probably furtive text messages – the thought makes her shudder. He will be home soon.

She thinks of the early days, her disbelief that he had actually shown an interest in her, that he was taking her out, going steady with her, of the excitement and terror combined, that at any moment she might lose him, this elusive and highly prized man who could have had his pick of girls. And then, remembering her horror as she had felt him slipping silently, but surely, away from her. She had never really thought about that – not really – but now she forces herself to. Had she been fair to him, really? To either of them? Had she allowed her fear of her own abandonment – and worse, much worse, her mother's bitter disappointment if she had lost him – make her tie him to her, wordlessly, deceitfully, without choice or consultation?

She remembers telling him, haltingly, that she was pregnant, making light of it, so close as it was to the wedding – the wedding that under no account would now be called off. She remembers the shock on his face, how he paled visibly, swallowing, and then rallied bravely, telling her everything would be fine, that accidents happened all the time. But he hadn't stayed long after that, making his excuses to leave once he was assured she was all right. She wonders now what went through his mind that night. Did he lie awake, worrying, feeling trapped, claustrophobic? Had she taken his freedom from him, nailed down the last opening through which a chink of light had flickered? Certainly, the last month before the wedding had flown by, and Abby was too caught up with dresses and veils and seating plans and her mother to give much or any thought as to how Edward was coping. If he seemed to be going through the motions somewhat mechanically, she reassured herself that that was what all prospective grooms did. The honeymoon in the glorious Caribbean island had been subdued, Edward exhausted from his residency hours and constant exams, and Abby feeling queasy in the intense heat. Neither of them dwelt on the spectre of their unplanned pregnancy, which here, in the almost stiflingly romantic atmosphere, seemed oddly incongruous.

When Rosie was born, Edward had been wonderful, falling instantly in love with his daughter and patiently taking time to reassure Abby that she was up to the job of looking after this tiny, helpless infant. He changed nappies and even shared night feeds occasionally, despite his gruelling schedule. Gradually their lives fell into a routine, and Edward's career began its steady and progressive ascent. Through it all, Abby was the perfect wife. If it seemed Edward spent more time at the hospital than at home, she never complained. If he was on occasion difficult to live with, being a rather compulsive perfectionist, she bit her tongue and instead devoted herself to keeping the show on the road as smoothly as possible. Five years later, the arrival of the twins completed their family, and although Edward was overjoyed with his identical boys, Abby suspects it is Roseanna who still holds a special place in his heart – for which Abby, annoying though her daughter can be, is profoundly grateful.

I trapped him, thinks Abby, miserably. Edward is a good man and I trapped him, now it's payback time. She hears his key in the door and resolves to say nothing, absolutely nothing, about the current situation. She will not think about it. She will just concentrate on dinner, swallowing mouthful after mouthful of it even though she has no appetite. She will be pleasant and make conversation just as if it's any normal evening. She will not, on any account, dwell on the possibility that her life as she knows it may be unravelling, that her karma has caught up with her, that she is getting what her mother would refer to as 'her just desserts'. Abby gets up, taking her glass of wine with her, and heads over to the oven, from which a reassuringly delicious smell escapes as she opens the door.

The Affair

*H*e *cannot go on like this, he is at his wit's end. Never in a million years would he have believed this could happen – to him of all people. He is sitting in the apartment, head in hands, a drink beside him, untouched. He gets up, checks his phone, paces the floor. She is late, and she usually lets him know if she is delayed. He is annoyed, not at her, but at life, how he, she, both of them, have ended up in this dead-end emotional alley. Because he cannot escape her, she is everywhere – in his thoughts, his dreams, his fantasies. No other woman will do. No other woman comes close. He has become irrational, obsessed by her. His friends are concerned, his family worry about him, he knows, although they do not suspect anything, but he is becoming more and more remote, even to himself.*

He hears her key in the door and her breathless apologies before she comes into the room, dropping bags, flings her arms around him. 'I'm so sorry, the traffic was hell, and I let my phone run down.'

He silences her with a kiss.

'Wait,' she laughs, 'there is food, I want to cook.'

'Later,' he mumbles, peeling off her wraparound dress, running his thumb under the silk strap of her bra, unclipping it with his other hand, cupping her breasts, caressing her shoulders, marvelling at the sheen of her skin.

He has waited this long for such little time together. Each time she leaves, he is even more aware of the pockets of loneliness she has left behind in his apartment. The indent of a pillow where her head was, the shadow of her perfume, the memory of her touch, the whispered promises.

He has waited this long, he can wait a few more weeks.

July 2011

Diana

'Hey!'

I felt a hand on my shoulder, and looked up from the array of colourful postcards I was choosing for Sophie, who had asked me to bring her back anything that might inspire her designs, when I heard Vonnie's voice. We had arranged to meet in the shop of the Chester Beatty Library. I had also felt compelled to buy some beautiful Islamic prayer beads, or worry beads as we used to call them. I thought maybe I could do with them.

'It's good you're early,' Vonnie said. 'It can get pretty crowded if a big tour group arrives.' She steered me out of the shop and towards the restaurant where we were to have lunch.

'I thought I'd have a look around before we met,' I said. 'It's really fascinating. You could spend hours here.'

We went in to the Silk Road Cafe and settled ourselves at a corner table.

'It's really great about Greg's television show, you must be thrilled.'

'I am, yes, of course, but, well, it's early days yet, Von. These things are notoriously precarious. The station is running it as a test pilot right now, there's no guarantee they'll take it on for another season.'

Vonnie nodded. 'Sure, but it's a start, right? You gotta stay positive, as they say in California.'

We were having lunch to celebrate, at Vonnie's invitation.

Abby couldn't make it – something about visiting a cousin of her mother's down in Wexford.

'To you and Greg and new beginnings!' Vonnie toasted, as the glasses of champagne arrived. 'What?' she said looking at my face. 'What is it?'

'Oh, God, Von, I don't know. I know I should be happy and grateful, but the truth is, I don't know how much longer I can go on like this.'

'Like what?'

'Living a lie.' There, I had said it.

'You and Greg? Are things that bad?'

I nodded miserably.

'Oh, Di.' Vonnie reached across and took my hand. 'I don't know what to say.' She shook her head. 'You *and* Abby, I'm finding it hard getting my head around all this.'

'What do you mean me and Abby?' My head snapped up. 'What's Abby got to do with it?'

'Well, she called in to me last week, she was in the area, and she told me she thinks Edward is having an affair. I assumed you'd know, don't you guys talk anymore?'

This was news to me, and my face obviously registered as much. 'No, no I didn't know that.' I took a quick drink.

'She's pretty upset, as you might imagine.'

'Has he said anything?'

'No, she hasn't confronted him about it. I'm worried about her, to tell you the truth. I don't know what's going on, but I don't think it's healthy having her mother living with them. Abs has always been too controlled by her.'

'Tell me about it,' I said dryly. 'But Edward? I just can't imagine . . .' I was surprised, and a bit peeved that Abby hadn't said anything to me about it, unless . . . unless maybe she knew something – oh, God.

'Are you okay?' Vonnie was concerned. 'You look a bit green around the gills.'

'I'm fine, perfectly all right. It's just that, it's all getting to me. I feel as if everything is resting on *my* shoulders and I try to think about it all logically and rationally but I end up going round in circles.'

'You can't possibly be rational about it, Di. This is your marriage, your family – you've got to listen to your heart. If there's anything I can do to help, anything at all.'

'Just listening helps. I don't think anyone can help when you're floundering in a relationship. You just have to find your own way through it, we all do. Look at us all! You were right not to get married, Von.'

'Don't say that.' Vonnie smiled ruefully. 'You don't really mean it. Not really.'

But I did. She had no idea how much I meant it.

Manhattan, 2011

Angela

I met with her, as she asked me to, how could I not? The venue was the restaurant at Saks, Fifth Avenue – busy enough to be impersonal, and open enough to make a quick getaway should either of us need to. I didn't know what to expect. For weeks before our meeting I was nervous, irritable; Ron didn't know what the heck had got into me, as he put it, and I had no intention of enlightening him. I had kept this secret for forty years of marriage, it could keep for a while longer.

She wrote to me. The letter arrived out of the blue, marked strictly personal and confidential, thankfully after Ron had left. It was the kind of letter that didn't go unnoticed, even before it was opened. I took it, with my coffee, into my small personal sitting room in our New York apartment and reached for the silver letter opener. I knew it was from her, of course, even before my eyes scanned perfunctorily to the end of the handwritten note. It was brief and to the point. She said she would be in New York in six weeks, suggested a place and time to meet and left a number to contact her on if I had any difficulty with that. If she didn't hear from me, she would assume I would be there.

I wrote back to say I most definitely would be there and that I looked forward to our meeting. There was no point in being gushy, I was careful to match my tone to hers, which was polite but unemotional. I had written to her many times since Carmel had let me know Vonnie had discovered the truth, but all my letters had gone unanswered. I couldn't blame her. This contact, however tentative, was a breakthrough, and I didn't want to scare her off with any kind of behaviour that might appear self-serving or phony. What was done was done, we all had to live with the consequences. Luckily for me, when the day of our meeting arrived, Ron was away on business for three days and that at least spared me something. I didn't have to act relentlessly, pretend that everything was normal. I was left alone to fret and to panic.

I focused instead on what to wear, a task that quickly assumed such gargantuan impossibilities as to render me senseless. And I had thought that would be the easy part. It wasn't as if I had never met her, my daughter, I had met her several times when she was a little girl, but then I had been the glamorous aunt, bearer of exotic gifts from the other side of the world. Not the vile mother who had abandoned her. No outfit fitted that bill. Whether I dressed as Doris Day or Cruella De Vil made little difference. I still felt as if I had the words 'Wicked Witch of the West' tattooed on my forehead. In the end, I dressed simply in neutrals, bisques and beiges, very bland, a cashmere sweater and pencil skirt with a camel coat and matching leather bag and boots. Then I wrapped a white silk scarf around my neck, because tones of beige can be so draining to the complexion. Old habits die hard – once a model, always a model, and I'm not going to apologise for *that*. I also made sure to wear my shades, the early spring sun can be lethal in New York, and, apart from that, I'm still quite well known, and I certainly didn't need any reporters following me and picking up on this. I mean, anything could happen. For all I knew Vonnie could hurl abuse and throw a glass of water at me – scream and shout, maybe even hit me, and she would have every right to.

So I got there early, fifteen minutes early. I ordered coffee, although I would have preferred a glass of champagne to steady my nerves, but I thought that would look too presumptive. There was plenty of time for champagne if things went well, and I was praying they just might. I forced myself to remember the last time I had seen her. It was 1976 and she had been ten years old. I remember how my heart ached for her then, not from longing, although there was that too, but because of the awkwardness that already emanated from her. My poor daughter, so big for her age and plump, seemed huge and ungainly beside Kate, who already held the promise of the blonde pocket-Venus she would embody as a teenager. I could see that, beside her, Vonnie felt hideous.

I couldn't tell her then, although I wanted to, that Kate's kind of beauty wouldn't last, wouldn't translate well into adulthood, she was one of those girls who would be at her best and prettiest at sixteen. From thereon she would outgrow her features, become ordinary. Those kinds of button-nosed, chocolate-box, cutie pie looks tended to mature into a kind of blandness. I had seen it countless times – when buoyed up by pushy mothers or hopeful boyfriends, these types of girls would show up at the model agencies only to be turned away, disbelief written all over their pretty faces. Vonnie, on the other hand, even then, had bone structure to die for, beautiful eyes and good, straight teeth. She was tall for her age too, and I figured and hoped she'd keep growing, and one day all that puppy fat would just melt away. My girl would be beautiful, she just didn't know it then, but I did. That's what I wanted to tell her, but of course I couldn't.

I looked up from my reverie as a tall, striking woman approached the table and my breath caught. There was no mistaking her, but, my, what a transformation. For a split second, part of me almost wanted to jump up and cheer, but another part was astonished, quite shaken in fact. I hadn't bargained on this, you see. It was not just that my daughter was quite, quite, beautiful – that I had hoped and expected – what took me unawares, and shook me more than I could have imagined, was that she had not got her looks from me.

Vonnie Callaghan had become the living, spitting image of her father.

July 2011

Vonnie

'Mommy!' Jazz is exasperated. 'You're not listening to me!'

We are in the garden and Jazz has been trying to persuade me to let her sleep outside in a sleeping bag under the stars. She's right, I wasn't listening, I was thinking about Abby and Di. Hearing about both their marital problems had unsettled me more than I realised. I couldn't say it was surprising – marriages seemed to have such a short lifespan these days, practically everyone I knew in the States was divorced or in a second or even third marriage – but it was distressing when it involved my two dearest friends. I could see how perhaps Di might feel constricted, or want to move on, she was always a bit of a free spirit (and I knew she would handle whatever decision she decided to make), but Abby . . . I just couldn't see her apart from Edward, it just didn't seem right.

'Sorry, honey, what did you say?'

'How long until Daddy gets here?'

'One more week, Jazz. Seven more sleeps exactly.'

'Yay! I can't wait.'

'I know.' I wrap a dark curl around my finger and tug it.

'Can he stay here with us, Mommy? In our house?'

'I don't know, Jazz, we'll see.'

'Why can't you just say yes.' She scowls.

'Because he doesn't stay with us at home, sweetie. It's best to keep things the way they are. Anyway, you can stay with him in the hotel if you like – it'll have a swimming pool and stuff.'

This seems to mollify her. It is hard for her, I think, hard to understand – and hard for me to see the pain it causes her. I had wanted everything to be perfect for her, to give her an idyllic childhood, what every parent wants, and yet Jake and I had ended up just another statistic. When I considered the cold facts, was I that much better than my own mother? Than Carmel and Colm, who I would be visiting shortly? I took a deep breath. I had a score to settle with them, I needed to set the record straight. Meeting my mother had made that possible at least. If nothing else, going to meet her that day had been worth it for that alone.

My birth mother is beautiful, but I knew that already.

I remembered her various visits to our house in Wicklow when I was young, inevitably preceded by a week of nervous irritability on Carmel's part while she presided over vigorous cleaning and preening, driving poor Barney and everyone else to distraction. There would be a flurry of clothes shopping too, where she and Kate would try on endless outfits and Kate's hair would be cut into the latest style. Colm and I would be considered critically, and sighed at, and both of us hustled into outfits which we wore with resigned misery. Colm because he loathed the cravat and navy blazer Carmel made him wear, and me because I felt enormous and shapeless beside Kate, my hair wetted and submitted into two tightly woven braids. We would stand, as instructed, stiffly uncomfortable, beside the fireplace in the drawing room, and I would listen, mesmerised, as Carmel became another person, putting on a different voice entirely (her posh telephone one) and gesticulating theatrically at every opportunity.

These visits of the woman I then thought of as my aunt never lasted long, but she always brought Kate and I wonderful presents. Dolls and games and clothes that seemed otherworldly in their sophistication. I wanted to ask her about America, and how one could go there, but I was never given the chance to talk to her alone. Beside Kate, I hung back afraid of sounding stupid, seeming dense. But she was always nice to me, always told me how well I looked and how tall I was getting (which I hated to be reminded of). I thought she was like a movie star, and I said so, blurting it out, immediately feeling foolish, even though she gave me a wonderful smile and a little squeeze. Obviously I had said the wrong thing, because Carmel's lips had tightened and an angry flush had suffused her cheeks. She was cold to me for days afterwards.

When Angela kissed me goodbye, her perfume lingered, and when she left, the house seemed airless, as if she had taken all the energy in it with her. I dreamed of her that night, and many other nights, and fantasised that one day I would run away to America and live with her.

Now here she was sitting before me.

She was still beautiful. Even though I had expected that, it still took me by surprise. This gorgeous, polished, carelessly expensive-looking woman must have been what . . . sixty-three now, but she could easily have passed for a woman ten years younger. If she'd had work done (and I was pretty sure she had) it was painstakingly discreet. As I approached her table, she looked up, smiled confidently and lifted her chin just a fraction, enough to let me know she wasn't going to be intimidated by this meeting. I immediately felt my resolve vanish. Faced with her, this personification of beauty, glamour and presence, my courage evaporated. Fuelled by anger and determination earlier, and encouraged strongly by Jake, I had made myself believe I could do this. It was my right. I had been riding high on a wave of self-righteous indignity – but now I crashed, hurtling into the familiar abyss of inadequacy and abandonment, but I wasn't going to let her see that. I shook my hair back and forced a smile. 'Angela,' I said, holding out my hand as she stood up, 'thank you for agreeing to meet me.'

I sat down and ordered coffee, and we chatted amicably about the weather and my journey. When the waiter poured my coffee I could feel her watching me, appraising me. 'You've turned out quite a beauty,' she said, smiling. 'I always knew you would.'

'Then you knew more than I did,' I said.

'I imagine you have a lot of questions.'

'Yes.' I took a sip of my coffee and tried to pretend that my heart hadn't started to beat faster. I was scared, panicked, part of me wanted to get up and run. I had done okay up until now – what was I doing here? Why now? What did any of it matter? And most of all, did I really want to know?

We kid ourselves you know, us children that were given away, we want to, need to romanticise it all. We tell ourselves our mothers were heartbroken to part with us, that we had to be wrenched from them, to be given cruelly away by some other, authoritative party, unavoidable circumstances leading to this tearing apart of mother and infant which would leave an open wound in our birth mother's heart, never to be healed. It is the only way we can cope. The other option to consider, that we were never wanted, that our fledgling presence was a source of such misery and unspeakable distress to our parents, is processed differently, silently, reminding us in a never-ending stream of destructive voices redolent with self-hatred how lacking we are, how inadequate, how hopelessly unlovable.

So yes, there are many questions we want to ask, but it really all boils down to the one we crave and fear the answer to most – why?

'Why? I whispered, the saucer rattling as I replaced my cup with inconveniently trembling fingers.

She met my gaze and held it. 'I'm not going to bullshit you, Vonnie, I promise.'

'Good,' I said, 'because there's been quite enough of that already.'

Diana

I took the afternoon off today, something I rarely do, in order to take my father to lunch. He has been low lately according to my mother and, anyway, it has been ages since we have sat and talked together properly. Today is their anniversary, which provided me with the opportunity to insist we have an outing. My mother was invited, of course, but she demurred, protesting she was suffering with a head cold and fever and had lost her sense of taste along with it. Personally, I suspected she just wanted me and Dad to have lunch without her. He suggested going to his club, on Stephen's Green, but I booked a table at our favourite restaurant, which is French. An expense I could ill afford, but the set lunch menu is quite good value if you don't go overboard with the wine, and I needed a change of scene to forget my troubles for a few hours and lose myself instead in the culinary delights that would be winging our way. They always made a great fuss of my father here, too, which in itself was almost worth the exorbitant prices. He could lapse into his native French and discuss in happy detail the merits of the wine, the tenderness of the lamb and the madness of not being able to enjoy a good cigar at the table with his after-dinner coffee.

I have agreed to meet him at the restaurant and, as I arrive, a waiter shows me to our table, where he is already seated. I order two glasses of champagne as an aperitif and my father puts on his reading glasses to peruse the menu. He is looking well, I think, if a little frail, but that is to be expected at his age. He is wearing a navy linen suit with a pale pink shirt and, of course, a cravat. His hair, still plentiful although his hairline has receded, is brushed back from his face, which is tanned from reading in his favourite sun-trap in the garden. He is still a very handsome man, still commands glances from women of a certain age, even younger ones regard him with curiosity and respect.

'Happy anniversary,' I say.

'Thank you.' He raises his glass to me. 'You are looking tired.'

'You always say that.'

'That's because it is always true.'

'Please,' I say 'can we talk about something cheerful today?'

'Of course.' He smiles and shrugs, an imperceptible movement, supremely Gallic. I immediately scowl.

'How is Mum? She didn't sound too bad on the phone when I spoke to her. It's not like her to turn down lunch.'

'We are getting old.' He sighs. 'It is not so easy to face the world.'

'It would have done her good to get out.'

'Your mother prefers to stay at home these days. She likes to cook, to look after the house. I think going out is becoming too much for her.'

This is news to me. 'Since when?'

Another shrug. 'I was always more of the extrovert in our marriage, like you I expect.'

We are tiptoeing, of course, around the big white elephant that is *my* marriage and which I have no intention of referring to.

'Does Greg make you happy, Diana?'

The question lands somewhere in the middle of our main course, accompanying a mouthful of my boudin of lobster cooked to perfection. My father, taking a sip of his Bordeaux, regards me speculatively.

'What sort of a question is that?'

'A very pertinent one, I would have thought. After all, we are on the subject of marriage.'

'*Your* marriage.'

'Your mother has made me very happy. I have been a very fortunate man.'

'You make each other happy.'

'Sometimes I wonder.'

'What?'

'If I was the right man for her, if she made the right choice.'

'Well if you're together almost fifty years later, I imagine she thinks she has made the right choice.'

'There are times in a marriage,' he continues, 'natural breaks, a drifting apart if you like, when it seems to me that one is offered an option of leaving, a natural opting out, or you make the decision to work to come back together.'

I take a drink of wine, washing down words I am afraid will escape.

'I think,' he says, 'that is where you and Greg are now. It is none of my business, of course, but I would urge you to reflect carefully on your position.'

Even by my father's standards this is a breathtakingly arrogant comment.

'Are you telling me you think I should leave my husband?' I ask incredulously.

He gives another imperceptible shrug. 'I am not telling you anything, Diana. I am merely giving you the benefit of my many years of hard-won wisdom.

We continue eating, and in the ensuing silence the question reverberates in my head. *Does Greg make me happy?*

Impossible to answer. And anyhow, isn't happiness something that is supposed to come from within? Aren't we all responsible for our own happiness? Don't all the troubles in every relationship stem from thinking or hoping someone else will supply the missing pieces, put us back together, make us feel warm and safe again? Except life isn't like that, as we find out sooner or later. Far from supplying missing aspects of ourselves, partners are more likely to bring demons of their own to throw into the mix, some of them unknown and unexpected, even to themselves. Add to that the curveballs life can randomly throw at you, and you have quite an eclectic mix of grenades that can go off in any relationship at any time, all with the potential to maim or seriously disable even the most robust partnerships.

'I don't love him anymore.' I shock myself with this answer. Not because it is true, but because I have not articulated it to anyone, least of all myself. Hearing the words aloud is no consolation, no relief; on the contrary, I feel even more bereft.

'That's not what I asked you,' my father points out gently.

'It's the only thing that matters.'

At this, my father gives a long sigh and smiles, nodding his head. 'Ah, love, *l'amour*, yes, perhaps it is the only thing that matters.' He seems to drift into private memories. 'We let it escape so many times, and then it is too late.'

'What are you talking about?' I ask crossly. He has made me admit my own relationship's shortcomings. Isn't this what he has always wanted to hear, that I was wrong and he was right?

'You knew when you met Mum, didn't you? You knew that she was the one. You must have because you pursued her relentlessly; you've said so, many times,' I demand.

'Yes,' my father replies, 'I knew she was the one for me, the right one to marry. I knew she was the person who would make me be my best self, and that's what she did. I am not sure I can say the same of Greg for you. Do you think he allows you to be your best self, Diana? You have so much to offer, so many talents, and yet it seems to me you spend most of your energy running after Greg and, if not cleaning up, then covering up his messes. Indulging his ridiculous projects. I thought at least there was some understanding that Greg was to allow you to take things easier, to take some time at home, with the children, but now, of course . . .' The comment hangs in the air, as my father gestures for the bill.

'This is my treat, my invitation,' I protest.

He looks at me kindly over his glasses. 'One you can ill afford, *ma jeune fille.*' He pats my hand. 'Allow me, at least, the pleasure of treating my daughter to lunch. I am an old man now, I may not be around for much longer. You must follow your heart, that is all I will say, but I won't always be here to advise you.'

I hate it when my father talks like this, and he is doing it with increasing regularity. Yes, he is old. Eighty-four is not young, but there is no sudden decrease in his health, which so far has been reasonably robust. Yet he is adopting more and more a sort of morbid sentimentality which is most unlike him. I find it both annoying and unsettling, and in a stroke he has gained the moral high ground, and I feel both guilty and ashamed for having invited him to lunch, and then allowing him to pay. We take our leave of the restaurant and I say goodbye to him, leaving him to meet some old friends in his club.

I have an appointment with my accountant, whose office is nearby. I had thought that lunch would be a boost to my self-esteem, a buffer to whatever financial woes lay in wait for me. Instead I feel unnerved, both cheated and exposed. I am aware that I am radiating resentment, and am less and less able to conceal it, least of all from myself. When did I become this person? And more importantly, why? What happened to my vision of our marriage? I saw Greg and I growing together, both of us creative, ambitious, tackling new challenges, new adventures along the way, making space for each other's passions and beliefs. Instead, I feel weighed down, trapped, burdened with responsibility, unable to turn to or rely on a partner I no longer believe in, who has robbed me of hope, of feeling he would provide for and protect us as a family. It is not that I mind doing all of the above for myself or my children – I don't – but I do mind doing it alone, in the framework of a lost and lonely relationship.

My father, with his ability to observe and dissect, has

exposed to me what I did not want to face. By always seeking to defend Greg and my marriage to him, I was forced to look at it up close, examine the cracks I could no longer paper over.

I had chosen to see creativity where there was lack of direction or conviction, and to focus on a laconic charm instead of the laziness and selfishness it so carefully masked. I had allowed myself to be blinded by a stupid list of physical attributes espoused by my fifteen-year-old self and, astonishingly, only my own capacity for stubbornness and pride kept me languishing in this partnership where love had long ago slipped quietly away.

I arrive at the steps of my accountant's office and shiver, pulling my light jacket closer. *I can do this,* I think. *This is the easy part.*

I end up staying for almost two hours, for which I will duly be charged.

He is a kind man, Alan, at pains to explain to me just how bad things are, that we can only continue as we are for perhaps three more months. Then I will have to make serious decisions. He asks after Greg, but neglects to suggest that I talk things over with him. An oversight, I'm sure, as Alan is relentlessly polite – or perhaps he too has always felt Greg is redundant. I dismiss the thought; I have simply been in my father's company for too long.

Eventually, I decide to head for home. Greg has promised to take charge of dinner tonight and said he would surprise me. So I stop off at our local off licence and pick up a nice bottle of red, one that's a particular favourite of his. Things might be bad, but there is no point dwelling on the negative. It is Friday evening, I can enjoy dinner and a bottle of wine with my family. I won't think about anything else, not for tonight.

I let myself in the front door, and pause as I stop to remind myself of my blessings. This house, the roof over our heads. The painstakingly refurbished interior, shades of palest Scandinavian creams, whites and greys, painted floorboards, scattered rugs, designer lamps and artfully displayed paintings and framed advertising prints. Greg, in fairness, has a great eye for colour and design. I look in the mirror over the hall table, run my hands through my hair and fix a smile on my face. Then I swing downstairs, bottle in hand, following the unmistakable aroma of an excellent curry, to the kitchen.

'Hey!' Greg looks up and smiles. 'Good timing, we're about to eat.'

I look at the table, which Sophie is setting with unusual care, and Philip is standing by the cooker, looking on with new-found interest. I look also at the vast amount of debris that has piled up in the kitchen sink and all along the stainless steel countertops. But most of all, I look at the strange man who is cooking in my kitchen, wearing my favourite apron featuring a glamorous-looking woman saying *Housework can't kill you – but why take a chance?*

'Diana, meet Rob,' says Greg, relieving me of the bottle of Chateau de Laussac and brandishing a corkscrew. 'I invited Rob to dinner, and he came only on the condition he could cook for us. Rob, this is my wife, Diana.'

Rob looks up from his curry making and simultaneously nods and winks at me. There is something oddly familiar about him, quite apart from the fact that he is wearing a T-shirt and a pair of combat trousers that belong to Greg. I have a slightly surreal sensation, where I feel I am standing in the middle of a set, that is in fact my own home, but I don't quite belong there. Something has changed, the props have been moved, but I know this Rob, where have I met him before? And then it dawns on me. We have not met, Rob and I. He is familiar because I have seen his face on television, more than once. Rob is the homeless man that Greg has interviewed regularly on *The Streets of Dublin*.

'I had dinner with a homeless man last week,' I say. I am sitting on the grass in Vonnie's garden, making a daisy chain, something I have not done for what seems like centuries, and finding it strangely soothing. Vonnie is stretched out, propped up by her elbow, her head resting in her hand. Abby is sitting cross-legged, mindlessly picking at tortilla chips which she alternately dips into salsa or guacamole. A little spider is painstakingly working its way up a strand of her hair, which I neglect to mention. We have eaten lunch, and are lingering over the wine and some glossy magazines. Jazz is playing at her friend Lindsay's house.

Looking at Abby and Vonnie, this scene could be just another version of many photographs I have of the three of us in various similar guises over the years, sitting or sprawled on some summer afternoon, contemplating life, dressed in anything from school uniforms to flares, sporting the odd dangerous haircut or style, and, fittingly enough, back to flares again, which I am now wearing. We have come full circle, in a fashion sense if nothing else.

'How d'you mean?' Abby asks.

'How – or where?'

'Both.'

'In my kitchen and awkwardly,' I say, piercing the stem of a daisy deftly with my nail and threading another one through.

'Did you invite him in? I don't remember you having a particularly fervent social conscience,' Abby continues.

'For your information Abby, I do a lot of work with home-less women.'

'What, hair and make-up?'

'Yes, as a matter of fact, I work with several shelters and hospitals.'

'I would have thought hair and make-up was the least of their problems.'

'It is, but you'd be surprised at the boost of self-esteem a good makeover can give a woman. Taking care of the outside is every bit as important as taking care of the inside. If you can put on a good face to the world, well that's half the battle.

'If you say so.'

I was about to ask Abby what the matter was because she seemed particularly crabby, when Vonnie caught my eye and gave an imperceptible shake of her head to warn me off.

'So how come this guy ended up in your kitchen?' she asked.

'Greg invited him.'

'That was kind of him,' Vonnie said.

'He all but asked him to move in too,' I said. 'Until I played bad cop and spoiled his little social experiment.'

Now it was Abby and Vonnie's turn to look surprised at the sharpness in my voice.

'I mean Greg doesn't know this guy from Adam,' I continued, 'and I'm not sure I want a virtual stranger hanging around the house if I'm not there, particularly with the children at home on holidays. I know it sounds mean, but there's something about him I just don't like, something shifty.'

'I've seen his programme once or twice, Greg's really good,' Abby said. 'He really gets through to those people, he's a great interviewer, that one when he—'

'Yes, yes, I know,' I snapped. 'Greg's wonderful, he's an inspiration, he's breaking new ground in reality television; believe me, he'd agree with you wholeheartedly.'

'Aren't you pleased for Greg?' Abby asks, looking bewildered as Vonnie reaches over to take the bottle of wine and top up our glasses. '*The Streets of Dublin* seems to be such a success for him, I thought after he'd been out of work for so long that you'd be—'

'I am, of course I'm pleased for him, it's just that, well, Greg is getting great publicity and visibility, and the ratings are good, but he's not making any money to speak of. He and his partner produce the whole thing, edit it, the lot, there really isn't anything left over.' I took a drink of wine, suddenly feeling the need to unburden myself. 'Not everyone in television is on ridiculous salaries, you know. Business isn't great at the studio either. We're ticking over, just about, but we're not generating anything like the income we used to, and Greg, well, he just doesn't want to know. He's so wrapped up with *The Streets of Dublin*, he's spending more time in his editing suite than he is at home, and when he is home, well, he's inviting his new buddies back home with him. Look, I don't mean to sound heartless, but after a hard week on my feet, when I'm looking forward to relaxing at home, I do not need to come in to find a stranger cooking in my own kitchen, wearing my husband's clothes.' I let out a long, pent-up sigh.

'He was cooking, in your kitchen?' Abby looks suitably incredulous.

'Yes. That is what I came home to on Friday evening, without any warning I might add.'

'Hmm,' Vonnie grinned. 'Interesting. How'd it go?'

'Great,' I said. 'He'd already had a good soak in the bath, very kindly leaving the bathroom in disarray, towels strewn on the floor, presumably for me to pick up. Oh, and his clothes were whirring away in my washing machine. Everyone raved about his chicken curry, which I'll admit was good, he went to a lot of trouble, apparently he's a keen cook, evidenced by the unbelievable amount of discarded cooking implements he left for me, again, to clear away. I couldn't very well ask him to clear up, could I? And then after dinner he regaled us with outlandish stories, none of which I believe to be true, but, of course, the children were enthralled with, particularly the one where he was pursued by gangsters believing mistakenly, of course, that he was an international spy with extra sensory mentalist-type powers. After that, he and Greg retired to drink another bottle of wine, discussing their theories about future episodes of *The Streets of Dublin*. When I eventually packed the kids off, and had finally got my kitchen back to resembling something approaching normality and called Greg aside to tell him I was going to bed, he had the nerve to say, "It's cool for Rob to stay the night, isn't it? No point him going back to the shelter at this hour." To which I replied if he didn't put Rob in a taxi and get him out of my house, he could accompany him.'

'Did he? Send him back, I mean,' Abby asked between bites.

'Reluctantly.'

'Well, that was something, I suppose.'

'Then we had the mother and father of all rows.' I took a swig of wine remembering the blistering anger I felt as Greg slung his hurtful accusations at me.

'How is it,' he asked, following me down to the kitchen where I had poured myself the meagre remnants of a bottle, 'that everything, but *everything* that happens in this house has to be on your terms?'

'Nothing appears to be on my terms,' I retorted coldly. 'I would have thought that was quite apparent from this evening's little episode in social integration. How dare you bring a strange man into our home without so much as telling me, never mind asking me!'

'Rob is not a strange man, he's a colleague of mine, a mate.'

'Oh please, Greg, even by your standards that's absurd.'

'Oh really, why? What is so absurd about that?'

'He's a homeless man you have interviewed on the street – other than that, as far as you know he could be a serial killer.'

'Now who's being absurd? For your information, Diana,
Rob is an out of work actor, he fell on hard times, lost his
house and all of his savings in a divorce, hit the bottle for a
while, and before he knew it he ended up on the street, living
in shelters. But you, in your wisdom, in your holier-than-
thou-I-know-best-about-everything policy, couldn't even
allow him the luxury of a decent night's sleep on a sofa bed
in the basement. Although why I'm surprised I don't know,
you haven't a charitable bone in your body.'

'How dare you!' I yelled. 'Me? Uncharitable? You miserable
sod! I work like a dog, a bloody dog, I look after this house,
I do the shopping, I drive people around like a taxi service
and I donate my skills to several shelters, so, in case it hasn't
dawned on you, I was volunteering with the homeless way,
way, *way* before you ever were – and you only do it because
it gets your big ugly mug on television. The only charity *you*
work for is the Greg O'Mahony Foundation, and by God
that certainly seems to require a bottomless pit of funding.'

Greg's face had gone white with anger, but I didn't care.
I hadn't meant to go quite that far, but something had snapped
in me and I was sick, sick, *sick* of shouldering all the practical
responsibilities of this marriage on my own.

Of course, I should have known that Greg, being a former
creative director and current scriptwriter, would twist everything I said.

'You're jealous,' he said, his mouth curving into a smile
that made me almost burst a blood vessel with rage. 'You're
jealous because for once in this marriage I am getting the
attention I deserve and you can't handle it!'

I gasped.

'See,' he continued gleefully, 'you can't even deny it. *Ms
Perfect Business Woman, Homemaker, One of Ireland's Most
Stylish Women*, can't hack it when her own husband gets a
bit of recognition for his undeniable talent. God, you're

pathetic, Diana. Anyone else, *anyone,* would be happy for me, supportive of me, but you— you—'

'All I've *done* is support you since you lost your job. *I* was meant to be retiring, remember? *I* was supposed to have some time out, a gap year, not *you.*'

'Oh, so that's what my foray into television producing is to you, is it? A gap year? How charming.'

'Well it certainly can't be counted as income, can it? I mean have you made anything at all from it?' I was quivering with anger, but despair was beginning to crawl around my stomach, which was already in knots.

'Of course,' Greg said wearily. 'Everything has to be about money, doesn't it? I can't even work my ass off trying to get what could be a money-spinning idea off the ground without you rubbing my nose in it that you are the sole earner now. That's a low blow, Diana, even for you.'

'It has to be about money,' I said, 'because soon there won't be any.' I thought about the meeting I had just come from with my accountant – things were worse than I'd thought, a lot worse. Add to that my strangely depressing lunch with Dad and coming home to find a strange man in my house, and I was suddenly all out of fight.

'What do you mean?'

'I had a meeting with Alan late this afternoon,' I said. 'Things are bad at the studio, I've been meaning to talk to you about it, but I thought it could keep, I thought it was just a bad patch, that things would pick up, but it doesn't look as if they will. I don't know how long more we can go on like this.'

'You never said.'

'No, I have to work out a plan for our finances and go back and see Alan in a couple of weeks.'

Greg said nothing, just nodded.

'I'm going to bed,' I said. I brushed past him, not caring any more, as he ran his hands through his hair and along the sides of his skull. He probably thought I'd been waiting for the perfect moment to drop this little bombshell, to rain on his parade yet again, but it had come as just as much of a shock to me. I had probably known, somewhere in the recesses of my mind, that things were deteriorating financially, but somehow, as long as we kept managing from week to week, I could lock the dark prospect of debt tidily away, but now it had reared its ugly head. I was grateful for Alan, he had been my accountant since I had opened the first studio, and I trusted him implicitly. If he said it was time to cut our cloth to fit our coat, well, that was all there was to it. But I didn't have to be happy about it.

'Rows are healthy,' said Abby. 'At least you're talking to each other. I can't remember the last time Edward and I rowed. In fact, I can hardly remember the last time we did anything together.' She pauses. 'Not that it matters, not now. I think it's only a matter of time before he leaves.'

'What?' I said.

'Edward's having an affair,' Abby said, matter of factly.

This was the first time Abby had mentioned this to me. 'Are you absolutely sure of that?' I said, carefully.

Abby shrugged. 'Vonnie knows, I told her. And before you ask why I didn't talk to you, Di, I've tried to, lots of times, but you're impossible to get hold of these days. You never have time to talk on the phone and pinning you down to actually meet is like organising a G20 summit. Things haven't been good between Edward and I for, well, for ages. It's not so much myself I'm worried about, but the kids. I can't imagine . . .'

'Did you talk to him?' Vonnie asked. 'Like you promised?'

'I don't have to ask him outright, that's probably what he wants me to do. I'm not going to help him. If he wants to end this marriage, he's going to have to do it himself.'

'*This* marriage?' I ask incredulously. 'Don't you mean *our* marriage? You sound as if you don't have any part to play in it, Abby.' I could hear my voice escalating angrily and Abby looking at me warily.

'As far as Edward is concerned, any playing he's doing certainly isn't with me.' She paused to draw breath. 'We haven't had sex for almost a year – ten months, I think it's been, to be exact.'

'Abby,' Vonnie looked at her. 'I can't believe you haven't talked to him, you swore you would. You have to hear his side of the story.'

Abby shrugged. 'I've seen her. She's young, pretty and pretty brilliant too, graduated from Harvard with honours.'

'They were together?'

'Minutes apart. They were discreet enough to leave the house separately. I saw all I needed to.'

'You followed him?' I asked incredulously.

'Yes. It was my mother's idea. She was right. We caught him red handed, pretty much.'

Vonnie and I exchanged glances.

'I'm sorry, I just don't believe it,' I said. And I didn't, I don't know why, but something about Edward having an affair just didn't ring true. I just couldn't see him being deceitful that way. Edward was the type of chap who would pompously *tell* you he was going to have an affair, give you ample warning, inform you that you were on final notification to improve things to his satisfaction or else. I said as much to Abby. 'They're like that, surgeons, they're all the same, they think they're God. The only people they have affairs with are themselves.'

'Edward doesn't operate any more, Di. Remember?

'Doesn't matter. Once a surgeon always a surgeon. It's the training, it's ingrained.'

'I preferred it when he was operating,' Abby said. 'He was

always maniacally busy, but he seemed happier somehow. Even though he said running the clinic would give him more flexibility, more time at home, he's more absent than ever. He's become withdrawn, never seems to be himself – not the man I knew, or married, at any rate. I suspect he's been unhappy for ages and couldn't bring himself to tell me, and now he's hoping I'll find out about this affair and confront him.'

'Is this your mother's theory too?' Vonnie asked, quite bravely I thought.

'No, she thinks I'm not being nice enough to Edward, that I've driven him away.'

'I thought she was driving you crazy?' Vonnie looked confused. 'The last time we talked you said you couldn't bear her being around.'

That, too, was news to me. I was torn between feeling very put out that Abby hadn't confided in me about any of this, and wanting to hear what came next. Abby and her mother had always been inseparable. Personally, I could never stand the woman, she was a total social climber and had been terrifyingly ambitious for Abby. She had a most unhealthy hold over her daughter, it seemed to me. Sadly, it appeared, marriage had done little to dissipate that. When I heard Abby and Edward had taken Sheila to live with them, I had thought it was a disastrous idea. Perhaps Edward had more incentive than I thought to have an affair.

Abby looked embarrassed to be reminded of this by Vonnie. 'Well, yes, she was driving me mad – but, now, well, it's nice to have someone on my side, some moral support.'

'Is she really on your side?' I risked.

'What do you mean?' Abby looked indignant.

'I mean, she may have the best intentions for you, Abby, all mothers do for their children, you know that, but maybe in this case she doesn't know what's best for you – or Edward.'

'Edward and my mother have always got on terribly well.'

'That doesn't mean it's healthy to have her living with you. Don't you and Edward find that a bit – claustrophobic?'

'Abby's mom lost everything in the banking shares collapse. They didn't have a choice,' Vonnie explained.

'Maybe it's just as well,' Abby said glumly.

'Why didn't you *talk* to me?' I asked her. 'I was here, just at the end of the phone. I could have helped, or tried to.'

Abby shrugged. 'Thanks, Di. But, like I said, you always seem to be so busy these days . . . and I wasn't ready for a lecture about how to handle my marital problems. Besides, I wasn't really up to talking to anyone about it.'

'I've never lectured you about anything!' I cried, stung by Abby's hurtful remark. Abby said nothing, just looked at her hands. That was when I realised she had no intention of talking to anyone at all about all of this until, as seemed the case, it was far too late. Poor Abby, I thought, living with her mother and without sex, it didn't seem fair. But then life was bizarre like that.

In the beginning, Greg and I had great sex – it was one of the reasons I married him. It's such a barometer of a relationship, sex, isn't it? I mean people make all sorts of excuses about it, having kids, not having the time, losing interest, but the fact is if someone is irritating you or you feel resentful towards them, or you've fallen out of love with them, well you can have all the time in the world, but sex will be the last thing you want to have with them.

'What are you thinking about, Diana?' Abby asks, looking at me curiously. 'You're miles away.'

'Was I?' I say guiltily. 'I was just thinking about sex, actually.'

'Lucky for some. What about you, Vonnie?' Abby looks at her. 'Is there a man in your life at the moment?'

'No.' She takes a sip of wine. 'There's been no one since

Jake. A couple of friends have tried to set me up on dates, but I'm not really interested.'

'But you and Jake are not together, right?'

'No, we're not. But he's a pretty hard act to follow,' she smiles. 'Besides, I don't really have time for a relationship, and I don't want to confuse Jazz.'

'Are you still in love with him?' I ask. The question takes her unawares.

'I . . . no, no I'm not. I love him. I'll always love him. We had some great times together and he's Jazz's father. But, no, that part of our relationship is over.'

Something told me Vonnie wasn't telling the truth, but I didn't push her. Maybe she hadn't admitted it to herself yet – often we don't – but I could tell by her body language, her closing up, her defensiveness, that she had a lot of unresolved feelings about this Jake. I'd put money on it. That's the thing about having been to boarding school with people. There's no hiding from them, not ever.

'Actually,' she said casually, 'he's coming over next week to spend time with Jazz.'

Both Abby and I perked up at this news.

'Will we get to meet the mysterious Jake?' Abby asked.

'Probably,' Vonnie grinned. 'I don't see why not. As long as you promise not to tell any stories out of school – literally.'

'Your secrets are safe with us,' I said. 'When is he coming over?'

'He gets in Friday morning. Jazz is beside herself with excitement.'

'Of course she is,' I smiled. 'Does she miss him?'

'She sees him every other weekend and we share holidays.' A cloud passed over Vonnie's face.

'But it's not the same, is it?' asked Abby, gently.

'No, of course not, but sometimes there's no other way.

And on the positive side, Jazz is too young to remember Jake actually leaving; he was always travelling with his work, she just adjusted to him being away more. I don't think she can remember things any other way. But yes, she misses him, she's a real Daddy's Girl. It's the Southern Belle in her.'

'What about you, Von?' I risked. 'Do you miss him?'

Vonnie bit her bottom lip and took a breath. 'Yes, I do miss him. I miss the way we used to be, but I don't miss what we were becoming.'

'That's a rather enigmatic way of putting it.' I raised my eyebrows hopefully.

'Jazz comes first with me. She's the most important person in my life, that's all anyone needs to know.'

'But you said Jake was a wonderful father,' Abby protested.

'He is,' said Vonnie. 'Look, if it's all the same to you guys, I'd really rather not discuss it.'

Ouch, I thought. Case definitely shut. Still, Jake was coming over, and, with a bit of luck, we might get to meet him. Maybe he would shed some light on things himself. And if not, well, it would be interesting to meet the guy if nothing else.

'Actually, I'm going to see Carmel and Colm tomorrow. Kate will be there too,' Vonnie said.

'Wow,' Abby replied. 'Will you bring Jazz?'

'No, it'll just be us. It's been a long time and there are some things I want to talk about. I'll see how it goes and then decide if I want Jazz to meet with them.'

Neither Abby nor I probed any further. We all had unfinished business, it seemed, with our families.

I thought about that afterwards, on the way home, how we used to tell each other *everything*, Vonnie, Abby and me. But now, well, with the benefit of hindsight, maybe it only seemed that way. Everyone has their secrets. As life goes on, your loyalties have to grow to accommodate other people – spouses and families. Much as we might want to share, to bear our souls about what is causing us grief in our lives, some things are just best kept to ourselves.

Vonnie

The house was pristine. Carmel had made sure of that. She had followed Barney around inspecting every surface while she hoovered and dusted until she had driven the poor woman mad with exasperation. 'Please, Mrs Callaghan,' Barney had begged, stamping her foot on the hoover switch to off, and regarding her long-time employer with a look that Carmel thought came dangerously close to defiance. 'I have cleaned and kept this house for nearly fifty years. I may be getting on a bit, but I am quite capable of doing my job without you following me around like an avenging angel.' She glared at Carmel, who took a reluctant step back.

'Yes, well, quite,' Carmel said. 'But I want everything to be absolutely perfect. Veronica is coming to visit and—'

'Vonnie is coming *home*, Mrs Callaghan,' Barney said firmly. 'She is coming home to the house she lived and grew up in for eighteen years. I understand you want everything to be just so, but, with all due respect, I doubt that Vonnie will be checking for dust or finger marks on the furniture. Won't she just want to have a look around the place, rediscover her childhood haunts? I've made her favourite treacle tart and lemon meringue pie, just the way she likes it; if she's the girl I remember, she'll be far more interested in that.' Barney's face broke into a wide smile, she looked hopeful. 'Will she be bringing the child, the little girl?'

Carmel stiffened. She hadn't wanted that little nugget of information to get out. God knows how Barney knew, Carmel knew she had certainly never mentioned anything about it in the village; no doubt Colm had been blathering to anyone who would listen. Carmel privately thought he had been adversely affected by the anaesthetic when he had his hip done. He was never the most talkative man when he was younger, but nowadays he was a regular chatterbox. You wouldn't know what would come out of his mouth. And when she wasn't there to monitor him, he could be a liability. Loose talk was dangerous, especially in a village such as theirs, where tongues wagged freely and the local gossips added liberally to what they knew or suspected.

'I've no idea, but I doubt it.'

'Why not? Why wouldn't she?' Barney looked crestfallen.

'It's been a long time since we've seen Veronica.' Carmel was guarded. 'I imagine she'll come alone. She didn't say.'

'All the more reason to bring her little girl. What I wouldn't give to see her. I'm sure she's gorgeous, it would be such a treat to set eyes on her and her mother. There's nothing like the sound of children's laughter to fill a house, it's not a home until—' Barney broke off, embarrassed at the sentence she left unfinished, hanging in the air.

'Kate will be coming too, of course, you know that. So we'll be four for afternoon tea.'

'Yes, Mrs Callaghan,' Barney said dutifully. She was looking forward so much to seeing Vonnie after all these years. It had been such a tragedy when she had left like that without saying goodbye to anyone. She had written to Barney, of course, saying she had to leave, that she couldn't stay another minute in the house. Although Barney didn't know the details, she could guess it was something to do with Carmel and Colm. She couldn't blame Vonnie for wanting to get away. She knew Vonnie had never seemed to fit in no matter how she tried, and it had broken Barney's heart watching her hide her pain as a young girl. And there had been nothing Barney could do except talk to her, reassure her and bake her favourite things for her. She shook her head sadly. Families were complicated things at the best of times, but this one would give most a run for their money.

Still, Vonnie would be here tomorrow, after all these years. Barney didn't know what the purpose of the visit was, but she got the impression it wasn't a long-awaited family gathering. And the way Carmel was going on, you'd think a visiting dignitary was coming to the house and not her own daughter. Still, Barney didn't care. She'd get a chance to see her favourite girl. She was an old woman now herself. She couldn't go on working for much longer. It would be a blessing to see her dear Vonnie before she died. Barney had always loved her. She tried very hard to love Kate, too, but she had never really taken to her – probably because the girl was far too much like her mother. Funny how life worked out, Barney thought. All those years, over twenty of them, and they had gone so quickly. Barney wondered if Vonnie would recognise her, she was seventy-five now. She hadn't thought she'd see her again. Then, to hear she had a daughter, a little girl, well, that had made her almost tear up and cry when she had heard from Monica Lavelle in the post office last week. Of course, she hadn't wanted to seem too surprised – she wouldn't give her the satisfaction – but afterwards, as she walked home, she had been furious. After all it was she, Barney, who had worked for the family for most of her adult life, and to think she had to hear that Vonnie had a daughter from the local gossip. Sometimes Barney despaired of the Callaghans. But she had wisely kept her mouth shut and said nothing. Not until today, when Carmel was following her around like Marley's ghost. Then she had asked about the little girl. Not that she got much of a reply, but still, the look on Carmel's face made up for it.

Kate had gone to a lot of trouble with her appearance. She always made sure she was well groomed and stylish; after all, in her profession as a dermatologist, how she presented herself to her patients and the world in general was important, but today – in fact for a whole week leading up to today – she had left no stone unturned. Her hair had been freshly trimmed and highlighted, her eyelashes and eyebrows tinted, and she had given herself a facial peel so her complexion looked fresh and dewy. She had even had a fake tan application at her local salon although she hated the stuff – messy though it was, it did give you a nice glow, and lately she had been feeling anything but glowy.

What to wear too had been minutely considered. Though why she was bothered she didn't know. I mean what did it matter how she looked, what she wore, for a meeting with a sister (who was in fact a cousin) who had left home so long ago and hadn't even bothered to stay in touch? Not that they had ever been particularly close, but Kate had had to put up with her all those years, share her childhood with an inter-loper, a very ungainly interloper at that, a girl who was more often than not an embarrassment to have around, never mind paraded as your sister.

Her mother had told Kate she should feel sorry for Vonnie, a big, plain girl whose own mother had left her, abandoned her, literally on their very own doorstep. What else *could* they do but take her in? Her mother had said she knew it was hard for her, but think how hard it must be for Veronica, having a sister as pretty and popular as she was. She would just have to be patient with the girl and feel sympathetic towards her.

But Kate hadn't felt sympathetic. It didn't matter that she was prettier or more popular or had more boyfriends. Once she had known that Vonnie was not her real sister, not even a properly adopted sister but a girl abandoned by her Aunt Angela, Kate had resented Vonnie all the more. She wasn't sure why, either. But even though Vonnie was tall and fat, she had an annoying way of seeming comfortable with herself that Kate couldn't understand (she would rather *die* than be that fat) and people seemed to like her for it. At boarding school, particularly, she had come out of herself and been sporty. She had been on the debating team and considered brainy. She had made some good friends, even that half-French girl, Diana something or other, who was considered rather seriously cool. Then to just leave like that for London – and never come back. Not until now at any rate. And Kate was annoyed at how disconcerted she felt about the whole thing.

She cast her mind back to that evening a few weeks ago when she had got the phone call, right out of the blue. It was seven p.m., and Simon and she were just finishing supper. It was the house phone that rang and not her mobile, so Kate assumed it was her mother as she always used the landline.

'Hello,' she said, rather irritated – she was in no mood for one of her mother's laments, which could go on indefinitely. Kate had planned to sit Simon down and ask him what exactly he intended to do about the amount of money they appeared to be losing in the property syndicate investment that had gone horribly wrong. When she had heard the cool, low-pitched voice with the slight American inflection say, 'Kate, hello. This is Vonnie,' she had all but dropped the phone. The same cool voice went on to inform Kate that she was back in Ireland for a couple of months or so on a work assignment and that she would probably catch up with her at some stage. Catch up with her! Kate could hardly believe her ears. The nerve of her! She who had waltzed off twenty-seven years ago leaving Kate to take responsibility for their now elderly parents. Vonnie had asked after Carmel and Colm, of course, but when Kate had announced that her father had had his hip done, all Vonnie had said was what a successful operation it seemed to be these days. 'So I believe,' Kate had replied dryly. Surely Vonnie would have heard that Kate was a doctor – a consultant – but just in case she made sure of it. 'Of course I made sure he was with the best orthopaedic surgeon in the country, one of my colleagues.'

'Yes, I heard you were in medicine,' Vonnie had replied. 'That's nice for you.'

Nice! Kate gritted her teeth. All those back-breaking years of study and internships and being worked to the bone on little or no sleep most of the time – nice? Vonnie made it sound like, well, she couldn't think what, but she certainly hadn't responded with anything like the respect and admiration she should have.

'What are you working at these days?' Kate asked. Last she had heard, Vonnie had been a secretary or some kind of dogsbody on a magazine in London.

'I'm a freelance writer.'

Well that covered a multitude, Kate thought, probably meant she was still a gofer.

'But I have a little girl now, so taking care of her is my main occupation.'

'I see, so we weren't invited to the wedding, then?' Kate said snidely.

'There wasn't one,' Vonnie replied simply.

'What, so you—?'

'Look, I really don't have time to chat right now, Kate. Maybe you could just tell Carmel and Colm that I'm back for a while, that I'd like to see them . . . and you of course.' She went on, 'I'll ring them, but it would probably be easier for them if they heard about it first from you.'

Then she had said she would be in touch when she had settled in. Kate had put down the phone wanting to punch something very hard. The nerve of her! The bloody *nerve*.

'What is it?' Simon asked, as Kate sank into a chair looking furious. 'You look like you need a drink.'

'Make it a generous one,' Kate said. 'That was my beloved long-lost "sister". She's back in town.'

Simon gave a low whistle and went to open a bottle of red. He had never met Vonnie, the mysterious sister/cousin person, but he was very relieved she was showing up again. Her timing was perfect. Judging by how his wife had taken the news, it would distract her from the ongoing bottomless pit of money the property syndicate investment was turning out to be.

Now Kate was in her car, heading for the Old Rectory where she and Vonnie had grown up – and where her parents still lived. She had promised Carmel to be down early, for moral support, she supposed, although why Carmel could be bothered to get herself into such a state about the visit, God only knew. She had been like an anti-Christ since Kate had told her Vonnie was back in the country. Since Vonnie had rung her and said she would like to call and see them, Carmel had become completely unhinged. So much so that she was now making Kate antsy. It was completely ridiculous. Vonnie was the one who had abandoned everybody, not them. Talk about the Prodigal Daughter. Carmel had been planning and organising things for weeks, she'd all but had the house redecorated, and all because she seemed to want to impress a thankless girl that had been taken in by them when her own mother dumped her.

Kate couldn't understand it. *She* had been the loyal one, the one who was always there for them, and she certainly never remembered as much fuss being made when she and Simon visited. It was most unfair, most irrational really. Well, whatever about Carmel, Kate was determined that she wasn't going to be taken in by whatever sob story Vonnie was peddling – and there was bound to be one. That was obviously why she had got in touch with them in the first place. No doubt it was something to do with the child, and her being a single parent; she was probably looking for money. Why, otherwise, would she be contacting her erstwhile family now, after all this time?

She took the turn off the N11 and drove down the familiar roads that led to the bustling village and beyond, eventually taking a left fork in the road and swinging into her parents' driveway.

Barney answered the door, wearing a freshly laundered overall and a hopeful expression, which became a fixed smile when she saw that it was Kate at the door and not her beloved Vonnie. Kate walked inside briskly, giving her the cakes she had bought in The Butler's Pantry. 'Mum asked me to bring these,' she said. 'Is she upstairs, Barney?'

Barney looked crestfallen. 'But why would she? I've been baking all week,' she said, sounding hurt and bewildered.

Kate was spared inventing an excuse by the sound of her mother's voice calling from the sitting room. 'I'm in here, Kate. Come on in.'

The house was gleaming in the midday sunshine, and a smell of fresh polish and delicious aromas from the kitchen wafted through the air.

'How do I look?' Carmel fingered the jacket of her cerise linen trouser suit and checked her newly done hair in the over-mantel mirror.

'You look fine, Mum,' Kate said wearily.

'Fine? Only fine?' Carmel sounded wounded.

'Why do you care how you look?' Kate said. 'It's only Vonnie, the girl took off twenty-seven years ago without so much as a thank you for bringing her up, and now she swings back into town and you're getting yourself all dolled up, for what, exactly?'

Carmel's mouth tightened. 'It's a matter of self-respect, that's all. I notice you haven't been exactly slap dash yourself,' she eyed Kate's hair and the large solitaire diamond ring that had been a present from Simon during the boom times. 'You've had your hair done,' she said accusingly.

'So have you.'

'Did you bring the cakes?'

'Yes, I gave them to Barney to put in the kitchen.'

'Good. She's been impossible since she heard Veronica was coming. I couldn't get her to concentrate on anything. I had to go over everything myself to make sure it was done properly. You'd swear it was *her* daughter coming to visit.'

Kate resisted pointing out the obvious fact that *she* was the only and rightful daughter of the house. Instead, she sat down and picked up a glossy magazine and began to leaf through it. 'I don't know why you wanted me to come down this early. What time is she coming?'

'Three o'clock,' Carmel said nervously.

'I had to cancel an afternoon's worth of patients.'

'You're very good, Kate. I appreciate it, you know I do.' She sat down beside her and patted Kate's hand.

'What on earth has you so jittery?' Kate looked at her, perplexed.

'I don't know.' Carmel's hand began to fidget with the pearls around her neck. 'It's been so long, I suppose, and, well, do you think she'll bring the child?' she looked even more anxious.

'How would I know?'

'Did she say anything, to you, you know, on the phone?'

'She spoke to you last.'

'Yes, I know, I can't really remember. I don't think she said anything. I didn't anyway.'

'Well we'll find out soon enough. Where's Dad?'

'In his study, where else?' Carmel got up and began to pace the floor.

'I'll go in and see him,' said Kate. She couldn't stand another minute of her mother's anxious fretting. Her father no doubt was very wisely hiding. Kate looked at her watch – over an hour and a half to go, how on earth would she stand it?

Jazz had her art class and, afterwards, Lindsay's mother very kindly agreed to take her for the afternoon until I would be back to pick her up. This was a journey I had to make on my own. I hadn't thought about it much, I hadn't allowed myself to, but now that the day was finally here, I was unusually nervous. I thought I had a handle on all this stuff. God knows I had talked about it enough, gone over it time and time again with my therapist, even Jake had made me talk about it over and over. But talking about it, putting it all in some nice tidy basket labelled the past, analysing it and finally persuading myself I understood it all, still didn't prepare me for facing it head on. In America I was removed from it, even talking to Angela hadn't been so bad.

But now, being back in Dublin, immersed in all the old familiar sights and sounds, meeting my old school friends even, well, it put me right *back* there – back to my early home life, back to being big, geeky, always-in-the-way Vonnie.

I had told myself time and time again that I could do this. Now I wasn't so sure. But I wanted them to know that I knew the truth. Of course, I am a different person now. I am armed with the truth, always a formidable weapon, but I didn't feel armed. I felt vulnerable, unwanted, not good enough, not part of this family and, most of all, not loved. And, of course, what I wanted more than anything was to be loved, to feel whole and worthwhile. That was where my trouble lay. And no amount of reassurance could help me – even Jake hadn't been able to. Oh, sure, I knew he had loved me, but I couldn't trust him – I couldn't trust anybody – and, in the end, Jake had proved me right. And that was the biggest let down of all. But I had to move on, leave all that behind. What happened, happened. The most important thing was that Jake *did* love Jazz. He adored her.

Maybe that's why we all make mistakes, so we can learn from them, from the hurt we cause others, unwittingly perhaps, so that we can be better friends and lovers in the future. But, right now, I had to face my past, and it was scaring the hell out of me.

I borrowed Lindsay's mother's car for the drive, allowing an hour for the journey, although she assured me it would take forty minutes at the most, what with the new road and all, but seeing as I wasn't even driving last time I had been in Carmel and Colm's house, I had no idea how long it could take me to get there. I might even need to stop off in a hotel or pub for a drink to give me Dutch courage, but I hoped it wouldn't come to that.

By the time I hit the motorway out of town I was forcing myself to breathe deeply, but my heart was in my mouth and my hands on the steering wheel were slippery with perspiration. I turned the radio up, and concentrated on trying to remember the lyrics of the song that was playing. After a while I began to relax. As the miles sped by, familiar memories began to surface, of days like this one, warm and sunny, along the same route, getting the bus back to school. Days golden with promise and the expectations of what our futures would hold. Back then, our only worries had been what would be for supper, a desperately awaited phone call from a boy, or frantically trying to get a tan, lining up like prostrate sardines against the school walls at every break, socks rolled down and skirts tucked into our pants, until one of the nuns would come by, red faced with fury, telling us we would go to hell for giving the gardener or maintenance man reason for impure thoughts.

We didn't know how good we had it.

Twenty minutes later I see the sign for our local village and take the exit. Now the terrain becomes more familiar, and the years once again fall away. The village, a town really, but always called 'the village', sits bathed in dappled sunlight, its houses and shops painted cheery new colours. Ample pots of flowers sit outside doorways or hang from lampposts. It has had a Celtic Tiger makeover in my absence, and is nothing like the drab, dreary place I left behind. I drive through the streets I once walked, ran and cycled, past the post office and past the three obligatory pubs, now with smart wooden benches outside and menus featuring up-to-the-minute dishes on blackboards. The other side of the village, I continue along a twisting road dotted with familiar trees and wreathed in hedgerow. I see the fork in the road ahead, the one where I will veer left – and I pull over and stop the car. I could still back out, abandon the whole thing like the bad idea it probably was, but then I thought of Jazz and the questions she would want answers to when she was older, and Jake, who had encouraged me, prodding me, nudging me for years to do this. I couldn't face him if I bottled out now. I took a deep breath and started the car. In an hour, maybe even less, it would all be over, I would have said my piece. Once I had decided, I felt better about it.

Diana

I was bad tempered all day – even in the studio, which was quiet. Usually I found going to work soothing, I could lose myself in familiar tasks, friendly faces and company, and doing what I loved. But today, nothing was working. The morning was spent bawling out a supplier who had messed up an order and trying to work out a resolution, and in the afternoon I had a ghastly third-rate celebrity booked in to have her make-up done for an awards ceremony. She was hard work at the best of times, but today, convinced she was going to win something for her part in a reality TV show, she was practically hyperventilating.

'It has to be this *exact* colour,' she was shrieking. And she proceeded to extract from her handbag a collection of lurid fabric swatches her stylist had given her instructions to match with eye make-up, blusher and lips.

'I won't do it,' I said flatly.

'What?'

'I won't do it, Moira. You will look hideous if I use those colours. For starters, they're tacky and even if I did like them, you simply couldn't carry them off. Nobody leaves my studio unless they look their absolute and utter best. Quite apart from having my clients' best interests at heart, I also have my own reputation to protect.'

'But my stylist—'

'I don't care what your stylist has said. She is not a make-up artist. And I doubt very much if she has worked with the major couture houses in Paris and Milan as I have. I will keep in mind the colours you are wearing, but I will make you up, as I always do, to flatter your own skin tone under the television cameras and enhance your features accordingly. Now if you have a problem with that you are perfectly entitled to leave and go elsewhere.'

For the first time in her life I suspect, Moira was speechless. She sat back quietly and let me get on with the job. My staff kept a respectful distance too, I noticed. When I was finished with Moira, I retreated to my office, intending to go through the paperwork I would have to put together for my accountant. But when I sat down at my computer and pulled up the appropriate spreadsheet, it blurred before my eyes and I realised tears were spilling down my face. 'Stop it!' I said to myself fiercely. 'Don't you dare cry! Not now. Not here.' I rummaged for a tissue and blew my nose. I couldn't go on like this – *we* couldn't go on like this. I would do it tonight. I would sit Greg down and tell him after dinner. Say we had to talk, that our marriage was clearly on the rocks, that I couldn't live this lie a minute longer.

The journey home was interminable. Why is it when you have come to an agonisingly difficult decision and need to act speedily with the courage of your convictions does the whole world seem to conspire to slow you down? I sat in rain-sodden traffic as the car inched its way forward, with my heart in my mouth and a boulder in the pit of my stomach. When I finally turned into our road, all the parking spaces were taken so I had to drive around for another ten minutes before I found one, about a mile away. Then I half-walked, half-ran, until I arrived on my doorstep like a drowned rat. I let myself in and walked down to the kitchen. Greg, Sophie and Philip were seated around the table, heads bent chatting and laughing over the script Greg was working on. They didn't hear me come in, and it was a minute before they realised I was there. A minute in which our intertwined lives seemed to flash before me. I watched Greg's smile, replicated on Philip's face as Greg ruffled his hair affection-ately. I saw Sophie's expression alight with fun and mischief, a childlike chink in the armour of her studiously sophisticated teenage sang-froid. I felt the love in my husband's eyes envelop our children as softly as sunlight.

'Hey!' Greg looked up to see me. 'You look like someone who could use a glass of wine.'

'I certainly could,' I agreed. 'Something smells good.' I sniffed the air appreciatively.

'Chicken casserole,' Sophie said. 'Granny's recipe, she gave it to me last week so I could practise for my Home Ec. competition.'

'We thought you'd be tired when you got in, you've been running yourself ragged lately.' Greg handed me a glass of red. 'Why don't you put your feet up for a few moments and relax?'

'That's a good idea,' I said. 'I'm just going to get out of these wet clothes, then I'll come down and do just that. And Sophie, *thank you* for doing dinner, it was sweet of you. Even if it is only Home Ec. practice.'

'No problem,' she grinned.

Upstairs, I peeled off my clothes and got into a steaming shower. I shut my eyes tight and let the water run down my body, wishing it could wash away once and for all the feelings of guilt, cowardice and deceit that clung to me like a second skin.

Not tonight, I think. *I will do it tomorrow. Maybe tomorrow . . .*

Vonnie

The Old Rectory was just as I remembered. I got out, noticed a smart 4x4 SUV and two other cars parked in the driveway, presumably Colm's and Carmel's. Then I took a deep breath and rang the doorbell.

Barney opened the door, just as she always had; she was older, now, of course, but she looked much the same as ever. I could tell she'd had her hair done that morning.

'Oh, dear God,' she exclaimed. The wide smile on her face faltered, as she put her hand to her mouth. 'I— I can't believe it. Vonnie? Is that really you, Vonnie?'

'It's me, Barney,' I said. 'Can I come in?'

She stepped back, laughing and tearful as I hugged her. 'What am I like? Come in, come in, we've been waiting and waiting, it's just that . . . Oh, my, but you look like a film star.'

'Is that Veronica?' I heard Carmel's voice from the sitting room.

'They're inside.' She inclined her head. 'Go on in and I'll bring the tea.'

Barney hovered behind me as I approached the sitting room, waiting, no doubt, to see the reaction I would get. I couldn't say I blamed her. Family reunions like this didn't happen every day. I took a deep breath and went in. They were all standing, Carmel, Kate and Colm, who leaned on a walking stick. The formality of the greeting, like a reception committee, struck me as both ridiculous and sad. There was no welcome, no warmth registered on their faces, just awkwardness, surprise, a ripple of unease.

'Vonnie!' It was Kate who spoke first.

'Hello, Kate.' I looked at the cousin I had remembered and envied, and saw a small woman, expensively but unimaginatively dressed, whose face, set in the comfortable beginnings of jowls, registered dislike despite the smile she forced.

'Carmel,' I smiled at my aunt, who was twisting her hands. She seemed unsure how to greet me, so I put a hand on her shoulder and kissed her cheek.

'Well, Veronica,' she said, 'it's nice of you to pay us a visit after all this time.'

'It's nice to see you too,' I said. 'Colm, I hope your hip is coming along well?'

'What?' he seemed flustered and older, much older. 'Oh, yes, thank you, very good, very good.'

'Well, sit down, why don't you,' Carmel said, lowering herself carefully onto the sofa, with Kate beside her, while Colm collapsed into his winged chair. I sat opposite, on the only other available chair. 'Barney, bring the tea in, would you?'

'It's on the way.' Barney disappeared reluctantly. For a moment, no one said anything. The air was heavy with unspoken accusations – theirs – not mine.

'I brought some things . . . gifts. They're outside, in the hall.'

'You're very good,' said Carmel. 'There was no need.'

I noticed Colm's face brighten at this. He would enjoy the cigars I had brought for him. I suspected, more likely than not, he didn't get the chance to enjoy much these days.

Barney arrived back with the tea and a tray full of sandwiches, buns, cakes and petits fours. There was enough to feed an army. She handed out plates watchfully, and I was careful to help myself to a slice of treacle tart, which won a smile of approval.

It was Kate who finally got down to business. 'Why now, Vonnie, after all these years?'

'I wanted to talk to you,' I said simply. 'I wanted to hear your side of the story.'

'What's to know?' said Kate. 'Mum and Dad told you what happened, that's obviously why you stormed off all those years ago without so much as a thank you. After all—'

'After all, what, Kate? After all they did for me?'

Carmel sat with her mouth pursed, but Colm began to shift in his chair uncomfortably.

'They took you in, you can't deny that,' Kate was warming to her theme. 'They made you part of this family when your own mother abandoned you.'

The word struck me as it always did, coldly, accusingly, and inwardly I flinched but outwardly I remained calm. I could do this. I was a different person now. I wouldn't let them – any of them – make me feel beholden any more.

'Yes, yes you did.' I looked at Carmel. 'And I believe I did thank you, several times.' I turned to Kate. 'It can't have been easy for you either, Kate. You got an unasked-for sister to share your parents, your home with. I'm sorry about that.'

'It was no big deal.'

'But it was for me. That's why I left.'

'What happened, happened,' Carmel said, matter of factly. 'You have a daughter yourself now, I believe?'

'Yes, that's right. She's seven years old. She's curious about her family, her grandparents . . . you can understand.'

'Is that what this is about?' Kate asked. 'You want to introduce her to us?'

'We'd like to meet her,' Colm sat forward in his chair, 'Wouldn't we?' He looked hopefully at Carmel. 'We wouldn't say anything, you know, we wouldn't tell her.'

'Tell her what, Dad?' demanded Kate. 'She's not your granddaughter to tell anything to.'

Colm slumped back, deflated. 'I just thought . . . have you got a photograph?' he asked.

'Yes, I do.' I fished for the one I kept in my handbag and handed it to him. He put on his glasses and looked at it, tilting it this way, then that. 'She's very pretty,' he said. 'She's got your smile. What's her name?'

'Her name is Jazz,' I said. Then Kate leaned over and took the photo from him. She looked at it, then looked back at me and smiled, handing the picture to Carmel. Carmel peered at it, inhaled sharply, and handed it back to me. 'I see,' she said. 'Well, there's no point is there?'

'No point in what?'

'No point meeting her. I mean Kate's right. There's no point at all pretending that we're—'

'Who said anything about pretending?' I said. 'I have no intention of pretending anything to my daughter. She is entitled to the truth, just as every child is.'

'Nobody hid the truth from you, if that's what you're implying.' Carmel shot a look at me.

'If you've come back to hurl abuse at poor Mummy, then I think you should leave now,' said Kate. 'You've never been able to face the truth, that's why you ran away.'

'I'm not hurling abuse at anyone,' I said, trying to keep my voice level. 'And I've never been afraid of the truth – that's why I'm here.'

'There's nothing more to be told,' said Carmel. 'If the truth's what you're looking for, you need to speak to your own mother.'

'I already have spoken to her.'

'Angela?' Colm sat up again. 'You met Angela? How— How is she?'

'She's very well,' I said.

'Why wouldn't she be?' Carmel took a sip of her tea. 'That woman thought of herself and no one else her whole life. She put our parents in an early grave with her carry on.'

'She said she was sorry about a lot of things.'

Carmel snorted. 'Sorry! Did she say she was sorry for lying, for running away, for stealing the money from our parents to get on that plane back to America?' Carmel's voice was rising.

'She said she paid that back, every cent of it.'

'The damage was done by then. And what about you? What did she say about leaving you?'

'She's not proud of it. But she didn't bullshit me.'

'Meaning?'

'She didn't try to defend herself. Except . . .'

'Except what?'

'Promise she'll be a devoted grandmother, no doubt,' Kate said snidely.

Carmel was studying her hands.

'Except,' I continued, 'except that she told me how much she paid you.'

I paused and looked at them. Carmel opened her mouth, then shut it. Colm flushed a deep red, and coughed – only Kate looked baffled.

'What do you mean?'

'I mean that my mother paid them handsomely for having me – keeping me, if you like. Isn't that so?'

'Angela wasn't short of money. It was the least she could do, to contribute to your keep.'

'But she didn't just contribute to my keep, did she?'

'What does it matter?' Kate sounded bored.

'She paid for everything, didn't she? That was the deal. She paid for schools, university, for you, Kate. I believe she paid several times over for this very house.'

'What are you talking about?' Kate was disdainful.

'I'm talking about the price you pay for marrying a gambler.' I looked at Carmel, who avoided my eyes.

'You're crazy!' Kate looked from one to the other of her parents.

'I'm not, though, am I, Colm?' I looked at him, shrunken in his chair, his belligerent expression looking strangely childish set amidst elderly, drooping features.

'That's a lie,' Kate said.

'I have the bank drafts to prove it. I have them right here with me, every one of them. Angela gave them to me.'

'I think it's time you left.' Carmel got up.

'You're not going to let her waltz in here and make outlandish accusations,' Kate looked at her mother, appalled, but Carmel said nothing.

I rose from my chair. 'I'm sorry you feel that way,' I said, 'but it's better to get the story straight – for all our sakes.'

'Just go!' said Kate.

'I'm sorry.' It was barely audible, as Colm stood up shakily.

'So am I,' I said. And I meant it. I did feel sorry for him. Addiction is a terrible thing. It breaks hearts and families. I should know.

I went into the kitchen, to say goodbye to Barney. I gave her my address in Dublin and asked her to come and see me, to meet Jazz.

Then I took a last look around the hall of the house I grew up in, that my mother paid for me to grow up in, that never came close to feeling like a home to me. Back in the safety of my borrowed car, I took a deep breath and started the engine, reversing, then swinging out of the driveway onto the road.

I felt lighter, if not happier (I had not expected it to be a happy occasion). I hadn't wanted to cause any trouble, but if Kate had been unaware of her father's gambling history, or the extent of it, then she would have to talk to her mother about it. But I wasn't going to let them make me feel beholden to them for one more minute. If Angela did me any favour, it was that one.

But as I drove away, a familiar emptiness stalked me. I had done what I came to do, but it brought me no pleasure. There was no regret either, only a vague bewilderment at my ability to shut people out. And I wondered, if it weren't for Jazz, if I would ever have known real love at all.

Diana

'Personal call for you,' Lizzie our receptionist said as I picked up my direct line in the office. 'It's a man, wouldn't give his name. He said you'd know.'

'Fine,' I said wearily. 'Put him through.'

It could well be Alan; I was expecting a call from him, although I could never remember him being this evasively discreet. But then with accountants you never knew, especially if there was bad news in the pipeline, and I was preparing myself for the worst.

'Hello? I said. Hello?'

A man was laughing softly down the line, a sinister sound. This was followed by heavy breathing, and the sound of something breaking, shattering. I hung up immediately, and gave instructions that no one was to be put through to me without identifying themselves.

'Crank caller?' Lizzie guessed correctly. 'What a waste of space, probably some school kids.'

'Probably,' I agreed. 'The holidays are way too long.'

Probably, or possibly not. The call wouldn't have bothered me in the slightest if it hadn't been identical to three previous ones I had already received this week on my mobile. All from an unknown number, also a mobile. Whoever this weirdo was, he knew my mobile number and where I worked.

Even then I told myself I was being stupid, paranoid – a crank phone call was just that, nothing more.

That was until the letter arrived, sent to the office the following day, marked private and confidential along with my other post. I opened it, and before I could even start to read it my hands began to tremble. It was on a sheet of A4 white paper, and the jerky, disjointed lines were made up of cut-out newsprint letters and words. It was a classic, old-fashioned, poison pen letter.

'I know what you're playing at Whore
I've been following you and I know
All about Your dirty little secret
Bitches like you need to be taught a lesson
Your family will be better off
Without you'

I sat down, my legs suddenly weak, feeling my throat constrict as I gasped and reached automatically for the glass of water on my desk. *Call the police!* The impulse rang loud and clear in my mind. But what would I say? That I was getting crank calls and poison pen letters? I would sound like something out of an Enid Blyton novel. No one had slashed my tyres, or put a brick through my window, which had happened to a woman I used to work with. Nobody had physically threatened me.

Besides, I reasoned, what in the name of God would I tell Greg?

Jake

There's this kid I meet with, once a week, called Ray. He's fifteen, going on forty-five, with a couple of DUIs under his belt, a conviction for car theft and a dead-end future if he doesn't clean up his act. Thing is, he's as smart as paint – but he doesn't get it and doesn't know what to do with it, because no one has told him, no one has showed him. His father was a dealer who got shot. His mother had a succession of boyfriends the latest of whom got her onto crack and onto the streets. His older brother is already in prison. He is very angry, very confused and in a lot of pain, but he's damned if he's going to let anyone see that, least of all himself. He'll get there when he's ready, with a little help from his friends, people who care about him, people who understand, who've been there – even though, right now, he won't let us in. That's okay, I know just how he feels.

You don't need an under-privileged background to begin pressing the self-destruct button, although it can help. Pretty much anything can tip you over the edge if the right circumstances align. For some people, it can be genetic, for others a trauma, a bereavement, a loss of some kind. For more, it can simply be having too much. And then there's the unbearable loneliness of not fitting in, whether it's with the people around you, or in your own skin or body, or someone letting you know, innocently or otherwise, that you are not good enough, that you are somehow wanting. There are as many reasons to begin hating yourself if you go looking for them as there are colours and shapes of people. And once you start, it's very hard to stop. That's when it becomes all about escaping, losing yourself, getting as far away from those feelings as you can, shutting them out, numbing them with the poison or destructive behaviour of your choice. That's where Ray is at.

His social worker is desperately trying to get him on the

Program, get him going to meetings and off the alcohol and drugs. He laughs at the idea. So I said I'd talk to him, spend some time with him, see what I could do to help.

Today, we are in my studio.

Ray is looking at my prized vintage Leica camera, turning it over and over in his hands.

'This is cool,' he says. 'How much?'

I tell him the price it would fetch and he lets out a low whistle. 'Man, you gotta be rich.'

'I just work hard,' I say.

'No shit?' he says derisively.

'No shit. That's all it takes.'

'Yeah, right.' He puts the camera down and shoves his hands in the pockets of his jailbird jeans, riding low on his skinny black hips. I look at him as he struts around the studio, radiating resentment, anger, beneath which a pitiable teenage curiosity is trying to surface, which he is equally determined to hide. My heart aches for him, this skinny, angry, clever, *clever* kid, hell bent on destroying himself, but I can't let him see that.

'Sarah told me you paint.'

Sarah is his social worker and graffiti is his form of self-expression, most of it angry, like him.

'She don't know shit about me.'

'Do you?'

'What?'

'Paint?'

'I don't do no artistic shit.'

'You ever thought about taking photographs?'

'Only on my cell.' He brandishes his iPhone.

'Which you stole, right?'

He grins, for the first time, his face transforming. 'No shit?' he says.

'You wanna learn?'

'What?' he looks wary.

'How to take pictures, proper pictures.'

'From who?'

'Me.'

'What, anorexic white models and kids in fancy dress? Forget it.'

'Well, you like to express yourself, don't you?'

'Meaning?'

'I was thinking more about something like this.' I take out my portfolio of award-winning shots – from Soweto to Iraq – and began to leaf through them.'

'Man.' He let out another low whistle. 'You took these?'

'They got my name on them. I was there.'

'Cool.' He begins to look, riveted. 'How many men you seen killed?'

'Too many,' I say. 'And it's always ugly.'

He looks at me, our eyes meet, and he nods, slowly. 'No shit?' he says. But this time the mask has dropped. There is a glimmer of interest. Something has spoken to him. We have a breakthrough of sorts, I hope.

'I can show you how to start,' I say. 'But you gotta show up – and show up clean, no drugs, no alcohol.'

'Why?' he looks belligerent. 'Why would you do that?'

'Because you remind me of me.'

'No shit?'

'No shit,' I say.

'Bullshit,' he says, grinning. 'Ain't no way you like me. You come from rich folks.'

'I didn't do drugs like you do,' I admit, 'but I drank, and I know what it's like to be angry.'

'You look like you doing okay. Don't think you owe me no favours man.'

'I was doing fine,' I say. 'Until I fell in love – had a baby girl, a family.'

'No shit. What happened?'

'I kept drinking, that's what happened. And I lost them. I lost the woman I loved and I almost lost my baby girl.'

'Families aren't worth shit,' he says darkly.

'Depends what you make of them,' I say.

'Didn't do me no favours.'

'You can start your own family one day, make your own rules.'

Ray looks doubtful, shrugs. 'Why? You lost yours.'

'I got my baby girl back, once I stopped drinking, once I stopped duping myself.'

'What about the woman?'

I take a deep breath. 'That's a work in progress.'

'You got a photo?'

'Sure.' I pull out the shot I carry with me always – me, Vonnie and Jazz, just about to turn three, just before we broke up.

Ray looks at it for a long time, before he says, 'You think I could learn to take shots like you do?'

'I think you can learn to do anything you put your mind to, young man.'

'Maybe I could go for it.' He narrows his eyes at me.

'Maybe you could,' I say.

Ray is wrong about a lot of things. He is especially wrong when he says 'families aren't worth shit'. They are worth everything. They form us, they ground us, they send us out into the world to become who we are. Sure they mess up, everyone does, but there is something powerful about belonging to, and coming from, the same unit, even if, at times, you could happily kill some or all of the members.

I certainly won't forget the day I lost mine.

Of course, I had been drinking. But this was no bender, no binge, quite the contrary. I had finished my work that morning and was heading out from LAX on the flight to San Luis Obispo as usual. At the airport I ran into an old friend, a former colleague of mine who worked on *The New York Times*, we hadn't seen each other in maybe ten years. I had allowed plenty of time to check in, so of course we headed to the bar for a couple of beers. We reminisced about the good old days, that we had managed not to get shot, and had held on to our hair. One thing led to another, and I was just about to leave when he persuaded me to stay for just one more beer. That's all it was, no big deal. We swopped email addresses, I said I'd look him up when I was next in New York and left for my gate. I wasn't drunk, not even tipsy, but when I saw the gate deserted apart from a lone stewardess, a chill ran through me.

'I'm afraid you've missed the flight, sir,' she said calmly.

'But I'm right on time,' I said incredulously, as I watched the plane detach from the walkway and inch towards the runway.

'It's leaving ten minutes early, we got an earlier take off slot. We called it three times, sir.' She smiled sympathetically.

'When's the next one?' I asked, my mouth suddenly dry.

'Four-thirty. I'm sure the sales desk can help you.'

She might as well have said next week. This wasn't just any day, it was Jazz's third birthday, and she was having a party. I was supposed to be there. I raced to the ticket desk to get on the next flight, which wasn't a problem, then rang Vonnie to explain what had happened. For the first time in our relationship, she hung up on me. I called her back, repeatedly, to no avail. Then I texted her, still nothing. There was nothing I could do, absolutely nothing, except wait for the next flight – and have another drink.

I rehearsed my speech many times before I got to Vonnie's house. But when I opened the door and saw her sitting on the sofa, I knew there was no point saying anything in my defence or otherwise.

The house was quiet. 'Where's Jazz?' was the only thing I could think of saying.

'She's asleep. She was exhausted after the party. I told her if she took a nap she could get up later.'

'How was the party?'

'It was fine.' She was curt.

'Vonnie, I—'

'Don't.' She put up a hand. 'Please don't. I want to talk to you.'

I sank down on the sofa and prepared for a heavy lecture, nothing more than I deserved. She had every right to be angry. But talking was good, that meant I was in with a chance.

I was wrong.

'When Jazz wakes up, I'm taking her to Jenny's with me. You'll have the weekend to get your stuff together, then I want you to leave. This isn't working for me, Jake . . . for us.'

I looked at her as if she was crazy. 'Vonnie! This is a three-year-old's birthday party we're talking about for Christ's sake! I know I should have been here, but it's hardly—'

'You don't get it, do you?' she looked at me coldly.

'What?'

'I don't care what your drinking is doing to me, to us, but I'm damned if I'm going to stand by and let my daughter's life be ruined by the precarious whims and notions of an alcoholic father.'

'Are you calling me an alcoholic?'

'You heard me. You have a drink problem, Jake, a serious one, one that's turning you into a different person. Someone I don't know any more.'

'Oh, for the love of—'

'My father was never around for me, but at least I know

he didn't even know I exist. I can't imagine what it must be like to know your father prefers the company of a crowd of drunks and a lousy bottle instead of showing up for his family, but I have no intention of letting Jazz go through the agony or instability of finding out.'

I was so angry I could hardly speak. Me, a drink problem? An alcoholic? Who the hell was she talking about? How *dare* she.

Instead, I retorted with what I knew would hurt her most. 'You're not exactly qualified to lecture on family life yourself, are you, Vonnie? What makes you think you're such a great mother to Jazz?' (Yes, I'm ashamed to say I really did say that.)

Vonnie recoiled as if I'd hit her. 'I'm going to take a bath.' She got up. 'Then Jazz and I are out of here.'

'Don't bother,' I said. 'I'm leaving. I'll come back for my stuff tomorrow. You can talk to my lawyer about Jazz.' I grabbed my bag and strode out the door, slamming it behind me.

Outside I got a cab, slammed the door and barked at the driver to take me to a hotel.

When I checked in and got to my room, I slammed the door there too, and slung my bag on the floor for good measure. Then I sat on the bed and cracked open a bottle from the mini-bar.

Sometimes, you're making so much noise in your life you don't hear the things that really matter. Like the shattering splinters of hurtful words, the quiet erosion of trust, or the breaking of a heart that makes no sound at all.

Vonnie

We are standing at arrivals in Dublin airport on a damp July morning. Jazz talked me into it, of course. I had arranged with Jake that he would call us when he got in to his hotel, which is five minutes from our house, and we would arrange to meet then – but Jazz was having none of it. It is just after seven, and I am scratchy from lack of sleep (I had disturbing dreams) and the early start, unlike Jazz who is fizzing with energy and wild excitement. There are only a few people here at this early hour, bravely waiting to greet loved ones who have made their way across the Atlantic. No wonder I feel awkward. I feel part-interloper, part-spectator in the blinding love affair between my daughter and her father. Sometimes, I am even a little jealous. Not of Jazz's love for Jake, but envious of the certainty she must feel in his love for her. *What must it be like,* I wonder, *to have a father who right from the moment he sets eyes on you, quite simply adores you?* I try to imagine and can't.

It is almost a week since my visit to Carmel and Colm's house and it has left me feeling pointless and rudderless. I want to finish up my work and go home, back to California. I have never fitted in here and feel I never will. That's just the way it is. If it wasn't for Abby and Di, I'm not sure I would have lasted as long as I have. We are due to catch up again in a couple of days at my place and I am looking forward to the distraction.

I see him before Jazz does, and involuntarily draw a breath. He is head and shoulders above the pale and weary travellers who trail through the doors before and behind him, he is carelessly, darkly, sleekly beautiful.

I bend down to Jazz and turn her so she can see him, catch his eyes, searching, scanning across the hall, and she takes off like a rocket.

I watch as she hurtles towards him, as his face lights up, and the part of me that can't forget aches to rewind, to go back to that place in time when we were a series of happy vignettes, like this one, spooling one after the other, revealing the movie of our love. But real life just isn't like that.

You think you know someone – someone you love more than you ever thought possible – and then it turns out you don't really know them at all. The picture has been torn, and you are left piecing together fragments that won't quite align. Part of me knew Jake had a problem, but I loved him so much, loved *us* so much, that I couldn't bear to admit it to myself. I wanted my happy ending. I had waited long enough for it, I couldn't face looking into the abyss of loneliness that waited for me in a life without him. So I told myself it would be all right. Everything would work out, things were just getting a little out of hand occasionally.

It's never only the addict who is deceitful in a relationship, there's usually a carefully constructed web of lies surrounding them, contributed to, and upheld by, lovers, family and friends. Well-meaning people, but all party to the lie, all for our own self-invested interests. It's just that we don't always see it like that. Not at the time, anyhow. Hindsight is twenty-twenty, as they say.

My interest? In retrospect, love. Clearly, I was madly, deeply in love with Jake, but beyond that, when I had time to examine my feelings, time (lots of long, lonely time) to really think it through, I began to wonder if I was so used to people with-holding from me, so used to not having an identity of my own as a point of reference, that maybe I would accept anything, any kind of love, however remote, as being enough, as only what I deserved. And maybe that was okay for me, but it certainly wasn't what I wanted for my, *our* daughter. I had had my parental mishaps thrust upon me, I wasn't going to do the same to her.

So we separated. I left him, after he didn't show for Jazz's third birthday party. Could happen to anyone, I know, but he wasn't the one there to see her puzzled little face, her constant demands of, 'When will Daddy be here, Mommy?' Until, worn out by the excitement and noise level of twenty-five under fives, she fell asleep on the sofa beside me when everyone had gone, still waiting for Jake. That's when I put her to bed. I vowed then and there that she was never going to be let down by him again. This time she would be too young to remember, to be hurt by it, but next time and the time after that she would not be so lucky. And there was always a next time. I knew that much. Life had taught me that if nothing else.

It was a few days after that awful weekend when Jake left that I found out something else about him. After he had come back to get his stuff (I had made sure to be out, I couldn't have watched him pack up), I was wandering around my house, echoing with emptiness, telling myself I had done the right thing, pulling out drawers and cupboards desultorily, when a couple of old newspapers caught my eye. I picked them up, to throw them out, and a clipping fell out of one. At first I thought it was a coupon, until I read the headline: 'Man (22) killed in car after student party'. Nothing so remarkable about that, sad to say, until I read the rest of the small paragraph and learned the man had been twenty-two-year-old Luke Kurkimaki, and his elder brother Jake, twenty-six, had been driving the car.

Later that night I called Gloria, Jake's sister, in New Orleans. 'I'm really sorry to hear about you guys,' she said. 'I hoped, we all hoped, that this was, well, you know, you've been so good for Jake.' She paused. 'How are you doing, honey?'

'I don't know,' I said. 'I can't take it in really, not yet, but things weren't good lately.'

'His drinking, right?'

'You knew?'

'Of course we knew, we were just hoping that maybe, well . . .' she trailed off.

'Gloria?'

'Umhm.'

'Your brother, who died in the car wreck, I never knew . . . is it true that Jake was driving the car?'

'He never told you?'

'No, we never discussed it. I found a newspaper clipping, just earlier today.'

'He was driving the car all right. It's not something we discuss a lot in our family,' she sighed. 'I'm sure you can understand that. It's hard, for all of us.'

'Was Jake drinking?'

'Good Lord, no,' she sounded surprised. 'That's why he was driving. But the other guy had been, he lost control of his car, came straight across the divide, ploughed into Luke and Jake. Luke was killed outright. It's amazing Jake got out alive, without a scratch. Both cars were totalled.'

I let out a long breath. 'That's terrible, I'm so sorry – for all of you.'

'It was real tough. But, no, Jake definitely wasn't drinking. But he blames himself, even though there was absolutely nothing he could have done. The highway patrol confirmed that. The irony is, that's what started him, and he's been drinking ever since.'

'I had no idea,' I said. 'Now at least it makes some sense, I suppose.'

'I'm sorry, Vonnie.' Gloria's voice was warm. 'Sorry he never told you, shared it with you – maybe now you could talk to him about it?'

'I don't know, Gloria; like I said, things haven't been good.'

'Without you in his life, I can only see them going downhill.'

'I have to think of Jazz,' I said.

'Of course you do.' There was a brief pause. 'Jake adores you both, I know he does, but he's messed up right now. I know that doesn't help anything, but maybe in a while things will work out. In the meantime, I'm here if you want to talk. Come and visit, bring Jazz, you will stay in touch, won't you?' A note of panic crept into her voice. 'You're family now, whatever happens. You know that, right?'

'Of course I will,' I said, thinking she had no idea how ironic those words were to me, especially now, when my only chance of real family had walked out the door. 'We'll come and visit soon, just give me a little time.'

'I understand; you take care, Vonnie.'

'Bye, Gloria.'

Jake

Last time I was here I was drinking. That's what I am thinking as the plane comes in low over the silver sea and banks towards that particular greenness that is unique to Ireland. Forty shades, right? It's been quite a while I remember, fifteen years or thereabouts, and I was stopping off on my way to the UK to see what all the fuss was about this little country that produced great writers, orators, and had a fondness for politics and Guinness, not necessarily in that order. I was with three of my buddies and we had a wild time. We were young, single and on vacation, you can imagine the rest. I always vowed to come back, but never got around to it, and now, well, I never imagined I would be going over to see my daughter, my own flesh and blood, separated and dictated to by a rote of calendar dates, suitable weekends or travel arrangements. That's how it is for the 'single father' – a term I have grown to hate – although I am grateful for any time I get to spend with Jazz, she is the light of my life. The only reason I held on through the dark times.

When Vonnie left me, I was so angry about it and what she had said to me that I wouldn't even talk about her or mention her name. I threw myself into my work, and drank with renewed vigour. Me, an alcoholic? I'd show her! I was simply resuming my bachelor lifestyle, without the hindrance of a nagging, neurotic woman in my life. That's what I told myself anyway. For a while, it almost worked. I made sure I always turned up spruce and sober for my outings with Jazz, and would drop her back to Vonnie without saying a word – enjoying the poorly hidden look of despair that would pass across her face. I even dated a few other women, briefly, but that was the worst idea of all. I told myself I wasn't the settling-down type, never had been, it had been stupid of me to delude myself. It would strike then, without warning, maybe while I was sitting in a cafe with my laptop, a feeling of such bleak loneliness and failure, it would take my breath away. Sometimes it was triggered by a scene in a movie, or the sight of a happy couple with kids, or the overwhelming feeling of loss when I returned to my empty apartment, and I would simply reach for the bottle. I could do what I liked, there was no one to stop me – I was in freefall.

That was how my sister Gloria found me. She and her husband were in LA on vacation. Luckily for me, she had a key to my apartment – one I had given her long ago. I had been supposed to meet them for an after-dinner drink. She had rung me a couple of times and I hadn't returned her messages. She was worried and decided to check on me.

They found me passed out in the early hours of the morning, a bottle of bourbon and sleeping pills beside me. I hadn't meant to do myself any harm, I just wanted oblivion, just for a couple of hours, that's how close I came. I was rushed to the ER, had my stomach pumped and told I had been lucky. Believe me, I didn't feel that way, not then.

My sister was crying when I came around, but she agreed when I begged her not to tell anyone, especially our mother, what I had done. There was one condition – that I go into rehab. I was hardly in a condition to protest. Her husband, Bryan, is a lawyer and said that if I wanted to have access rights to Jazz, I needed to clean up my act or I would lose her. I knew he was right. In a way, it was a huge relief. Terrified though I was of a life without alcohol, the realisation that I didn't have to pretend any more was hugely comforting. They kept me in the hospital overnight for observation. In the morning, I agreed to check in to the hotel my sister and brother-in-law were staying in for a couple of nights until I got into rehab. Six weeks later I came home to a beautifully cleaned apartment, complete with home-made freezer meals and fresh flowers. I took a long look around. I was on my own, one day at a time.

That was four and a half years ago. Not easy years, I won't lie to you, but good years that I am grateful for. I stopped hating myself, it took me a while to realise that I did, even more time to stop beating myself up for surviving the car crash my brother and my best friend didn't. But, little by little, with a lot of help from my friends on the Program, I began to put my new life together. Of course there are regrets, but who doesn't have those? And they are more than compensated for by the joys.

We get off the plane and I wait for my bag, which comes through surprisingly quickly, and make my way through customs to arrivals. I have told Vonnie I will get a cab to my hotel and call her when I get in. But as I walk through the sliding doors I hear the shriek of an unmistakable voice, and a small figure with dark hair flying behind her hurls herself at me.

'Daddy!' Jazz yells. 'Daddy, Daddy, Daddy!'

I pick her up and swing her around and around until I am

out of breath, as she laughs out loud and onlookers smile fondly at us.

'You're here!' I can't believe you're here!'

'I sure am, kiddo,' I say, putting her down to pick up my bag. 'You better believe it.'

'C'mon, hurry, Mommy's over here.' She takes me by the hand impatiently.

Like I said, the good times far outnumber the regrets.

Angela

The phone call came right out of the blue. Ron had his head buried in the *Wall Street Journal* and was still half asleep before he'd downed his third coffee – and that's just with breakfast. I've tried so many times to get him off caffeine I've lost count, but he's a stubborn guy about some things. I picked up my cell phone wondering who could be calling so early, and had a slight intake of breath as a deep, resonant voice asked if I was Mrs Angela Douglas. When I said that I was and moved from the table to take the call in my room, the voice apologised for the intrusion at such an early hour, and introduced itself. Then I understood. It was Jake Kurkimaki, Vonnie's partner.

We had never met, but she had spoken about him, the father of her little girl. Since that first meeting in Saks, Vonnie had only communicated through the odd card, very occasionally a phone call; there had been no suggestion of meeting my granddaughter – nor did I moot it, it was not my place. I would let Vonnie set the pace of our fledgling relationship, if there were ever even to be that.

There was also the small matter of telling Ron about her. And try as I might, I quailed at the thought. Perhaps if we'd had children of our own it might have been easier but, somehow, it was bad enough to think I had abandoned my own daughter in favour of a new and infinitely better life than I would have had at home, but it seemed even more cruel to tell him (never mind try to explain why) when we hadn't been blessed with children of our own. Even though technically speaking that wasn't my fault, I still felt to blame. *The Lord giveth and the Lord taketh away* . . . I had deserted my own flesh and blood daughter from a silly, youthful, romantic escapade, and was, in turn, denied children with a good man I loved and who loved me.

That's why my first reaction to that phone call had been alarm. I thought something must be wrong with Vonnie for Jake to call me, and my heart turned over. But he quickly reassured me that everything was okay. Instead, he asked if he could meet with me. I was taken aback by this; I knew he and Vonnie had split up some time ago, so I couldn't think why he would want or need to meet me. I was also afraid it might anger Vonnie, who clearly didn't know anything about this.

'That's the point,' Jake went on in that rather hypnotic voice. 'This is about Vonnie. I need to talk to you about her.'

'Well that's very good of you, I'm sure,' I said. 'But to be quite frank with you, Jake, I've told Vonnie everything she wanted to know, there's really nothing I can add to the story that she hasn't already asked me. And, beyond that, I'm ashamed to say I really know very little about her. Perhaps it's her aunt and uncle she grew up with you might need to talk to?'

'No,' he said. 'It's definitely you.' There was a brief pause. 'I need to talk to you about Vonnie's father.'

I sat down on the bed, my knees suddenly weak.

'I really don't think—' I began.

'Please, Mrs Douglas – Angela – at least agree to meet me, for Vonnie's sake and our little girl. We really need to talk. I promise you I'll never bother you again as long as I live but, please, just meet with me this once.'

Just at that moment Ron called to me from the dining room.

'Angie? You all right?'

'Yes,' I called back. 'I'm just in the bathroom, I'll be right there.'

'I have to go,' I whispered to Jake.'

'Tomorrow,' he said urgently. 'Anywhere, anytime, I'm here in New York.'

I said the first place that came into my mind. 'The Empire State Building, eighty-second floor observatory, ten o'clock sharp.'

'I'll be there.'

I went back to the dining room, sat down and poured myself a cup of coffee, wondering what had possessed me. Was I out of my mind?

'You okay, honey?' Ron looked at me over his reading glasses.

'Just a headache,' I said. 'That's all.'

'Sure?'

'Sure. Why?'

'Your hands are shaking.'

Abby

'I wish Abby would confront me,' Edward says, miserably. 'It would make it so much easier, but she won't, she doesn't say a word – not a word.'

'Do you think she suspects anything?' Olivia asks gently.

'I don't see how she can't.' Edward runs his hands through his hair and shakes his head. He is beginning to sound desperate. 'I mean we barely talk to each other, never mind anything else.'

'That must be . . . difficult,' Olivia says tactfully, not probing.

Edward looks at her gratefully. Olivia is full of understanding, she never employs the art of silent accusation, of quiet martyrdom the way Abby does.

'What about your mother-in-law? What's her name?

'Oh, Sheila.' Edward gives a short laugh.

'Yes, Sheila.'

'I thought it would help, you see, having her to live with us. I thought it would show I wanted to make an effort.'

'And has it? Helped?'

Edward shrugs. 'Not so you'd notice. It's a relief in a way, though, having someone else in the house. I find Sheila very easy to relate to, she's very supportive, I suppose.'

'And Abby isn't?'

'She's been a wonderful wife, a wonderful mother, it's just that . . .'

'What?'

'Well she's always looked up to me so much. In the beginning I was flattered, of course I was, but then it began to feel like a sort of responsibility, a burden, and then when – well I couldn't tell her, you see, I couldn't bear to do it to her, to see how devastated she'd be. And I was afraid . . . afraid she'd leave me.

'What will you say if she does confront you? Have you given it any thought?'

'I'd have to come clean, wouldn't I?'

'About everything?'

'Everything.' Edward gets up and begins to pace the floor. 'About me?'

'Especially about you.' He pauses and looks at her intently. 'I don't know how I'd manage without you. I was at the end of my tether when— when . . .'

'It won't be easy,' Olivia says. 'She's going to feel betrayed.'

'I'm already betraying her and the kids.' Edward begins to pace again. 'Oh, God, it's such a mess. Everything's such a bloody mess.'

'It will get better.'

'Will it?'

'I think so, once you make a decision, once you face up to it.'

'She might leave me. She might put me out.'

'Would that be such a bad thing?' Olivia lowers her eyes.

'I don't know,' says Edward. 'I really don't know anymore.'

Olivia holds her breath. Then she says, 'You see, I can't possibly advise you, Edward. This has to be your decision and yours alone, you have to be sure, absolutely sure. There's a lot at stake here, not least your future happiness.'

He looks at her with gratitude. 'I don't know what I'd do without you, Olivia.'

At home, Edward takes a deep breath before putting his key in the door and letting himself in. Things have not been good for a long while, but they have been especially tense since the Atlanta trip. When he came back, he noticed a distinct deterioration. In fact, you could cut the tension with a knife.

He goes into the kitchen, and the easy chatter that was going on between Abby and her mother comes to an abrupt halt.

'Hi,' he says, to nobody in particular.

Roseanna is reclining on the sofa with her legs up watching television. The twins emerge from the utility/shower room with towels wrapped around their waists, fresh from training, their hair still dripping.

'Hey, Dad,' they say, simultaneously. Timothy high fives him, Tom flicks water at him, making him duck.

'Hurry up, boys,' Abby says, 'dinner's in five.'

'Shouldn't you be helping your mother?' he says to Roseanna, who looks at him as if he has taken leave of his senses.

'Sure, isn't she only in the door before you, Edward.' Sheila rushes to her defence looking flustered. 'Here, let me get you a drink. Everything's done now; anyway, we're ready to eat in a minute.'

Abby carries on, studiously ignoring the exchange.

Sheila hurriedly hands Edward a glass of red wine. 'There, sit down and relax now. It's Friday, the end of a stressful week for you, I'm sure.'

'Thanks, Sheila,' Edward says wearily.

'Anything I can do to help?' he says hovering, as Abby takes out a pasta bake from the oven. She shakes her head.

Dinner is strained. Abby is mostly silent, Sheila talks too much and Roseanna is sulking. Fortunately the twins, unaware of any undercurrent, argue vigorously about team selections and Edward tries to join in.

Abby pours herself a large glass of red wine.

'I would have done that, you should have—' Edward begins.

'No need,' Abby retorts brightly.

Sheila coughs discreetly and Edward obliges, topping up her empty glass. She smiles in gratitude, and the two red spots on her cheeks increase in colour.

'This is delicious,' Edward says.

'It is, isn't it?' agrees Sheila. 'Abby used to moan about learning to cook but I was determined to teach her. Nothing worse than a woman who doesn't know her way around a kitchen.'

'Nothing, indeed,' says Edward, looking pointedly at his daughter.

'What?' says Roseanna indignantly. 'What's the matter with you lately? Get off my case, will you? Mum?' She looks to Abby, who remains silent.

'This sucks.' Roseanna pushes her chair away from the table and leaves in a huff.

Edward is inclined to agree with her, but he cannot bring himself to say so. He tries to apologise but it falls on deaf ears. 'Rosie,' he calls after her. 'I'm sorry. I didn't mean to—'

Sheila gets up and begins to clear the plates.

'Leave that, Mum. Please,' Abby says.

'I was only trying to help.' Sheila is wounded.

'Boys, your turn to clear up. Everything in the dishwasher, please.'

Something in their mother's tone makes the boys move smartly and efficiently.

'Sheila,' Edward begins, 'would you mind giving us a moment? I need to talk to Abby about something.'

Sheila's eyes dart nervously in Abby's direction. 'Of course, I, um—'

'Here,' he says. 'Let me bring you a glass of wine up to the sitting room.'

Sheila looks at Abby, who will not meet her eyes. She is torn, but does as she's told, following Edward and the glass of wine up the three steps along the corridor and into the sitting room where he makes sure she is settled comfortably and the television is tuned to her favourite soap opera.

When he returns to the kitchen, the boys have cleared up and off and Abby is sitting alone at the table.

'We have to talk, Abby,' Edward says.

She had been doing alright up until that moment, just a few minutes ago, when he had asked Sheila to leave the room, to give them some time together. She knew things were bad, but she hadn't realised how bad until he had picked on Rosie. Edward never criticises Rosie, never. This proves how much he is feeling the strain. She has done it herself, she acknowledges, feeling a wave of guilt wash over her – been narky and bad tempered with Rosie and the boys for no reason other than dreading facing the truth. She has been taking it out on her children and her mother. Now Edward is doing it too. How dreadful.

But Abby doesn't want to talk. Her blood has run cold at the prospect. She would rather anything than that. She does not want her clever, erudite husband to articulate how sorry he is that they have grown apart, that he has met and fallen in love with someone far more suitable than her. Someone he has intellectual conversations with, who can debate the finer points of medical advances and the current state of the health service, a woman with a multitude of attributes and accomplishments that Abby could never hope to acquire.

Instead, she would rather put her head in the sand. Ignore it all, hope it might go away, this unprepared for eventuality in her marriage. It always worked before, this method, Abby reasons somewhere deep in her subconscious.

It worked at home, when she was just a small child and heard her mother's voice raised too often in frustrated disappointment in her father. It worked at school when she would retreat to her books and her daydreams rather than get involved with some of the more risky adventures of her companions. And when those same girls got into trouble with the nuns or their parents, it was Abby who always managed to smooth things over. It worked later, as a teenager, when she would lie awake waiting for her father to come home, listening for his sometimes faltering footsteps as he came up the stairs, and she could relax, and finally go to sleep. Nothing terrible had happened then, and nothing terrible had happened yet. Because Abby was a peacemaker, she had played by the rules all her life and they had not let her down. She had not upset anyone, until Edward of course. Then she had been underhand. She had deliberately stopped taking the pill, but only because she loved him desperately, and wanted to – was sure she could – make him happy. But she hadn't, had she? He was miserable, and it was all her fault. She was willing to admit this to herself, but she was not willing to talk about it. That would make it real. And Abby wasn't ready for real. Nothing terrible had happened yet, but Abby had the distinct feeling it was about to.

'I don't want to talk,' she says to her husband.

'Abby, we have to talk, we need to – it's imperative.'

'Not tonight we don't.' Abby gets up from the table, and takes her glass.

'But surely you want to know—'

'No, Edward, I do not.'

'But that's the problem, we need to communicate, I need to explain—'

'You don't. Really, you don't.' Abby is resolute. 'I know. I just don't want to talk about it.'

There is a loaded silence.

'You know?'

'Yes, Edward, I know. So you see there is no point at all in talking about it. Let's just continue as we are, and make the best of things.'

Edward is flummoxed. 'But don't you want to know why—'

'No. I don't want to know anything. No details, no confessions. I just want to go to bed and wake up tomorrow and the next day and go on as we are.'

'But we can't go on like this, Abby. It— It's not fair to either of us.'

'I didn't sign up for fair, Edward. I signed up for better or worse. Things aren't good now, I'll admit, but that's the way of things. That's life. There's no point discussing it.'

'But Abby, I need you to listen to me, to let me explain—'

'No, Edward,' Abby says with finality. 'That is exactly what I don't need. Now, if you'll excuse me I'm very tired and I'm going upstairs to have a hot bath and go to bed. I'm not angry with you. I want you to know that. I just don't want to discuss any of it. I really don't see what good can come of it.'

And with that Abby takes her glass of wine and leaves Edward in the kitchen, staring after her in bewilderment.

The Affair

*S*he *can be herself with him. It was not until she had fallen in love with him – truly, completely – that she realised how lost she had become within her marriage.*

Every time they are together, she is rediscovering things about herself she had all but forgotten. How she loves to feel the grass beneath her feet, the sound of children's laughter, the tear-pricking gesture of being given a bunch of hand-picked flowers.

They are having a picnic, sitting in the shade of a large oak in a park on the other side of the city. She has made him take off his shoes and socks – just like the scene with Richard Gere and Julia Roberts in Pretty Woman. *She leans against him, looking up at the sky, wondering how many other lovers have sat here, sheltered, just like they are. They do not have long, just over an hour, then he has to get back to work, but the day was so lovely she had to see him, to share it with him. They leave separately, arranging to talk later. She gets the Dart, listens to her iPod, tapping her feet and wanting to sing along, aloud, about how happy he makes her. She walks home a different route from her normal one, feeling carefree in her summer dress and Converse trainers. She looks around once or twice, just to check . . . crossing the road and, again, at a junction approaching her house. She sees a flash of blue, has an impression of something there – then not. For a moment, she almost imagines she is being followed.*

She shakes her head and smiles, she is becoming paranoid.

Who would be out on this beautiful summer's day following anyone?

She turns in her gate and runs up the steps of her house. Not long now, she has promised him. She cannot bear to be apart from him any longer.

Vonnie

The house is quiet without Jazz. Jake has taken her out for the day and although I was invited to join them, I thought it better to give them some quality time alone. Jazz is in seventh heaven to have her dad here, to the extent that she has conveniently forgotten she has a mother. But that's always the way, isn't it? We get to stay up nights worrying when they are sick, bandaging scraped knees, doing endless jigsaw puzzles, making ridiculous costumes or cajoling vaguely healthy food into small, stubborn mouths, then Daddy shows up and you don't exist anymore. That's little girls for you.

This evening, I am having the girls around. Just me, Abby and Diana – a simple dinner of pasta, salad, fresh baguette and some nice red wine. I have been looking forward to it all week. They are due to arrive shortly but I have just enough time for a quick shower and to freshen up.

Twenty minutes later, the doorbell goes. Abby is the first to arrive, complete with a bottle of chilled Prosecco, which she thrusts at me.

'Abby, how lovely,' I say. 'You shouldn't have.'

'Of course I should,' she says, grinning, 'and I don't know about you, but I'm gagging for a drink.' She seems flustered and slightly out of breath.

She is wearing jeans and a loose, white, linen shirt, no make-up and her cheeks are flushed. Her hair is tied up in a youthful ponytail. She reminds me, just in that instant, of exactly how she used to look at school, and I feel a rush of affection for her, except then, of course, she was a regular beanpole, always giving out about her lack of curves. Well, the hormones kick in sooner or later.

It is a warm sunny evening, so I open the Prosecco and we sit outside. Then Diana arrives, with a bottle of red and some chocolates. She is looking lovely but seems stressed, and there are dark shadows under her eyes which her concealer has failed to mask.

We chat about the usual things, and I potter in and out of the kitchen, still party to the conversation as the small French doors are wide open.

'Where's Jazz?' asks Abby.

'She's been out with Jake all day.'

'Jake! *The* Jake?' That's Diana.

I poke my head around the door and give her a look. 'Yes, Di, *the* Jake. He's over this week.'

'Of course,' says Abby. 'You told us, I'd forgotten. Will we get to meet him?'

'I don't know.' I am non-committal as I pour the boiling water into the saucepan and add a dash of olive oil for the pasta.

'What do you mean, you don't know?' Diana again. 'Isn't he dropping her back? Won't he come in?'

'Yes, and I don't know, respectively,' I tell her, stirring the pasta in.

'Will you at least ask him in?' Abby wants to know.

'Of course I will. What do you take me for?'

'Well then, of course he'll come in, won't he? He couldn't possibly miss meeting us, your oldest and dearest friends, could he?' Diana says triumphantly.

'Well, we'll find out soon enough,' I say.

'Oh, I wish I'd worn something more . . .' Abby pauses.

'More what?' Diana is grinning.

'Well, you know . . .'

'You mean you don't bother to dress up for me anymore?' I ask archly, putting some freshly baked focaccia on the table.

'Well I'm glad to see there's life in the old girl yet,' says Diana. 'I'd almost given up on you, Abby.'

'Speak for yourself, Diana. You're the biggest flirt I've ever met.'

'I'll take that as a compliment.'

'You take everything as a compliment. I wish I had the knack.'

'It's easy. Just tell yourself you are a divine goddess, especially when you look in the mirror.'

'I would, but my backside would laugh out loud at me.'

'That's just your internal critic, you have to learn to silence it or at the very least ignore it.'

'And how are you supposed to do that?' Abby enquires.

'Tell it to eff off. Sooner or later it will, and even if it does chatter away occasionally, you recognise it for what it is – just negative energy.'

The pasta is ready so I drain it and spoon it into a nice ceramic dish and pour the sauce over it, giving it a good stir. I call the girls in to sit down, and get Diana to open the bottle of red. I have just put the salad on the table and am about to sit down when the doorbell goes.

'I'd better get that,' I say, sounding calmer than I feel.

'You better had,' says Diana, mischievously, as she wrestles with the cork, which gives with a satisfying pop.

I open the door and Jazz runs past me into the kitchen clutching bags, Jake hovers uncertainly on the doorstep. 'I thought I'd worn her out, but it doesn't look like it,' he says wearily.

'Come on in, my school friends are here, they want to meet you.'

'*The* school friends? Abby and Diana?'

'The very same.'

He follows me into the kitchen and I try not to look self-conscious. Jazz is already deep in conversation with Diana, who has never met her before, examining her purchases. Abby is smiling at them, and eating a slice of focaccia.

'Girls,' I say, 'this is Jake. And Jake, this is—'

'*You're* Diana, and you *have* to be Abby,' he finishes for me, shaking his head as he grins and runs a hand through his dark curls. 'Hey, it's great to finally meet you girls. I've heard so much about you.'

'Well I hope we don't disappoint,' says Diana, looking up from her conversation with Jazz. Her eyes run over him discreetly and she sits back in her chair and smiles. Abby swallows her mouthful of bread, almost chokes, then takes a quick swig of wine. She blushes.

I am used to this, the ridiculous effect Jake has on women (I was one of them after all) but back here in Ireland amongst my closest friends it seems weird – magnified and incongruous. Why does the cosiness of the small house suddenly seem claustrophobic instead of intimate? And why do I feel uncomfortable watching my girlfriends practically squirm with delight as he talks to them?

'Sit down, have a drink,' says Diana, grabbing a glass and about to pour some red wine.

Jake pulls up a chair. 'Thanks, but I'll just have water.' He takes the jug sitting on the table.

'Oh,' Diana looks disappointed.

'I'm a recovering alcoholic,' he explains, as he tops up Abby and Diana's glasses. 'But don't worry, I love watching other people drink.'

My back is turned, so I don't see the girls' reaction to this. Personally, I am quite taken aback, I didn't think Jake would be so upfront with complete strangers – but then, in a way, Abby and Diana are not strangers to him. He has never met them before, but he must feel he knows them intimately, seeing as they are the closest thing to family I ever had. All the same, some uncomfortable part of me wishes he'd kept the information to himself.

I am about to dish up, which is awkward.

'You'll stay and join us, won't you? Have something to eat?' Diana says.

'Oh, yes, you must,' Abby agrees.

'I couldn't possibly. This is a girls' evening; I know the drill, believe me.'

'Oh, but you must stay, mustn't he, Vonnie?' Diana appears horrified at the thought of him leaving.

'Yes, do,' I say, trying to sound enthusiastic. It's not that I don't want him to stay, exactly, just that I'm not ready for Diana and Abby to scrutinise him, as they most certainly will.

'There, that's settled then,' says Diana.

'Well if you're sure I'm not interrupting your evening, I'd love to eat with you – then I'll leave you girls to it.'

'We couldn't think of a more welcome interruption, could we, Abby?' says Diana, shooting me a sly look.

You see? This is exactly what I was trying to avoid.

Two hours later Jake finally gets up to leave, despite Abby and Diana's respective protests.

'It's been great meeting you guys finally, but I really have to go. I have some work to finish up that's due in tomorrow,' he says regretfully, smiling as he stands up from the table.

I notice how his white T-shirt contrasts against the deep coffee colour of his skin, the rippling strength of arms that I always thought would protect me against a thousand hurts, the muscular length of his legs in jeans that made him the first man to make me truly feel small, feminine even, beside his reassuring height. I catch Abby and Diana noticing too, and look away quickly, but not before they have caught me too.

Abby

It is just about midnight when Abby gets home from Vonnie's house – late enough by what she rather amusingly thinks of now as their 'middle-aged' standards. Although there has been nothing staid about the evening – far from it, it was more like electric. For starters, she thinks – undressing quietly so as not to wake Edward, who is sleeping soundly – she had not anticipated meeting Jake. Nor had she appreciated quite how handsome he would be, not to mention charming. Not in that oily, fake way, either, that some good-looking men have, but genuinely, pleasant, interesting and good fun. He also oozed sex appeal, so much so it had made Abby feel almost uncomfortable in his presence, she wasn't sure why.

She climbs into bed and shivers, wondering what must it be like to make love with a man like that. A man who clearly made women weak at the knees, through no effort on his part. Even Diana, the most accomplished and seasoned of seductresses (if you were to believe her!) had practically simpered at him all evening. Vonnie had taken it all very well, Abby thought. She wasn't so sure she'd have liked it if it had been *her* husband. Women had always found Edward quite attractive (well he was a *doctor*), and although she would like to have felt flattered by this, it only made her feel more inse-cure, even though Edward, to be fair, had never encouraged any of them, not openly at any rate – not until now.

Thinking about Vonnie, she couldn't help going over why things had gone wrong between her and Jake. He was quite open about the fact he was a recovering alcoholic (though Vonnie hadn't mentioned this), but he had been sober for over four years now – so even if that had been a problem, it seemed to have been resolved, at least on Jake's part. Abby wondered briefly if he was physically abusive perhaps and shudders at the thought. Somehow she doubts it, it doesn't seem to fit and, besides, Vonnie denied it. Anyhow, Jake didn't appear to be one of those charming but closeted women haters. He clearly enjoyed women's company and it was plain he adored Jazz. Come to think of it, Abby would bet he still adored Vonnie too. He had listened earnestly whenever she had been speaking (on the few rare instances that Diana had paused for breath), and looked speculatively at her when she wasn't watching. Vonnie had been on edge too, with him unexpectedly being there with them, Abby could tell. She wished she and Diana could have talked more about what was going on with her as regards Jake but Vonnie had become quite upset when they had broached the subject and hadn't wanted to discuss it. Whatever was going on, the chemistry between them was potent, you couldn't help but pick up on that.

Abby drifts into a restless sleep punctuated with decidedly erotic dreams, none of which feature Edward.

Diana

'Nice evening, love?' The taxi driver I have been assigned on my way home from Vonnie's is chatty, just my luck.

'Yes, thank you. Very pleasant.' I gaze out the window, avoiding eye contact.

'Out on the tear, were you?' he says cheerfully.

'No.'

'Oh, right.' He gets the message and blows out his cheeks.

I am not in the mood to chat. I have had quite a lot to drink, not intentionally, but it was a very interesting evening, thanks in no small part to Jake. Not that I wasn't looking forward to seeing Vonnie and Abby, I was, but I'm not going to say I don't enjoy the company of a gorgeous guy – and as guys go, Jake was *hot*. The whole thing has left me feeling quite . . . rattled really. I mean, I just could never have imagined Vonnie pulling such an incredibly handsome guy, highly intelligent too – apparently he's quite famous in the world of reporting, Abby Googled him on her phone when we were going to the loo upstairs. I suppose I still think of Vonnie the way she used to be, the way we *all* used to be, when things were comfortable and predictable, and all our roles seemed unchanging. Now, I realise, I feel a stab of jealousy, which comes as a shock. It's usually me who has the guys eating out of my hand, but this one, attentive and polite though he was, only had eyes for Vonnie, who must be the only woman in the world determined to ignore his constant glances in her direction. Personally, I think she's still in love with him, I mean who wouldn't be? Whatever she says about co-parenting and being just good friends. Men like Jake don't do friendship with women, not because they don't want to be friends with them but because women can't help falling for them.

After he left, Abby and I stayed for about another hour and a half (although it only felt like twenty minutes).

'Is that why you split up with Jake, Vonnie,' Abby asked her, 'because of the alcohol?'

'That was part of it, a big part.'

'Was he violent?' I ventured.

She looked appalled. 'Jake? God, no, never.'

There was a pause while presumably Abby was wondering about the same thing I was – why, then?

'He let Jazz down. He missed her birthday party when he was drinking.'

'But that was over four years ago, wasn't it?' Abby remarks.

Good point. I had forgotten that, and Abby's meticulous memory for minute details.

'Which means . . .' She does the maths. 'Jazz was three?'

'That's not the point,' Vonnie snaps.

'That was *it?*' I say.

She sighs. 'There was something else he kept from me, something important. I couldn't— I wasn't able to trust him again.'

'An affair?' I wonder.

'I really don't want to talk about it.'

'Don't tell me he's gay, because I won't believe it.'

'A cross dresser?' Abby suggests helpfully.

'His brother was killed in a car accident, years ago.'

'He never told you that?'

'He told me, he just left out one significant detail – that he had been driving the car.'

'Oh, my God, was it his fault? Had he been drinking?'

'No.' Vonnie shook her head. 'But the other guy had, he lost control of the car and it ploughed across the road. It was nothing to do with Jake, but he blamed himself for it.'

'And this is why you broke up with him?' Abby's face says it all.

'I told you,' Vonnie says, her voice escalating. 'I couldn't trust him.' She pushes her hair back distractedly. 'He hid a drink problem from me, he couldn't tell me the truth about how his own brother was killed. What else is he hiding from me?' She begins to clear the table, banging plates and cutlery into the sink, pausing to grip the counter with both hands. 'I've had nothing but lies told to me my whole life!' she shouted.

I had never seen Vonnie like this.

'Why *couldn't* he confide in me?' she demands. 'What's *wrong* with me? My own mother runs away from me, my family tell me I'm adopted, then that I'm not. I mean what *is* it with me? Huh? Do I have *lie to me* tattooed on my forehead or something?'

She collects herself as quickly as she lost it, resuming her plate stacking and brushing her hair off her face. 'I'm sorry.' She chews her lip. 'It's just that sometimes it all gets to me, you know?'

Abby clucks sympathetically and goes over to give her a hug. 'I know it's hard, Vonnie,' she says, 'but you really need to let yourself trust more.'

It strikes me then, ironically, that the instructions we give others, however well intended, are often the very ones we most need to follow ourselves – or to use the words of one of Greg's spiritual gurus, 'accusation is almost always confession'.

We arrive at my house, eventually, and I pay my taxi fare and get out. The house is quiet when I get back, Greg is out working one of his late-night stints on *The Streets of Dublin*, and the kids are in bed asleep, my sitter Kitty who is a neighbour informs me. Kitty lives a couple of doors down and is a very active retired widow. She is happy to hold the fort between times when Greg and I are both out of the house. Sophie, my eldest, resents this bitterly, feeling more than adult enough to oversee her younger brother, but autocratic though she is, rules are rules and, to be fair, it is usually only for an hour or two at most.

'Nothing to report,' Kitty says, pulling on her raincoat, 'good *Cold Case* and *CSI* though.' Kitty is a crime fan.

'Thank you, Kitty. Safe home,' I say, seeing her out the door.

'Not at all, your two are a pleasure, even though I know they're too old for babysitting; they're always polite, always well mannered. Sophie even made me a cup of tea.'

I am glad to hear that, as I wave her off. Even if our children can be vile to us parents, we always hope secretly that this is a front, a tactic, that they will be charming at best, or at the very least polite, with others. I heave a sigh of relief and take off my coat, wandering down to the kitchen to make a late night cup of coffee before I go to bed – and that is when I hear it. At first I think it sounds like a scratch, coming from the basement, a sort of faint sawing noise, and I ignore it, spooning coffee into the cafetiere and pouring on boiling water. But the noise continues, then stops, followed by a noise I can't ignore – footsteps, soundly planted, coming up the basement stairs. The spoon freezes in my hands as I force my brain to compute a variety of plausible explanations all of which I know are improbable if not impossible – that it is Philip and one of his friends, or Sophie (ludicrous, the footsteps are too heavy), or even perhaps Greg, who has come back, unbeknown to me or Kitty, and has been pottering in the basement. They pause, and I am rooted to the spot. The key unlocks, the door handle turns, and slowly the door opens.

'I thought it would be you,' Rob says, rubbing unfocused eyes and smiling. He is wearing Greg's clothes, which are obscenely tight on him. I fight the urge to register disgust. I must keep calm.

In his hand, hanging loosely by his side, is a hammer. He knocks it mindlessly, repeatedly, against his left thigh.

'Greg's not here,' I say, frantically trying to sound normal.

'I know.' He grins, and puts the hammer on the kitchen counter, folding his arms. 'He gave me a key. I gave it back, of course, but I took a copy, just in case I might need it, y'know.'

'Yes,' I mutter. 'Of course.'

'You don't like me, do you?' He looks me up and down, lewdly.

'Why do you say that?' I try to back away, but I am blocked.

'I can tell.'

'I don't have any reason to dislike you,' I say, falsely cheerful, playing for time. 'I don't have any feelings one way or the other, to be honest.' *Where is my phone? Oh God, where is my phone?*

'Oh, but I think you do.'

'I'm sorry, but I don't know what you're talking about. Now if—' I look frantically for my bag. *If I could just get it.*

'You think Greg is a loser, don't you? You think you know it all. I saw it, that night I cooked for you, it's written all over your pretty, entitled face, little lady.' He steps closer to me and leans in, his breath rancid. 'But I've been watching you, following you. I know your dirty little secret. I was married to a woman like you once. A woman who cheated on me, betrayed me – just like you're betraying Greg with your fancy man.'

My blood, which is pounding in my ears, runs cold.

'I— I don't know what you're talking about. You must be mistaken, you—'

'Don't lie! You're all such liars. Do you think we're stupid or something? Greg would be better off without you. You're ruining his life, just like she ruined mine. I was an actor, a good one. I had my whole career in front of me – and she *ruined* it.' His eyes are ablaze.

'You don't understand,' I whimper. 'I'm sorry but—' I try to call out but my mouth has gone dry . . .

'Shut up,' he hisses. 'You're all the same. I don't like seeing men made little of.' He reaches for the hammer, never taking his eyes off me, and my throat constricts.

'Please,' I gasp, clutching the countertop behind me. 'I love my husband. My— My children . . . they're upstairs. Please, I'm begging you.'

Abby

The next day Abby wakes to an empty bed. It is Saturday, Edward is probably at the gym and although she would normally have a lie in, today she feels restless. The house seems unnaturally quiet, and then she remembers. Her mother is visiting her brother in Bath, the twins have gone to some unsuitable-sounding festival and Roseanna has gone to Galway to stay with a friend. Bliss. She showers, has a leisurely breakfast and decides to do an early supermarket shop. While she is in the shopping centre, she pops in to a hairdresser to see if they can fit her in for a blow-dry. They can, if she will wait ten minutes. Abby says she will come back, and goes off to buy herself a couple of magazines. It is not her regular hairdresser, so she finds it relaxing to read and not be subject to Dermot's far too intuitive brand of psychoanalysis. The stylist does a good job, and Abby is so pleased with the result that she wanders around a few more shops, taking sneaky glances at herself in mirrors. She thinks she doesn't look half bad.

She is drawn to a rail of summer dresses, floral prints and bright, blazing colours and decides to try a couple on. One of them, a rich coral red, takes her fancy; it drapes cleverly, flattering her curves but cunningly seeming to make her look more svelte at the same time. She decides to buy it and wear it out of the shop, bringing her jeans and T-shirt up to the desk to put in the carrier bag. Then the shop assistant directs her to a pair of funky sandals, which match the dress perfectly, and a soft leather bag.

'Colour blocking is all the trend this season,' the girl tells her reassuringly, ringing up her purchases on the till.

Abby walks back to her car with a slight sashay, tosses her hair and smiles demurely at a man who gives her an appreciative once-over. She feels unexpectedly buoyant, and has put all thoughts of her fractured and flailing marriage out of her head; she will not think about it today. One day at a time, and today feels like a good one.

She drives home, humming along to a song on the radio, and is surprised to see Edward's car outside their house, alongside another one she doesn't recognise. This strikes her as unusual. He is not normally home at this time, even on Saturday.

She lets herself in and walks down to the kitchen with her shopping bags.

'Abby.'

She jumps as Edward's voice cuts across her meandering thoughts, turning around to face him as he stands up from the kitchen sofa – and that's when she sees her.

For a second, Abby is frozen – a second when time seems to slow down and distil a scene that will forever remain printed in her memory. Her husband and another woman – *his* other woman, together – confronting her. Not caught red-handed, no sign of clichéd behaviour here, rather the clearly thought-out and no doubt much-rehearsed scene where she, Abby, would be forced to come face to face with a situation she had done her damnedest to avoid. Eyeball to eyeball, she was looking at her husband's lover.

She says the first thing that comes to her. 'You've brought her here?' her voice is incredulous, panicked. Whatever else, she could not have anticipated this act that goes beyond cruelty on so many levels for Abby.

'Abby,' Edward says again. 'We have to talk, you know we do. You won't talk to me, God knows I've tried, so I thought perhaps if Olivia was here it might help.'

'Did you?' Abby says icily.

'Please, Abby, at least hear Edward out. It's important for both of you.' Olivia's face is wreathed in concern, which makes Abby's stomach lurch disconcertingly. Up close, she is even prettier than Abby supposed. Clear, unlined skin, large wide-set eyes, hair shiny and natural – and she is thin, definitely thin.

'Is it?' Abby hears herself saying. 'I suppose you'd know, being a psychologist and everything, wouldn't you? I suppose you both feel sorry for me, have given great thought as to how you'll approach this awkward situation with me.'

'Yes, well,' Olivia frowns, 'that's true, in part. But there's so much more to discuss, won't you sit down? Please?'

'No,' Abby says. 'I will not sit down. Although thank you so much for asking me to in my own house.'

'Please, Abby.' Edward takes a step towards her. 'At least hear me out.'

'Why?' She backs away. 'So you can feel better about it all? So you can offload your guilty conscience and your underhand behaviour?'

'Two can be underhand in a marriage, Abby,' Olivia says. 'It's rarely just one person, there are many ways of being distant, unavailable, passive.'

'Are you implying that I am to blame for this?'

'Nobody's blaming anyone,' Edward says, looking at Olivia helplessly.

'You really need to listen, Abby,' Olivia says insistently.

'I hated being underhand about it all.' Edward looks at her pleadingly. 'I hated deceiving you, really I did, you have to believe me.'

'He did,' says Olivia. 'I can vouch for that.'

'I'm sure you can,' Abby says.

'He's been worried sick, stressed out of his mind. You must have noticed.'

'Must I? Really?'

'Please, Abby,' Edward shakes his head. 'I'm asking you – *we're* asking you, Olivia came here especially, begging you to listen, just let's sit down and talk about all of this.'

Abby has seen and heard enough. 'Let's not.'

'You're unbelievable!' Edward says. 'Stubborn, selfish – I just don't get you any more. I thought our marriage mattered to you.' He is becoming angry.

'Did you? Did you really? Well, you know what, so did I, but you've managed to change my mind about that, Edward. You and your fancy woman psychologist. I can't believe you'd do this to me – both of you. It's the lowest, most underhand thing I've ever heard of! How could you?' Abby turns on her heel.

'Abby, wait! Where are you going?'

'I don't know, but I know I've seen and heard enough. Do what you like Edward, that's what you've always done.' And with that Abby runs up into the hall and out of her house, leaving Edward and Olivia stunned behind her.

'Well that went really well,' says Edward.

'You didn't prepare me for how resistant she would be,' Olivia shakes her head.

'What am I going to do now?'

'You'd better go after her. I have to get back. Let me know how it goes.'

Diana

My head hurts. I try to open my eyes, but they hurt too. When I do open them, my vision is blurred. I am aware of voices, machines, snatches of conversations, comings and goings, the swish of a pulled curtain, and I drift in and out of consciousness.

'Visual changes . . .'

'Balance difficulties . . .'

'Fatigue – if the frontal lobe has been damaged, she could have memory problems, attention issues . . . mood-related changes. We'll just have to monitor her . . .'

I struggle to sit up, pull the mask from my face, but I'm immediately overcome with nausea and am sick. A nurse quickly gives me an injection and I sink back into blackness.

There are nightmares, terrifying ones, and I cry out, calling for Greg, my children, for help. I do not know it, but I am going through the textbook beginnings of coming around from a serious concussion and beating. Kind voices soothe me, medication dulls the pain and I succumb to depths of tiredness I could never have imagined. When I try to speak, my tongue feels like cotton wool and my throat is swollen and bruised. I must rest, I am told.

Abby

Abby is belting down the M7. She didn't think, she just got in her car and drove. Now she is on the road to God knows where. All she knows is she has to get away. She doesn't think about Edward, her mother or her children, they are perfectly well able to manage without her she reckons – for a few days certainly. She is definitely not going to worry about them. She looks down at her new dress and sandals, and wonders why she bothered, she is ruining them both sitting in the car. Then she remembers her jeans, T-shirt and trainers are in a bag on the backseat. She pulls over at the first exit and finds a lane to stop in, then wriggles out of her dress and pulls on the jeans and T-shirt. Then she folds the dress up carefully and puts it in the bag along with the sandals. Back on the M7, she keeps her eyes firmly on the road ahead. She stops in a pretty village full of thatched houses on the other side of Limerick, and goes in to a well-known pub for a light lunch. It is quiet, there are a few businessmen, some couples with children and an older lady, alone like herself, sitting with a glass of red wine and the newspaper. There is a turf fire crackling in the grate and wooden beams give the place a cosy air of times gone by. Abby orders a sandwich and a bowl of soup and sits at a small table by the fire, stretching her legs.

A mournful-faced waiter brings her food. 'Going anywhere nice?' he asks.

'Just passing through, really,' Abby says.

'That's all anyone does,' he confirms sadly, 'mostly on their way to Cork. Sure why wouldn't you? There's nothing here, Cork is a great place.'

It is years since Abby has been to Cork. Her grandmother's old house was on the outskirts of a village there. She thinks maybe she will go and take a look at it, spend a couple of days in Cork. Whatever else, she is not going back to Dublin, not yet, anyway.

Vonnie

I was finishing up an important part of my work on the Chester Beatty collection at home when I got the news. Jazz was watching a movie on television. I saw Diana's number flash up on my phone and grinned, no doubt she wanted to have a post-mortem about our dinner. Since there was no avoiding it, I thought I might as well bite the bullet.

'Hey!' I said. 'Your timing's perfect. I've just finished work.'

But it wasn't Di's voice that answered me. It was Greg's, sounding desperately tired. 'Vonnie, this is Greg. I knew your number would be in Di's phone which is why I'm ringing from it.' He paused.

'Greg, is everything okay?'

'No, no, I'm sorry to say it's not. Diana's in hospital, she was attacked last night, Vonnie. She's been badly beaten up.'

'Oh my God,' I gasped. 'Is she—? How? Where? What happened?'

'She was attacked at home, in our house.' His voice was leaden.

'Dear God, how? I mean, was it a burglary?'

'Not exactly, it was a break in of sorts. The guy was mentally unstable, has a history apparently. Look, I can't talk about it right now. I just wanted you to know. Oh, and I've been trying to get Abby, too, she doesn't seem to be answering her phone – could you try her, maybe?'

I assured him I would.

'Can we see her?'

'Not just yet.' He was hesitant. 'Maybe in a couple of days.' He told me which hospital she was in and the name of the consultant she was under. 'They're concerned about internal abdominal bleeding right now, and she's pretty badly concussed.'

'Oh God, poor, poor Diana,' I said. 'Tell her we're thinking of her and praying, and I'll get in to see her as soon as they allow it.'

'Of course I will. Bye, Vonnie.'

I could hardly take it in. I called Abby immediately, who, as Greg said, didn't seem to be picking up. 'Abby, call me as soon as you get this. It's important.' I left the message at that. Then I went and poured myself a glass of wine, called the hospital, and gave them Diana's name and the date she was admitted.

'One moment, please, I'll put you through to the ICU nurses' station.'

The intensive care unit! Greg hadn't said she was in ICU; oh God, she must be really bad.

'Hello, I'm enquiring about Diana O'Mahony,' I said.

'Are you a family member?' a clipped woman's voice replied.

'No but I'm—'

'Then I'm afraid I can't give out any inform—'

'Oh, please, please don't hang up on me,' I begged. 'I'm her best friend, her husband has just told me. He rang just now,' I was babbling. 'Please, I've known her since we were twelve years old.' And to my horror I began to sob.

There was a brief pause. 'She's taken an awful battering, she's critical, but stable at the present. We're taking good care of her; try not to worry, she's in good hands. Now, I'm very sorry, I have to go.' And the line went dead.

Critical, *critical!* Greg never said, oh God, where was Abby? I dialled her again, still no answer. I left another message. 'Call me, Abby, it's urgent. It's Di. Abby you need to call me!'

I tried her home number then and got her daughter. 'Hi, Rosie, it's Vonnie. I need to talk to your mom,' I said.

'She's not here.'

'I've tried her on her mobile but she's not answering. Do you know where she is?'

'No, hang on. D-a-d!' I heard her call. 'Dad's just coming to the phone.'

'Hello, Vonnie?' It was Edward.

'Yes, hello, Edward. I've been trying to get Abby. She's not answering her phone.'

'Tell me about it.' He sounded almost as tired as Greg had.

'Is something the matter?'

'I don't know, to be honest, we had a row of sorts. Abby took off this morning and I haven't seen or heard from her since. Frankly, I'm sick with worry, but if you can't get hold of her, well, that's even worse. I think I'm going to have to get on to the police.'

'I'm sorry to hear that, Edward, really I am. I'm sure Abby's all right, but the reason I'm trying to get hold of her is Diana – she's had an accident, she's in hospital, in the ICU.'

'Diana?' he repeated sharply. 'Where?'

'St Vincent's, she must be in a bad way.' My voice was tremulous. 'They wouldn't say, they couldn't tell me—'

'What on earth happened?'

'She was attacked, beaten up apparently, in her own home.' I heard him suck in his breath.

'And Greg?'

'He was out when it happened, working, I think.'

'I see. Give me your number there, Vonnie.' He sounded calm and collected. 'I'm going to get on to one of my colleagues attached to St Vincent's, I'll find out what the story is. I'll get back to you.'

'Oh, would you, Edward? That would be so great.' I felt hugely reassured. I had all but forgotten he was a surgeon himself.

'Leave it with me, and I'll tell Abby the minute I can get hold of her, but you may hear from her first.'

'I'm sure she'll be in touch soon,' I said. I gave him my number then sat down to wait, and pray. Suddenly I felt guilty for all the times Di and I had been mean about Edward. I didn't know what was going on between him and Abby, but I could tell that he was genuinely upset about her, frantic with worry. Which was more than Greg had sounded . . . oh, that was unfair of me – but alone, in her own home, and the kids – had they been there? I hadn't had time to ask.

But Edward had been calm and helpful and I was grateful for that. I knew Abby would be too.

Then I remembered Jake, and thought he would want to know. So I called him. *What bullshit!* my inner voice mocked me. You *want* to talk to him, to hear his voice. You just *need* him, girl.

'Hey, what's up?' he answered at the first ring.

Diana

My family are around my bedside. It must be serious, because I can hear my mother and Sophie crying. I want to speak, reassure them, but I am somewhere light and drifting. I cannot find my voice, but I hear words now and then, breaking through the fuzzy edges of my consciousness.

'I'll never forgive myself,' Greg says, hoarsely.

'Beautiful Diana, my lovely girl.' Mum strokes my forehead.

'Mum, you have to hold on. Mum, you *have* to,' Sophie says through her tears.

Philip clutches my hand. He doesn't say anything, his grip is full of unspoken desperation and I find this hardest of all. If only I could speak, tell them all how much I love them.

I see snapshots of my life in soft focus – being carried on

my father's shoulders as a little girl, feeling as if I was on top of the world . . . running down to the lake at school with Abby and Vonnie, shrieking with laughter . . . walking hand in hand with Greg on a beach . . . feeding my children, reading them a bedtime story, kissing them goodnight . . . then Harry, Harry, he won't know, they won't understand – I have to tell him . . . I was wrong, I need to tell him before it's too late – I love him so much.

'She's trying to say something.'

'Shh, Diana, you mustn't try to talk, darling.'

But they don't understand.

An alarm goes off somewhere in the distance, a siren wail of bleeps. I look around and find it is coming from below me. I seem to have drifted up to the ceiling from where I have a clear and detached vantage point. Consternation unfolds as a medical team rushes to a bed, pushing family members out of the way, shouting 'She's arresting. . .'

'She's bleeding out. Get her down to theatre, *now*.'

I watch, bemused, untroubled, and realise with an over-whelming sense of calm that the woman in the bed is me.

The Affair

He is at home, out of his mind with worry, he hasn't heard from her in two days, and when he rang her mobile, her husband answered her phone – so he hung up. Something has happened, but what? Has Greg found out? Has he confronted her? Is she telling him, now, this minute – is she all right? He longs to go to her, to rescue her, to protect her, but he is helpless, impotent. There is nothing he can do but wait.

The past five years flash before him, meeting her again, after all that time, fifteen years later. He had been just a kid really, twenty to her (very sophisticated) twenty-five, the first time, at Edward's wedding, when she seduced him. He had been devastated then when she had refused to have anything to do with him afterwards, she hadn't even wanted to dance with him. He smiles ruefully, remembering. But then, when they met again, everything was different. He was thirty-five, he was confident, successful, on his way – and the sexual chemistry between them had been as electric as ever. He had been dating a lovely girl back then, blonde, good-looking, a couple of years younger than he was, and she had been devastated when he broke up with her – but there was no point, no future in it. Once he and Diana fell in love, he knew she was the only woman for him.

They had split up several times throughout the affair, she couldn't bring herself to break up her marriage, her family. In the interim weeks or months, he'd go on the tear, meet other women and try to forget her, but never succeeded. No one even came close. He knew people wondered about him, why he hadn't settled down, begun to raise a family of his own – after all, he was turning forty now – but he just didn't have any interest. One of his sisters had even asked him if he was gay, 'You can tell me, you know, Harry.'

Sometimes he thinks that might have been easier, anything would be easier than this. But now he senses a conclusion at hand. If Diana hasn't called him, and Greg picked up her phone, he must know, they must be having it out. His fate is being decided one way or the other. He jumps as his phone rings, but it is only Edward. He takes a deep breath and tries to sound upbeat, 'Ed, hi.'

'Are you alone? Can you talk?'

'Yes, why?'

'There's something you need to know. There's been an accident – Diana—'

He doesn't get any further, the unthinkable has just exploded in Harry's brain.

'What? Is she hurt? What's happened? Jesus, Edward, tell me.'

'I'm trying to, Harry, just calm down, will you?'

He listens, as the blood begins to pound in his head, his hands sweat, his heart races. 'I have to see her, I have to go to her.'

'You can't, Harry,' Ed's voice is gentle. 'It's out of the question . . . no one knows about you and Di, not even Abby, as far as I know. Her family are with her—'

'Oh God,' Harry says hoarsely. 'But what if . . . she needs me, Ed. She may be asking for me.' He is aware of the hysteria in his own voice but he doesn't care.

'You would only be making things worse for her, for them, surely you can see that?'

Ed is right. Harry sits down suddenly, all the wind is knocked out of him. There is nothing he can do – nothing. The woman he loves, would give his life for, is fighting for her life, a life he cannot even exist in.

Through a fog of misery it occurs to him. 'How did you know about us, Ed?'

'I saw her going into your house once, you opened the door, it wasn't hard to figure out. After that, I couldn't help but notice the lack of women in your life, how you never seemed interested in anyone. It all fell into place.'

'You never said anything.'

'None of my business, Harry. Besides, I've had my own worries lately,' Edward sighs. 'I have to go.'

'You'll tell me, Ed, won't you? Let me know anything, any change good or bad. You're all I have to— to . . .' his voice catches.

'Of course I will. Her medical team are keeping me updated.'

'Be straight with me, Ed. What are her chances?'

'Right now, it's anyone's guess, Harry, and that's the truth. The next twenty-four hours are crucial. Try not to worry. I give you my word, I'll let you know. I'm only sorry I can't do more.'

As his brother hangs up, Harry breaks down, leaning his head against the wall, sobbing hoarsely, brokenly. The painful lament of a heart for what might have been, what was, and, most cruel of all, what now may never be.

Abby

Abby stops at Dunnes Stores on her way in to Cork to buy some fresh underwear. Then she checks in to a hotel in the centre. It is four o'clock in the afternoon and the sun is shining as she decides to take a stroll through the city. She realises she has left her phone in the car, where she threw it on the back seat earlier. She heard a few message alert bleeps while she was driving but didn't want to look at them. It would only be Edward, or her mother, wanting to know where she is and what she thinks she's doing. Abby is not sure she knows. That is what this detour is all about. She needs time alone, away from the house, from her responsibilities so she can think.

She is having a 'Shirley Valentine' moment. The thought makes her smile, although she feels she has very little to smile about. Little did she think, she muses, when she was writing her petition to St Valentine all those years ago that she would find herself in this predicament. All she had wanted was to marry a doctor, raise a family and to make her mother happy, of course. It was quite simple and straightforward. Little did she know, then, all the loopholes she had left unchecked. She couldn't blame St Valentine, he had given her exactly what she had asked for – if only she had thought to be more careful, more explicit in her request. She didn't realise he would take it literally. She wanders through the English Market, overflowing with every kind of food, then pops into the Crawford Art Gallery to look around and have a cup of tea. She is back in her hotel room at six, feeling suddenly tired and a little shocked at the enormity of what she has done. It was horrible, awful, of Edward to bring that woman into their home and confront her, corner her the way he did, but perhaps she had over-reacted a bit? Going AWOL didn't really feature much as a solution to anything in the problem pages she constantly read. She would text him in the morning, let him know she was taking a couple of days to think. She was still in shock, after all. Tonight he could sweat a bit.

Vonnie

Edward was as good as his word and rang me back about an hour later.

'Edward,' I said, eagerly, 'any news?'

'Yes, but I'm afraid it's not good.'

'Oh God.' I felt the strength go from my knees, and sat down on the arm of a chair.

'She's in a bad way, Vonnie, head injuries, broken ribs, concussion. She's not fully conscious, but there's internal bleeding.' He paused significantly. 'That's not good; in fact, while I was at the hospital she started to haemorrhage and was rushed to theatre, they're working on her now.'

'I just can't believe it. I can't take it in. Only last night she was here . . .'

'I spoke with her mother,' Edward went on. 'Apparently the guy who did it was some hobo friend of Greg's, one of the guys who featured on his show. Apparently he had a history of violent behaviour, psychotic episodes. Lord knows how he got into the house, or even knew where Di and Greg lived. I can't believe anyone would be foolish enough to give out their address.'

'No,' I murmured. Remembering all too clearly Di telling us how she had arrived home one night to find a strange man cooking in her kitchen. That must have been him. 'Was his name Rob, by any chance?' I asked. 'The man who attacked her.'

'I've no idea. Greg seemed to know who it was, and the guards have tracked him down – not that that'll be much use to Diana now.'

'And Abby, have you heard from her?'

'No, I'm afraid not. It's turning out to be one hell of a day.'

'Well, keep me posted and thank you, Edward, for checking up on Di, I'm so grateful. I know she would be too.'

'It's a pleasure, Vonnie. I'm only sorry I can't be the bearer of better news. If it's any consolation, she's with the guy I'd choose for myself. He's a superb surgeon, if anyone can pull her through this, he will.'

I felt a lump in my throat. 'All we can we do is hope and pray.'

'I'm afraid so. I have to go, if I hear anything I'll let you know. Goodbye, Vonnie.'

'Bye, Edward, and thanks again.'

I put down the phone and tears began to stream down my face. I just couldn't believe it – Diana, our beautiful Diana, lying in some theatre, having been battered and beaten to within an inch of her life; it just couldn't be happening, but it was.

At that moment the doorbell rang and Jazz hurtled downstairs to open it. 'Daddy!' she said, thrilled at the unexpected appearance of her father. 'You never said you were coming around, come on in.'

Jake took one look at me and took me in his arms, where I began to sob.

'What's the matter, Mommy?' Jazz looked alarmed.

'One of Mommy's friends is very sick,' said Jake. 'Diana, you met her yesterday.'

'Oh, Jake, it's bad. Edward rang, he says she's in theatre now, she's haemorrhaging. She might not make it.'

'Hey, we don't know that yet, let's take this minute by minute. She's strong, she's healthy. She has a good chance, Vonnie.'

'You're right,' I sniffed. 'I just can't take it in, only last night she was sitting right here and now . . .'

'I think we should go and get something to eat, it could be a long day.'

'Oh, I don't want to go out, Jake, suppose—'

'Suppose what? You'll have your phone with you if anyone calls. There's no point sitting in going crazy, we might as well get some food – we need to eat anyway. If nothing else, it will pass the time and take your mind off things for an hour or so.'

'Okay,' I said. 'Jazz, go get your jacket.'

'Yay!' said Jazz, and rushed upstairs.

Abby

Abby is lying on her bed in her hotel room debating whether or not to order room service. She is suddenly overwhelmed by tiredness, by her unfamiliar behaviour and surroundings. At the time, it had seemed like a good idea, now she wonders if she is losing her marbles. What on earth is she doing lying on a bed in a hotel room in Cork when her family must be out of their minds with worry? What would Edward have told them? *Well that was his problem*, a petulant inner voice reminds her, it was all his fault anyway. But still . . .

She pulls herself together and wonders what Shirley Valentine would do. She certainly wouldn't sit around feeling sorry for herself in a hotel room, Abby is sure. She gets up and has a good, hot, shower, taking care to pin up her blow-dried hair so it doesn't get wet. Then she rubs in some of the moisture cream provided, puts on some make-up, and takes her new dress, which is the only item of clothing in the wardrobe, from its hanger. When she is dressed, and wearing her new sandals, she feels better, more in control. Picking up her handbag, she takes a last look in the mirror, pulls her shoulders back and says firmly, 'You are a divine goddess, you got that? An adorable, absolutely divine in *every* way goddess.' Then she jumps as there is a loud knock on her door, followed by another. Housekeeping, presumably, although they needn't be so insistent, she thinks crossly.

'Yes,' she says, opening the door, and then freezes.

'May I come in please?' says Edward, wearily. 'If you're alone, that is?' His eyes dart into the room.

'Of course I'm alone. What are *you* doing here?'

'I thought I heard you talking to someone.'

'Must have been the television, I've just switched it off.'

'You look as if you're dressed up to go out.'

'What if I am?' Abby is beginning to rather enjoy this.

'I've been trying to get you all day. You're not picking up your calls.'

'I didn't feel like it.'

'No, quite.' Edward walks into the room and over to the window.

'How did you know I was here?'

'I didn't. I was out of my mind with worry. I went to the police, it wasn't hard to trace you.'

Abby is not sure whether to feel pleased or ashamed.

'I have to talk to you, Abby.'

'Have you brought your psychologist friend with you?' Abby asks archly. 'I suppose she's going to jump out of the wardrobe any minute and shout, "Gotcha!"'

'Please, Abby, I've just driven non-stop from Dublin, I'm tired and I'm stressed, is it too much to ask you to just listen to me?'

Abby feels chastened. Edward looks a wreck and she can't very well throw him out, even if she would quite like to.

'Have you eaten?' he asks.

'No, I was going to order room service, then I changed my mind. I *was* going to go out.'

'That's a lovely dress,' Edward remarks, rather sadly.

'Thank you.'

'Can we go out together then? Let me just freshen up and I'll be ready in five minutes. We can go somewhere to eat – and talk.'

'I suppose so.'

'Where's your phone?' Edward suddenly asks.

'I left it in the car, why?'

'Nothing, I'll tell you over dinner.' And he disappears into the bathroom.

Abby sits down on the bed, feeling all the fight seep out of her. It is very sad, she thinks, how couples who were so much in love can drift apart. She is in a hotel room with her own husband, and all they are going to talk about over dinner is the demise of their marriage. So much for love.

Vonnie

'She's asleep, finally.' Jake comes downstairs after almost an hour and sinks down into the opposite corner of the sofa, which suddenly seems pitifully small.

He has been reading Jazz a bedtime story, something she always exploits shamelessly, making him do endless voices and faces until shrieks of laughter float downstairs from her room. It couldn't help but make you smile, even though I know her sleep routine will be shot to pieces. I focus on that, in order to avoid the other creeping feeling of guilt, that I should be denying her this right, that I am keeping them, my daughter and her father, from one another. But Jazz has adjusted well to our separation; she is happy and healthy, I reassure myself. She loves us both, I know that, but the decibels of joy in her voice and her laughter are saved for when Jake is around.

'Any news?'

'None.' I have been ringing the hospital on the hour, every hour. 'She's out of theatre, stable at the moment, but the next twenty-four hours are critical.'

I think of Di, lying there in intensive care, fighting for her life, and a horrible fear grips me. The fear of grim reality, the possibility of the unthinkable, that she might not make it, that she may die, and I begin to cry. 'What if I don't get to see her again?' I sob. 'What if we never—'

'That's not going to happen.' Jake pulls me to him, and lets me cry and cry.

Gradually, in the safety of his arms, the fear recedes. I can be hopeful again, I can think *yes, she will get better, come through this* . . .

I take the tissue he offers, dry my eyes, blow my nose and look up at him.

'I'm sorry.'

'Don't be. You have nothing to be sorry about.'

I look into the depths of slanting black eyes that scan mine, searching for an answer, or maybe a question. My daughter's eyes. Eyes that have always mesmerised me.

Jake leans in, kisses me, pulls me tight and something inside me unfurls, prevents me from saying the words I know I should.

I take his hand, and wordlessly follow him upstairs.

He undresses me, silencing me with a kiss when I try to protest, although I do not try very hard. I think I will be awkward, shy, it has been over four years since we have made love, and I know this is madness. But lying beside him, I can only silently marvel at the glorious sculpture of his body, and its ability, just like the first time, to make me forget myself, my inadequacies, insecurities and all the reasons why I shouldn't do this. Instead, I revel in the familiarity of our togetherness. Every touch, every caress a cherished memory, alive again in the pounding of my heart, the trembling of my limbs, the building heat between us.

We are still awake as dawn breaks and birdsong fills the air. Jake leans over me, takes my face in his hands, looks into my eyes. 'Marry me, Vonnie.'

Those words . . . the ones I thought I'd never hear. I want to say yes, I really do. I have always, somewhere deep in my unconscious, been waiting for those words, from childhood fantasies, through teenage longings, even in the worst depths of my self-loathing years, I have always dreamed that someone, somewhere, would want me, *really* want me, to have and to hold, to love and to cherish . . .

Say yes, just say yes.

'Vonnie? Look at me.'

'I– I'm sorry Jake, I can't . . .'

Jake looks at me, hard, and sees right through me. Then something in him shuts down, there is a flash of scorn, a light that flares and just as quickly goes out in his eyes.

'Wait, Jake, please . . . where are you going?' I ask as he gets up, pulls on his jeans and T-shirt.

'I have to get back, and I don't want to wake Jazz.'

'Please, Jake, can't we talk about this, I need to—'

'There's nothing to talk about, Vonnie. You don't trust me – correction, you *won't* trust me – but worse, far worse, you won't even trust yourself. It's not just about you, Vonnie, you know, there are other people's lives involved here too.'

He is angry, and I don't blame him, but I need to make him understand. 'That's not fair, Jake—'

'That's your answer to everything, Vonnie, and, you know what? I'm tired of it. Life isn't fair, it's messy and dirty and it hurts like hell sometimes, but if you shut down on it, you're shutting out a lot of other people too. That may be fine for you, but it's not a great legacy for Jazz, is it?'

I feel as if I've been hit, and rage at the fear and confusion that are roiling inside me, not to mention the horrible turn things have taken, overcome me. 'That's a low blow, Jake,' I hiss. 'I'd do anything for Jazz, anything, you know that. I adore her – she's my life, my whole life.'

'Exactly,' said Jake.

I listen to his footsteps echoing down the stairs, then the front door shuts behind him.

Abby

Abby cannot sleep. She did briefly, after their extraordinary evening, for about an hour or so, but now she is wide awake again. Awake with worry for Diana and wonder at what has just passed between her and Edward, who is out for the count beside her. He was so exhausted she doesn't want to wake him, even though they had agreed to set off for Dublin as early as possible. It is only six o'clock, she will let him sleep for a little while yet. She curls into his back and he sighs imperceptibly in his sleep, reaching behind to hook his hand around her thigh. Abby smiles and, remembering the previous evening, thinks that life is surely full of unexpected surprises.

'A large gin and tonic,' Edward says to the waiter, 'and I'd like to see your wine list, please.'

They are sitting in Isaac's, one of Cork's smartest restaurants, and the place is buzzing. Abby has ordered a glass of Prosecco, but is surprised at Edward having a gin and tonic, whatever about wine. It must be bad, what he has to say to her, but since she knows already what has been going on it can't be any worse than what she has been thinking about day and night herself. If she is to listen to the final death knoll of her marriage, then she will do it to the accompaniment of good wine.

When their drinks arrive, Edward begins. 'Promise you'll listen to me, hear me out, without interrupting?'

Abby sighs and nods, taking a sip of her sparkling wine.

'I know you think I'm having an affair with Olivia, which in itself speaks volumes about our marriage, but I'm not.'

Abby opens her mouth to protest, and is silenced by a look from across the table. She scowls, annoyed. She had expected apologies, explanations perhaps, but not denials.

'I am seeing her on a purely professional basis, although I won't deny that she has been a huge help to me under extremely difficult circumstances.'

'You really expect me to believe that – that you were seeing a therapist? You don't believe in therapy, you've said so often.'

'You're right, I didn't – not until I needed it. Not until I thought I was going out of my mind. Even then I tried to fight it.'

Abby looks at him as if he *has* lost his mind. She wonders what will come next. The wine arrives and the waiter fills their glasses.

'You remember when I set up the clinic, when I retired from my vascular surgery?'

'No!' Abby says, exasperated. 'Of course I remember, how could I not? Two and half years ago.'

'Yes, well.' Edward takes a deep breath. 'I wasn't quite truthful with you at the time.'

Now he has her attention. 'What do you mean?'

'Just what I said. I didn't tell you the truth.'

'About what, exactly?'

'About why I left the hospital, why I gave up surgery.'

'You said you were fed up with the HSE and the way

hospitals were being run, you said you wanted to work for yourself, to run your own business, a private clinic.'

'Exactly. That was a lie.'

Something in Edward's tone makes Abby listen very carefully. She has the feeling she is going to hear something she would rather not. But there is no running away this time, not unless she wants to make an embarrassing scene in a crowded restaurant, and she does not. She is also weary, too weary.

'Go on.'

Their first course arrives, oysters for Edward, prawns for Abby. Edward waits until the waiter has gone.

'I left because . . . I lost my nerve.'

A prawn pauses in midair, en route to Abby's open mouth.

'Lost your nerve?'

'Yes, I was unable to operate. I lost my nerve completely. It happens, you know. Not often, but it's not unheard of.'

'But you're a highly trained surgeon,' Abby says incredulously.

'Yes,' Edward agrees, 'I am. And I like to think I was one of the best, in my day, but it doesn't matter how good you are if you can't face an operating theatre, never mind an actual operation or even a scalpel.'

Abby couldn't be more shocked if he told her he was a cross-dresser.

'But, how . . . I mean, how did you manage?'

'They were very good about it. Everyone was very patient and understanding. The board wanted me to take some time off, get to the bottom of it, and that's how I began seeing Olivia – on their recommendation. So I had to, you see, and then, well, I began to find it very helpful.' Edward swallows an oyster and washes it down with some Pouilly-Fumé.

'Not helpful enough to go back to operating though.' Abby does not like the image building in her head of the helpful and sympathetic Olivia, which can only mean . . .

'No, but that was part of the problem. I had never wanted to operate, I'm not even sure I wanted to be a doctor, it was my father's dearest wish, I was just trying to make him happy. It took quite a while to unearth that, to dig it up, so to speak.'

'But you never said . . . you never told me. How could you not talk to *me* about all this?' Abby hates the whiny tone that has entered her voice, but she cannot help it. Suddenly she is unworthy again, not good enough. Her own husband couldn't turn to her in his hour of need.

'I couldn't bear to,' Edward says. 'I couldn't bear to let you down. I tried once or twice, not very hard I admit, but I just couldn't bring myself to. You always looked up to me so much. I couldn't bear to shatter your illusions, if I'm honest. I didn't want you knowing I was a mess, that I was unravelling. I was the surgeon, the supposed alpha male, the head of the family. I was supposed to protect you all, not heap chaos and prospective unemployment on you – so I had the idea of starting the clinic, where I wouldn't have to operate at all, just manage it. A cop-out, I know, on the emotional front, but, as solutions go, it hasn't been a bad one.'

'I— I'm having trouble taking all of this in.'

'Of course you are. If I couldn't face it myself, how on earth could you be expected to grasp it?' Edward says gently. 'And I want you to know, you've been wonderful.'

The waiter brings their main course, but Abby finds she has lost her appetite. Nonetheless, she tries to play with her food half-heartedly. She takes a swig of wine.

'That's not all,' Edward goes on. 'There's something else I need to explain.'

Here it comes, thinks Abby, her chest constricting. The scene has been nicely set up – stressed, misunderstood husband meets kind, empathetic young therapist and unconsummated love blossoms. Oh God, this is worse than she could have ever dreamed up.

'I struggled with all of this, but it was taking its toll. I know I wasn't easy to live with then, but that's because I began to suffer from depression and it was getting worse. I had to go on medication – anti-depressants. They took a while to work, about three months I think, looking back, and when they did kick in, well, the relief I felt was enormous.' Edward pauses. 'There was light at the end of the tunnel again. I could see a way forward. Except for one rather debilitating side-effect.'

Abby listens, mesmerised. 'What?'

'I, um, wasn't able to perform . . . in the bedroom department.' He looks around furtively to make sure no one can overhear their conversation. 'As I'm sure you must have noticed.' Edward takes a gulp of wine. Then he continues quickly, as if he is afraid to stop, now that he has started. 'I couldn't believe it. First I can't perform in the operating theatre, then I find I can't perform sexually. I felt as if I was in a waking nightmare. Naturally, I went back to therapy.

Olivia said I had to talk to you – explain – and, in the meantime, look at changing my medication. But it was working so effectively to combat the depression, I didn't have the nerve to come off it. So I'm afraid I stuck my head in the sand and threw myself into the clinic, into my work, and now, well, here we are.' Edward looks at her, rather beseechingly. 'I know the past couple of years must have been awful for you, I'd do anything to have avoided that, but I'm afraid I was just concentrating on keeping my own head above water and keeping the finances on the straight and narrow. If it's any consolation, it hasn't been easy.'

'Oh, Edward.'

'I knew you were slipping away from me, and I was totally at sea about how to deal with it. And then when I tried to talk to you, well, you just didn't want to know, and I thought you'd made up your mind that you'd had enough. When you left the house this morning, well, I've been out of my mind with worry. So has your mother by the way.'

The spectre of Sheila floats for a second before Abby, who had clean forgotten about her mother in the light of Edward's revelations, and is quickly banished. She is suddenly beginning to understand the meaning of the saying 'the ring of truth'. She feels as if a great fog is lifting. 'I thought you didn't fancy me anymore, that you wanted *her*. I've got so fat and unattractive.'

Edward takes her hands, not seeming to care that he has dunked his shirt cuff in mint sauce. 'Abby, I'm crazy about you. I always have been.'

'B— But I trapped you into marriage.' Abby's lip wobbles and tears spill down her face.

'Rosie was an accident. A very wonderful, occasionally challenging, accident, I grant you, but one I give thanks for every day.'

'It wasn't an accident, I mean *she* wasn't an accident.' Abby takes a deep breath and looks her husband in the eye. 'If tonight is about confessions, then I have to tell you that I stopped taking the pill – I *wanted* to get pregnant. I'm so sorry, Edward. I know you were having second thoughts and I couldn't bear to lose you.'

Edward leans in to her, still clasping her hands. 'I was nervous, Abby, I'll admit to that, but I never entertained any second thoughts. I was only ever worried that I wouldn't live up to your expectations, that I wouldn't be good enough for you, might not be the husband you deserved. I know I can be withdrawn sometimes, but it was never, ever about you, about us. But now that you've told me I must admit, I feel pretty chuffed.' Edward leans back and grins.

'You do?'

'Yes, I certainly do. I love you, Abby, whatever shape you are, you're always the sexiest women in the room to me.'

'I am?'

'Most definitely.'

'You're not just saying that?'

'No, I'm not. And if you come back to the hotel with me now, I'll prove it to you,' Edward says with a gleam in his eyes.

'But what about your anti-depressants?'

'I've been off them for almost a month, I don't need them anymore, not if we're okay again – we are, aren't we?'

'Oh, I hope so.'

'Let's get out of here then.'

'Yes, let's.'

It is in the taxi on the way back to the hotel that Edward gently tells Abby the news about Diana, though he does not say anything about Harry. Diana will address that herself if she needs to, if that time ever comes.

'Oh God! I can't believe it. Poor, poor Diana, can we go back to Dublin now?' Abby pleads. 'We must!'

There's no point, darling, really. I rang the hospital before dinner, there's no change, she's stable but still critical. Let's get some sleep and set off at the crack of dawn tomorrow, there's nothing to be gained from going back now. But you might give Vonnie a call, she's been worried about you too. She was trying to get hold of you.'

'God, I'm so stupid and selfish, I can't believe it.' Abby is horrified.

'No you're not. There's been a lot going on the past couple of days, for all of us. You were just doing what you had to do. You couldn't have known.'

Upstairs, in their room, Abby feels dazed by all this new knowledge, and sits down on the bed. She cannot take it all in. Edward is not having an affair, he's still in love with her – and Diana, hovering between life and death in a hospital bed in Dublin.

'Abby?' Edward hooks his hand around her neck and leans down to kiss her.

And suddenly she needs to do something, anything, to affirm the fact that they are here, alive. That her marriage that she thought dead is still a living, breathing entity. Edward pulls her up, so she is standing before him, and slowly begins to ease her dress off her shoulders, burying his face in her neck.

'I've missed you,' he murmurs. Abby takes his face in her hands and kisses him hungrily. Then they are pulling each other's clothes off, falling on the bed, and behaving very much like any couple in love who have been given a night off in a nice hotel away from the kids.

Diana

I am back in my body, feeling clammy and oppressed. It is dark and I want to open my eyes, but my eyelids are too heavy. I cannot speak. I am aware, though, awake and listening. It is late, into the small hours. I know that Greg has taken the children home to get some sleep and will be back early in the morning. My father is at home. He cannot bear to see me like this. It has made him very upset, my mother has said, and he is too old. My mother and sister speak in low, hushed voices, one sitting on either side of my bed, each holding one of my hands, a conspiracy of women.

They must be exhausted. I want to tell them to go home, that I will still be here tomorrow. A nurse comes in to check on me. 'No change,' she says. 'Her vitals are stable.'

'It's his fault,' my sister Corinne says. 'Who else but Greg would give the key of their house to a stranger, a madman?'

'He didn't know that . . .' My mother tries to defend him.

'Papa was right about him. I don't often agree with him, but he was right about Greg. He always said he was weak and self-obsessed, that he never put Diana first. Now look what's happened.'

'She loves him.' My mother strokes my hand. I wish I could squeeze hers in return, but I have no strength. 'Love is not always easy.'

'In this case, she has almost loved him to death, her own death,' Corinne says bitterly.

'Corinne!' my mother whispers. 'Be careful what you say!'

'Why wasn't *he* at home? Why didn't *he* get beaten to a pulp? Huh?'

'Shush.'

'You say love isn't easy, well no one pretends it is, but surely you don't have to risk your life for it. You and Papa have had a wonderful marriage but, if you ask me, I don't think they come along very often.'

'You're right, they don't. And ours was no different.'

'What do you mean? You and Papa adore each other – he worships you, everyone knows that.'

'Your father is a wonderful man, but he is not perfect. For a long, long, time I had to share him.'

'What do you mean? That he worked too hard?'

'That too.' My mother pauses. 'But, no, that's not what I meant. I had to share him with another woman.'

I hear Corinne gasp and, for a minute, there is silence. 'Papa? Papa had another woman?'

'For over twenty years,' my mother says, mildly. 'She lived in Paris. She died recently, about two months ago from cancer. That's why your father has been so melancholy lately. Even though the affair was long over, they remained friends – I was more jealous of that than anything. But she's gone now, finally – too late for me to care really.'

I want to shout, to sit up and demand to know what the hell is going on. Has my mother taken leave of her senses? Is she hallucinating? On drugs? This is preposterous! It couldn't possibly be true, but then I remember. A wisp of memory, a conversation, a closed door and me, twelve years old, confused and frightened, listening, not understanding, but now the words reverberate in my ears, 'I love her, yes! I have always loved her. I love you both. Please, Pauline, don't force me to choose.'

And I had thought he was talking about me.

'Why did you stay? Why didn't you tell us?' Corrine asks gently.

'Things were different in those days, Corinne. Women didn't have the options they do now. What would I have done? Where would I have gone with two small girls? And we were happy, you know, he adored you both, and you him. I couldn't have stood to split everyone up.' She sighs. 'Besides, I loved him, I really did, and I believed him when he said he loved me. It was just unfortunate that he loved her too. She was an old friend, they had known each other from childhood, that's a very strong bond between lovers.'

'I can't believe it,' Corinne whispers, echoing my thoughts.

'So, you see, our marriage wasn't so perfect after all, but we got through it. We stayed together. Nowadays, well, who knows what would have happened. But I sometimes wonder if I have been a good example to you girls.'

'Oh, Mum, of course you have.'

'But not a truthful one, hmm?' You have chosen not to marry and Diana, well, I often wonder if she can't bear to admit to her father that he was right, that Greg is not right for her, just because she wants to prove she can make a marriage work as well as ours did. Maybe I should have spoken to you both before, perhaps this might not have happened.' Her voice catches and I hear her stifle a sob.

'No, Mum, don't say that!' Corinne whispers across me. 'Diana will get better. She is strong, determined, she will fight for us, for her family, for her children.'

'Yes,' says my mother, rallying. 'You are right. My girls are fighters.'

I am trying, I want to tell them. *I am trying so hard.* But part of me is crying too.

Vonnie

Jake has gone. He came back to say goodbye to Jazz, who is, as always, heartbroken that they are to be parted, even though she knows they will be reunited in less than two weeks when we are back in the US. He told her he had an important assignment that meant he had to travel immediately. Only he and I know the truth, and I can't go there.

Instead, I focus on Diana and ring the hospital the first moment I can. No change. Stable, but critical. Oh God. At least Abby called me last night, but I was so relieved to hear her voice, to talk to her. Edward was with her, they were in Cork, I didn't ask why, but she said they would be travelling back early this morning and would ring me again then. I call Diana's mother, who asks us to pray for her, and assure her I will. Jazz is in the garden, playing with Lindsay, and I am trying unsuccessfully to work. I get a notification of new email, so I abandon my notes and open it. It is from Jake. I inhale sharply:

I'm sorry about how I left the other morning. I was angry, it wasn't your fault, I take full responsibility. I probably shouldn't have put you on the spot like I did, but it was something I had to do, and it felt like the right time to say what I did.

Here's the thing: I can accept that maybe I'm not the right man for you. You seem to be pretty definite about that. But I think I might have found one who is.

His name is Gus (Gustav) Petersson, and his email is gus14@indimail.com. He's your father, Vonnie. Angela has confirmed this, and both she and Gus would really like it if you would contact him. He's waiting and hoping you will. I realise you might find this overly intrusive on my part, but it was not intended that way. Ideally, we could have done this together. I wanted, obviously, to give this to you personally.

I just want to open a door for you – for you *and* Jazz, and fully accept that you don't want me in your life apart from being Jazz's dad. That's okay, I couldn't think of a greater privilege than having her as my daughter. I think we were meant to find each other, Vonnie, if for nothing else so that our wonderful daughter should come into this world. But I also know you were part of my salvation, and I like to think I might, in some small way, be contributing to yours.

I love you, you know that, I always have. I want you to be happy and find the missing pieces of yourself. Making contact with your father seems like a good way to begin.

Love, always

Jake

My heart is racing by the time I finish reading it. I pick up the phone to my mother, Angela, checking the time, it must be about ten a.m. on the east coast. I know she will be in The Hamptons at this time of year.

She picks up on the first ring.

'What the hell do you think you're doing?' I demand. How *dare* you interfere in my life. How *dare* you conspire behind my back with Jake. I never expected you to play happy families, but the least you could do is respect my privacy, my boundaries.'

'Hello, Vonnie,' she says calmly. 'So I guess Jake talked to you, or tried to talk to you, about your father?'

'No he did not,' I hiss. 'I just got an email from him this minute with my father's address, saying you had given your blessing that I should contact him.'

'I thought Jake was with you, in Ireland.'

'He was, but he had to go suddenly with work.'

'I see.' She pauses. 'Well it must have been very important work to take him away without discussing this with you. I know he intended to.'

'Really?' My voice is icy.

'Yes. Really. He came to see me, you know.'

Silence. I couldn't believe it, how dare he. How dare she! My blood boiled.

'How nice for you both,' I say, spitefully.

'Oh, Vonnie, really, there's no need to take it like this. Jake obviously cares a great deal about you—'

'And you'd know all about that, wouldn't you?'

'I know when a man is in love with a woman, yes.'

'That's not what I mean,' I snap.

'I know that's not what you mean, I'm just telling you.' Another pause, then she sighs. 'You turned him down, didn't you?'

'What? How did you know anything about—?'

'He came to ask me for your hand in marriage, as well as to enquire about your father. He was very charming. As regards your father, I could only give him a name. I have had no contact with your father, he didn't know about you. Jake tracked him down through his journalist contacts. It was his idea of an engagement gift to you. He went to a lot of trouble.'

'If I had wanted to know about my father, I would have asked you, don't you think?'

'I'll tell you what I think, Vonnie. I think Jake is a good man. I think he loves you deeply, and I think you're a very foolish woman to have turned him down, which you obviously have if he's not with you. He's kind and he's honourable, and he's trying very hard to make up for any mistakes in his past. You can't ask for more than that from any human being. I think you're a very foolish woman to turn down a man like that. I mean, for heaven's sake, you're already a little family, you, Jake and Jazz. What's the harm in making it all legal?'

I gasped. 'You have no right – you—'

'Maybe not. But life goes by very quickly, Vonnie, and I have every right to give you some good advice which I've come by the hard way. Men like Jake do not come along every day, you know that as well as I do. He loves you, he's Jazz's father and I think you love him too – only you're too damn cowardly to throw caution to the wind and go with your feelings. It's much easier to moan about how you've been abandoned and treated unfairly. I know it hasn't been easy for you, Vonnie, and I know I was a rotten mother, but, believe me, you're going to regret losing Jake a whole lot more. Maybe not fully until you see him with another woman who'll appreciate him the way you can't – or won't. And that's gonna hurt, believe me. Forget about your father, if you don't want to meet him, that's up to you, but if you want my advice, call Jake up the minute you put down the phone and tell him you acted in haste and made a huge mistake.'

'I don't believe you—'

'I don't care what you think. I'm too damn old to listen to a daughter ranting on the telephone. This is neither the time nor the place to discuss all this. And I might remind you, you're not getting any younger yourself. I can tell you that precisely because I *am* your mother, however bad a one I've been. I can only hope that you'll come to see that maybe this time I'm doing you a favour. Goodbye, Vonnie.'

And with that, my mother hangs up on me.

I have never thrown my phone at a wall before, but there is a first time for everything.

When it rings, sometime later, I have a senior moment, rummaging in my handbag until I realise my phone is resting on the floor. It's Abby. 'Vonnie? Are you there? You sound breathless.'

'Yes, I'm here; sorry, I just dropped my phone.' I struggle to my feet.

'Wonderful news, Von. Diana's mother has just rung me, she's awake, she's conscious. We're allowed to go and see her for a few minutes. Edward and I are on our way, shall we swing by and pick you up?'

'Oh, would you, Abby? That'd be great. I'll drop Jazz off at our neighbour's.'

'See you in twenty.'

Half an hour later, we are at the hospital. We get out of the lift and walk to the nurses' station on Diana's floor, and are directed to a small room of four beds, three of which are occupied. Diana's mother meets us at the door. She has been crying. Abby and I hug her.

'I'll leave you girls alone with her, she's been asking for you. She's turned the corner, thank God.'

'Only five minutes,' says a nurse. 'She's very tired, not able for much.'

'I'll wait here,' says Edward.

The nurse pulls back a curtain and waves us in behind it, and Abby and I sit on the chairs on either side of the bed. Diana is hooked up to drips and various machines. She is resting, but her eyes flutter open when we sit down beside her. Looking at her, I try not to wince. Her face is twice its normal size, and covered in purple and red bruises. Her eyes are swollen, there are welts on her throat and neck. Her ribcage is bandaged. I want to gasp, to turn away, but I can't, I force a smile instead.

'Hi,' she croaks. 'What took you so long?'

'Look who's talking,' Abby says. 'You've only just woken up!'

'That's what they think, I've been awake all along, just too tired to open my eyes.' She attempts a grin, which turns into a lopsided grimace. 'Ouch, that hurts.'

'Oh, Di, you must be in so much pain,' I say.

'I've felt better, but the drugs are good,' she says drowsily. 'See? Morphine on tap.' She holds up the hand-held pump.

We stay for barely five minutes, and already she is closing her eyes, nodding off. We say our goodbyes, kiss her forehead and promise to return tomorrow. Outside, in the corridor, Di's mum and Edward are talking. She looks all done in, poor woman.

'He left her in quite a state, hmm?' she says grimly.

I nod, afraid if I try to speak I will cry.

'But she's back with us, that's what matters,' says Abby, 'and she'll make a good recovery, I'm sure of it.'

I keep forgetting that Abby was a nurse and would have seen many injuries in her time, but the sight of Di battered and bruised has left *me* shaken. We ask after Corinne and the children, her father, and thank Di's mother for ringing us to let us know so quickly.

It is not until we are back in the car that I realise no one has mentioned Greg's name, not even Diana.

Edward has some business in town, and offers to drop Abby and me off so we can have lunch together. We pull up at the Grafton Street end of Stephen's Green, and Abby and I get out. Edward gets out too, and kisses his wife lingeringly, before getting back in the car and driving off. When I look at Abby with raised eyebrows, she blushes.

'Well,' I say. 'Aren't you two the love birds?'

'I'll tell you all about it over lunch,' she says, grinning.

We choose a little restaurant off Grafton Street which looks quiet and slip into a corner table. When our food and wine arrive, Abby raises her glass to me. 'I have to admit you were right and I was wrong. I should have talked to Edward when you told me to, I should have ages ago, but I was too scared of what I'd hear.'

'And now?' I ask.

'I was wrong, he wasn't having an affair. It was something else entirely.'

I listen as she recounts the events of their night in Cork.

'Oh, Abby, I'm so pleased for you, and so relieved. You had me worried there for a while, Di too.'

'I know, I got myself into such a state about it I couldn't even think straight.'

'Promise me you'll never do that again, that sticking your head in the sand thing.'

'You have my word. How's Jake liking Dublin?' she asks.

'He, er, had to go back – work, you know.'

'Oh, I thought he had another week here, I was going to ask you guys over to dinner – Edward would really like him.'

'Well that was the original plan, but something came up.' I toyed with my salad.

'Vonnie?'

'Mmm?'

'What happened?'

'Nothing happened.'

Abby gave me her 'as if' look. 'You're holding out on me, I can tell.'

'He asked me to marry him.'

'Oh, Von, that's wonderful!' Her face lit up. Then she looked at me. 'Not wonderful?'

I shook my head and to my horror found tears spilling down my cheeks. I put my hand over my mouth and sniffed loudly enough for the waiter to look over and away again hurriedly.

Abby handed me a tissue, then made me take a drink. 'Tell me what happened.'

So I did. I told her everything.

'Do you love him?'

I nodded.

'Well, then, what's the problem?'

'Oh Abby, I'm such a mess. I'm not good in relationships, I find it so hard to trust . . . and Jazz and I, well, everything is working so well this way. She's been through enough already. If Jake and I didn't work, I couldn't bear to put her through losing him again.'

'But she wouldn't be losing him, she'll never lose him.'

'Maybe not, but she'd have to go through another break-up and now she's old enough for it to really upset her.'

'Vonnie, you can't *not* do something because it might not work.'

'It didn't work before.'

'That was different and you know it,' Abby said firmly. 'Jake was drinking then, you didn't know the truth about his brother's car accident – and, from what you've told me, you've done a lot of work on yourself the past few years.'

'That's what I mean, Abby. I'm in a good place now, so is Jazz, she's used to how things are. I couldn't bear to get it wrong again. Jazz is everything in the world to me, she's everything I ever wanted, dreamed of. I won't do anything that might compromise her happiness.'

'That's a cop-out.' Abby sits back in her chair. 'And what's more, you know it.'

Whatever else I had expected her to say, it wasn't that.

'And there's no use you looking reproachful, either, Vonnie. I'm your friend, so I'm going to give it to you straight, that's what friends are for. Children are wonderful, I know that, but that's what they are, Von, kids – who grow up and lead lives of their own. I think it's unfair of you to use Jazz as an excuse to opt out of every part of your life except motherhood, and it's not healthy either.

I open my mouth to protest, but Abby holds up a hand to silence me.

'Just let me finish. There's nothing worse than parents who define themselves by their children, and that's what you're going to turn into if you carry on like this. Right now, Jazz is seven years old but, before you know it, she'll be seventeen and leading her own life. Jazz is not going to want, or appreciate, a mother who threw away a chance for happiness with the only man she ever loved because she was scared, a man who loved her back and who was her daughter's father. Jazz will find out, or figure it out, one way or the other, and you know what? She's going to think less of you for it. Even if you and Jake don't work out, at least you can say you followed your heart, gave it your best shot. That's an example worth setting, whatever way it turns out. That's what you'd want for her, isn't it? If you had been this cautious the first time round, Jazz wouldn't be here at all, would she? Don't short change yourself just because your family has already done that for you. That's in the past. Only you can create your future. And I for one think it should be a future with Jake in it – so does Di, by the way.' Abby pauses for breath. 'I'll shut up now. But think it over carefully, Vonnie. Jake's a good man, they don't come along every day.'

'That's what my mother said,' I say, listlessly.

'Well, there you are.'

'Bit late in the day for her to be giving maternal advice.'

'Leave the maternal thing out of it, Vonnie, that's your mental block. Just think of it as advice from one woman to another. I won't mention it again, but don't let your chance for happiness with a good man pass you by because of what other people have done. This is about you, and about what you want. That's the way you have to think about it. Not, Jake, not Jazz, not your mother, just you, Vonnie. What do *you* want?'

There wasn't a lot I could say to that; besides, I was still sniffling. We had coffee and paid the bill.

'You know what?' Abby says.

'What?'

'We're just five minutes away from Whitefriar Street. Let's go up there and pay St Valentine a visit – it's years since I've been in.'

'Years. Jeez, Abby, I haven't been in since, well since we went in to make our wishes.'

'Thirty years ago.'

'It's never—'

'Yep. Thirty long years. C'mon, Vonnie, we can light a candle and pray that you make the right decision, and that Di makes a full and speedy recovery. I need to say thank you for Edward and me sorting things out, or at least beginning to.'

I follow her out of the restaurant. What have I got to lose? I figure.

The church is exactly as I remember. Part of me feels fifteen years old again, another part infinitely older, but not wiser. How is that? We make our way over to St Valentine, where he still presides over his little altar, the casket of his relics slumbering in the glass case below. Unbelievably, there is a wire A4 copybook, just like the one we wrote in, with the page turned to the latest entry. I wonder, as I sit in a pew and say a silent prayer, whatever became of the one we wrote in, thirty years ago? What secrets did it hold? And did everyone who wrote in it get their longed-for petitions? Just like before, Abby is writing away fluidly. She smiles and motions for me to go up, and hands the pen to me:

Thank you, St Valentine. Thank you so much for Jazz, and thank you for Jake, even if maybe we were wrong for each other. But please, St Valentine, if we're meant for each other,

*let me know, don't let me mess it up this time. It's Vonnie
again, by the way, and I'm sorry it's taken me so long to come
back and thank you. I asked for a chance to be loved, all those
years ago, and even though I never thought it was possible, I've
experienced the most wonderful love imaginable. I'll always
be grateful to you for that, no matter what happens, as long as
I live.*

With love and gratitude
Vonnie

Abby and I stroll back to Grafton Street and go our separate ways, arranging to meet up when we visit Di the following
day.

When I get home I make a cup of tea, and lie down on the
sofa, kicking off my shoes. Jazz will be back in an hour and,
until then, I savour the peace and quiet. Recent conversations
swirl around my head. Angela, Abby, Jake. And one accusation keeps recurring, is common to them all – *fear*. I think
about the email Jake sent, and the trouble he must have gone
to to track down my father, and how ungrateful I have been.
And more, more than all of this, I think of how empty the
house seems without him, how much I miss him, have always
missed him, when he's not around. I sit, bolt upright, and
see it all clearly for maybe the first time – how stupid I've
been, how selfish and how I keep managing to press the
self-destruct button, resolutely determined not to allow any
happiness enter my life. Abby was right, it is a miracle Jazz
ever found her way to me – to us. The thought of not having
her, of not having our time together with Jake fills me with
the bleakest of despair. All at once, I know what I must do.
I will ring him, right now, and tell him that I would love to
marry him more than anything in the world, if he'll still have
me, that is.

Before I can get to it, my phone rings. Could it be telepathy?

Could it be him? I grab it, not looking at the caller display, and hear a man's voice.

'Is that Ms Callaghan? Vonnie Callaghan?'

'Yes. This is Vonnie Callaghan,' I don't recognise this voice, which is clipped, businesslike.

There is the briefest of pauses. 'I'm calling from the *Los Angeles Times*. Jake Kurkimaki has listed you on his file as his partner and mother of his daughter, Jasmine Kurkimaki-Callaghan, his next of kin.'

'What? Why are you calling me?'

'The vehicle Jake was travelling in was ambushed, Ms Callaghan, just last night. There was an explosion. He and his group are unaccounted for. There's a possibility they may have been taken hostage by Libyan separatists. I'm going to give you a direct line to call for any further information.'

'Wait, please.' I scrabble for a pen and piece of paper, still clutching the phone, taking down the number with my other hand, which I can barely read because I am shaking so much.

'What's happened, exactly, I mean, can you tell me—'

'I'm afraid we have no other information at this time, Ms Callaghan. I've told you all we know. Our people are working on it. Like I said, the number I gave you will update you and family members as regards the situation. I'm sorry I can't tell you more. Goodbye.'

And then the line goes dead.

I want to scream. I want someone to shake me and slap my face and tell me that I'm being hysterical and that this is all a bad dream, some weird delusion, my mind playing tricks on me. But I have a little girl coming back home in less than twenty minutes who is far more vulnerable than I am. If she can't have both her parents, then she needs the only one available to her to be calm and strong. I cannot think the unthinkable, that the pattern is repeating, that Jazz may have to grow up without her father, and there isn't a damned thing I can do about it.

Upstairs, I splash cold water on my face, and say out loud to no one in particular, 'Please send him back, I'm begging you, please send him back. Don't take her daddy away, whatever about me, she doesn't deserve it. And I need to tell him I still love him.'

I cry, holding on to the basin, until there are no more tears, until I have no more strength. Then I blow my nose, wash my face and go downstairs wondering what in the world I am going to say to Jazz.

Morro Bay

Diana

It is October, three months since my beating and Jake's
disappearance. Abby and I are in Vonnie's house in Morro
Bay. We arrived three days ago and are still adjusting to the
time difference. I am up making coffee, Vonnie has gone to
take Jazz to school, Abby is still asleep.

I have recovered sufficiently to have a holiday, my doctors
tell me, as long as I take it easy, no wild parties, no abseiling.
My arm is just out of cast, I need my walking stick less and
less, and my face is more or less back to normal, except for
a few scars that, I am told, will become more faint with time.
Abby reminds me I am in the right place for some plastic
surgery if the mood takes me. I laugh and tell her I am just
happy to be alive. For once, my appearance, my beauty
routines, have taken a back seat.

This is more than a holiday, of course, for all three of us.
It feels more like a rite of passage. We are here for Vonnie,
who cut short her visit home when she heard the devastating
news about Jake. She left so suddenly, she barely had time
to say goodbye to us. Sadly, there has been no happy breakthrough, no resolution. Jake, along with two other journalists,
was investigating reports that abducted Libyan civilians were
being forced to give blood to NATO militias and mercenaries.
On their way through Sirte, there was an explosion, their
jeep was wrecked and they were taken hostage by Gaddafi
loyalists.

There was a video, apparently, proving they were still alive, but in bad shape. Vonnie didn't want to see it; Jake's sister Gloria and her husband watched it, said it was grim. Thinking back to my own attack and my early days in hospital, I'm glad Vonnie didn't watch it. There are some things you don't need to witness about a loved one, some images better not engraved on your memory, your soul. Though now Vonnie says she wished she *had* watched it, saying what she imagines couldn't be any worse.

We were shocked, Abby and I, when she picked us up at the airport. She was tanned, but too thin, and sadness was palpable behind her wide smile. Although she was trying hard for us and, of course, for Jazz, loss had enveloped her, was stalking her silently with every step.

'I'm worried about Vonnie,' I say to Abby, who is making her way downstairs, yawning.

'Me too. Mmm, is that coffee I smell?'

'Yes, freshly made.' I pour her a cup.

'Where is she?'

'She's taken Jazz to school, then she's going to pick up some groceries; she said she'd be about an hour, that was forty minutes ago.'

'She looks awful.'

'I know, but what can we do?'

'Nothing, except be here for her. I feel guilty, though, I mean we're here in Morro Bay, in the sunshine, with the Pacific on our doorstep, it's hard not to go about with a goofy smile on your face. I have to pinch myself. Not so long ago it was you we were sick with worry over, and no sooner were you out of the woods than this has to happen.' She helped herself to some fruit and berries. 'I keep telling myself it's a mercy mission, but it feels like a holiday.'

'I know.'

'That's because it's meant to be a holiday.' We jump guiltily, not hearing Vonnie come in. 'Look, I know you mean well, really I do,' she says, 'but I don't want to be morose. We so rarely have time together like this, just the three of us, let's make the most of it. And it *is* meant to be a holiday, we've all been through stuff lately and having you guys around is great for me and Jazz.'

'I just wish there was more we could do,' Abby says.

'You're here, that's all you can do, all I want you to.'

'So, what are we going to do today then?' I ask.

'What everyone does around here, go to the beach of course.'

'Again?' Abby rolls her eyes in mock exasperation.

'Unless there's something else you'd prefer?'

'Nope, beach is fine by me.'

'Me too,' I say.

We drive to the beach and set up our place, and I huff and puff until I make myself comfortable. Abby rubs sun block on the places I can't reach, and Vonnie opens a book, which Abby and I have no intention of letting her read. I lie back and soak up the rays, mindlessly watching the surfers and beautiful young girls and men frolicking in the water.

'Oh, to be young again,' I say.

'Speak for yourself,' says Abby.

'What would you do differently?' Vonnie asks.

'I'm not sure.' I take a moment. 'Everything and nothing.'

'Are you sure about what you're doing, Di? You've been through so much lately, maybe—'

'That's exactly *why* I'm doing it, Vonnie. You of all people should understand.'

'I do, of course I do, it's just—'

'What?'

'I guess you're right, it's your life. But it all seems so . . . sudden.'

'Exactly, it is my life, and I very nearly lost it.'

There is nothing anyone can say to that.

When I came round from the coma, I felt as if I was waking up from my whole previous life. I can't explain it very well, except to say that things took on a clarity that was glaringly simplistic. I know what happened wasn't Greg's fault, but it was the wake-up call (literally) that I had needed. I wanted to change my life, I had wanted to for so long, but I hadn't been able to face the fact that changing it would mean changing my marriage. Now I had. I was never going to have a gap year, a sabbatical, a chance to explore what I want to do, as long as I was waiting for it to be the right time for Greg – because it was always about *him*. And that's the way it would have continued.

'How has Greg taken it?' Vonnie asks, while Abby remains tactfully quiet.

'He's shocked, naturally. Wanted to talk me out of it, try again, but I was certain. That's one thing a near-death experience does for you. But he's been decent about it. He's pretty cut up about what happened, but he knows I don't blame him. I think the biggest shock he got was when I said I was selling the business, and that I wanted to sell the house.'

'Poor Greg.' Abby shakes her head. 'I don't think he'll cope without you.'

'He'll be fine.'

'What about the kids?'

'They've been fantastic about it. I think they're so relieved I'm still alive that anything else is taking a back seat. Philip is off to Irish college this year and Sophie is going to Paris for her transition year. It's not going to be easy, but they know we both adore them, and plenty of their friends' parents are divorced or separated. They don't know about Harry yet, obviously,' I pause. 'One hurdle at a time.'

'Will it come to that – divorce I mean?' Abby asks.

'I think so, Abby. Whatever happens, I just know I want to be in control of my own life for a change, discover who I am again – all those clichés – before it's too late. Maybe that will mean a life with Harry, or maybe it won't, maybe it'll just be me on my own. But whatever the future holds for me, I know I've got to tackle it now.'

'It's so weird,' Abby reflects. Three months ago I thought *I* was on the brink of divorce, now it turns out you might end up being my sister-in-law.'

'And look at you, Abby, having a second honeymoon!' Vonnie teases. 'I'm surprised Edward was able to let you out of his sight. How many times has he texted you already?'

Abby grins, and I take this opportunity to be serious.

'I'm really sorry, I want you both to know that. I hope you can forgive me – you, Abby, especially . . .'

'You don't have to apologise to me!'

'I do.' I took a deep breath. 'Harry's your brother-in-law, for God's sake, it was too close to home. I hated myself for the deceit, but we, I, couldn't tell anyone. Can you understand that?'

'I wouldn't have said anything,' Abby sounds reproachful. 'You could have trusted me, you know.'

'I do know, Abby,' I reach for her hand. 'Of course I do, but talking about it, admitting it to anyone, even you, would have made it real. And I couldn't have coped with that. As long as nobody knew about it, well, it kept it a secret, a fantasy, something that was just between us. In the real world it didn't exist, that's the only way I could deal with it. Can you understand that?'

'Yes, yes I think I can. It was sort of like me and Edward, as long as I didn't tell anyone what I was thinking, it wasn't real. I tried so hard to run away from it – even when Edward confronted me with it, I ran away – so yes, I can understand.'

'Thank you for that, Abs. It means a lot.'

'Do you love him, Di, really?'

'Oh yes, yes I do.'

Abby smiles. 'That's good, because Harry's a sweetie.' She looks at Vonnie. 'You know I could never understand why he was never interested in any of the girls we tried to set him up with. Now it all makes sense. Edward couldn't believe it either!'

'Is he okay with it?' Harry had told me that Edward had known about us, but he had obviously been a gentleman and left me to divulge what was happening to the girls. I was grateful to him for that.

'Yes, I think he is. I mean he was surprised, we all were – you can hardly blame us. But I think he's happy for Harry. He's just . . .'

'Just what?'

'Well, no offence, Di, but I think he's worried you might be stringing Harry along. You know, playing with him,' she sounded embarrassed.

I took a deep breath. It was a fair comment. 'No, Abby, I'm not doing that. You can reassure him on that score.' I paused. 'Harry is the love of my life. I know that's not a guarantee that we'll make each other happy but, for what it's worth, I'm going to give it my best shot.'

'Good,' Abby smiles. 'That's good.'

'Time for a toast,' Vonnie says, brandishing a bottle of chilled sparkling wine.

'But we've only just got here!' I say.

'Sun's over the yardarm.' She proceeds to fill three glasses from the picnic basket and hand them out.

'What'll we drink to?' asks Abby.

'To friends, forever friends, and St Valentine, of course,' says Vonnie.

'To the best of friends and to love,' says Abby.

'Yes, to life-long friends and life-long love,' I say, and mentally offer up a prayer that Jake, wherever he is, is safe and makes his way back home to Vonnie.

Vonnie

That last night with the girls was harder than I thought. Morro Bay was home to me for sure, but Diana and Abby are the closest thing I'd ever had to family, apart from Jazz and Jake. Now, after dropping them to the airport to catch their flight to LA, the house seemed hollow without the echo of their warm voices and laughter. Even Jazz was tetchy, she blamed it on George. 'He won't talk to me today,' she said.

'Why not?' I pulled her to me and stroked her hair.

'He doesn't feel like it.'

'How about we go to Fred's for a pizza?' This was usually a cure-all.

But Jazz just shook her head. 'Not without Daddy.'

'But we do all these things when Daddy is away working, honey.'

'This is different.' She looked at me defiantly. 'This time you don't know when he'll be coming back.'

That had been the hardest thing, telling Jazz, trying to explain that Jake would be away and I wasn't sure how long for. Ever since she had looked at me with distrust, retreating from me day by day, sensing I knew more than I was telling her – which really, I didn't. The only thing I was keeping from her was my worst fear, that she would never see him again – that *we* would never see him again. That was the thought I only allowed in as night fell, as the wee small hours ticked slowly, painfully by, but it stalked me like a shadow throughout the day.

Then the phone rang. I thought it might be the girls calling from LA or maybe Jake's sister, but when it flashed up, I didn't recognise the number.

'Hello.'

'Is that Vonnie Callaghan?'

My hand tightened on the phone. The voice was deep, warm, but it wasn't Jake's.

'Yes, this is Vonnie.'

There was a pause and then the voice continued. 'I wasn't planning on doing this, Vonnie, but since you didn't seem to be getting in touch with me, I figured maybe I should try calling you. My name is Gus, Vonnie, Gus Petersson. I'm your father.'

'Oh my God.' I sat down, while Jazz looked at me curiously from the floor.

'I'm sorry if this has come as a shock to you, but I'm not getting any younger, and I thought it'd be a good idea if we met. How would you feel about that?' The immediacy of the question floored me, and yet it was a simple one, requiring only a simple answer.

'I guess so.' It was all I could think of saying.

Gus chuckled. 'Well, that's a good start. I understand I have a granddaughter.'

'Yes, yes you do, she's right here beside me.'

'Well, well, well. Look, I'm gonna suggest something, you take as long as you like to think about it. I'm based in Colorado these days, I have a small ranch. It's really beautiful up here at this time of year, why don't you and your daughter come visit? I'd love you to stay with me or, if you'd prefer, I'll put you up at the local inn. What do you say?'

A million things were whirring around my head but only one word made any sense. I'd shut down on people enough in my life, I wasn't going to do it anymore. 'Yes,' I said, slowly. 'I think that would be a good idea.'

'Well, now. That's just great. If you'll give me your email address, I'll send you all the details. I have to tell you,' he continued, 'you came as a real surprise to me, Vonnie. I had no idea about you. I want you to know that; if I had known, well, I would have—' his voice caught.

'I understand.'

'You know, I tried to stay in touch with your mother all those years ago. I wrote her several times, but I understand she never got the letters. Life can be cruel like that. I have a lot of regrets, but I'm hoping to make it up to you – better late than never, right?'

I could hear the smile in his voice. 'Right.'

'Well, you've made my day, Vonnie. I can't wait to meet you and . . . what's my granddaughter's name?'

'Jazz. Her name is Jazz. She's seven years old.'

'We'll see each other real soon, Vonnie. Goodbye now, it's been a blessing to talk to you. You take good care of yourself.'

'Goodbye, Gus.' I put down the phone.

'Mommy?' said Jazz, clambering up beside me. 'Why are you crying?'

'I don't know,' I say, wiping my cheeks, laughing and hugging her. 'I don't know, honey.'

My father is tall, six foot three, maybe four, standing head and shoulders among the throng at arrivals. I spot him immediately, lock eyes with this man I have never seen before, but who seems instantly familiar. He is handsome, craggy, grinning broadly, wearing jeans, a plaid shirt, leather jacket and a cowboy hat, which he takes off and waves.

'Who is that man waving at us, Mom?'

'That's your grandfather, I say. That's him.'

'He doesn't look like Daddy.'

'That's because he's *my* daddy, not Daddy's daddy. You already know Grandpa Kurkimaki.'

'Oh-o-o-kay.' Jazz is a little confused. I can't blame her.

'You made it!' he says, standing back to look at us. 'My, I can hardly believe it. Look at you.'

'Well, neither can I,' I say awkwardly, not knowing what

to do with myself, awash with shyness. Then I am enveloped in a bear hug that all but squeezes the breath out of me, and Jazz is hoisted up onto his shoulders, from where she squeals with delight, and my father leads the way out of the airport and to the waiting car.

The drive from Denver airport took about an hour and twenty minutes, moments which will always be precious to me. Cocooned in Gus's Jeep, we are a micro family – new, yet not new, shy, finding sudden bursts of humour, a genetic disposition perhaps, a gesture, a word, not yet familiar. My daughter falling asleep in the back to the reassuring rumble of his voice. We feel safe, it is a primeval thing, the same blood is coursing through our veins.

'I hope you don't mind, but I called your mother, just to straighten out some things. She tells me you're going through a tough time.' Gus glances at me as he drives. 'I'm very sorry to hear that. I never met him, but your Jake sounds like a mighty fine guy.'

My Jake. I swallow. 'Yes, yes he is.' There is no disputing that. Gus, perhaps sensing more, does not follow up.

'I know he contacted you,' I say.

'Yes, he did. Although how he tracked me down, God only knows,' he smiles, 'but I'll always be grateful to him for that.'

'Me too.'

My father reaches over and squeezes my hand. 'Good, I'm glad.'

Angela

He left me, of course. Can't say I blame him. Lost a husband, lost a daughter, what does that say about me? Except, of course, I couldn't lose or gain Vonnie. I had just left her behind, now it was my turn to be alone. But that was the easy part, it was facing Ron that had been hard. I had to tell him, sooner or later, and after that meeting with Jake, I couldn't keep up the pretence a minute longer.

'I need to talk to you,' I said to him, that night after dinner. We had been out with friends, had a good evening and were settling in at our cottage in The Hamptons for a nightcap.

'I figured something's up with you, Angie, you haven't been yourself lately. What is it?' He sat down, looking at me quizzically as I poured us both a brandy and handed one to him.

'There's no easy way to tell you this,' I began. 'I have a daughter.'

'A daughter?'

'From before I met you.'

'Before?' I saw him do the maths, and disbelief flicker across his face. 'But that must be—'

'Forty-five years ago now. I was just turning eighteen.'

'A daughter,' he repeated.

So I told him everything. I stood with my back to him, looking out the window, taking a swig of brandy occasionally to smooth words that threatened to lodge in my throat and, without stopping, I got through the whole unedifying story.

'I'm not proud of any of this.' I turned to face him. He was sitting dumbfounded, looking at me like I was a stranger. That's when I knew I'd lost him.

I lay awake that night, while Ron slept, or at least spent the night, in one of the guest rooms. Never, not in the whole of our married life, not through any of his affairs, had we spent a night apart under the same roof. This was a first.

At first light, I got up, unable to lie with my guilt and imaginings a minute longer. I went outside, swam, came back in, fixed myself up, dressed and made breakfast, dismissing the housekeeper for the day.

I was sitting having coffee at the breakfast table when he came in, stood at the door, fully dressed. His face was ashen, his eyes sunken.

'Why?' he asked. 'Why didn't you tell me before?'

I put my face in my hands. I had pondered this question for years, and how I would reply, but now that it was levelled at me there was no sensible response.

'I don't know. I guess I was scared, scared that you wouldn't want me – us.'

'I would have loved her, your little girl, Angie. I would have loved her.'

The words cut through me like a knife, along with his bewildered tone, the confusion on his face. 'Was I really that much of an ogre to you that you thought I wouldn't have wanted her – you – both? I *loved* you.' The hurt in his voice was palpable, as was the past tense he used that screamed out at me.

There. *Me.* You see, that's my problem, it's always been about me. I knew, deep inside, that I'm selfish, but I never wanted it to be like this, really I didn't. I was just scared back then. I would have loved a little family of me, Vonnie and Ron. But, for all his talk, it was easy for him to say that he would have loved Vonnie now, I'm not so sure I believed him. Things appear very easy with hindsight. Back then, and after, when we discovered Ron couldn't have his own children and he didn't want to adopt, well, I don't think he would have accepted Vonnie either. That was my call. Maybe I got it wrong, we'll never know.

Anyhow, that's when he left, to go back to New York.

I got a letter from his lawyer the next day. It didn't come as a total surprise. I knew this would hit Ron hard. Living with someone for forty years who's been keeping a secret like mine comes with its own repercussions. I'd been feeling the vibrations for years, now came the explosion, the after-shocks would take a while. Poor Ron, it was all new to him, I couldn't blame him for being blown away, for looking at me like I was a monster.

I had got used to seeing that reflection quite some time ago.

Vonnie

The ranch is a series of low, wooden buildings attached to the main house, approached by a mile-long driveway. On either side, acres of pasture and land stretch to the horizon and the Rockies beyond.

We pull up and I wake Jazz, take her from the back seat, where she rubs her eyes and looks around. A Hispanic couple emerge, the man takes our luggage and the woman stands at the door to welcome us.

'This is Carlos and Esperanza, they keep house for me,' Gus explains. 'This is my daughter, Vonnie, and my grand-daughter, Jazz,' he says proudly. 'We have an awful lot of catching up to do.'

'Welcome to Lazy River Ranch.' Esperanza takes my hand and exclaims over Jazz.

I let the word 'daughter' wash over me, settle, and silently own it.

'Why don't you go to your room and freshen up,' Gus suggests. 'Then come down and have a drink. Just let Esperanza know when you're ready.'

'Well, sure, thank you,' I say, a little dazed.

Esperanza shows us upstairs to our room, which is down a long, curving corridor and overlooks the back of the ranch. It is decorated in blues and whites with hand-made quilts on the beds. There is an en-suite where I freshen up and attempt to brush Jazz's curls, which have developed a life of their own. George is propped up on the bed. He looks as exhausted as I feel.

We make our way downstairs, where a smiling Esperanza silently reappears.

'Follow me, Miss Vonnie, your father is waiting for you in the great room.'

We walk along oak floors, scattered with rugs, past paintings and polished furniture with gleaming silver and hundreds of photographs, old and new, which I will examine later in detail. I have learned I have four half-brothers, my father's late wife, Louise, lost her battle with cancer five years ago. He told me she would have loved a daughter.

We come to a set of heavy wooden double doors, which Esperanza pushes through, and I stop in my tracks and gasp.

There is an eruption of noise, a room full of faces, smiling, laughing, crying. Arms outreached. A huge banner reads: 'Welcome Home, Sis!' Another says: 'Vonnie and Jazz, we love you!' There is singing and someone banging on a piano, but I cannot make out the tune or song. I stand, paralysed on the threshold, joy fighting shyness and shock.

Jazz shows no such reticence and dives into the fray. 'Look, Mommy, it's a party!' And she is gathered up by strong arms and swung into the air. My father shoulders through faces which are beginning to blur, as tears threaten. 'Come on in, Vonnie, honey. Your family are waiting to meet you.'

I take his hand and a deep breath and, for the first time in my life, step into a room full of love.

Later, much later, I am reeling with new names, faces, gratitude and tiredness. Relatives have reluctantly dispersed, arranging to meet us tomorrow and over the next few days. I am sitting in the den, with Gus (I can't yet call him Dad), my half-brother Ryan and his wife Keelan. Jazz has gone from being wired to flaking out, and I must put her to bed, where I will follow shortly.

'Here, we go, Princess,' her grandfather picks her up easily from the sofa where she has passed out, and she blinks awake and grins. 'Time for bed, young lady,' he says, holding her to him, as she leans her head against his shoulder. They are standing in front of the enormous fireplace, over which a large portrait of my father hangs. 'It was a gift from my boys for my fiftieth birthday, when I was young and handsome,' he jokes.

Jazz sleepily fingers the brass bar on the portrait frame where his name is printed. 'Gustav V. Petersson,' she reads, haltingly. 'What does the 'V' stand for, Gramps?' she asks.

Ryan chuckles. 'Go on, tell 'em, Dad. She's gonna find out sooner or later.'

My father shakes his head and grins. 'It's become a family joke,' he says. 'The 'V' stands for Valentine. That's my name, Gustav Valentine Petersson. What can I tell you, Vonnie? Your grandmother was a hopeless romantic.'

Ryan slaps him on the shoulder, laughing.

I say I will be back just as soon as I have put Jazz to bed. I climb the stairs, retrace our steps along the low-lit corridor to our room where the beds have been turned down and fresh towels and flowers placed on the wooden chest. I get Jazz to undress and put on her white cotton nightdress, which has been laid out on the pillow. She snuggles under the sheets with George and is too tired even for a story. I know how she feels. I leave the bedside light on and she falls asleep instantly. I tiptoe quietly from the room, leaving the door ajar.

It's been a long day – a long and sometimes lonely journey. But I have finally made it home.

Epilogue

The woman and the little girl stand in the throng at LAX arrivals. The woman looks anxious, craning her head to see through the crowd. The little girl, clutching a worn-out toy monkey and a balloon, hops from foot to foot, darting back and forth impatiently. 'Can you see him? Can you see him yet, Mommy?'

'No, Jazz, not yet,' the woman says, for what seems like the thousandth time.

Then her face changes. She takes a breath, something in her relaxes, unfurls.

A man has come through the doors. A very tall, dark man, but the little girl has not seen him just yet.

He walks through the crowd, thin, lean, his face hollowed out, intense, until a smile lights it up. Something in his demeanour makes people make way for him. He heads straight for the woman, drops his bag, takes her in his arms and they cling to each other. Then they kiss, lingeringly, and break apart laughing as the little girl shrieks and makes noises of disgust.

He lifts up the little girl, carrying her easily as she wraps her arms about his neck. Then he reaches out to take the woman's hand.

People around them watch and smile as the little family walks out into the bright LA sunlight.

Acknowledgements

Grateful thanks as always to the wonderful team at Hachette Ireland, and Hodder in the UK, and in particular to my editor Ciara Doorley. We got there, finally! Your patience, expertise and insight made *The Love Book* so much better . . .

Thanks also to my delightful agent Felicity Blunt – who makes me laugh when I want to chuck it all in, and believes in me when I can't believe in myself. I hope many more enjoyable and productive (even frivolous) projects beckon!

If I have forgotten anyone, which is entirely possible – lunch is on me.

Finally, grateful thanks to you, dear reader, I truly hope you enjoyed *The Love Book*, do let me know – I love hearing from you. www.fionaobrien.com

Let's do it all again soon.

With love and gratitude,

If you like happy endings . . .

You have just come to the end of a book.

Before you put it aside, please take a moment to reflect on the 37 million people who are blind in the developing world.

Ninety percent of this blindness is TOTALLY PREVENTABLE.

In our world, blindness is a disability – in the developing world, it's a death sentence.

Every minute, one child goes blind – needlessly.

That's about the time it will take you to read this.

It's also about the time it will take you to log on to www.righttosight.com and help this wonderful organisation achieve its goal of totally eradicating preventable global blindness.

Now that would be a happy ending.

And it will only take a minute.

Fiona O'Brien supports the right to sight and would love if you would too.